LADIES' OWN BAKERY
SEASON TWO

The Collected Episodes

JUDITH LYNNE

JUDITH LYNNE

Books by Judith Lynne

<u>Lords and Undefeated Ladies</u>

Not Like a Lady

The Countess Invention

What a Duchess Does

Crown of Hearts

He Stole the Lady

No Titled Lady

<u>Maids Done Waiting</u>

The Lord Trap

The Lady Escape (Forthcoming)

<u>Cloaks and Countesses</u>

The Caped Countess

The Clandestine Countess

The Castaway Countess (Forthcoming)

<u>Ladies' Own Bakery</u>

The Regency romance comedy serial

This is for the Ladies' Own Bakery readers, and all women building lives of their own.

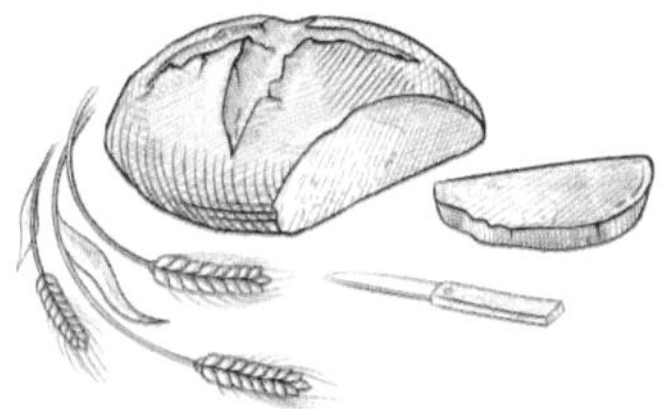

Preface

Welcome! The Ladies' Own Bakery is something a little different: a Regency romance comedy serial. It's a comedy sandwich stuffed with tasty Regency romance filling. My faithful readers got the episodes right to their inboxes. Now that the season is over, I'm delighted to bring you the collected season.

Like your favorite show, the season isn't over at the end of season 1 *or* 2. The loves and lives of our Bickering sisters will go on, planned now for three more seasons. **So you've been warned—this story doesn't end at the end!**

Rose, Emery, Jane, and Anna, and their whole world, will return in Season Three!

Learn more about Judith Lynne books, or sign up to find out when more Ladies' Own Bakery is released, at judithlynne.com!

Episode 1: Where Paths Lead

The shop was bustling, as it usually was now, with much noise of patrons' conversation and rustling of skirts.

The Bickering sisters wove among them with baskets of bread, careful plates of cake, and whispered messages to each other.

The sisters still had plenty to say. Things that could not wait till the bakery might be empty.

"Why don't you go home?" Anna whispered to Rose as she whisked away empty cake plates.

Rose could not find ears to whisper in, nor was she tall enough to reach them, so she was left to call out odd things and hope no one would notice. "Thank you, I feel very loved!" she told Anna's departing skirt-rustle.

"Well, I should hope so!" The lady before her smiled. "You must be enjoying your new married life! I so want to hear about it all."

"*No!*" chorused eight other women in the shop who just wanted to buy bread and go home.

Rose bowed her head to hide her smile. "Tell me how

"

many pounds to cut for you, Mrs. Lacey, and we'll have that chat another day."

In truth she had no intention of having that chat, today or any other day. Mrs. Lacy already doubtless knew whatever wives were supposed to know, perhaps from some school Rose could not attend.

All Rose knew for certain was that she herself had no idea how to be a wife, except in the ways to which Mr. Russell had finally persuaded her.

Thinking of *that* made her blush so hotly that Rose worried someone would think she had a fever, and Anna would send her out.

"I'll take two pounds." Mrs. Lacy leaned in conspiratorially over the new counter, already pocked with the grooves of the knife despite the sisters' best efforts. Rose needed one groove to help her line up the cuts she made through the bread, but she tried not to make it too much deeper.

Mrs. Lacy said under her breath, "Makes me worry for some of them, if they don't want to hear a new wife sing her husband's praises."

Rose showed her smile, adjusting the big heavy loaf. The toothy foot-long knife nestled against her left knuckles so that it was impossible for her to cut herself, and she began to saw through the crust to the soft white body of the bread itself. "Mr. Russell is a lovely husband," was all she said.

Mrs. Lacy sighed. "I'll just bet. With those big square shoulders and those big strong hands? I bet he—"

"Mrs. Lacy. Will you have any cake today?" Emery interrupted from behind Rose as she slid fresh *gâteaux Bretons* to the shelf.

The shock of Emery trying to sell anyone any cake straightened Rose's back and startled Mrs. Lacy out of her daydreams. "No thank you, Miss Emery, not today."

Rose wondered if she ought to be grateful for the interruption, or wave her long knife at Mrs. Lacy. How dare the woman think about Mr. Russell's hands?

It all led to Rose to thinking about Mr. Russell's hands too, and she felt herself blush again.

"If you'll step over here, Mrs. Lacy, I will take your payment." Jane, at the cash box, insisted on being closer to the door. She'd become convinced that she'd seen customers come in then just leave after staring at Lady Arnold's vase stuffed with bread. Jane wanted to herd them closer to the counter.

Once Jane had Mrs. Lacy's coins firmly in hand and the lady had left, Jane still kept both hands on the cash box as she leaned and whispered, "If you don't like him, Rose, you don't need to go home."

"Of course I like him!" Rose's outburst made her drop the knife, its metallic rattle on the wood causing the chatter among the patrons to lull.

"Hope so," Mrs. Grogan gruffed, pushing her way to the counter next. "You've married him now. Pound of the white, please."

This was unsupportable. Rose hadn't wanted to talk to her sisters; she came to the shop so she *wouldn't* have to talk. It was so busy there was no time to talk, much less fret.

But now she felt moved to speak. She didn't want to tell them anything about the astonishing things married people could do once they were alone; she didn't want to tell them Mr. Russell was both endlessly patient yet still expected her to do all the housework in his little rooms on Castle Street. She didn't want to tell them she had never once thought what married life would be like before she embarked on it.

And she didn't at *all* want to tell them she missed them.

"I'm coming to supper." She slid Mrs. Grogan's bread toward Jane, who asked for the money with an authority that reminded Rose of a simpler life.

"I'm shocked," murmured a re-appearing Anna. "Mrs. Billings, do come this way. You want a quartern loaf, don't you?"

Now Rose's face felt hot in a different way. None of her sisters ever said anything to make her feel like their home wasn't her home.

But it wasn't.

"We must do something about the number of customers," Jane announced that night over their cabbage soup.

It was a very different room now, with a table and chairs enough for all to sit and eat. The fare was different too, with the Talbourne dishes; they had bowls for things like soup.

Jane felt it elegant, to sit on a chair with one's feet on the floor. Such a simple thing had never seemed elegant when she'd worn pretty dresses to parties every night, using Aunt Eden's money to try to attract a husband.

Jane would never take chairs for granted again.

"I miss sharing a plate with Emery," Rose sighed.

"I don't." Emery felt strongly enough about this to say it with her mouth still partly full of buttered bread. But she swallowed before she went on. "What do you want to do about the customers, Jane? Shove them out? We worked ourselves to nubs to get them."

"This isn't the way Mother made cabbage soup." Anna stirred her bowl decorously, never touching the porcelain sides, but with a little frown between her brows. Jane could see the frown's little pucker past their mother's candlesticks, which sat atop their very own table.

Soon the nights would be longer, and they would need to

light a candle to see their suppers. Already the days were colder, with a nip that said the winter would be icy.

"Just once," sighed Jane, "I'd like to finish my thought before you all leap on it to argue."

"Once we're all dead," shrugged Emery.

Emery's assumption that their future must be exactly like their past pricked Jane's temper.

"That's just what I mean. We are ladies of business. Established. It's childish simply to do the same thing over and over again just because it's brought us success so far."

"*Success?*" Anna's jaw dropped. "We still count every penny!"

Jane remained firm. "We have pennies to count. We have food to eat. We have *chairs* on which to sit."

"Exactly. What else do we need?" demanded Emery around her next bite of bread.

"You are developing some unpleasant habits," Anna observed, pointedly staring at Emery until the bread disappeared entirely.

Jane wanted to smash a damn bowl if it would get their attention. "Listen, all of you. We cannot serve quickly enough. Our patrons stand waiting in the store. We need help."

"We do have Tilly," Anna reminded Jane with the diffidence of a person who knew Tilly was very little actual help.

Jane conceded with a nod. "We have Tilly, and her cousin's patronage, and the attention of Tilly's hand-selected cabbage vendor. I concede her value. But in the shop, our patrons need more help. And Emery, I think you should hire more bakers."

That idea plopped in the middle of the table like an unwelcome muddy boot.

"I don't need any bakers." Emery chased peas around her

plate, clearly signaling where her attention lay in the battle between dinner and this conversation.

"You do."

"I don't."

"It wasn't a question, Emery."

"I've told you my answer, Jane."

"All right now." Anna's older-sister tone bustled into the stalemate without her ever leaving her seat. "Jane, you must have a reason behind the idea."

Jane tried to catch Emery's gaze across the table, but Emery pointedly looked only to Anna. She'd sat back in her chair and folded her arms across her chest, green eyes blazing the way the rest of theirs never did.

How should Jane put this? In front of Anna? She didn't want to mention Emery's work at the tailor's, or any of Emery's secret... socializing.

But Jane wasn't stupid. Lady Arnold hadn't just hosted Rose's wedding due to a sudden burst of civic pride. Her lady-ship supported the bakery, clearly because she liked Emery. Jane had no idea how *much* she liked Emery, but she didn't want Emery to have to say anything about it she wasn't ready to say.

Well, she'd tried to pull Emery aside and have this conversation for most of the last two weeks. Emery had brushed her away each time. So here they were.

"Emery." Jane could try to be delicate. "You simply cannot bake day and night, all day, every day. You must want to do *something* besides be locked up in the bakery. You've been sleeping on the flour sacks."

That made Emery meet her eyes.

Jane wanted to reach out her hand. But Emery looked so... so bricked away. They used to know what each other was thinking. They were the unpleasant ones, the difficult ones, different from Rose and Anna.

And Jane wouldn't gain Emery's confidence by blurting out any of her secrets.

"Don't you want an hour or two to yourself?" she asked Emery softly.

"No." Emery's eyes warned Jane off the topic.

Rose shattered the tension between them. "I don't want to live in Mr. Russell's room."

Whether Rose had captured center stage to forestall further conflict between Jane and Emery, or merely because she couldn't hold it in any longer, her revelation effectively gained control of the conversational battlefield.

Anna's spoon clattered in her bowl, and she winced. Anna was clearly working hard to recapture the habits of their younger years, when such things as eating from porcelain bowls were commonplace. "You don't have to do anything you don't want to do, muffin, but you know... you *married* him."

Rose threw up her hands. "I know! And I like him fine. I love him. I do love him. But you can't imagine what it's like! Alone there in that little room all day, with no one to talk to, and it's not as though Emery is washing his collars while I iron and Jane takes the money. There's no swirl. It's too *quiet.*"

Anna's own hands clasped her cheeks. She simply stared at her littlest sister. "You *married* him, muffin."

"I didn't bury myself," Rose said with rising exasperation.

"Doesn't he mind all your time in the shop?" Jane was truly curious. "Lord Boislegrand mentions every time he visits that soon Anna won't need to come at all."

"This isn't about Lord Boislegrand," Anna shook that alternative conversation away with a flittering hand.

"Mr. Russell doesn't *mind*, so to speak. He knows what this shop means to me. And all of you, of course. I just think he also thought perhaps his collars would be clean and his supper cooked."

"Good Lord." Jane immediately clapped a hand over her mouth.

Now Emery and Anna both stared, and Rose's jaw dropped open. Such an imprecation had never been uttered at the Bickering table, not even by Aunt Eden, whose insults could wither ivy.

If Jane weren't careful, her sisters might start to wonder where *she* spent all those hours she claimed she needed to do the shopping.

"My apologies. I only mean, Rose, I--I suppose it makes sense, but... what are you to do?"

"We have the most intense conversations about it, he and I." Rose's shoulders slumped. "Long into the night, and he reads me long sections of *Wealth of Nations* and Sir Hale's treatise on the poor. I even brought it up at the women's meeting, but they just sound confused."

"They must have thought you wanted to be married when you said you wanted to be married." This Emery seemed to find very amusing. Forsaking her soup, she leaned back in her chair till its front feet left the floor, but her eyes twinkled.

"None of the ladies in the meeting ever started a bakery," Anna observed with a sharpness that Jane suspected was more about Lord Boislegrand's attitude than the attitudes of the Quaker ladies.

"But what do I *do?*"

"Rose, you haven't whined like this since you were eight." Straight and sharp, it was clear Anna was disinclined to baby their baby sister.

"I'm not whining. I am concerned. I have a concern." Sitting straighter herself, Rose tried to look very tall and married at the table.

"Easy enough. Rent the rooms upstairs." Emery went back to conveying her soup into her mouth as fast as possible.

Her sisters were forced to pause in astonished silence.

"Can Mr. Russell afford it?" Jane pounced on the question of money. It wasn't a room, it was an entire apartment of rooms, between them and Lord Zachary's painting garret.

But all Anna's crispness melted into puddles of smiles. "Oh, Rose! Wouldn't that be lovely? Right upstairs! You'd be back here with the shop! And all of us!"

Rose, however, seemed less delighted. "How does that help anything? It's still a question of what I do all day!"

"No, it isn't." Emery sounded disgusted. "You've lost all your sense. We'll do his laundry with all of ours. Cook the meals with all of ours. It's five people instead of four, that's all, and you do your share like you always did."

"It's a lovely dream," Jane said slowly, weighing each word, "but men like things of their own. And *my* point remains. There is too much work here for the four of us to do."

"Plus Tilly," put in Anna, re-addressing herself to her soup.

"Plus Tilly. Bread to bake, four times a day now, cakes from the wee hours, and all the customers all day, besides the chores here that we must do to live. With or without you, Rose, there is simply too much work."

"Jordan and Sal work like demons all day." Emery, folding her arms again, looked back at Jane like a firing line of soldiers.

"And we can't have that. Sal should be in school. And even if Jordan only aspires to be a journeyman baker," Jane cut off the argument all the sisters had repeated many times before, "he must know his history, and well enough to read and do arithmetic that he can't be cheated. Just think of all the bakeries that opened and closed in this spot."

"I think Mrs. Scrope had something to do with that," muttered Anna more darkly than she ever did, and Jane considered her oldest sister's ability to hold a grudge against their landlord.

"Well, we've done what they said we could not do. We are making the bakery pay." *Just barely,* Jane wanted to add, but didn't. There was a world of difference between where they had started and where they were now, and she knew they all felt they had climbed a cliff and reached the top. She wouldn't take that away from them, any of them. They only had to see what the road looked like from here. "We need more help for that, or *we* will pay, in exhaustion. Emery, if you could only see the circles under your eyes."

Jane didn't expect an appeal to Emery about her looks would carry any weight with her sister. Emery had decided when she was still small that if she didn't intend to marry, she didn't have to look ladylike, and Jane didn't remember ever seeing her look in a mirror.

So it took Jane aback when Emery muttered, "I'll sleep more."

"I don't wish to be ungracious to the concession, but we still need more help."

"Jane, you're overlooking something. We are not of the Baker's Guild. They haven't concerned themselves with us because they haven't *seen* us." Anna's soft brown eyes were deadly serious now. "If we do too much business, they will have to notice us."

"I thought we followed all the rules." Was it always to be some new horror?

"We are not members of the guild," Anna said quietly, as if reluctant to admit it aloud.

Jane was tired. If none of the rest of them were, she would admit it. She was tired. When she snuck out of the bakery for some time to herself, she spent too much of it doing things she could not tell her sisters about, and that made coming home tiring too.

If only Rose would be more forthcoming about being married. There were things Jane really needed to know.

Her paving man had a wicked way with a kiss and chuckled things into her ears that he must think Jane understood. Jane didn't. If Rose didn't explain them, who would?

Emery finally slowed her chewing, only to lean her elbows on the table. "All I know about the guild rules is what I could get from Mr. Gruninger when I visited his shop. None of us even knew then if we could do this."

"I remember." It had been a whirlwind of speculation, of *what ifs* and *maybes,* and they'd all pictured survival as the end of the race.

Well, now they'd arrived at survival; what happened next?

"We should reach out to the Guild before they summon us." Jane believed the best defense was always charging forward.

"Should we talk to the Captain?" Rose sounded even less sure about this than about being married.

"No!"

When Jane's violently quick answer made even Rose's mouth fall open, Jane took a deep breath.

"We can't simply run to the Captain every time we have a problem, Rose. He's not our guardian. He's not our father."

He wasn't their anything. Jane was painfully aware of that.

"He's our friend, and he's been terribly helpful." Staunch in her defense of Captain Brice, on that Rose would not be moved.

"All right, all right." Anna tried to rap her big-sister voice against the table without doing anything so unladylike as actually using knuckles. "Nothing drastic need happen today. We really should look into more help, Emery. You may not wish to hire more bakers, but I do. Let me inquire whether any other women in the neighborhood could be good at helping with the cakes. I, at least, don't enjoy waking in the small hours every day to bake cakes, and the Hotel requires them to look perfect. We must think more about what to do regarding the Guild. And Rose. You know we will always be here for you. Of course, it's between you and your husband." Every time Anna mentioned Rose's husband it seemed to get a little easier for her; it still wasn't easy. "But we would love to have you as a neighbor. Wouldn't we all?"

Jane chimed in her *of course* as Emery took Rose's hand and squeezed it, and Rose, at least, looked a little calmer.

"At least until you marry, yourself." Jane couldn't stop the words. They'd run away from her.

Why couldn't she be glad for Anna, as long as Anna was determined to go through with what Jane knew was a terrible mistake?

Anna's fingers just fluttered that idea away too. "Who knows when that will be?" she shrugged, looking down into her soup.

Episode 2: The Men

"The suite is so large. The rent is so reasonable," Mrs. Scrope repeated to Mr. Russell for the third time.

As if it were a chant, and rent was Mrs. Scropes' church.

She'd insisted he come to the Scrope house and conduct his business with Mr. Scrope himself.

The prospect of meeting the mysteriously absent Mr. Scope would have drawn Mr. Russell's inescapable curiosity, even had he not been set on renting the rooms Rose wanted.

As it turned out, the much-vaunted Mr. Scrope was eighty years old if he was a day, and could barely hold himself upright under his lap robe. Wisps of white hair sprang out from under the edge of his damask cap, and his lap robe, a heavy bearskin from the colonies, seemed likely to crush him.

He was as still as his wife was inexorable. His rheumy eyes turned back and forth between his wife and Mr. Russell as if they were playing tennis, and he had no idea which side was his.

In his personal dealings, Mr. Russell preferred to be liked. He always had, and never more so now than when the vote for his possible seat approached. He did not wish to make an enemy of Mrs. Scrope, who had stamina and stern eyes that would be the envy of a prime minister.

"Perhaps..."

Mrs. Scrope flicked her eyes toward her husband, silently instructing Mr. Russell to address *him*. Mr. Russell duly began again, addressing himself to the skeleton wearing a bearskin.

"Perhaps you would be good enough to consider reducing your rate, as the rooms have been empty this half year and more." Somehow Mr. Russell thought his audience would find this more persuasive than the idea of letting his wife reunite with her sisters.

Economic realities that had previously been only topics of discussion had become manifestly real since his marriage. He could not feed his wife and still pay a servant to iron his collars. And he was growing tired of dining on bread, which was the only food in never-ending supply.

His standing had benefited greatly from the grace of Lady Arnold herself, the beneficent widow of Leicester Square, hosting his wedding.

Now, neighbors' opinions were sliding backwards. The men grinned at him in a way that wasn't wholly friendly, and the women just shook their heads in puzzlement. Every day Rose appeared in the bakery, it chipped away at that benefit.

To Mr. Russell's credit, he valued very little in this earthly life above the happiness of his sweet, pretty little wife. And if she wanted to work in the shop, he would find a way to make it right. After all, the Friends believed that women were equal to men before God in their ability to serve His goals. Why not equal to make our daily bread?

His heart and mind were clear. He needed only to sort out the practical realities. Faith did not win a seat in Parliament; and he still needed clean collars.

All of that would be addressed once Rose had the rooms

she wanted. All that stood in his way was stiff, suspicious Mrs. Scrope.

Who parried his gentle point. "If we reduced our rates every time a place was empty, we'd soon have only pennies."

"Yet if the establishment remains empty very long, it brings you nothing at all."

"Hmmm. Let us meet in the rooms, then, in perhaps an hour, and discuss it."

That sounded hopeful to him.

BRICE HAD A POLICY NOT TO HOVER OVER THE BAKERY SHOP or constantly check on his charges, as he thought of them.

He had serious affairs to address. Until this year he'd never begged a day in his life, and now it seemed all he did. Months of begging might be ready to bear fruit; and if fruit there was, he'd win the right to put his life and many others in danger.

But the damp autumn day he left his hotel and spotted a gang of men approaching the shop door at the end of the street, he waved away the waiting carriage and walked down the pavement to see what was the matter.

As he drew closer, he realized he probably needn't have bothered. The residence door, just this side of the shop door, had two men in it, lounging and obviously watching the goings-on.

Brice spoke first. "It's Lord Zachary, isn't it?"

The man unfolded his bare forearms and bowed slightly, his formality at odds with his jacketless, hatless state. "It is, sir. And you are Captain Brice."

"Indeed." Brice looked at the other man, who didn't offer his name. Brice had seen him at the wedding. He'd had clean hair then. He didn't now. "What goes on?"

"Apparently the Misses Bickering have decided to hire." The man's accent was faint, suggestive.

"Hire what?"

"Bakers." Lord Zachary had resumed leaning against the door frame with his arms folded across his chest against the chill air. He nodded toward the shop door; it held a pinned notice. *Journeymen wanted,* it said.

Two thick-shouldered men shoved their way out, grumbling.

Brice thrust out his chin as the grumblers passed. "All right, men?" He made it a point to ask grumblers about their grumbles. It stopped many a shipboard fight before it started.

"Lady told me I didn't have the right attitude. My *attitude.*" The applicant said this in many syllables: *a-ti-tyooood.* "Because I wouldn't take orders from a lad."

"Oh la." The second one waved an exaggerated pinky. "That's what we get, Harry, we shouldn't've tried. What do you expect of a bakery with only women?"

"What's goin'ta happen to that lad living in that bakery? Women around him all day, and him thinkin' he knows what to do?"

They meant Jordan, realized Brice. Jordan, who had put on at least a stone since he'd been roaming the park hungry. "He does."

"He does what?" The bakers clearly hadn't expected Brice to join in.

"He knows what to do."

Both men puffed up their chests to argue, but Lord Zachary, still leaning, just nodded. "He does."

One baker glanced at the nameless neighbor, as if assuming anyone so disreputable-looking would offer support.

But the neighbor only narrowed his eyes. "Why are you so determined to question it?"

The rejected applicant just settled back on his heels.

His friend didn't. "See here, he doesn't half know how to bake bread! Harry and I have worked in two bakeries. Eighteen years between us. We know how to do it."

A faint memory stirred. Brice mused aloud, "The Ladies' Own Bakery has a unique prescription for bread, I do believe."

Lord Zachary shrugged his free shoulder. "If you can't follow orders, you can't bake here."

The baker made a rude noise. "We ain't about to take orders from a bunch of women on how to bake bread!"

"Then why did you come?" The nameless neighbor had not stepped forward; if anything, he'd moved farther back into the shadows, behind the jamb of the door and Lord Zachary's shoulder. But his voice issued forth with inescapable insistence. "Did you not intend to work here? Do you think you can intimidate the ladies? Extort them? Where did you hear of the bakery? Do you live in the square?"

"Here." The quieter journeyman wrinkled his bent nose, its burnt tip peeling in the daylight. "We don't have to tell you anything."

"Not right now you don't," the man's voice issued from the door, a bit eerie because his face was unseen, "but I will find out the answers all the same."

"Bollocks." The louder one nudged his friend's elbow, and without a goodbye, they walked down the pavement, fast, not looking back.

The neighbor stuck his greasy head out of the doorway and peered after them, as if he could derive the direction of their destination from the backs of their shoes.

It surprised Brice that, with all he *had* heard about from the Misses Bickering, he had not heard about this disquieting fellow. "Have we met?"

The man's eyes turned to Brice. They were piercing in the

truest sense, in that they made Brice want to look away, lest he find himself impaled. "Wouldn't you remember if we had?"

"Don't even try to find out anything about him." Lord Zachary was still peacefully leaning against the painted wood, shaking his head toward Brice. "I live here, and all I know is what room is his. And what he drinks."

Brice was used to facing down much larger men on his ship... and in battle. "And the Bickering ladies are fine with that?"

The nameless neighbor didn't back down either, nor did he study Brice up and down. Just kept his eyes trained on Brice, unmoving, nearly unblinking. As if Brice were a spider that might suddenly leap. "I am on good terms with my neighbors."

Knowing the discomfort of Her Majesty, as Brice thought of Anna, with anything inappropriate, Brice doubted that was completely true.

The neighbor, however, just tilted a regal nod toward Lord Zachary. "I include you, of course, good sir."

Perhaps that was a flicker of a smile at the corner of his lordship's mouth? "We like to keep an eye on the ladies, especially that blighted viscount who thinks he's going to marry Anna Bickering."

"As I understand it, she fully intends to marry him." If they knew anything about their neighbors, they knew that what mattered was what the *ladies* intended.

The neighbor's profile emerged again from the shadows into the light of day. "Matters of the heart are rarely simple," he said, with that lilt that said English was not his first language. "The smallest motion can set the whole world on a new path; why not a heart?"

Brice stared at him. "Poetic, aren't you?"

From inside, they heard a bellowing voice that could only be Miss Emery Bickering. "*Next!*"

Another disgruntled-looking beer-scented bag-lifter shouldered his way out the door, muttering darkly about women, using words that got him a glare from all three men waiting outside.

He drew himself up with a sharp stop, seeing three men watching.

"We live here," Lord Zachary took obvious dark pleasure in saying to the man, who picked up his steps and hurried off with no more swearing.

At the sound of the man's boot leather on the paving stones, notably loud even among the quick steps of the rest of the passers-by, Lord Zachary turned to his compatriot. "You must let me scare off one or two."

"I didn't even get to show my teeth," said the other, and Brice decided that for at least this moment, the Bickering sisters were well defended.

THE SEA CAPTAIN SEEMED RIGHT ENOUGH, THOUGHT ZACH, but their conversation was broken off by the arrival of a barouche at the edge of the paving, its stop damming the flow of carriages and horses around this busy corner of the square.

Zach couldn't help his scowl. It was Lord Boislegrand.

Who didn't even see three men standing an arm's length from him as he hurried into the bakery shop, hat in hand.

Zach felt his forehead furrowing. He forced it smooth.

By the time he looked back to Brice, the Captain had turned, toward his hotel.

"You're not going in to the shop?" he asked Brice.

"No; the ladies will do well enough, and they're familiar with his lordship."

Zachary's next words betrayed his pressing need to deal in some gossip. His sister was absorbed in planning to be married, his mother obsessed with his older brother's *lack* of marriage plans, and his father hadn't paid attention to anything outside White's club since his own marriage a thousand years ago.

Zach had gathered pocketsful of details, with the eye of an artist, but had nowhere to discuss them. He was desperate.

He blurted out, "The man comes every day to ask Anna Bickering to marry him."

That paused the Captain. His dark eyes came back to study Zach, with less sympathy than Zach had hoped. "Does he?"

"No!" The nameless neighbor scoffed. "He does not ask; he has already asked, and she accepted. He comes to see *when*. Every day."

"Does he?" That seemed to interest the Captain more.

"He has the license," added the nameless neighbor.

How he knew *that,* Zach didn't bother to guess or ask. It was apparent that whatever the man wanted to know, he'd find out.

Captain Brice, however, was less familiar with their neighbor. "How do *you* know so?"

"Why would I tell *you*?" was all the neighbor said, scowling in the dark doorway.

"Go in and see," Zach exhorted the Captain. He and his neighbor had each heard the speech half a dozen times, without even trying. Every day Lord Boislegrand arrived in his carriage and asked Anna Bickering to come away with him, in short sentences sprinkled with words like *diamond* and *heart* and *forever,* and every day Anna Bickering told him she was busy.

That, however, apparently didn't interest the Captain enough to go see. "If you gentlemen are looking out for the ladies' interests, I feel secure in going about my business."

Zachary's aim was to paint well enough to give his mother

fainting spells and draw an actual word of disapproval from his father. Yet here he was standing in his doorway. From having no interest in the Bickering sisters at all, he now found them more interesting than any other society. His sister Cecily was obsessed with reporting about decorations on silk slippers and false curls that had slipped into salads, but she was missing out on the real drama on life's stage.

It made a real difference to the Misses Bickering that their bakery now bustled from morning till night, that a footman came from Jacquier's every day to take away cakes, that the chimney of their bread oven now constantly trickled smoke into the sky. The ladies walked taller, and Zach thought he saw different cares carved into the corners of their eyes and lips.

He found that maddening, as he knew he wasn't a good enough painter to capture them. And he wanted to. They were true evidences of life.

A barrel of a man came rolling down the sidewalk, fat and sturdy at the same time. His scarred knuckles had seen many a brawl.

Even Zachary felt a bit of consternation as he approached, but the nameless neighbor just said, "Owen," and the man nodded as he went inside.

If the Captain weren't to help him keep an eye on the bakery ladies, at least Zach had one near friend. Of a sort.

"Gentlemen," said the Captain, fingers moving to lift his hat and then, realizing he wasn't wearing one, dropping as he nodded and departed.

"Damn." Zachary kept his swearing under his breath. "I honestly wanted him to go in and see what that lord-toad was saying today."

"Should I go in?"

Zach looked over his shoulder. "Do you want to scare the customers half to death? I'll go."

At that moment, Mr. Russell, the new husband of the youngest Bickering sister, rounded the corner from Bear Street, their landlady on his arm.

Avoiding the landlady would be good, as Zachary was a bit behind on his rent. "You watch all *that*," he said as he opened the door to the shop proper and slipped inside.

THE SECOND COUNTER, PUFFY SAW, HAD BEEN GIVEN OVER to Miss Anna and Miss Emery, who stood behind it interviewing potential bakers for their new positions.

The distressingly striking Miss Jane was at the till, leaving Miss Rose--Mrs. Russell to wait on the customers.

Puffy knew it would serve him to notice all the sisters, but his eyes, as always, went to Miss Anna and stayed there.

She looked so pretty and golden with the sunlight coming through the Bear Street windows behind her, making the crinkled frustration of her brow look like that of an angel come down to scold mere mortals into behaving.

"I've been baking twelve years," said the stout young man, staying, Puffy noticed with approval, on his side of the counter.

"And we want that experience," Miss Anna said, nodding in that flower-like way of hers, "but you must understand that Jordan Collier has already been with us for some time, and knows how we bake."

Puffy had no idea who Jordan Collier was, but immediately felt jealous.

He shouldn't; he knew that. But Anna had admitted him to no intimacy at all. He was terribly hungry for her time, for her attention; and she had no conception of a date when he could claim her as his very own married wife. "Miss Bickering."

She heard him; her sweet brown eyes flicked his way, and she bobbed her head, very proper, but she made no move to come to his side. Instead, she went on questioning the heavy-shouldered young man. "You understand, Mr. Wiggs, that Jordan will guide you through learning Miss Emery's methods, and he will in a sense remain senior to you, older though you may be."

"Miss Emery?"

"Me," said Miss Emery, simply.

The young man looked her up and down, tall tower of plain cloth and plain hair that she was. He shrugged. "I've done dumber things."

Puffy considered that a lack of commitment, but Anna seemed to accept it.

"Very well. If you wish to begin at those wages, you can start tomorrow."

"One question. Do you have rats?"

"What would we do with rats, Mr. Wiggs?" Anna wrinkled her nose prettily.

"You don't do with them, you *have* them. I can't stand a bakery with rats. When you sleep on the floor by the oven all winter, it's bad enough one side's always cold. If there's rat bites as well--I won't do it."

"Sleep on the floor? Yes, I see." Miss Anna pretended it wasn't news to her that she was hiring men to sleep on the floor of her bakery year-round. Puffy thought that adorable. "We haven't seen any rats, Mr. Wiggs, and if we do, I assure you they'll be forcibly evicted."

The man blinked. "I guess that means no rats."

"No rats." Miss Emery nodded.

"Fine." The young man nodded familiarly to Puffy as he took his leave.

"They're going to sleep on the floor?" Anna whispered to her sister once the man had gone.

"Just like I do. *Next!*" shouted Miss Emery.

Puffy drew closer to Anna. "Miss Bickering. Won't you come take a drive with me?" If he could get her alone, he could get some promises out of her, he was sure of it.

"Oh no, my lord, I'm terribly sorry but you see how busy we are."

Another thick-chested young man elbowed his way through the women buying bread on the other side of the shop and shoved forward. "Next is me."

Miss Emery sounded bored as she said in a sing-song voice that showed how often she'd asked the question that day, "What work have you done baking, and where?"

"I've had positions at--"

Anna interrupted him, flying out from behind the counter. "Never mind, go ahead!" she called back breathlessly to the young man as she dashed away. Their possible baker just gave Emery a quizzical squint and started again. "I've had positions at--"

Across the shop floor, Anna flapped her apron at a young man by the counter holding a tuppence loaf in a state of undress. Him, not the bread. He wore no coat, no hat, and wore his shirtsleeves rolled up. Nameless stains marred his waistcoat.

"Lord Zachary! Go away!" Anna hissed; Puffy heard it quite clearly as he followed her.

"I need my dinner. Lord Boislegrand." Coatless, the man executed a flawless bow in Puffy's direction.

"Have we met, Lord Zachary?" Puffy didn't know anyone interesting enough to buy his own bread while coatless.

"Indeed. My father is Lester Vane, Earl of Tasseton. I believe we met last season. At Lady Villeneuve's *soirée.*"

Well. No one went there who didn't want a wife. Puffy didn't understand why, if a brash young lordling like this wanted a wife, he didn't have one already, and why he was buying his own dinner at the Ladies' Own Bakery.

"Go away," Anna hissed again, and it took Puffy a moment to remember she wasn't talking to him. "You set a bad example for the kind of man we want to hire."

"If they can't handle a man buying bread, I don't see them working for ladies," said this Lord Zachary, using both hands to toss his loaf up to spin in mid-air.

"See here, lad, if Miss Bickering wants you to go, you must go." It was only his duty, Puffy felt, to enforce his lady's wishes.

Which duty Anna immediately dismissed. "No no, Lord Boislegrand, you needn't chase Lord Zachary away. He's going." Her eyes hardened. It was impossible for sweet, soft eyes like hers to be hard, yet they did. "Aren't you?"

"Do you want your *other* neighbor in here instead?" Lord Zachary asked lightly, leaning an elbow on the counter, clearly prepared to wait his turn to pay for his bread no matter how long it took.

That inflated Anna with true horror. Her indrawn breath was quickly stifled, but loud enough that several patrons turned to look.

"Fine, but go away immediately soon as you can," she said, all in a rush like one word, before turning to Puffy. Elation!

Quickly crushed as she added, "And you, my lord. Not today."

"But--"

"Not today."

"*Next!*" Miss Emery shouted behind them, and Puffy knew he'd spend one more day dissatisfied.

F ROM THE WINDOW ABOVE , M R . R USSELL SAW L ORD Boislegrand leave the bakery.

Just the sight of him, his fine beaver hat, his elegant carriage, all made Mr. Russell bristle.

He knew Anna had accepted his proposal, and decided that until his wife gave him any specific instructions about the man, he should leave Lord Boislegrand to the Bickering sisters.

Any sister but Rose.

"Mrs. Scrope," he wrested his attention back to the matter at hand. "The bakery is working hard both day and night, with a certain amount of bustle. You must consider that when calculating the rent."

"Yes, I know," said the landlady darkly, with a sour eye down to the bakery door.

Seeing no reason for rancor in that direction, Mr. Russell changed course.

"Of course the Misses Bickering themselves are then on the next floor—"

Over her shoulder, Mr. Russell caught sight of a man's hair peeping in the doorway.

That was all he could see, a tuft of hair just at the edge of the open door, dark against the darker air of the corridor.

Who the hell was out there?

He gathered himself. "—meaning we shall have the ladies below us, and isn't there a tenant in the garret?"

"An artist!" Mrs. Scrope dismissed him as if he were no more substantial than air. "He is hardly ever there. A lord."

Saying *a lord* clearly delighted the woman.

She opened the door of an empty side room—a bedroom, perhaps—and Mr. Russell saw not just the light coming in the dusty windows, but a place where his little wife could be happy.

With her old home right downstairs.

"You really must make more allowance for the empty state."

Over her shoulder, Mr. Russell saw the man in the hall—it was indeed a man—slide more into view, an eye, the side of an elegantly sloped nose, an unshaved chin.

He looked toward Mrs. Scrope, then back toward Mr. Russell with a questioning gaze. As if asking if he should *do* something to her.

Mrs. Scrope did not see. "I don't *have* to make more allowance than I have, sir."

The man put his hand to his belt. Then, as if surprised he wore no weapon, began feeling around himself for one.

Mr. Russell burst out, "Don't!"

The man stopped. Raised his eyebrows questioningly. *Hadn't I better?*

Mrs. Scrope just raised her chin. "Don't what?"

"Don't... pretend to a harder heart than you have, madam." The man in the hallway wasn't moving; neither was Mrs. Scrope. One of them held his future in their hands. "Surely you wish to be kind to young newlyweds. I can see it in your face."

Her gray, grooved, implacable face said no such thing.

"Mr. Russell, this is an affair of business, not charity. Do you wish to engage the rooms or not?"

Frantically Mr. Russell wondered if the rooms came haunted by the unshaven maniac in the hall.

Knowing that he wanted them even if they did.

"Very well, madam, I accept your terms."

The man in the hall just shrugged and disappeared.

Mr. Russell thought first of how happy Rose would be.

Then he thought of the size of his savings and wondered if he had perhaps just made a mistake.

Opening the bakery door, its tall visitor with his flour-spattered hat surveyed a scene of bustle and noise.

There were ladies of all sorts in various states of dress, from maids in starched aprons and old-fashioned caps, to women with buttoned spencers snug on strong shoulders and skirts that showed the ink, blood, and whiskey of various trades.

Indeed, he was taken aback at the crowd's variation. Then he noticed two other things: the largely bare shelves, with only big half-peck loaves left at this time of day; and the stunning, jewel-like, black-and-flowered vase in a nook of pride, high up on the empty shelves.

Behind a counter two young women, one slender and blonde as ash-wood, the other round and curly-haired, noted his arrival; then the tall one waved him away.

"No more today," she said with an air of infinite weariness.

"I take it you are the owner," he said, making his way to her counter.

"One of them."

Her curly-haired companion just fanned her own face with her hand. "Truly, sir, no more interviews today."

He placed his hands palm-down on the counter. His hands were indeed thick and strong, as were the wrists above them disappearing into his ill-fitting sleeves. There was flour under his fingernails, too.

"I am not a journeyman," he said, setting his poorly shaven jaw. "I am a freeman of the Worshipful Company of Bakers, and you are not."

Episode 3: Such a crowd here

Winter was on the doorstep. Summer was long gone. And the Misses Bickering were no longer easily startled.

There was no gasping, no display of nerves.

Emery just closed the space between her shoulder and Anna's. "That's a rude way to meet," she said, more quietly than usual.

The man straightened. He looked a bit surprised the ladies hadn't cowed before him. "I am Josiah Keales, and I am here to represent the Worshipful Company of Bakers."

"We're glad to meet you, sir," Anna said, but without a single bob of her head.

Even Jane felt steady. One man couldn't rock them. Not after all the knocks they'd had in the last half-year.

"Perhaps you would like to take some tea with us. Perhaps next week?" Rose inquired without leaving her place at the counter.

"You're offering me tea? *Tea?* You women haven't an inkling, have you? I could have you prosecuted in court for selling bread without the approval of the guild!"

The broad-shouldered young man who had been speaking to Emery began to sidle toward the door.

Mr. Keales bristled a high, judging eyebrow at him. "Well you might sneak! You can't become a master if you work in such a place, you know!"

"Don't want to be a master," muttered the young man, still sliding one foot, then the other along the quickest path to the front door. "Just want to work."

"As do we." Even as Anna said it, the young man slipped out the shop door, pulling it silently shut behind him as if they wouldn't notice that a man the size of a bullock had just left. "There, you see what you've done? You've frightened away our possible help."

"No loss there," muttered Emery under her breath to Anna, "not overburdened with brains, that one."

"True enough," Anna muttered back.

Before them, Mr. Keales spread his arms as wide as a skinny man could. "Now *see here*."

Rose chuckled, and at that gentle noise, Mr. Keales tottered, his arms dropped.

She pushed a hank of bread across the countertop to her patron, and then spoke up clearly, so Mr. Keales and everyone else could hear. "We've invited you to take refreshments with us, Mr. Keales, where we will be happy to take a long, hard look at anything you require." The shoppers near her tittered, taking this for a joke about being blind. Which Jane thought it was.

Mr. Keales clearly grasped that he was in some way being made fun of, but couldn't figure out how.

"For the moment," Rose added, "we must attend to our patrons. Surely you understand."

Mr. Keales slumped. Then his wide-knuckled hands with the white margins of flour stuck under the fingernails waved, their uncontrolled flapping punctuating his dismay. "You can't just do this!"

"Sir," Jane said, wondering if she would have to summon help to eject the man or if some of the customers might help her, "we're doing it."

He blinked at Jane, blinked again, then muttered, "Fine, I'll be back," and left, threading his way through the silent, unfriendly glares of customers.

"Honestly," said one good woman as she stepped up to be waited upon. "A pound of the maslin."

"This is a problem," Jane heard Anna tell Emery, just before Lord Zachary in his shirtsleeves finally left the shop too.

"Mm hmm." The nameless neighbor treated Zach's report of the entire conversation with the solemnity of a general receiving a field report. "And that's every word he said?"

"I've told you twice through." Zach had thought the neighbor might do something—follow the man, at least. He ought to be useful for that. Instead, he'd let the fellow go, stomping south on the pavement until he was out of sight.

Zach sighed. "I suppose the ladies ought to consult a solicitor." Surely such a disreputable-looking man knew a solicitor or two.

"A solicitor? *Bah.* The question is not what the law prescribes. The question is what people actually *do.* One can make a law forbidding anything. But most of them are paint on paper, just for show."

Zach considered this. It was certainly true regarding the things gentlemen did; he supposed it must apply to ladies' bakeries as well. "You can help them?"

"Sir," said the neighbor, voice trailing away into a whisper, "I have already begun."

"THEY SIMPLY MUST ACCEPT US, THAT IS ALL."

The bakery proper never had privacy any more either, now full of people dashing here and there constantly working. The sense of space, of empty tables, was no longer unlimited. At any moment the big room held any number of Bickering sisters, always, of course, including Emery. Jordan and Sal were there in the mornings, sent off to the cellar from time to time to read lessons.

Anna was giving this reassurance to Wiggs, the man disturbed by rats. He was now disturbed by the Worshipful Company of Bakers.

He *had* come back, though, along with a Mr. Bailey, gruff and burly. "I just want work, ma'am," he'd insisted to Emery, not out front, but at the door to the mews, as if wishing to avoid being seen. He'd clutched his hat in his hands.

"Bugger the Guild," Bailey had said more succinctly, spitting at the sewer drain.

Emery had explained that language at the Ladies' Own Bakery had to be suitable for any children who might be listening, and Mr. Bailey's eyes had popped a little. But he'd promised to watch his tongue, and Emery had set them to learning her prescription for bread.

This morning, besides all these, the bakery also held the former Mrs. Baby, whom everyone tried to remember to call Mrs. Wallace.

Plus all three of her children.

Mrs. Wallace had answered Anna's inquiry about women who might bake cakes with what Anna could only call a desperate pounce. She had been such a good friend to them, and seemed so violently interested, Anna could only accept her.

But Anna hadn't specified that baking meant leaving her children at home.

"Toast!" Jimmy demanded, as he did every ten minutes, and Anna sighed.

"Sal, I don't suppose you could take Jimmy into the mews to let him run about?"

"Do you want me to read this book, or do you want me to keep charge of Jimmy?" Sal asked with the bitterness of a young person who had already taken Jimmy into the mews a dozen times in the last week, and who didn't care for her book.

"You don't like Virgil, do you?"

"I never met him," Sal said with a sniff, "but I think hiding in a horse and then jumping out and killing everyone is very rude."

"Virgil didn't suggest the idea," Anna reminded her reluctant pupil. "He only wrote about the Trojan War."

"Well, it was rude, and here he is telling everyone about it, and you just know that's going to encourage someone else to try it."

Anna contemplated Sal's point as she peeked at how Mrs. Baby creamed the butter.

"I must help Jane in front. Rose's move will take her all day, surely." Anna was very aware of Emery's squint-eyed look. Emery had opposed letting Mrs. Baby bake cakes, and Anna had sworn she'd ensure that it worked.

The littlest baby was happy enough in his basket, and the toddler cheerful enough playing with the baby's toes, but Jimmy was insistent, loud, and concerned only with his stomach.

Wiggs had a wonderful way of ignoring everything, but Bailey seemed constantly astonished, never more so than by the sight of small children in a bakery. He looked like he was about to say something to Jimmy, and Anna shuddered at the thought of what it might be. "Don't worry, Mr. Bailey, we'll find Jimmy some company in a moment."

Mrs. Baby—Mrs. Wallace, Anna firmly reminded herself —had a wonderfully light touch with mixing the cakes, though, and Anna was not about to give up on her.

Perhaps if she ignored all the children, they would sort themselves out.

Emery's thin lips said she didn't care for *tiny* children in her bakery, she didn't care for Anna leaving her alone with them to serve out front with Jane, and by the way, she didn't care for the Worshipful Company of Bakers.

Anna tried to be reassuring about the one thing she could. "The guild cannot reject us; clearly, we are a bakery."

"The *guild* doesn't have any members who are women."

"That's not so. We know there's a Mrs. Forrest."

"Mrs. Forrest inherited her place from *Mr.* Forrest, who died."

Since that was so, Anna needed a moment to marshall further arguments. She didn't see the point in despairing before time. The guild simply had to accept them, because they must continue. What good it did to be as grim as Emery all the time, Anna didn't know.

"Jimmy, let's walk outside." Jane would kill her. There were probably a dozen patrons waiting to be served.

Apparently Jimmy had not learned more words, from Mr. Bailey or anyone else. "I want *toast*," he said firmly.

"Everyone knows that." Anna took his hand and led him out the rear door into the cobbled mews, wondering when her position as oldest sister began requiring minding someone else's child.

"Where have you *been*?" By the time Anna appeared in the bakery shop, Jane had served what felt like half of Leicester Square, choosing bread with one hand and taking money with the other.

Her mind was chopped in so many directions she feared she was developing *paranoea*. She could swear she'd seen a little woman slip a twopenny loaf under her cape and disappear. But since she couldn't remember what the woman looked like, mightn't her mind have made it up?

"I do apologize. We all do as best we can when *you* are off doing the household errands, you know," Anna said crisply, nodding to a lady who wished to see the bottom of the half-peck maslin.

Those simple words iced Jane's bones.

She simply must stop sneaking out of the bakery to see Hughes. He was like a drug, winding his way into her blood. There was something peculiar about his kisses. They left her feverish, hungry, yet less interested in food. There was something wrong with her. Like tobacco, he was a habit that smelled delicious and yet left a sticky residue. She must stop venturing out to see him.

"It's the middle of the day."

Jane surveyed the loose paving stones, the digging and tamping tools in a barrel alongside the bare dirt, and the man with the kissable lips. All of them were annoying her.

"I know it's the middle of the day," she hissed, "I cannot pretend to be shopping in the middle of the night."

"I can't stop working just because you want a buss in the middle of the afternoon."

Why did he look so good? Even the way the ropes of muscle in his neck, browned by the sun, glistened with sweat from the work he'd been doing, made Jane go a little weak in the knees.

Yet she still didn't know his first name... and didn't care.

This must be what it felt like to be dogged by spirits, or devils.

No angel would cause this.

Behind him, the other paving-men were giving Jane knowing leers, and that didn't make this fun at all.

In fact, Jane wasn't sure that kissing Hughes *was* fun. It meant chasing after him at odd hours, trying to catch him by the inn where he liked to drink of an evening, or even pretending to cross his path, literally, in the street.

It was just so *good*.

"Come by the inn tonight." He was impatient; peeling off his cap with one hand, he wiped the sweat from his brow, then quickly replaced it. The air was getting chill, more than usual this time of year, or perhaps it was just that Jane was so often out of doors.

She just nodded, and walked on, pretending to all and sundry who might care to look that her urgent errand was thread to mend a stocking, and not the kind of kiss where his hands went round her waist and made her feel tiny and big all at the same time.

It was the nature of devils, or addictions, that they made one feel ashamed of one's cravings.

IN INVESTIGATING THIS WORSHIPFUL COMPANY OF Bakers, he'd crept around their great hall, twice.

It was on Harp Lane. Glass and spice, coffee, wine, corn and seed and paint, the looming buildings swallowed them all thanks to young boys with trucks and burly men carrying crates upon their shoulders. All their scents were in the air, the sour and sweet, mineral and earth, all overlaid with the gut-calling scent of British *semoule*. The corns of wheat-stalks, whole and milled.

He assumed that the lane was orderly because its masters wished it so. Otherwise, this close to the Thames, it would not have been. He saw several wary men who looked healed of past bruises, the look of men hired to keep the peace; but he wasn't interested in any of them. He wanted to see if there were women.

There were, but he couldn't tell just from looking at them, unfortunately, if any of them had business there. Nor could he follow them all.

He did approach one. "Madam," he said courteously before she shrieked.

"*Gaaah!*" squealed the woman in her corsets and brown wool. "It's the Monster come again!"

She seemed genuinely rattled, and he didn't wish to upset her further, but he had to ask. "What Monster?"

She paused amidst drawing in her skirts. "The Monster. That man what stabbed women in the rear. The streets were full of 'is stories."

This caused him to shy back. He had some recollection of those stories. The man had terrorized London for months, cutting ladies' skirts, and, cruelly, ladies' *derrières*. He'd also been described as thin, pock-marked, with a large nose and brown hair.

In *1790*.

Offended, unable to deny that he had a pock-mark or two, a largish nose, and nondescript hair at best, he summoned his defense. "Madam," he said, pulling himself upright and displaying his chest, "how old do you think I am? That was twenty-three years ago!"

"You look right suspicious!" she insisted, causing him to tip his battered low hat and walk away. This was no place for remaining unobserved.

Then he stopped, turned back. "Do you do any business with the Bakers' Guild?"

Her eyes narrowed. "My 'usband's a respeckable business-man, he is!"

Discouraging.

He needed a drink.

"Here." Mr. Morley's pin-pricked hand appeared at the closet door waving a waistcoat, half-made. He dropped it on the chair and disappeared.

Emery still worked for Mr. Morley. Especially now that the bakery was always full of so many people, Mr. Morley's closet had become a welcome refuge.

Also, the nights were growing long and cold, and the closet was so small it was always warm.

Emery hadn't visited Lady Arnold again. Her ladyship had not visited the shop in weeks... not that Emery would know if she did, as the new journeymen kept her baking. There was no chance for her to be in the shop alone any more.

Perhaps Lady Arnold had recovered her good sense.

Trying to find satisfaction in the way the needle slid, with only an occasional slight *pop* of friction, through the wool, Emery contemplated returning to the kitchen salon.

She had no time to walk about, either, and therefore had not seen Jasmine in what seemed like forever.

She ought to simply announce she was going for a walk. Jane did it all the time. Why couldn't Emery? She wasn't afraid of her sisters knowing anything... though Jane knew something.

No, Emery simply wasn't sure what to do next. With any of it.

In her mother's house, she had often felt like a broom, or a candlestick. Always there, nowhere to go, nothing to do but exist.

Her mother had seemed happy enough. "With four daughters," she'd once said, "it's only a blessing if one of them wants to stay with me."

Emery felt guilty remembering it. Because she *hadn't* wanted to stay with her mother. It wasn't that she minded, exactly; it was only that she had felt more like furniture than family.

Now there were all too many new people to see, and things to possibly do, and the more Wiggs and Bailey baked, helped by Jordan and everyone else, the less Emery felt needed. The less she felt *critical*.

Her bravado about continuing to sleep by the ovens had evaporated the first night she'd gone down and found two huge men, snoring, sprawled on flour sacks by the banked fire. *Her* flour sacks.

She wondered if it would be cruel to send them to sleep in the cellar.

They looked odd, they smelled odd, and Emery wished them gone. If she'd wanted to be that close to a man, she'd have married.

And her bedroom, without Rose's warm presence, was cold.

It shocked her, but Mr. Morley's closet was a welcome bit of heaven.

ROSE HEARD THE DOOR CLOSE AND SOMEONE CROSS THE wooden floor with unusually direct stride.

"Miss Bickering," she heard Lord Boislegrand address her oldest sister. "I cannot take your delay for an answer any longer."

"What? Oh Mrs. Meade, do come again. Your pardon, your lordship, but I must—"

"Dinner on Sunday."

Rose held her breath.

She wasn't the least bit alarmed by Lord Boislegrand, but she had never heard him take that tone with Anna.

She'd never heard *anyone* take that tone with Anna, other than perhaps Aunt Eden.

Truth be told, now that she was married, she had an indecorous interest in others' relationship maneuverings. As if she'd climbed down into a hole and now just wanted to see if anyone else would climb down in with her.

Not that she minded being married; she didn't.

Anna seemed to grasp that Lord Boislegrand had reached the end of some sort of tether.

"Do you mean to say that you invite me to dine at your house on Sunday?" she asked, a little frostily.

"I do."

"My sister and I will be glad to attend."

Clearly her easy capitulation delighted his lordship. His display of backbone dissolved into giddy pleasure. "*Won*derful. I shall send the carriage."

And apparently he had no more to say, as, victorious, he celebrated by marching out.

The little jingle of the shop's new door bell told Rose he was gone.

"What sister will you be taking to dine with you, Miss Bickering?" Rose asked, as formally as possible for the benefit of the customers, all of whom had just witnessed the very personal conversation.

"Mrs. Russell—"

"I ask out of interest, since I of course won't be able to attend."

Rose was interested in others' romantic affairs, but not enough to give up a Sunday dinner with her very own Mr. Russell. Not even to watch Anna make a fool out of her betrothed, herself, or both.

Episode 4: Two sisters and tea

"Mr. Keales. Will you have another sandwich?"

Mr. Keales, sitting at their dining table with Talbourne crockery in front of him, looked calm enough; but he was growing red.

It was curious, Anna thought with detachment as she passed him the little crock of honey for the tea she'd just poured. He gave away nothing with movement of his face, yet the flush of blood in his cheeks grew darker and darker the longer their conversation went on.

"The Guild doesn't admit women. Except as mercy to a woman whose husband in the guild has died."

"And in those cases? Does not the woman direct the bakery?"

"Mrs. Forrest is the daughter of a master baker. She knows how it's done."

"But not a master baker herself."

"Well, she can't be."

Anna wanted to tap his saucer with her knife and admonish him not to be rude. But he wasn't Lord Boisle-grand; he was an unknown quantity, really.

And she wasn't sure what it said about her supposed betrothed that she would have felt perfectly comfortable correcting him like a child.

As she contemplated her best approach, a creak above them made her think of Rose; but it must be Lord Zachary, or their other neighbor. Rose and Mr. Russell, of course, would be at their Quaker services.

Anna would have preferred Rose be here, but she had not wished to delay this conversation, and Rose had said she was quite happy to leave it to the rest of them. Being a married lady took a great deal of her attention, Anna thought with a little acid, forgetting that said married lady worked in the bakery nearly every day.

Emery ought to be here too, but when asked had simply said, "No." On a Sunday morning, with the journeymen and children and Mrs. Baby all gone, Emery was likely downstairs petting the oven in peace and privacy.

"I know you don't mean to be insulting, Mr. Keales." Anna sipped her tea. "After all, we are doing you the courtesy of meeting with you on a Sunday."

The man stopped himself rolling his eyes. "Don't you have Sunday dinners to bake?"

Feeling simultaneously pleased and guilty, Anna looked toward her sister.

Jane simply said, "When we opened the bakery, we decided for it to be very modern. We do not take in dinners to bake on a Sunday. This is Leicester Square."

In truth, Anna hadn't been able to bear the idea of working on the day of rest—not because of the rest, though it had later proven to be critical, but because she could not bear the pitying looks of their customers for working on a Sunday.

In truth, they had baked on Sundays, sometimes, when they were desperate to make just a few more pence for the week; but they had not wished to make a practice of it. Had they opened their bakery on a Sunday like bakeries of yore, like the small ones in poorer streets like Spitalfields still did, they would have been subject to all manner of people bringing in dishes to be baked. Emery hadn't liked the idea of other people's dishes in her oven.

Anna couldn't tell if Mr. Keales wanted them open on a Sunday or not.

Everything about the Guild seemed to be difficult. From apprenticing as a child, to the time one must serve as a journeyman, to the submission of a masterpiece for judging; it all seemed quite unnecessary to Anna, who had baked bread all her life, though admittedly only recently in any large amounts.

Mr. Keales clearly believed his gospel of difficulty.

"Our government of the food of London has served for centuries, madam, to safeguard the health of the public. Our sacred duty is to survey all London bakers, and prevent unhealthy greed. I have seen bread mixed with peas, or chaff; I've seen it mixed with *chalk*. Flour is dear, has been these last two years, and that just makes things worse."

"Yes, quite so." Jane added nothing more, only sipped her tea, forcing Anna to conduct as much conversation as she could.

As long as the man was here, Anna could at least understand the Guild better. "I am so glad to meet you, as our interviews quite confused me. I thought journeymen served only for seven years, yet several told us they had worked in that rank for ten years, twelve, or more."

"You must recognize the need to maintain the number of journeymen. If journeymen become masters, who will bake the bread?"

Anna felt her back straighten. "I see. So why then should such journeymen not strike out for their own interests? I imagine if they had the funds, they would open their own bakery."

Her eyes met Jane's over Jane's teacup. They knew perfectly well that some must have done so; why else had this spot housed so many bakeries the last few years?

Mrs. Scrope definitely had evil intentions, but the fact remained that this bakery had passed through several hands. They couldn't all have been master bakers. And what did it say about the rank if they were?

"Miss Bickering. The Guild has overseen these *critical* affairs for over *six hundred years*. Surely you recognize that the need to preserve it outweighs any one man's wishes!"

He tugged at his shirt cuffs, as if irritation made his arms swell.

Anna wasn't in the mood. She and Jane were to dine with Lord Boislegrand; she didn't like admitting it to herself, but the anticipation wasn't pleasant. She wished Lord Zachary hadn't told her Lord Boislegrand's friends called him Puffy. It was unfortunately apt.

Yet she still had not begged off the betrothal.

Honestly, this Guild man was only one of her problems. A bothersome betrothal put things in perspective.

"If you instruct us on how to appeal to the Guild to join, Mr. Keales, we would be more than happy to take your advice." She wasn't, but it sounded well.

His eyes darted toward the silent Jane. He seemed unnerved by Jane's stark beauty, which served Anna's purposes just fine.

"Ladies," he said as if explaining things one more time while a thunderstorm raged over his head, "you *cannot*."

"Nonsense." Puffy—Lord Boislegrand would be here soon, and Anna felt her insides pulling tighter and tighter, as if wound on a spool between her ribs. "The very nature of its charter permits people to apply; that is its method of operation."

She had chosen those words specifically to make it hard for him to insist that she and her sisters were not people.

Go ahead, say it, she warned him silently in her head with uncharacteristic sharpness.

He didn't say it.

"I cannot help but notice that you ladies are quite young," he tried to say instead. "Surely one of you must be inclined to marry a baker in the Guild? Or who could petition to join it?"

"No," Anna said frostily, "we are not."

"Does your wife bake?" Jane's conversational dart was swift.

And poisonous, apparently. "Yes," Mr. Keales began with real enthusiasm, "she was my master's daughter, and as good a hand as you ever saw at... uh..." Realizing the conversational trap too late, Mr. Keales abandoned praise of his wife as a baker and examined the walls for artwork on which to comment. It clearly pained him that there was none.

"He wants to tie everyone to a six-hundred-year-old wagon full of rules and flatten them!" Anna was tidying up from tea with a vengeance, thumping things around till something might break.

Jane couldn't recall seeing Anna so hot in a long time, not even with Aunt Eden. Oh, her temper had been pricked by Mr. Russell marrying away their sister; but after all Rose was about to live right upstairs, so Anna was well on her way to forgiving Mr. Russell.

Perhaps.

Something about Mr. Keales just clearly rubbed her the wrong way.

Jane didn't argue; all men rubbed her the wrong way. Even Hughes. When he wasn't kissing her, he constantly said things in which she had no interest at all.

"How does my hair look?" Anna gave her own curls a twist.

"Lovely." And Jane meant it.

Gone were the days of sleeping in rag curls, or making them with paper and iron. Lacking Anna's natural curls, Jane simply braided her hair and twisted the braid against her neck, securing it with a bit of string.

It wasn't particularly comfortable or lovely, but with the ends of the string tucked under her hair, they barely showed. She'd seen a bronze hairpin in a shop window on Green Street; but it was as far from hers as the moon.

The bakery was always warm, and now that the cold weather had come, Jane felt more comfortable in the outside air. Inside the air had become dense and ashy; or perhaps it was simply the smell of baking bread that seemed to permeate everything, even her skin, till she longed to smell something different.

Hughes' breath was different, and surprisingly pleasant, when his arms were around her holding her close. He had a knack. One hand cradled her head *just* right, the other went round her waist and *just* fit, and when she was there, it was as though Jane was made to fit right there.

Not a spot where one could spend the day, but very nice.

Jane wished for that bronze hair pin. And for a wild second, she wished for lace and gold thread and pearls and silk.

Perhaps that was what she really liked about Hughes' kisses. How luxurious they were. She couldn't afford pearls and silk, but his kisses were free.

She touched her hair, then determined to forget it. She needn't be frilled up for supper. It was only her sister's wrong betrothed, she told herself firmly. She didn't need that bronze hair pin for a day like this.

She just wanted to feel... nice.

Anna, on the other hand, wasn't thinking of her betrothed at all. She still steamed over Mr. Keales. "He wants us to impress a seal mark upon our *bread*. We must buy the seal from the *Guild*. We must pay for a new one if ours wears *out*. There is nothing about the operation of the Guild that is for *our* good."

"That bakery to the north, the one closest to us," Jane mused. "I don't recall seeing any marks on their bread."

"We ought to have gone with Emery when she spoke to Mr. Gruninger."

"You were frightened someone might see you speak to a tradesman." Jane didn't bother to soften her cool tone.

"Oh. Yes."

Had Anna looked at her, had they exchanged any unspoken understanding, Jane might have felt more in charity with her sister.

But Anna only put the rest of the plain butter sandwiches under an upturned bowl, waiting for one of their sisters, or perhaps even Mr. Russell, to eat later.

THEIR PRIDE IN OFFERING MR. KEALES BREAD AND butter on Talbourne plates shriveled, became dust, and blew away by the time they arrived at the Boislegrand table.

Lord Boislegrand himself had arrived in his carriage to attend them, and showed them into his home with obvious pride.

"I hope it is to your liking," he said diffidently, following them up the front stair to where the butler held open the door for them. "If it is not, anything can be changed, of course, Miss Bickering."

Anna couldn't begin to imagine what, if anything, one would change. The house was a treasure chest of beautiful engagements, from its peonies and birds painted on its wallpaper, to the deeply polished oak planks of its floors, to the gilt-edged, marble-topped sideboards that bore huge Chinese vases and polished mirrors.

Everything sparkled, everything glowed, everything had a million perfect little details.

"The home is lovely, Lord Boislegrand," Anna told him as warmly as she could, admitting no ownership of anything she saw.

This felt like the valley of temptation.

She had only wanted safety. She had wanted her sisters to be able to eat. She *needed* those things.

But deep in her heart Anna had also wanted the gilt and glittering mirrors. She *wanted* the rich Ottoman carpets in their glowing reds and greens.

With one finger, she touched the cool edge of a blue-figured vase, then quickly pulled away. What if she broke it?

Lord Boislegrand—*Puffy*, the name unfortunately crossed her mind—did not make them wait. He showed them to a dining room as grand as any Anna had ever seen. The fine old timbers in the ceiling reminded Anna of the days of Queen Elizabeth, and its windows, glazed with new flat glass, looked out over an overgrown garden, a secret little vault of green struggling to be gay despite the approach of November.

Before the windows stood a table, its snowy linen field ranked with a full court of silver candlesticks, crystal goblets of all sizes, delicate porcelain dishes and glittering forks, spoons, and knives.

And between the just-lit candles, surrounded by their scent of smoke and beeswax, lay a white Grecian temple stuffed with dried rosebuds, the flames burning on either side like altars at a pagan rite.

A temple made of sugar.

"Oh, my lord," breathed Anna, intending it as a prayer.

Puffy took it as a compliment. "Pretty, isn't it? I wanted the nicest things laid on." He pulled out the chair on the right of the master's seat. It was clear he wanted to give her the best impression of everything he offered.

How could he be so thoughtful, so genuinely kind, and so ignorant of how hard Anna and her sisters had worked to avoid using, eating, or purchasing sugar?

Sitting was like avoiding the sight of someone nude in the middle of the room. Anna didn't know where to look. What was bare to everyone's sight—surely Jane noticed—was that Puffy had made an embarrassing choice, whether out of ostentation, carelessness, or simple cruelty.

Not cruelty, thought Anna as his lordship waved over a footman to unfold her napkin and pour her wine. Puffy— Lord Boislegrand wasn't capable of being cruel. Something else had motivated him; but that something was not attractive.

She resolved to enjoy the food.

Puffy settled back into his heavy gilt chair with a wide smile of benevolent comfort.

He waved to the footman again, and a parade of young men in spotless livery began to remove dishes from a warm- ing-cupboard by the fire.

EVEN BOLSTERED AS THEY WERE WITH THE RELATIVELY recent memory of Aunt Eden's table at Walbey Hall, Lord Boislegrand's table overwhelmed the senses.

There was a full platter of sliced boiled beef. The most

exquisite luxury at Rose's wedding had been Lady Arnold's generously provided roast beef, and Anna's mouth watered at the sight of so much meat in one place.

Around it lay smaller dishes of gently stewed carrots, cut into amber cubes; cooked greens; and a plate of poached salmon surrounded by tiny fried rolled smelts. Anna could smell their salty goodness from where she sat. The fifth spot of the French square service held two pots, one of melted butter, the other of delicate brown sauce.

"I chose the bill of fare," said Lord Boislegrand, still awash with pleased pride, as he handed the dishes first to one lady, then the other. "My housekeeper swears on Mrs. Mason's table book as though it were the Bible, and I've come to enjoy paging through it myself."

Anna had swirled through the *soirées* of the titled. Gentlemen entertained themselves by gambling, shooting, and drinking—sometimes at parties. She could not imagine a gentleman so wanting for entertainment that he would read a cookery book; nor could she imagine him admitting it.

Well, she no longer had to imagine it.

"I'm not familiar with the book," she admitted, resisting the urge to ask for more carrots.

"No? But you must have a copy! I admire her prescription for curry and chicken above anyone else's. Say! You must have visited the Hindoostane Coffee House? I am bereft since its failure. But it wasn't terribly far from your bakery."

"No, sir." Anna had no help from Jane at all, who applied herself with diligence to the beef and everything else. "Sadly, we did not."

"That *is* sad. Exquisite tastes. Can't imagine how the fellow couldn't make it pay. Of course one can have a curry brought in, but it was so much better hot."

"Did you go often?"

Lord Boislegrand's face fell a little. "It's no pleasure always dining alone," he said shortly, before launching into a tale of the glories of the carrots.

BY THE TIME THE SECOND REMOVE ARRIVED, EVEN JANE had loosened a little. Whether it was from the wine or the excellent food—Lord Boislegrand could certainly boast of an excellent cook—at least she was helping to keep the conversation afloat.

Anna had never contemplated the sheer effort of holding formal conversation, and dining, when there were only three people.

"What sort of exercise do you take in the winter, sir? As I could imagine you much plumper now that I have seen your table." Jane's eyes practically glowed with a softness Anna had never seen except over money as fresh dishes were laid in the French square shape on spotless cloth.

The second remove included two chickens *fricassées*, the rich sauce thick with cream, nestled together on a platter opposite an entire roasted piglet. Anna ought to have remembered that the first course was meant to be the lighter one, but that boiled beef had made her lose her head.

Now she studied these two plates, imagining all the room she would make for them because they looked *delicious,* when the footmen set down a dish of white cheese laced with damson plums, a cold custard in its silver bowl resting on a bed of chipped ice, and a plate of *jaune mange.*

Something gave way inside Anna at the sight of it all. She wanted the creamy custard to melt on her tongue. She wanted the orange-laced *jaune mange*, its delicate, citrusy jelly cutting away the richness of the pork so that she could taste the luscious chicken, and then to begin the dance of flavors all over again.

She wanted it all.

Lord Boislegrand rubbed his hands in sheer delight. "Only a spoon of sweetness in the *jaune mange,* you know; I made sure it was done with honey. Custard too. Must admit I tried them both last week when I thought I might have the pleasure of your company, and I think I prefer them that way."

Anna's hunger crushed itself flat under a heavy weight of guilt. He had remembered the honey *then*. And eaten it alone. How many times had he prepared this dinner thinking she might be here?

And yet what came out of her guilt-free mouth was, "So thoughtful of you, sir. I wouldn't have expected you to remember, given the sugar sculpture on the table."

"Oh?" Lord Boislegrand looked up, as if noticing the Grecian sugar temple for the first time. "Never thought of that! Everyone has them, you know."

Not everyone; the Duke of Talbourne, Anna knew for a fact, had table sculptures of plaster rather than sugar.

So her betrothed did as everyone else did, unless it occurred to him to do differently; and it seldom occurred to him to do differently.

"Lord Boislegrand." She felt she had to broach this topic. "Will you be quite comfortable, when we are married, to be associated with a woman of business affairs?"

His face-splitting grin at the mention of marriage could not be feigned. "Quite, quite! There are ladies who have investments in the five per cents, always. And an heiress here and there."

He didn't seem to quite follow. "I meant, *conducting* business."

"There'll be no need for that once we're married, of course."

Anna very carefully did not look at her sister.

Gentle, generous Lord Boislegrand couldn't even seem to

hear her proposal that she might wish to do something different.

"Do you not know any ladies with more pressing business concerns?" she tried again.

He frowned, chewing his flawlessly roasted pork. "Hmph. There's a rumor the new Countess of Rawleigh is one and the same with that Clockwork Heiress in last winter's papers. But that can't be true."

Faced with his refusal to believe even what was published in newspapers, Anna felt quite overmatched.

Wishing for someone else to carry along the conversation, she said, "I suppose when you are married you will want to entertain more."

Puffy looked around.

He shrugged. "It's an idea. My wife's old associates wouldn't attend, of course, but we should find someone who would do."

Anna gripped her spoon. "Why wouldn't they attend?" She tried to sound light. "They must have a fondness for you, too."

"Don't know as they do," he said, his downcast expression belying the lightness of his own voice. "Not likely enough to come back, and certainly not once we're married."

"Of course," Anna managed to say.

JANE FELT LIKE SHE WADDLED AWAY FROM THE TABLE. Surely it was a good plan to stand before she burst.

Anna, too, looked sleepy and full, while Lord Boislegrand fairly bounced in his excitement.

"And now you must let me entertain you! We might take a turn in the garden, or if you'd care for music—"

"No garden," Anna waved that idea away, a little bleary—

How many glasses had she drunk of Lord Boislegrand's excellent sack?

"Well..."

The door that he opened led to a room lined with warm autumn-colored carpeting, stripes of satin in the wallpaper, and a bas-relief that might have been Cupid staring down above the chandelier. The carved face that looked down from the ceiling was certainly plump and surrounded by roses.

On one side stood an exquisitely gilded blue-sided harpsichord, its lid standing open to display that its inside bore a delicate painting of a willow tree.

Opposite was an adorable little square *pianoforte*, also with its lid open to show the harp-strings cunningly laid so that the keys fit within their curves.

Jane immediately went to the *pianoforte*. She had always preferred its smooth sound, and this one was the color of Anna's hair.

"Do you play, Miss Jane? I had so hoped." Puffy wasn't short of energy despite the soporific amounts of food.

Jane swallowed a tart smile. He hadn't hoped, he'd *expected*, because they were young ladies and should be able to play.

Well, in that he was right.

It had been so long that Jane began by just playing with the keys. Each one made such a lovely sound, soothing and ringing all at the same time.

"Don't feel you must entertain us," Anna said languidly as she sank to a settee.

"Well, I must entertain Lord Boislegrand, mustn't I? He has given us such a good supper."

"Yes, he has, I'm so—" Anna sat up straight. "Do you recall how to play anything... suitable?"

That tweaked Jane's pride. She might have used some raw language lately, but she still recalled how ladies behaved in fine houses. She just wouldn't have married Lord Boislegrand to get here.

The idea of a bronze hairpin seemed so small now. And much less attractive once one saw what it would take to get it.

His lordship sat at the edge of a high-backed chair, literally on the edge of its seat, hands on his knees, just waiting.

It might have pressured Jane to be good, but she was too full of food to be pressured. It was such a pleasure listening to each key as they followed one another.

Of course they needn't follow, she could make jumps... One and two, one and three, one and four, one and five...

When Jane had learned piano it was by rote, as all young ladies learned. Strike the keys in this manner in this order with this rhythm.

Now full of wine and peace, Jane saw the keys apart from her childhood lessons. They stood alone. One and two and three and four—

No, four wasn't quite right. That was what the flats were for.

She played with the keys so long that Anna fell asleep.

"I remember one tune," she said, a little guiltily, to the still rapt Lord Boislegrand. The soft little snores stopped and Anna jerked awake. "Our mother used to hum it all the time."

She couldn't remember any chords to accompany it; indeed, she couldn't recall if she'd ever learned any. But the *pianoforte* sounded pleasant on any note, and she did not attempt anything complicated. Just hummed a little to remind herself of the tune, then sang quietly,

'Tis Love, 'tis Love, 'tis Love
that has warmed us.
'Tis Love, 'tis Love, 'tis Love
that has warmed us.
In spite of the weather

He brought us together.
'Tis Love, 'tis Love, 'tis Love
that has warmed us.

"Oh." Anna sounded awake now, and much brighter, but her voice was quiet too. "Mother's Cupid song."

"Was it Cupid?"

"Yes. They are literally thanking him for keeping them warm."

"Ah."

Jane didn't remember much more—perhaps there wasn't much more—but she sang the chorus again, thinking of Anna's determination to wed in order to stay warm, and wondering if it had been the work of Cupid her mother had meant.

"No, your lordship, you needn't accompany us home. We are so grateful to you for the evening. The food was exquisite."

Puffy looked pleased enough to burst his buttons.

In an attempt to build goodwill in the butler, Anna turned to him as they paused in the hall. "Please do convey how delighted we were to the housekeeper and cook."

"Madam." The lean old fellow bowed, but Anna detected no warmth in his face.

Perhaps, like all the old Lady Boislegrand's friends, he was loyal to her memory; or perhaps, like all the old Lady Boislegrand's friends, he had no intention of welcoming in a trollopy baker from Leicester Square.

Anna was grateful that Jane said nothing as they climbed back into the lacquered carriage for the ride back to their bakery.

Lord Boislegrand's house wasn't far from Claremont

Square, a fashionable neighborhood of peers who took an interest in government, though Puffy did not. He'd offered to show them the view of the Thames from the uppermost floors, but Anna had declined. From anyone else, it might have sounded indecent; from him, it was only obvious that he wanted to extend their company.

They were nearly home before Jane spoke. "I feel sorry for him."

She was right. It was impossible not to feel sorry for lonely Lord Boislegrand.

As impossible as it was to imagine herself married to him.

With a burst of energy that came from not wishing to think, Anna thumped upon the roof of the carriage.

When their conveyance paused and the footman, surprised at the peremptory summons, opened the door, Anna said, "His Lordship wished us to be conveyed wherever we liked, did he not?"

"Indeed, madam."

"Then we would like to visit a bakery." She mentioned the general direction of the bakery they knew to be their closest neighbor. "Can you take us there?"

"As you say, madam." Wide-eyed, he closed the door.

Anna met Jane's questioning eyebrow. "Do they seal their bread? I have never noticed. We must visit Mr. Gruninger again as well, though perhaps not tonight."

"It is a Sunday. Will their doors be open?"

"That," Anna said with a sort of grim determination, "I would also like to know."

Business affairs had become a welcome distraction from her betrothal, which was fast changing from bothersome to burdensome. Anna might soon be positively grateful to Mr. Keales and the Worshipful Company of Bakers.

By the time the Boislegrand carriage stopped near the Ladies' Own Bakery, full dark had fallen. The chill had turned into genuine cold, and Anna and Jane, in their thin gowns and shawls, hurried in.

Rose dashed down to meet them, one hand trailing along the railings to keep her place, shoes clattering on the wooden stairs as the Boislegrand carriage rolled away. "We have the most delightful sitting room! I've been waiting for you for hours! Do come see!"

Above them, Emery also bent over the railing. "It took you this long to eat a fancy dinner?"

"I think we've been to every bakery north of the Thames," Jane said, utter exhaustion apparent not just in her voice but the way she lifted one foot to the stairs, then, slowly, the other.

"What?" That brought Rose to a stop.

Anna, her head full of everything she'd seen, let it tumble out. The carriage had become a rolling conveyance seeking bakeries; they'd spent the entire late afternoon and into the evening. "There were bakeries still cooking neighbors' dishes, late as we were. There were bakeries that were closed. There were bakeries selling day-old bread, and one fresh—I'd swear they baked it this morning. Yes, on a Sunday. Some loaves were marked with a seal, and some weren't. There were bakeries selling only white bread, and one with bread I wouldn't give to a pig." The scent of moldy flour had been strong.

"Why! What does it mean?" Rose waited till her sisters reached her on the stairs; Emery still leaned down from above.

"It means," said Jane with grim delight, "that Mr. Keales can claim whatever he likes about how carefully his Guild watches over the foodstuffs of London, but he is, if I may use the word, a bare-faced liar."

Episode 5: Two sisters and tiny trees

Emery didn't know why she hadn't said at breakfast that she intended to go to Sunday services—to the meeting, as it was called—with Rose and Mr. Russell instead of meeting Mr. Keales for tea.

It had seemed a wiser choice, as the past months had convinced Emery she had no head for the ups and downs of money or its regulation. She had made some new bread, and that made more money, but having accomplished that, Emery had lost interest in coins.

Somehow, the revelation that Lady Arnold... liked her had also distracted her from earning money.

She must have been mistaken. She hadn't *done* any of the things. No love tokens, no protestations. None of the things she'd been sure she must do if she wanted a woman's attention.

Of course, if she were to... woo that lady (why were all these words so hard to think?), money would hardly help. Lady Arnold was rich. A few ribbons would not turn her head.

Had love been a method, like baking bread, she might

have had a chance at grasping it; but as it was, the whole affair was too mysterious.

The Friends' meeting room was delightfully peaceful, and Emery liked sitting among silent thinkers. Even if the mysteries they contemplated related to God and her mysteries were different.

Sometimes the Friends did speak, about God, and things they had felt God called them to do, but Emery didn't really mind. Everyone's mysteries could be unique, for all she knew.

By the time people started shaking hands, signaling the end of the meeting, Emery had decided to surprise Lady Arnold with a visit.

Miss Hayes and the kitchen salon had been, in different ways, readily available. Lady Arnold was walled up in her elegant stone castle on the south side of the square, and approaching her was a different matter.

Whether from lack of schooling, her life with her sisters, or her own inner substance, Emery hated delay. If she could see a path to her target, she took it. Lady Arnold had *asked* her to call; she would call. There was no method, only action. The way to handle the grandeur of it all was to ignore it.

She turned south as they reached the square, calm but also quietly exhilarated, and muttered something about calling on Lady Arnold, only to hit a traitorous obstacle she hadn't expected: Rose.

"Oh, we should *all* go! We can never thank her enough for her kindness in providing our wedding breakfast, and we must try. Mr. Russell, don't you agree?"

That amiable man was ready to bumble along wherever Rose bumbled. "I do!"

Every step along the freshly-laid paving stones added weight to Emery's resentment. She had not *asked* them along. Why did her sisters always assume she wanted what they wanted?

Because she didn't tell them the truth.

She batted the traitorous thought away.

And all her careful plans, to announce herself with the right sort of humility and hopefulness, were wiped away, because once they arrived Mr. Russell assumed the job of speaking.

"Mr. and Mrs. Russell to see Lady Arnold, if she will receive a call," he told the butler, blithely ignoring his own lack of calling card. "And Miss Bickering."

Emery had imagined Lady Arnold running down the steps to see her. Not that she really expected Lady Arnold to run; she just liked the picture, the elegant little lady running to see *her.* Miss Bickering.

Likely her sisters would all change their names, and leave Emery sole ownership of that title. That could be pleasant. But at the moment nothing felt pleasant.

Her mood reversed immediately when Lady Arnold appeared in the door. Not running, of course, but with color in her cheeks that suggested she might have hurried.

Or was simply very pleased.

Titles be damned, Lady Arnold came to *her* first. "Miss Emery! What a delightful surprise. Truly, I am grateful for your distraction."

Emery felt very tall as Lady Arnold drew near, looking up at Emery with those flushed cheeks.

Emery shattered her morning's silence. "Are you well? Is there some difficulty?"

"Not at all." And her ladyship put a hand on Emery's.

The shock of being touched with that fine little hand was swept away in a flood of worry. "Your hand is like ice!"

"I am trying to better arrange the heat for my glasshouse. The nights are too cold. My more tender trees are suffering."

"How can I help?" It was as though only the two of them stood together, and the urgency, the *need* to do something useful, from the early days of the bakery came flooding back and concentrated in the little person standing in front of Emery on golden Arabian carpets.

"Never trouble yourself! I am only trying to rearrange things. I have no good plan and it takes forever. The larger trees are difficult to move. I thought this afternoon would be a better time to address the situation, as the children are out walking with their governess, but so many of the footmen are taking their day—"

"Let me help."

It was very gratifying to see Lady Arnold flush again, and suspect that neither cold nor heat had caused it.

The moment between them snapped as Mr. Russell spoke up. "Quite. Show me heavy things to lift, Lady Arnold; I am beholden to you for far more. Surely we could assist you."

"Oh!" Called to remember all her guests, Lady Arnold's hands fluttered away from Emery's. It was a hollowing feeling. "Not at all! You are kind to visit, I should be delighted to provide you with entertainments. Max, do bring some refreshments," she told a young footman, who dashed away.

"Not at all!" Mr. Russell insisted, sounding hearty, and Emery wished him at the bottom of the Thames. "We have spent the morning in quite pleasant contemplation, and would enjoy the exercise."

"We would indeed," Rose added. "Surely we can be of some use?"

Biting her lip, Lady Arnold nodded once, and turned to go. Clasping her cold hands, she flushed a little, and reached out again to Emery, taking one of Emery's hands in hers to lead her to the staircase.

Feeling as huge as a castle herself and yet full of light air, Emery squeezed her hand.

Her ladyship smiled a little as she led Emery upward, letting Rose and Mr. Russell follow.

THE VAST BALCONY EMERY HAD SEEN DURING preparations for Rose's wedding was empty but for a few heavy pots.

Everything was crammed into the adjacent little greenhouse.

Its delicate tracery of ironwork firmly offered each pane of glass up toward the sky, magnifying the light and its heat too. Still, the air was chilly.

"It has been *so* cold, and the dahlias are still flowering. I don't want to chill them; they'll stop flowering, they may die." Clearly, Lady Arnold found the idea alarming.

Emery could see why. The lemon trees were not small, and beside them were even larger shrubs, each one spouting fat blooms in colors of pink and mauve.

She reached up to touch one's petals. "They are like daisies and yet somehow... more."

Lady Arnold beamed as Mr. Russell guided Rose's fingers up to trace one low-hanging bloom. "They are so lovely, aren't they? And I know it's trivial, but I am terrified they will die. The botanist in Spain who sent them to my father hasn't written in two years; I fear what might have happened in the war."

"They are from Spain?" Emery let her fingertip stroke one velvety petal. It was more intimate than she expected, and she felt her own face get a little warm. And wished Rose at the bottom of the Thames with her benighted husband.

"*New* Spain. There's war there too. Everyone is at war now, aren't they?" The little woman looked up to where blooms bobbed over her head.

The flowers bore petals wider than daisies, their cool purplish color glowing in the autumn light. Emery touched one stem. It was four-sided, sturdier than she expected.

Lady Arnold saw her. "Strong, aren't they? The plant is called *water cane* where it comes from."

"You don't call it water cane?"

"No, the Spaniard who sent them named them *dahlias*, after a Swedish botanist." Lady Arnold shrugged a little shrug as if admitting how foolish this sounded.

"That's a beautiful name."

"Thank you." Lady Arnold flushed again. "It's mine."

Emery blinked, mind scrambling to understand. She remembered when Lady Arnold had first shown her the lemon trees, mentioning her father was a botanist and how that explained her first name. But she hadn't mentioned what her first name *was*.

"Dahlia? That's lovely," murmured Emery, dropping her hands from the plants.

Her ladyship's flush deepened. There was indeed a marked resemblance to the cool pink of the flowers. She nodded.

The tension was intolerable. Why had Emery spent so much time worrying about gifts, money, love tokens, when the difficulty was facing someone fascinating and being unable to speak?

Jasmine had done all the speaking, a part of Emery's brain put in bitterly, remembering all her encounters with Miss Hayes in the salon and in the street.

Then Rose spoke, which was even more intolerable. "How may we help you, Lady Arnold?"

Mr. Russell looked about. "It's a bit jumbled, but not as cold as I expected."

"There are channels that run under our feet from a fireplace below. But it's been *so* cold..." Renewed worry over her plants brought her ladyship's attention back to the problem at hand. "It's too dark farther from the glass, but so cold right against it... I don't know what to do!"

Emery couldn't offer any clever conversation on New Spain or botany. But problems? Problems she could solve.

The lemon trees had little tree-like shapes, with their branches spreading largely at the top. The dahlias looked like they wished to do something similar, but for now had more of a shrubby shape, leaves as wide as Emery's hand spreading below the equally wide blooms.

"Have you any stools or tables?" Hefting one of the enormous porcelain pots in two hands, Emery lifted a dahlia slightly, showing how if it were higher, it would fit in the open space between the lemon tree pots and their spreading branches. "If you could lift these a bit..."

"Stools! Yes! There are some in the kitchen..." Lady Arnold's face fell as she realized that those were likely often used. But then she brightened. "There must be tables or stools somewhere in the house that would serve. How clever you are, Miss Bickering. Here I was, too tangled in the problem to solve it."

Feeling very clever indeed, Emery put down the pot.

It was odd to be admired for something other than bread, or shifting sacks of flour. Indeed, as Lady Arnold darted away, no doubt to scour the house for spare tables, Emery felt that she could still put her muscles to use, lifting whatever pot her ladyship wanted lifted.

But it was a nice change to be admired for her mind.

"Here, Miss Emery, you must let me lift them when our hostess returns." Mr. Russell looked worried. About Emery lifting things?

Half of Emery wished both he and Rose were at the bottom of the sea, and the other half was abashedly glad they were here, so at least she would not have to embarrass herself with too much further conversation. Things were going well; no need to press her luck.

"I KNOW I OWN ANOTHER COLLAR."

"Perhaps it's with the pressing in my sisters' rooms. I'll go search for it." Rose didn't sound the least concerned.

"It feels awkward to have one's clothing at one's sisters' house."

"Not to me."

Emery listened as Rose and her husband mildly bickered all the way home. She was not at all interested in whether Mr. Russell felt awkward if she or Jane ironed his collars.

When they reached the sisters' rooms, Rose didn't go looking for the collar. Instead, she went straight up to her own with her husband, and perhaps out of perverse annoyance still that they had attached themselves to *her* visit, Emery followed.

Rose was a busy little picture of domestic bliss, arranging things stacked in their rooms the day before but which, with one thing and another, she had not yet had time to sort.

It felt odd to watch Rose handling Mr. Russell's plates, his stewpot, his drinking glasses, as if they were her own. They were her own, after all. She and Mr. Russell were one now. One *what,* Emery couldn't guess.

Whatever it was, Emery didn't have it in store for her.

She wanted to kiss Lady Arnold. *Dahlia.* Very much. She wanted to sweep Dahlia's little person up in her arms, hold her when she was cold, smell the greenery with her and the scent of her hair.

She didn't want to sort crockery with her.

Yet didn't one go with the other?

"I'm going out," she muttered, knowing it sounded as sullen as Sal with a history lesson, but unable to make it any brighter.

"Oh, would you look for Mr. Russell's collar when you go down?" Rose's chitter-chatter followed Emery out the door. "Mr. Russell, where do you want to have your desk?"

Where do you want your desk? So intimate. Homey.

Terrifying.

Emery didn't go down at all. At the end of the hall, she went upward instead.

There was no door at the top of the stairs, but she knocked, suddenly realizing that this was an insane thing to do by Anna's standards and perhaps other people's.

But "Come," Lord Zachary's voice floated down out of the topmost space in the house, and Emery went on up.

Easels stood everywhere bearing half-painted canvases, and Emery found it odd to see their piles of apples and water pitchers richly painted in thick oil colors for half the space, then tapering away into blankness. Small tables stained with dribbles of costly color stood about, and Emery couldn't help thinking some of them would have been the perfect height for Lady Arnold's dahlias.

Lord Zachary had been putting a roll of cloth into an open leather valise. He paused, one golden lock of hair flopping across his forehead, surprised.

"Miss Emery. I didn't expect you. Have I done something loud?"

"No, no." Emery could well imagine that her sisters had given his lordship the impression that their only interaction was complaint.

She herself simply had no interaction to offer, so she hadn't. Until now.

"Lord Zachary..."

The straightest path to her target.

"What do you know of wooing women?"

His lordship seemed to choke a little, dropping the rolled

shirt in his hand into the valise before sitting on the edge of the narrow bed beside it.

"Not much," he admitted, brushing his hair out of his eyes with a blue-stained thumbnail. "If you are looking for an expert, that's not me."

"Why not?" Was there another person in the world with a complicated romantic life?

"Ah..." Peering behind her. "You sound as though my mother sent you. Ah... I suppose because wooing a lady involves offering marriage, and I don't wish to offer that yet."

"Mm-hmm." Emery stepped farther into the room, letting it envelope her with its boil of colors on every surface and its earthy smell of linseed oil. "And without marriage?"

Lord Zachary snorted. "Without marriage you're simply offering to dishonor a lady. I didn't mean—not *you,* of course."

Emery had to wonder if she did indeed wish to dishonor a lady. That didn't sound appealing. And it didn't sound right, not for her, and certainly not for Dahlia.

"Isn't there any room between marriage and dishonoring?"

Making a more violent noise, he stood again and turned back to his task, packing an oilcloth roll of brushes into the valise. "Not according to society, Miss Emery. There are rules, and there are the lowlife scofflaws who break them. Follow the rules and you are deserving of all that God offers; break them and you deserve—well, nothing."

This didn't sound like the God Emery knew, but perhaps the peerage knew another one.

When things were complicated, Emery preferred to uncomplicate them. "But say you did wish to woo a lady, how is it done?"

He stared over his shoulder. "*Have* you been speaking to my mother?"

"No."

He tossed into the bag a large wad of India gum, suitable for wiping pencil marks from a canvas. "I don't know. The chaps I know seem to become someone entirely different whenever they try it. *Yes, I'd love a game of cribbage. Here's a diamond.* All that shite. I beg your pardon."

Emery just waved her hand. "Go on."

"I've nothing to tell you. That's all I've said. My sister's soon-to-be-husband arrived at the house with a calling card, danced with her at two assemblies, and *boom,* suddenly I'm to have a brother." He didn't look delighted, wrapping a collar around one hand before shoving it in the bag. Emery was glad he knew where his own collars were.

Then she finally noticed he was packing. "Are you leaving?"

"Just a short journey with a friend of mine. For no reason, apparently, except that he must make it. I'm hoping to try some landscape painting in the country. I can't—" He shook his hands at the room in general. "I can't find my eye."

Emery had no idea what that meant, but it sounded painful.

He must have seen the puzzlement in her expression. "I'll tell you one thing, Miss Emery. There's a new feeling among the artists, and the writers too, that *feeling* is more important than rules *or* breaking them. If we are worth anything as human beings, it must *matter* what we see, how we *feel* about what we see, at least as much as rules of perspective. Maybe more."

"Makes sense." Emery nodded. "I just came to ask about courtship."

"It's not unrelated." The window, dark already, caught his eye and he seemed to lose track of where he was, thoughts flying, perhaps somewhere in the night outside the window. "What if how one feels about a person is the most important element of the relationship? What then, eh?"

Indeed, thought Emery. *What then?*

Coming back to himself, he tossed a box that looked the right size for pencils into the valise. "How about Miss Bickering and Miss Jane, have they returned from supper at Puffy's yet?"

"I don't think so." Realizing that she ought to go look and see if her sisters were in their apartments, Emery decided it would be a good place to go think if they weren't. "I'll tell them you're going."

"They won't notice, surely," and his lordship shrugged the offer away without noticing that Emery had only made it in return for his very scanty information.

WHEN JANE AND ANNA RETURNED, SO LATE THAT THE moon cut through the dark and no one walked the streets but the watchman, Emery followed them into the rooms, with Rose following.

"Come see my sitting room!"

"Yes, muffin," Anna said, her exhaustion showing. "We must all go do that." In contradiction, she sank into a chair.

"What does it mean that Mr. Keales is a bald-faced liar?" Emery was glad to wonder about something else after a long day contemplating divine inspiration and the difficulties of courtship. She thanked all that was holy that the ovens would fire up again the next day.

"It means," said Jane, "that *plenty* of bakers in London don't follow the Guild's rules. I doubt they are even members."

"That makes no sense." Emery leaned on the wall behind Anna. Despite lifting a few pots at Lady Arnold's, Emery had had her fill of rest; she needed to stand. "Either there is a guild, or there isn't."

"I don't think so." Jane slid forward on her seat. "It's like Aunt Eden's gate. It's so covered with ivy it's more a garden than a gate. But who can say only looking at it? It's a tower of ivy, yet one drives through it to reach the hall."

"Even if there truly is a guild, it doesn't sound as though its bakers are all in charity with one other," observed Rose. "So many people not following the rules!"

"I think," Anna said slowly, "that it is like Vauxhall Gardens. A veneer of civility, but all manor of riotous chaos within."

"I think it's a load of what horses drop, that's what it is," Jane insisted with a toss of her head. "Bakers with no seals, or who simply don't use them. Baking on Sunday. Baking the neighbors' suppers at all hours. Bakers selling horse bread using peas and rye for people to eat. Bakers selling *bad* flour. I mean, what rule of the guild are people not breaking? According to rule, the bread is all supposed to be a day old when it's sold, too. Or was that law changed?"

"I wish we'd brought back a loaf from everywhere we visited and weighed them." This Anna said with a genuine sense of spite.

They had all worked so hard to follow the assize laws, never charging more than allowed, never shortchanging their customers on the weight of their bread. It certainly didn't look as if other bakers were going to such lengths.

"You know..." Jane folded her arms and leaned back in her seat. "Mr. Keales said the Guild surveyed all the bakers. But are they? How many bakeries did we see today that they *can't* have seen?"

"Millions." Anna's sigh was weary.

"But then..." Rose, sitting at Anna's feet, straightened her back. "Why did Mr. Keales come *here?* Why bother us about joining the Guild when he knows we can't, anyway?"

"You know why," was all Jane said. "We're women."

"All right, we're women. But how did Mr. Keales *know?* Out of the millions of bakeries in London breaking the rules—"

"It's not *that* many, truly, muffin." Anna patted Rose's arm.

"—out of all those doing all those things, why did Mr. Keales come *here?*"

"Someone sent him."

This short speech was perhaps the most bile-filled, bitter speech of Jane's whole life.

Everyone turned to her.

"That's the simplest answer, isn't it? Someone told him to come. The crawling little toad."

"All right," Anna said with a touch of concern, "someone ought to pour you some sherry."

"We can't afford *sherry.* One afternoon at Lord Boislegrand's house and you've lost your head." Jane tossed hers again. Perhaps it was the effect of their grand supper, perhaps it was a pent-up dam of anger against all those rule-breaking bakers, or perhaps it was six months of strain beginning to crack. "Why do *we* have to follow the rules if no one else does? We need to find Sal a decent school. Anna must plan her wedding."

"There's no rush," muttered Anna.

"We are too busy to play games with Mr. Keales and his silly Guild!"

Several moments of silence followed.

None of them were exactly following the rules they'd inherited, thought Emery. She should remember how much in common she had with her sisters.

A shy knock at the door broke the silence, and Emery went to open it.

"I expect it's Mr. Russell in search of his wife, or his spare collar," put in Rose from the floor.

But it wasn't. It was their nameless neighbor, sober, with his waistcoat entirely buttoned.

"I could not help but hear, ladies," he said with a little bob of his head, "I know you are concerned about this worshipful company of bakers, and though it is little, I do have a report."

Episode 6: Fireworks

"I'd like to be happy."

This, out of the blue, from Jane, quite brought the sisters' breakfast table to a halt.

"What was that?" asked Anna in between bites of porridge.

"Excuse me?" Emery was even more abrupt.

"I'd like to be happy."

The silence at the table grew even more awkward as neither Anna nor Emery quite understood why it felt so awkward for Jane to say so.

"Of course you do!" Anna patted her hand.

"Well I mean, you never *have* been," Emery added, half under her breath.

"I'd *like* to be happy, but I may not have the knack. Rose adores being married, that's clear. Anna will be soon too, and Emery... loves bread. What about me?"

"What *about* you, darling?"

But Emery interrupted Anna by putting down her spoon. "What is more important than bread? Anyway. No one really believes Anna will really be married soon, do they?"

"True."

"Excuse me!"

Neither sister paid Anna the least attention, so Anna decided to ignore the point herself. "Jane, aren't you simply on pins and needles waiting till you can buy a new dress?" For though the table bore plates *and* food, all their hems were still shockingly short, and the weather had grown very cold.

Jane seemed relieved not to discuss her outburst. "No one may buy a new dress unless your betrothed gifts you with the money—"

Anna pointed a warning finger before they could make one more remark about her betrothal.

"—or we have the coin in hand for one quarter's bills and sufficient free money for the fabric."

Jane had said this before. Still, Anna raised hopeful eyebrows.

"Not yet," was Jane's blunt verdict.

A knock at the door and it opened, revealing Rose.

"I can't get the porridge to boil," announced their sister, followed in by a sheepish husband.

"One must have an oven bigger than a thimble." Anna clearly wasn't much interested by failures of porridge.

"And more than a stick burning inside it," Emery added helpfully.

"Coal isn't free," said Mr. Russell, more than slightly chagrined, clearly, at interrupting his sister-in-laws' breakfast to beg some porridge.

"Jane would like to be happy," Emery told him.

"It wasn't to share with the world."

Emery just *hmmphed* and subsided to her bowl. It was impossible to tell what people were supposed to say and what they weren't.

"Happiness is complicated." Mr. Russell addressed the

question, and the porridge Rose gave him, with equal solemnity.

"Oh, then, I don't want any." Jane, disgruntled, stood up and led Rose, returning from the stove with a dish of porridge for herself, to the free chair.

Before anyone answered, another thump at the door drew their attention, and this time Jordan opened it without waiting for them to answer.

"You'd better come see to the journeys," as he insisted on calling the journeymen bakers. "They're not adding enough water."

"What now? I thought Mr. Bailey understood." Emery found Mr. Bailey less biddable than Mr. Wiggs, but he seemed to grasp what his job depended upon.

"He says it's an interesting idea but I don't know shit."

The silence that settled over the room at this news was heavy.

Anna pushed back her chair. "I think I had better speak to Mr. Bailey."

"I'll talk to him." Emery didn't sound as though the idea excited her.

"I'll have a talk with Mr. Bailey." Mr. Russell stood, his porridge untouched.

At the silent stares, he just shrugged. "Surely it must be of some use to have a man in the family."

"Thank you, Mr. Russell." Anna sounded faint but grateful, as if being helped down a very tall ladder.

Once he and Jordan had left, Emery went back to the topic at hand. "What can we do to make you happy, Jane?"

Jane's scowl melted away like honey in the porridge. She leaned over to hug Emery hard. "It's not for you to do. I don't even know why I brought it up."

"You know," Anna mused, "when you played the *pianoforte*

for Lord Boislegrand, you looked as happy as I've seen you in years."

"You played the *pianoforte* for Lord Boislegrand? That must have been heavenly! How did it sound? What song did you sing?" Rose looked transported by the very idea of a *pianoforte*.

"That old song of Mother's." Jane didn't need to hum it; they all knew the one. "We ought to have more music. No criticism of the Friends, Rose, but I do miss music at services."

"No insult taken; I do too."

"We must find some entertainment." Anna was still dipping her spoon into her porridge and out again, without taking another bite. "We have had none, and the bakery is working well now, isn't it?"

"Or will if Mr. Bailey does as he's told." Emery said this darkly.

Anna shuddered. "We ought to have some fun. The year's been hard, and midwinter not for weeks yet."

"It's Guy Fawkes day!" Rose bounced a little in her seat like when she was a child. "If you want some entertainment, why not begin with that? What shall we do to celebrate?"

"Are Quakers allowed to enjoy fireworks?"

"You'd better be teasing, Anna, or you'll see what this one can do for a firework. It's our first Guy Fawkes day in Leicester Square! Surely there will be some entertainment."

"The prospect is slightly alarming. Mother used to lock the windows against the bonfires." Anna didn't look half as excited as Rose did.

"Mother was a bit timid, though, wasn't she?" asked Jane.
They all fell silent.

"Was she? I don't think of her so." Rose clearly didn't like even the idea of someone criticizing their mother.

But Jane wasn't deterred. "I think she was."

Anna flapped her hands, then addressed herself to her porridge. "She was a grown woman with four children. Women in her day were more restrained."

"She was no Lady Godiva," mumbled Emery, swallowing a bite of her porridge.

New information about something other than bread from Emery stumped them all.

"Who," asked Anna, "was Lady Godiva?"

"Very pious woman who rode through town with no clothes on," said Emery briefly.

There was another pause while they all digested this news.

"That story must be longer." Jane said what they were thinking.

"How did you hear of this Lady Godiva?" Anna wanted more. "Does she live here?"

"I called on Lady Arnold on Wednesday, and we passed an hour or two with her reading. *Eccentric biographies of women,* it was called."

"Well, there you go, she was eccentric." This seemed to settle the matter for Anna.

"I didn't know you'd called again on Lady Arnold." Rose, who was eating her porridge with hungry enthusiasm, dimmed a little at the news she had missed the event. "Mr. Russell and I ought to have gone. How are her trees?"

"Her trees are fine. I trust you'll allow her to be a friend of *mine,* if you please. In fact, she's asked me to go with her to the theater next week."

A burst of excited noises round the table greeted *that* news.

"My stars, what will you wear?" Anna addressed the practical concern first. "Here you are planning entertainments without us!"

"She's loaning me a dress." Emery's voice got quieter and more sullen with every sentence.

"Well, I don't know why you shouldn't be pleased at that! What excitement." Rose's smile said how pleased she truly was. "You see? That's just what we all need. Fun."

Emery looked more and more uncomfortable. "We all need it. It shouldn't be just me that goes. If anyone goes, in fact..." With a kind of squashed grimace that looked like she'd stepped on a bed of thorns, staring into her porridge, Emery said, "...it ought to be Jane."

"Oh no!" Taken aback, Jane's spoon clattered into her bowl. "I wouldn't think of disturbing your friendship with Lady Arnold, Emery, truly."

The look that passed between the two sisters seemed to say more than their words, and Emery relaxed, but shrugged. "You just said you wanted to be happy."

That made Jane laugh. "But not by stealing your friend! Or Anna's betrothed, or Rose's husband."

"Those aren't the same things at all," Rose said with a little frown, but Jane just pressed on.

"I didn't mean I needed any of *you* to be *un*happy. I just wonder what might make me happy. If anything," she added quickly. "As you say, Emery, it's no great skill of mine."

Rose preferred a sensible approach to happiness. "Well, we've never tried a bonfire night before, so at least we will try it tonight."

"Yes," said Jane, with a visibly lighter expression. "Let's see if we can find cheer tonight in setting things on fire."

THE STREET ROUND THE SQUARE WAS LARGELY EMPTY, ONLY a few walkers here and there, and a horseman or two.

As the sisters left the Bakery and walked south, the air was thick with the smell of wood-smoke. It mixed with the peculiar scents of cold fog, wet paving-stones, and dirt.

"I hope no one sets fire to the park in the square, it's a jungle," Anna fretted as they walked past Jacquier's Hotel.

The park was indeed overgrown as always, some few branches bare in the November air but the rest still green and forbidding, bushing up over the iron railing and up to the metal feet of the gilt triumphant horse-rider in the center.

"Look." Jane pointed at the statue's metal glowing with reflected light. "The King is orange. Someone has a fire."

Sure enough, when they turned the corner, there was a magnificent heap of flame right in the middle of the street.

A little crowd ringed the fire, largely keeping a safe distance, though one fellow danced close to it with a jug on his head. One from which he'd presumably been drinking.

Emery spotted Mr. Morley.

He had a respectably bundled-up woman with him who must be his wife, and the two of them stood together on the far side of the fire, united in their disapproving stares at it. His eyes flicked her way, she noticed, but he said nothing, nor did he approach.

Well, that was about what she expected from Mr. Morley, though a bit chilly on a holiday.

Emery wondered for the hundredth time if she hadn't better quit sewing for Mr. Morley. Not because it was *eccentric,* but because he just wasn't pleasant. It was not entertaining *or* fun.

It had never been about putting food on their table. It had been about aspiring to something more. A life with more.

Trailing behind Anna and Jane, Emery saw Mr. Russell speaking to Dr Shelton, one of their customers. His forehead and chin curved toward each other, like the crescent points of a bitten cookie, but he was attractive enough in his tall beaver hat and heavy woolen scarf.

"I do agree with you, Russell, I just don't see casting you my vote," Emery heard as she moved closer.

The look on Mr. Russell's face—disappointment, chagrin, and most of all, worry—hit Emery in a way that felt cold and foreboding.

But Mr. Russell's voice was hearty enough as he said, "If you agree with me, Dr. Shelton, I hope you send your vote the same way. If everyone voted their conscience, I'd carry the day without problems."

Dr. Shelton just shook his head, loose silver-flecked locks of hair escaping his neck-scarf.

The two men moved closer to the fire, and Emery leaned down to Rose. "He looks worried," she said, knowing that Rose could only hear Mr. Russell's utterly assured voice.

"He shouldn't be." Rose *was* utterly assured. "The war has changed things, Emery. People want more of a hand in the running of the country. They are ready for a new candidate."

"A new candidate, perhaps, but not necessarily a new member of Parliament."

"That is the sort of negative thought that makes you morose, Emery. No wonder Jane can't work out how to be happy. When did this family become a box of nay-sayers, anyway?" Rose, nettled, put her hands on her hips.

"I think when Anna was born. Say, don't you think Mother was a bit... timid? Truly?"

"Was she?" Rose slid her arm through Emery's. "Or wasn't Father the timid one?"

"What makes you say that? You can't remember him nearly as well."

"I just feel like perhaps Mother would have done more, said more, if she hadn't had to please Father in everything."

"Well." Emery looked across the fire at the only other married couple she knew. Mrs. Morley didn't even look her way, had never said a word to her. Probably didn't even know she sewed in Morley's shop. "You're the one who knows about marriage."

Running hand in hand down the pavement, Sal and Jordan waved before Sal pulled her brother over into the street. A plume of greener wood-smoke blew over them as they came, and Sal coughed. But her eyes shone. "Isn't this splendid?"

Emery had to smile. She'd been doing that more lately. She felt guilty for it if Jane wasn't happy, but she couldn't help it. "It is, a bit."

"It's so peculiar seeing everyone outside in night-time." Jordan's eyes were big. He'd been filling out and up lately, but his eyes were still those of a boy.

"And less crowded than seeing them all in the shop, isn't it?" teased Rose.

Sal rolled her eyes. "It isn't the crowded shop that's the problem, it's the bakery."

"Mr. Bailey hasn't done anything unpleasant, has he? Or Mr. Wiggs?" Emery belatedly remembered that she ought to cast doubt on everyone or no one.

"They're fine," Sal said without conviction. "I just liked the shop better when it was only us."

Emery smiled again, almost hugged her. "Family?"

"Yes. Just like that."

Emery *did* hug her. Who cared? It was a holiday. "I know what you mean," she whispered to Sal, because she did.

river and see if there're fireworks."

Tilly announced this with the confidence, and volume, of an army general directing the troops.

Anna wished she'd go and be done with it. But no, Tilly was moving along behind *her,* waving her coat-tails to herd Anna in front of her as if Anna were a sheep.

Well, cow. Goat? *There is no flattering herd animal*, thought Anna darkly.

A tall figure stepped off the pavement moving toward the fire, and Anna stiffened. "*Monsieur* Boucher."

"Miss Bickering." The *executif* of Jacquier's Hotel was no warmer than he had ever been before, despite the steady stream of cakes that traveled between the bakery and the hotel daily.

Why didn't Tilly herd *him* somewhere?

He paid his accounts on time, but had done nothing to stop the shouting of his men. They still hurled insults at the Bickering sisters in the street. Or at least at Emery, Jane, and Anna; she noticed they were too cowardly to shout at Rose, whether or not she was with her burly new husband.

"We're walking to the river to see if there're fireworks," Tilly told him, flapping her coat-hems again.

He simply looked down his nose at her. "*I* am not."

Someone down an alleyway set off a rocket. Its shrill cry was followed by a volley of red sparks, shooting into the alley off Green Street.

Anna didn't find it all that entertaining. She found herself hoping the rocket-owner wouldn't accidentally burn down Lady Arnold's house. Of course, London didn't burn down every bonfire night; but it did have fires.

Why had she never worried about fires when she was younger and dancing at *soirées* where fireworks were used to celebrate the attendance of the Prince or one of his *coterie?*

She needed entertainment, but she felt too old and responsible for the kind that exploded.

"Tilly, go on ahead, if you want." Nor did Anna wish to spend bonfire night next to an icy Frenchman, but she didn't want to be herded anywhere by Tilly, either. "Who is going?"

Tilly's head turned, yellow curls under her head-scarf blowing in the hot air coming from the fire. "I guess the

Russells won't, and Dr. Shelton is with 'em. There's your sisters," she pointed at Emery with Sal and Jordan, and Anna didn't bother to correct her, "and they're looking comfortable right where they are. Those other men are drunk. Guess no one's going to the river." She was clearly disappointed.

Past her shoulder, by the iron garden fence, Anna saw her nameless neighbor.

And she had a very entertaining thought.

"You should please yourself, surely, Tilly. Do excuse me, won't you? *Monsieur* Boucher." And with those brief acknowledgements, she sailed away.

Tilly just looked the Frenchman up and down. "Don't suppose you *do* want to walk down the river to see if there's fireworks?"

"No," said the gentleman, and stalked away.

"Hmmph." Tilly muttered to herself, trying to assuage her disappointment. She kicked a pebble out of the dirt. "Lot of effort shooting fire about and very little actually burned down, if you ask me. Guess I might not bother."

"Miss Bickering." Captain Brice seemed to melt out of the dark mass that was the central park of the square, his tricorn hat separating from the trees.

Anna barely paused. "Captain. If you'll just excuse me." And rushed on past.

The Captain stood astonished as she took the arm of a man he recognized as their bedraggled nameless neighbor.

He must have stood there long enough to be noticed, as it was Jane who walked up to him next. Unlike Anna, she stopped. "Captain."

"Ah. Miss Bickering." He couldn't seem to tear his eyes away as Anna walked—not arm in arm with the man, that seemed inadvisable given the state of his coat, but side by side, away from the fire and toward the side of the square, just opposite the entrance to Lady Arnold's house.

Jane followed his eyes.

Oh, if she could hope for things, she'd hope that he would still do something about Anna's dastardly betrothal.

But she only said, "Did you need to speak with my sister?"

"No, not really." He turned back to her. The dark of his skin had faded with wintertime, and when the orange light of the fire fell on him, his face took on a weird night-time glow.

"Bidding us goodbye?" Jane wasn't sure why she wanted to tease him, but she did. "You're always threatening to be gone soon."

He sighed. "Hope and hubris, Miss Bickering. Now I fear I won't get the *Halia* into open water before spring, and by then I'll likely be bankrupt."

"Never say so!" All teasing fell away and Jane just stopped herself from touching his sleeve. "Is there no shipping at all this time of year? No one with a decent cargo?"

Captain Brice's brow was hidden under his hat, but Jane could see from the set of his face how his expression shifted with puzzlement. "I don't carry cargo. Or haven't this past year."

"No? I thought that was what you were waiting for." Head spinning, Jane wondered if she had grown a bit dizzy with smoke from the bonfire. It hung in a hazy cloud about every-one's head, making the world look unreal.

"No. I'm waiting for permission from the Crown to take the *Halia* and a sister Portuguese ship off the coast of Dahomey to stop slaving ships. I thought you knew."

The air had all gone, thought Jane as she pressed on her feet in an attempt to stay upright. "No," was all she said, and faintly.

"Everyone in this damned square—I beg your pardon—

seems to know everyone else's business," the Captain said testily, but without real rancor.

"Do they?" Jane looked across the fire.

Hughes was there, his black hair curling with the sweat of the fire, dancing, and drinking, as he and his compatriots were all doing around the fire.

As if touched by her look, he turned and met her eyes just then, his grin through the flames a demon's portrait.

He saluted her with his jug, as if knowing she wouldn't accost him with her sisters about.

The Captain still spoke. "I can't beg any more ships till this war is won, and no one in any government position is stupid enough to hazard a guess when that will be. Until the Continent is freed, I can't expect any ships from the Royal Navy, but I can't get any coin either. I thought I could, but I've exhausted every support except my Portuguese sponsor."

"I won't be sad you can't go," Jane said without censoring herself. The idea of him on board a ship in the endless sea locking guns and swords with desperate men had crushed all her conscious thoughts. "But I am sad if you will be bankrupt."

"I won't starve." He sounded angry, not frightened, which eased something in her. "Only sorry to lose this chance to do something needed. My family has a farm. Hell, I may end up behind a plow after all." His chuckle was a little bitter. "Twenty years of insisting on a different life, and I may well end up back there after all."

"I don't see that happening, Captain." She didn't. She couldn't picture him doing anything he didn't want to do.

She was so confused now about whether to be glad he hadn't persuaded Anna to marry him.

Happiness seemed even farther away than it had over breakfast.

"IF LADY ARNOLD WILL SEE ME, MR. SPARKS." EMERY WAS no longer intimidated by the front door or the butler, just waved to him that she'd keep her gloves and hat.

But her ladyship appeared much too quickly to have been summoned by the butler. Perhaps she'd been watching out the window.

Emery grinned at the sight of her. She couldn't help it. "Is the bonfire helping keep your trees warm?"

Lady Arnold's laugh was as beautiful as the bowl she had made for the shop. "Very likely!"

They were interrupted by a boy in a dressing-gown, a copy of a grown man's *banyan,* stepping down the stairs. "Isn't it late for you to go out, Lady Arnold?"

Lady Arnold's back stiffened. The convivial air Emery had brought inside with her shattered. Emery herself felt brittle. Her ladyship said, "It's a bonfire-night, James. Lord Arnold. Oughtn't you be in the nursery?"

The boy's hair flopped over one eye, destroying his serious look. "I'm only trying to look out for you, Mother."

"I'll be fine." The formality cracked and Lady Arnold smiled again, waving him back up the stairs. "You'll be asleep in five minutes. Don't worry about me."

He went.

Once Lady Arnold was wrapped in a thick wool shawl and a heavy hat atop her head, Emery escorted her down her front stairs.

"What was that?" Emery murmured as they reached the pavement.

"He's getting older, that's all. Such a shame children have to grow up. He has been stretching his wings by trying to give me orders, that's all. Look at that fire!"

And Lady Arnold dashed for the fire, taking Emery with her, concern and all.

ANNA WALKED BESIDE THEIR NEIGHBOR BACK TO THE pavement. It was colder there, but quieter, and Anna found it easier to breathe.

"My apologies, miss," her neighbor said. "I ought to have come tell you what I have learned about the Guild."

"Never mind that." He reared back; Anna shook her head. "I don't mean never mind it, of course you must come and tell my sisters and me one of these evenings. We will be very grateful. I just meant, I only wanted to see how you were. You so seldom are out in the evening, and not..." She trailed away, unsure how to remark upon the fact that it was good to see him when he wasn't drunk.

The idea that someone simply wanted to talk to him was clearly startling. "Kind of you, madame. Though not necessary."

"It *is* necessary. Honestly, at some point you must let us do something to repay you for the kindness of locating our candlesticks."

He, recalling that their acquisition had little to do with kindness, demurred. "It is not necessary, truly. We are only neighbors."

Claiming a distant relationship when his bed was perhaps four feet from their stove struck Anna as wrong. She might not be able to entertain herself with assemblies and gowns, nor had she any idea what to do about Lord Boislegrand or her betrothal.

But this fellow needed *something* and if she knew him better, she might know what.

"Sir." Anna folded her hands, in gloves, tightly together at her waist. "Lord Zachary takes every chance to embarrass us in the shop, and Captain Brice throws himself thither and yon however he pleases. Mr. Russell, well." She clearly thought it impolite to point out that Mr. Russell had committed the unforgivable sin of marrying her sister. "But *you* have always been a gentleman, sir, and we are in your debt, even though we don't even have a name to call you."

He almost looked down at himself. But there was no need. He knew his waistcoat was missing two buttons, his stockings were stained, his coat collar torn and his chin as rough as one expected after a week's distance from a razor. A random straw hat, suitable for summer, was jammed on his head, failing to keep off the cold November fog.

Anna had a knack for ignoring all this *déshabillé* even as she talked about it. "There must be *some* advantage for you of being housed so near a group of ladies. Perhaps we could advise you on, well, grooming perhaps, and a few points of dress, and you could—you *ought to* go out in the world with more regularity, and let people see who you are."

The last thing he wanted was for anyone to see who he was.

This moment had been inevitable, perhaps, from the second the Bickering sisters walked up the stairs. The danger of it was exactly that it did feel so inevitable, so reasonable. Ladies tidied things. That was what they did. It was the simplest thing in the world: they wished to tidy him. It would be easy to let them do it.

He was still alive because he didn't do what was easy.

Still, he liked these ladies. Their lives had a spark to them that had kept him stirring. He couldn't simply ignore the offer.

"Miss Bickering. I wish I could feel comfortable taking all your advice. But what have I to show the world? Nothing fit to see." He raised a hand to forestall any false compliments.

He knew what he looked like. "The truth is that sometimes a man's life is done and yet he keeps walking. In such a case, what can he do?"

Anna's eyes snapped fire the same as the piled wood did.

"I don't believe in giving up anyone's life. You are *here*, Mr. — Well. Even if I don't know your name. You're *here*. I don't know what has brought you here, but your life hasn't just *stopped*. Eventually you must *do* something."

Everything she said rang his soul like a bell. He had been drinking, sleeping, waiting to die, for so long he'd forgotten that it wouldn't just *happen* because he willed it to.

If the war were really over soon—

But the war would never be over. Would it? It couldn't be. For more than half his life it had raged on, flaring up again when it looked ready to die out, more dangerous and impossible to smother out than that yards-high bonfire in the street.

He'd finished his task and hid in the room over the bakery for more than a year. No one would ever know what he'd done. Yet she was right. *He* still existed.

"Madame."

Anna had looked like she was about to work herself up into a larger speech, but his one word stopped and deflated her.

Having begun, he wasn't sure how to continue.

"Miss Bickering," he said, his accent becoming a little more pronounced. "Would that we could use first names like children do. How simple a name seems then." He had plenty of names, after all; he would just give her one. What harm could it do? Just give her one.

Instead, he gave her three.

"If we could simply be children together, innocent little ones, I would ask you to call me Remy-Claude and we would be friends." Even saying so much, he felt his shoulder-blades tense for a blow, but when it didn't come, let his breath out and kept talking. The smoke from the bonfire had begun to make his eyes water. That would be his story about that, if anyone asked. "Such as we, of course, must be grown and formal. Call me Mr. Laurent. Would that do?"

Her smile was slower, wider, than he had seen on her before. "Of *course,* Mr. Laurent," and she kept her voice low, "we would call you Mr. Pickle-pot if you wished! It's only so much *easier* if we have a name."

"Easier?" He felt lightened, and wary too.

"You know, to invite you for some supper. Oh, to talk about the Guild if you like, but also to simply be neighbors. I think we can help you a bit, Mr. Laurent, I really do."

Wondering how much help he would be getting, and if he would survive any of it, he noticed her eyeing the length of his hair and realized with the savvy of a long-time maneuverer that he had just been out-maneuvered.

Some Bickering sister, or perhaps all of them—yes, including that Mrs. Russell—wanted to fix him up somehow, like one shored up a ratchety house with new beams. He could smell it.

They might as well stack him in the street like cordwood and set him afire.

He'd been so long wary of serious dangers, he told himself, that he'd failed to remember the simpler ones of a woman bent on getting a man to bathe.

Episode 7: Adventures in drinking

"Yah!" Hughes slammed his beer-pot down on the table; droplets went flying. "Another!"

The innkeeper laughed and, uncorking the barrel balanced on two poles so he could easily put tankards beneath, drew another draught.

Jane, from her precarious perch on Hughes' lap, jumped at the noise.

But it was all soon lost in the room's cacophony. Men were shouting at a faro table, their eyes fiery enough to burn holes in the cards, and beside them were women.

Women of all ages, shapes, sizes, and as far as Jane could tell, degrees of virtue. They ranged all the way from the woman wearing beauty patches and an old-fashioned laced gown... that wasn't tied all the way to the top, to a tightly buttoned wife in a coat and pinched hat pulling weakly at a man's sleeve and exhorting him to come away from the table.

"Expected this?" Hughes downed a quarter of his beer in one swallow, then slammed it on the table again, making Jane jump and the white froth slosh back and forth in the vessel.

The two men playing the pipe and violin at the next table

took no notice of beer flying. What with the cards, the dancing, the man at the next table shouting for a better knife to
carve his ham, and the unconscious drunkard being carried
out the door, there were any number of distractions more
pressing than flying beer.

"I didn't expect anything," said Jane, just as Hughes' hand
landed on her ankle.

She'd come to the pub because he'd taunted her. Like a
schoolgirl, she'd let herself be persuaded.

"You're too tightly laced," Hughes had accused, his eyes
snapping, as they had one of their hurried conversations
around the corner from the paving crew. "I don't fancy being
your dirty secret. Or should I say, I don't fancy it any longer."

Jane awkwardly rested her elbow on his shoulder. "What
do you want? I'm hardly taking you home for supper."

"No, I can see that ain't in your plans." A flash of hurt said
that perhaps he had hoped for just that, but then it was gone,
lost in the grime streaking his face. "And I'm not likely to buy
supper for the likes of you."

"Well then, we've nothing to say, do we?" The frustration
had pushed Jane to a breaking point. She simply could not go
on sneaking out of the house to steal kisses, and then too,
Hughes' kisses had *grown*. There were hands now, hands that
roamed places she knew she shouldn't let them roam.

How was she supposed to feel about such brazen treatment? His hands felt good. He had a *knack*. But it was the way
he did it, with smug satisfaction, that she didn't like.

So how to escape the moment? Jane wondered, looking into
dark eyes rather like her own. There seemed only two ways
out of a moment like this: back, or through.

Jane wasn't ready to give him up.

"Buy me a beer, then," she told him, the heaviness inside
lightened by the delighted look on his face. It made him seem
boyish.

"Truly?"

"Why not?" She tried to look careless when she shrugged. "I've never had one."

And now she was here, both containing and wearing some of the beer. The taste was pleasant enough, reminding her of both bread and flowers.

She'd been afraid she'd have to talk to Hughes, but there was clearly no danger of that.

When his hand crept slowly upward, callused fingers scraping the light cloth of her stocking, Jane shivered.

She still didn't know how to be happy. But *he* knew how to make her feel… *good.*

Across the room, the pipe player fell back against his table, clearly exhausted, and motioned for a woman to step forward. She was slight, with mousy hair under her cap, but she had a good complexion and, once she sang, a sweet voice that carried.

The moon on the ocean
was dimmed by a ripple
affording a checkered delight;
the gay jolly tars
passed a word for the tipple,
and the toast -
for 'twas Saturday night

Of all the things Jane had thought might happen in a pub, a new song never occurred to her. Yet how natural it was. Well-chosen, the rollicking little song went with the wave and fro of the men shouting and subsiding over cards, and it drew in the dancers, who'd stopped when the fife quit.

Some sweetheart or wife
he loved as his life;
each drank, and wished
he could hail her.
But the standing toast

that pleased the most,
was 'The wind that blows,
the Ship that goes,
And the lass that loves a sailor!'
Jane's skin went cold.

"Don't let them sing that."

"Why not?" Hughes was rocking to the song, rocking her on his lap along with it.

Jane suddenly had the sick sensation that this was all wrong. Being here, his hand, all of it.

Shoving away and on to her feet, she shouted over the din. "Sing anything but that!"

Confused, the violin stopped, so the girl singing stopped, to a chorus of *boos* from the listeners. They thumped heavy boots on the worn floorboards, a chorus of disapproval.

"Listen, sister, we paid our fee, and a woman singer is part of the price!" someone yelled from a farther table.

Jane flattened her hands on the table, leaning close in desperation. "Play something else. Anything else."

"Mildred don't know anything else," the man said, still in thick confusion. His partner, fist gripping his fife, returned.

"Ah..." Jane looked around. The dancers were scowling, and Hughes just sat where he was, arms crossed across his chest. "Sing *There's nothing to be had without money.* Everyone knows that."

The girl just wrung her hands. "I don't know how to start it!" she whispered.

Jane, desperate to hear any song but the previous one, gave the girl a wobbly smile, and sang.

You gallants and you swaggering blades,
give ear unto my ditty,
I am a boon companion known
in country, town, and city,
I always lov'd to wear good clothes,

and I ever scorned to take blows,
I am belovèd by all me knows,
but God a mercy penny.

Waveringly, the girl joined in by the third line, and they finished the verse pretty well together.

But then the girl stopped, and one of the men beyond the little crowd of dancers, his ragged sleeve opening flapping around his hand as he gripped a deck of cards, waved his arm. "Keep going."

The girl looked at Jane, panicked. Jane went on. The girl joined in.

My father was a man well born
who loved to hold his money,
His bags of gold, he would declare
far sweeter were than honey,
But I, his son, do let it fly
in tavern and ordinary,
Yes, I am beloved in company,
but God a mercy penny.

Jane had always liked singing at home, but never at society functions. She was too conscious of the French and Italian lessons of those white society blossoms, the elegant shape of their notes and demure downcast eyes.

Here she could sing as loud as she liked, and no one expect her to be girlish.

The sounds of the card game faded, and the dancers had quieted too. When Jane tried to gesture for the girl to keep singing alone, one of them shouted out. "You sing too, miss. It's right pretty."

So Jane kept going, the wavering girl dropped silent completely, and only Jane's voice, warm and rich, with a flutter on the high ends of verses like a bird's wing, carried to the far corners of the silent tavern.

All parts of London I have tried,

where merchant's wares are plenty,
The Royal Exchange, and fair Cheapside,
with speeches fine and dainty,
They bid me in for to behold
their shops of silver and of gold,
That I may choose what wares I would,
but God a mercy penny.

Realizing that everyone in the pub was staring at her, Jane stared back and stopped.

"Why aren't you dancing?" she asked.

The fife player trilled a few notes and the violin joined in, the young girl following Jane on the tune and giving it richness.

One dancer *whooped* and swung his lady round by her waist, and then they were all dancing.

Hughes, confused, watched her sing and forgot about the dregs of his beer.

"THIS IS GENUINELY AWKWARD."

"Why?" Lady Arnold darted out of her chair. "Is there a pin stabbing you?"

Emery tugged at the satin edge of the brown velvet sleeve. Its deep coffee color warmed the color of her skin, and it was so soft to touch that it made Emery notice where her own fingers were rough.

It was the opposite of *Emeryness* in every way. She waddled toward Lady Arnold with arms outstretched like a cranky tree, leaving the seamstress kneeling behind her. "You said you would loan me a gown."

"And so I am. We're only adding a panel at the bottom— obviously, you are so many inches taller than me."

Emery wasn't arguing that, though she did feel a little

chagrined that the thing otherwise fit her. She was so skinny for her height. Lady Arnold was tiny and perfect. If only Emery had stopped growing at a seemly point.

But Lady Arnold made no criticism, and now that Emery was standing still, the seamstress pinned the last of the gold brocade panel she'd added to the hem, then trimmed it with swags of golden tassels.

From her knees, she surveyed her work. "We'll put the same tassels on the shoulders, and it will just look as if I designed it that way."

"One set at the waist, Mrs. Hilliard, and one at the shoulder. That will be more elegant."

"Of course! Excellent taste as always, Lady Arnold. Let me see if I have a ribbon to match."

Emery waited until the seamstress was head-down in her trunk of fittings. "This is an extravagant expenditure," she whispered to Lady Arnold, trying not to be distracted by the way a wisp of her ladyship's hair fluttered with the motion of Emery's breath.

"Is it? No, I don't think so." The littler woman waved the concern away. "I have not worn the dress for two seasons. It ought to get use."

"It's not just that, it's—" Emery tried to indicate the seamstress with her eyes. "A draper visiting the house?"

"But you are at your work during the days! This is the only time that would do, and Mrs. Hilliard doesn't mind."

For Mrs. Hilliard not to mind, she would have to be making enough money.

"You needn't—" But Emery stopped.

She did need. If Lady Arnold wanted *Emery* to accompany her to the theater, Emery had to look at least as respectable as a lady's companion, if not a lady.

This was more than respectable.

When the seamstress emerged with her ribbon, Lady

Arnold drew delicate brows together and frowned with a tiny shake of her head. "I think I have a better thing."

She dashed away, leaving Mrs. Hilliard and Emery to wait awkwardly with one another.

Mrs. Hilliard attempted to start a conversation. "How do you curl your hair?"

"I don't," said Emery.

That ended any attempts at conversation.

When Lady Arnold returned she was breathless. She must have run. "Yes, this will work splendidly!"

And she held up a chain of golden topaz stones, each one backed with silver foil to ensure it glowed.

"No, honestly—"

"We must try it!" And with that, Lady Arnold reached up to put the treasure around Emery's neck.

Bending her knees a little so the shorter woman could reach, Emery felt soft fingertips brushing away the trailing hair at the back of her neck, presumably so that she could catch the clasp of the thing.

Emery shivered.

"Do they work?" Emery asked. The lady had spoken of the topaz stones as if they were a steam engine, driving wheels around. Whatever work they were supposed to do, Lady Arnold must judge whether they did it.

"Of course," was the subdued answer. Emery turned to catch her just pulling back her hand, as if she'd reached out to touch the topazes—or Emery's hair—again.

"See?" Lady Arnold reached up to touch one stone with her fingertip. "The neck of the velvet is quite high, and the stones rest on it like they were made to go there."

"Lady Arnold." Emery had dropped her arms and her voice. "You needn't. If I were to embarrass you—"

"That's not possible, Emery."

And that, thought Emery, encased in her terrifyingly soft gown, was that.

How on earth had she gotten into this?

"MR. COLLIER, WE BELIEVE WE CAN ARRANGE A PLACE FOR Sally at quite a good school."

"Who?"

Rose, who hadn't met Mr. Collier before, didn't know what to say. Finally she realized there was only one thing *to* say. "Sarah, Mr. Collier. Sally. Your daughter?"

"Oh, is she?"

Sally, standing next to Rose, slipped her hand into Rose's and squeezed it gently. Rose found it odd that the girl seemed to want to comfort *her*.

Mr. Russell was not daunted. "The ladies in the committee—"

"The ladies' committee," Rose added, trying to help.

"—they sometimes fund students, and there are generous ladies among them who are interested in funding education for a girl who is not a Friend. Sally has been very intelligent in her lessons, and this will make it possible for her to learn much more."

"Has she?" The man, his long lank hair hanging down over his collar this time but his shirt still mis-buttoned, looked at Sal with a detached puzzlement. He clearly didn't question her ability to use schooling; he just questioned who she was.

Mr. Russell surveyed the chamber. It held more amenities in it this time. The pallets on the floor had quilts on, both of them, and the laundry was washed. Bowls of butter and peas sat on the table, along with, of course, an excellent loaf of Ladies' Own Bakery bread, begun and standing on its cut end to stay fresh.

But Mr. Collier seemed no more collected than he had at the previous Bickering visits.

Sal was unfazed. "I'm going to be schooled, Dad."

He patted her shoulder gently, clearly wishing her well, whoever she was.

Sal continued. "The bakery ladies said I got a choice. I could go learn to be ladylike; but I don't want that. Reading, writing, and casting of accounts. That's what I'm to get. Miss Jane says I can spell good enough now for a charity school." Sal clearly doubted this but didn't want to gainsay Jane. "Otherwise I would have had to go to some lady who would teach me reading and like that."

This jumbled account of the societal layers of schooling available to poor girls in London rather captured it, thought Rose.

She was so terribly proud of Sal, and of Mr. Russell for arranging this. The sisters had wanted to do something about Sal's school for ages, but hadn't known where to begin. Mr. Russell had known exactly whom to ask about charity, and options, and even the dame schools where children who couldn't read and write got their start.

My life would have been different, Rose thought, *if I had gone to school*. There was a school for the blind, in Southwark; it had opened just before Rose's illness. Had they money, she could have gone. But then, had they money, would she have suffered so with the illness that scarred her?

It didn't matter. Her life was perfect as it was now, so what did it matter?

"Mrs. Russell and I will be in touch with you constantly, Mr. Collier. There will be a direction to which you can write, if you wish to."

Secretly Rose still thrilled to that new *Mrs. Russell*. But the thrill seemed wasted on Mr. Collier. "Sounds fine," was all he said.

Seeing them out the door like the little lady of the place, Sal said, "See what I told you?"

She had certainly been right about how little such a visit would accomplish.

"That's all right, Sal; at least he knows."

"No he don't." Sal seemed unperturbed by this, but Rose doubted that she was as unaffected as she seemed. "If Jordan's going to bed down with the journeymen, it's time I found myself something to do, anyway. It's lonely here with just my Dad. As long as the ladies from the church look in on him from time to time, and you can see they do."

She gave Mr. Russell a shyly grateful look, something a bit out of place on her little sharp-eyed face, and closed the door.

As they walked home arm in arm, Mr. Russell patted Rose's hand in the crook of his elbow. "Are you well?" he asked softly.

"I can't imagine a worse fate than to have bright, lively children like Sal and Jordan and forget who they are," Rose admitted. "I feel so sorry for him."

"Well..." He drawled the word out a little, changing the tone of their conversation with it. "If we have children and you *remember* who they are, might you feel better?"

Squeezing his strong arm, Rose felt her face warm, but only nodded. She still couldn't bring herself to discuss what married people did behind closed doors, and even referring to it left her mute.

But yes, that idea was very, very appealing.

Soon the special election for the seat Mr. Russell was standing for would be accomplished, and Rose felt that the world would lay before them like a carpet, soft and cushioned for their feet.

LORD ZACHARY, IN A FOUL MOOD AFTER A CHILLY, STUPID trip to the country with men he wasn't sure he even liked, charged up the stairs at number 17 Leicester Square in a mad dash to be done with it.

He stopped, aghast, on the landing.

Miss Anna Bickering was coming out of the closet-room of their neighbor, and in her hands she carried what was clearly his clothes.

"Lord Zachary," she bobbed her head politely to the man as he stood staring, then disappeared into her own door.

Zachary put out a foot as if to keep going, then pulled it back. Reconsidering, he shook his head and tried to step forward again.

Then gave up and just opened the neighbor's door.

His neighbor sat on a pallet on the floor, wrapped in a quilt and clearly disgruntled. "Thank the heavens you're home. She's half killed me."

"What the devil?" Remembering his manners, despite standing in the door of a closet staring at his unclothed, unnamed neighbor, Lord Zachary revised himself. "Your pardon. What on *earth* is going on?"

The man sat forlornly, his ragged hair now short to his head and his beard bristle gone.

It gave him more of an eagle-eyed look, masterful nose and piercing eyes under slicked-back hair. But no eagle ever looked so suspiciously forlorn.

"She shaved you?" Lord Zachary's voice rose in both pitch and volume.

"No, she's made me go to the barber. And I had to *bathe.* And now she's taken my clothes to mend them."

"She's *what?* No, never mind, I've heard you. But I mean —*what?*"

"A man tries to fight and die for what he believes in. He tries to stand tall. And like that—" He snapped his fingers, then quickly grasped the quilt again before it fell off his shoulder. "He is brought low."

"We are talking about Miss *Bickering*. Miss *Anna* Bickering."

"Well, it's too late to do anything about it now." He regarded the walls of his little cell sadly. "Unless she doesn't bring back my clothes."

"Miss Bickering is washing and mending your clothes."

"Yes." The neighbor didn't seem to be half as surprised about that as he should be, thought Zach.

Then it hit Zach differently. He *wasn't* half as surprised as he should be. "Have you been importuning Miss Bickering?!"

His neighbor took in a quick breath with flared nostrils and started to rise. Then he thought better of it, as he needed both hands to hold the quilt, and subsided. "Sir. Do not insult a lady."

Zachary wanted to say that was just what *he* meant. His neighbor had better not be insulting a lady. Then he, too, settled himself. He'd spent hours with this man watching over their baking neighbors. They were allies, if not friends.

Still. This was not the way he'd left things.

Not only had this trip been pointless, clearly he ought to have been managing things better at home.

By *home* he meant Leicester Square.

ANNA HAD MR. LAURENT'S CLOTHES WASHED AND PRESSED fairly quickly, though she wished she had more time; some of the stains ought be soaked. She'd buy some vinegar.

She could hardly insist Mr. Laurent leave her his clothes more often, or that he buy another suit.

A year before she couldn't have imagined requiring a man to turn over his clothes so *she* could mend them.

But now, with the hem of her dress so high that her ankles were in constant danger of showing, and every stocking and glove in the house mended four and five times, she knew exactly what it was like to have one's garments give away too much about one's situation.

It was as if Mr. Laurent trusting her with his name had put them on an equal footing she'd never experienced with a gentleman, or any man, before.

Creating cakes for sale had been born of desperation. There had been no time to enjoy the process, when every moment felt like it was slipping off the edge of a knife.

Now that her next meal was assured, and she even had plates from which to eat it, Anna had time to feel pride in her cakes, in the sale of them, and the steadier running of their business venture. She liked the feeling.

And she felt pride, too, in making a neat patch of the gentleman's waistcoat where it was torn on one side, and setting a fresh button at the top that didn't match but co-ordinated very prettily.

She was just contemplating the repair of a frayed spot of lining when the door opened to admit Jane.

They froze for a second, staring at each other across the floor. Jane in the pale green gown she shared with Emery, nameless stains dotting the skirt and her gloves; Anna holding a strange man's waistcoat.

What Anna remembered later was how oddly clear the moment felt, as if they were immersed in cold glass, preserved in a second.

She saw Jane's eyes shutter, saw her unwillingness to say where she had been or what she had been doing. She knew, as Anna knew, that there were no more plausible excuses regarding shopping.

Nor did Anna feel any need to explain the waistcoat. Mr. Laurent might well share his name with any of them, but this project of hers, like her cakes, rested with her, and she didn't wish to share it.

"Do you think," Anna asked her sister, "that we are all drifting away from each other?"

She didn't wish to blame the bakery, or Rose's marriage, or anything. Or anyone. She just, in that moment, felt farther from Jane than she had ever felt, even though they were only two yards apart.

She would have been happy with any answer.

But Jane only dropped her eyes and retreated to their room, no doubt to bathe and wash the gown.

Episode 8 Cliffs and falling

"Mr. Choate! Come in." Mr. Russell opened the door wide to his apartment on Leicester Square, but the gentleman outside did not come in.

His face, under his hat, was worn with cigar smoke and concern.

"I've just come from constituency counting, Russell," he said, and the air grew even heavier inside than the cold, gray air outside.

Jane was bent over her slate at the Bickering table. "Why won't these figures come right?"

Anna pulled tight the darn she was putting into Mr. Laurent's one worn pair of gloves. "You must have done it right, Jane. Numbers never defeat you."

"This says we have made more money for the last two weeks than I expected."

"Can we not question the benefit of making *more* money?

Honestly, Jane. It's as though you always look for the worst in everything."

Jane's head whipped around, but Anna wasn't giving her any pointed looks. Only darning.

Jane *did* wonder if there was something wrong with her, seeking out the lower points of life. Kissing Hughes in alleyways. Visiting beer-stained inns. Would she soon be in a public house every night, sucking down spirits till her teeth fell out?

Till she staggered home, smelling of alcohol and despair?

Till she turned into Mr. Laurent?

"Whatever are you up to with that poor man?" she snapped, bending again over her slate.

Anna's reply sounded surprised. "He could use some feminine help, surely? He's a decent man, drinking his life away."

"Perhaps he has reasons."

"What possible reasons?"

"Perhaps he lost the love of his life. That's a good, romantic reason to drink one's life away, don't you think?" Jane didn't think it for a second, but it could have happened. She didn't know what their neighbor thought. She didn't know what Hughes thought, or any of the people who had clapped so when she sang. She didn't know what *anyone* thought. "Or perhaps he killed someone."

Anna seemed unperturbed. "Someone like the love of his life? What a romantic soul you are today."

Jane felt the opposite of romantic. "Perhaps he didn't mean to, but the other person... fell off a cliff. Or onto his knife."

"Such ideas! It's much more likely that he has been to war, Jane. He has... a bit of violence to his personality, and a strong moral bent."

Jane stared at her sister. "So you are mending his gloves because you like his bit of violence, or his small moral bent?"

Anna frowned. "I am grateful for his help. We would not have survived the summer without his help."

"No, we would not have survived the summer without the *Captain's* help. We would not have got back Mother's candlesticks without Mr. Laurent."

Her sister's eyes bent down to her sewing, and stayed down. "Mother's candlesticks matter to me."

They mattered to Jane too, but that wasn't the point.

Voices on the stairs interrupted her thoughts. Voices that clearly did not belong to Rose or Mr. Russell, or their neighbor.

Jane darted to the door to peek out.

There was Lord Zachary, following an... undone sort of woman up the stairs.

She had hair of all kinds of shades of brown and gold, and Jane wondered what gave her the *undone* impression. Her curls were tied up in a ribbon, but several dangled down to her shoulder. One small sleeve slid partway down her shoulder under the heavy gray shawl she wore. A woolen muff dangled from one gloved wrist. But it was really her smile; she glanced back and giggled at Lord Zachary as if her garters were untied, soon to be followed by her dress laces.

Jane shut the door.

"Lord Zachary is bringing in a trollop," she whispered to Anna, a loud boiling hiss.

"*What?*" Anna leaped to her feet.

Waving her back with hard-flapping hands, Jane tiptoed to her chair. "There's a trollop. In the hall. Lord Zachary is bringing her in."

Anna glared at the door. "He can't be!" She too kept her voice nearly silent.

"Oh I assure you, he *is*."

"He can't do this! We are a respectable house. Why, the neighbors will have seen!"

"Yes. Past tense." Jane moved to the window and peeked down. All below was the usual bustle of a dark autumn afternoon. No one seemed to be looking at their house; but then, how many people had seen?

"This is unconscionable. I must tell Mr. Russell. Or perhaps Mr. Laurent—"

"Shhhh!" Jane flapped her hands again. "Mr. Laurent? What are you thinking? The man is like a loaded gun. Who knows what he will do?"

"He does seem a bit... Well there you are, Jane! He must have fought in the wars."

Trollop forgotten, the sisters stared at one another.

Then Jane said, "But on which side?"

Anna scoffed. Then looked worried. Then she scoffed again, and sat back down. "A lady of the Friends told me that this square used to provide residence for the French ambassador. I mean, a hundred years ago. That is why there are so many Frenchmen in the area; there have long been Frenchmen living here, traveling back to France, and back and forth."

"That only means there are likely spies everywhere. Not that Mr. Laurent has fought for Britain."

"Look at his treatment of us!" Anna steadfastly ignored the sounds of footsteps climbing further in the house and flicked a finger back towards Jane's slate. "He's been so kind."

"We're not Britain, Anna."

Anna folded her lips together. Perhaps she felt their household and Britain were equivalent. "Your slate. What can possibly be wrong with making more money?"

Slowly, Jane sank down into the high-backed chair.

"Well, two things. One is that I miscalculated our rate of return somewhere. I expected having journeymen would make us more money because they are making more bread, but it earns back more than I expected."

"So?" Anna had picked up the glove again and taken the needle back up, and stabbed it into the glove with determined focus.

"I'd like to know where I went wrong. But two, what do we do now? How can we best grow, given we have a little more money to put back into our business? I'd like to know when it would be profitable to fire up more ovens. These figures make me nervous. What if we invest in that much more wood, and our profits are lower than I expect?"

Unexpectedly, Anna nodded. Her hands, and her mending, dropped to her lap. "If only the Guild offered practical advice, instead of demanding we close."

Their neighbor had offered a thorough, but unhelpful, report on the Guild house operations. They had grand rooms that they let out for different affairs; they had meetings and owned a large amount of good silver plate. The women who went into the house were all wives of some elected officer of the guild or another, and many conversations went on about London's food and London's money that the Bickering sisters had found very interesting, but not helpful.

Their neighbor had been apologetic, but they'd given him a plate of lamb stew and many, many thanks.

So they had some idea of what the Guild did, but still no idea of what it might do, especially about them. And certainly it had offered them no help.

"We ought to talk to some bakeries we saw while riding in Lord Boislegrand's carriage."

That night had felt endless, the bakeries everywhere. "You will borrow his lordship's carriage again?" Jane asked, with some dry disbelief.

Anna's lips folded tight. "Perhaps. We are *betrothed,* you know." Then she bit her lower lip. "He expects me to have supper with his mother sometime soon."

"His *mother?*"

Anna didn't elaborate.

Befuddled at the idea that Lord Boislegrand had a mother, Jane subsided, erasing her slate to copy over the figures she had in the ledger and try again.

She had plenty of problems, but she had to admit Anna had a few of her own.

"IT'S SO SOFT." ROSE LET HER FINGERTIPS STAY ON EMERY'S velvet sleeve a moment longer; then she let them drop away.

The velvet fit Emery snugly, all the way down to its smooth satin edging. Rose had never felt something so sumptuous, let alone formed into a gown that one could wear.

That Emery was wearing it kept astonishing Rose.

"Is it soft to wear?"

Emery sounded uncomfortable, though Rose would bet it wasn't because the dress was stiff. "It's too fine. I'm afraid to touch it, and I'm *in* it."

I wouldn't be afraid, Rose thought, then squashed the thought. She was jealous, that was all. She'd never had a dress this fine, and Mr. Russell wouldn't be providing one, either.

They counted every lump of coal that went into the stove, and practically every grain that went into the morning porridge.

But she loved him, and that balanced any inconvenience. She loved him more every day, which she hadn't expected to happen. She loved the way he chuckled in the morning when he drew her against his chest, loved the way his voice sounded against her ear. She loved how he was constantly looking for people to help. She loved how quietly sure he was, and then how flustered when she mentioned darning the holes in his stockings, as if embarrassed by a flaw.

She loved him.

But she let herself sigh a little over Emery's dress.

"You must go home and show Anna and Jane," Rose said, making Emery feel that much more awkward.

She was not an exhibition. She didn't expect people to look at her. In this dress, she felt like a circus show, as if she'd soon be surrounded by racing horses and acrobats.

But then Lady Arnold came in.

Her eyes shone as she crossed the blue-and-pink patterned carpet, looking only at Emery in her made-over velvet dress.

"That's *lovely,* Miss Bickering, don't you think? That brocade edging worked *just* as I'd hoped. And the tassels are elegant."

Emery reminded herself that it was the tassels that were elegant, not her.

But then Lady Arnold drew closer, looking up at Emery with her eyes still shining that way, and Emery had to admit to herself that the lady wasn't admiring the dress.

Lady Arnold put up a small hand and ran one finger down Emery's braid, pulling it forward over her shoulder. "I'm not sure how we should dress your hair," she said quietly.

The shiver that went through Emery from a touch she could barely feel was peculiar. It was different from all the shocks she'd had meeting women like her, women with no intention of marrying. Those had been shocks of recognition.

Lady Arnold wasn't like her. Lady Arnold had been married. That was confusing, but her touch was not. Lady Arnold felt something that Emery could feel too. There was no question it was true; the only question was whether either of them would ever admit it.

Or perhaps, Emery realized, that touch was Lady Arnold admitting it.

Slowly, Emery put out her own hand and let one finger slide down the shining edge of Lady Arnold's hair where it swooped, smooth and glossy, over one ear.

She felt the answering shiver.

"Perhaps..." Something had gone wrong with her voice. She cleared her throat, tried again. "Perhaps you'll choose for me."

Rose was paying no attention, still studying the way the stitches had attached the new brocade panel to the bottom of what had been a skirt a foot shorter. Emery felt like she was about to be discovered; but discovered doing what? She only stood near her ladyship. Only touched her hair.

Only wanted to touch it again.

Perhaps Lady Arnold felt the same constraint and freedom. She said, "If I were to choose, I would leave it down your back. It would be a glorious golden shawl."

"And warmer," Rose put in from the floor, proving she was listening. Emery considered giving her a kick.

Well, a nudge with her toe.

She didn't have any clever subterfuges. She never had. "If you like it that way, I shall wear it that way."

"It's a style for a young girl," put in Rose again from the floor, which made Emery even more frustrated. Rose's hair, when wet, still reached her hips, and brushing it was her daily way of shutting out the rest of the world.

Plus, who was her younger sister to call Emery old?

Lady Arnold must have seen some of this in Emery's face, because she laughed. "It does tend to be. But I haven't any idea how else to arrange it on short notice, and there's no need to fuss with natural beauty."

The phrase *natural beauty* plucked a string somewhere in

Emery. No one had ever used those words in connection with her. Not remotely.

"Go and preen for your sisters," Lady Emery said, "and meet me back here. I'll have a plate ready for you. It will be such a late night for you, but hopefully a pleasant one!"

Pleasant, Emery decided, was a weak and inadequate word.

ON THE SHORT WALK UP THE EAST SIDE OF THE SQUARE, Rose would not stop talking, apparently not noticing that Emery had little to say.

"And her son is so gallant, walking with his mother around the square as if he were the lord squiring a lady. I mean, he *is*, but he seems so self-conscious about it. But Lady Arnold isn't self-conscious at all, is she?"

"No." Emery had some work to do, handling the heavy skirt and two petticoats underneath in some way that still let her walk up the stairs. It was astonishing how warm they'd made her walk, but this many layers...

Rose preceded her, opening the door to the sisters' apartments. "I hope when I have a son that he is as wise and as sweet to his mother. I suppose some of that will be my fault. I mean, if I teach him the right things."

Jane's slate clattered to the table and Anna, sitting in a chair near her, shot to her feet. "You're having a child? A *son?*"

Rose waved her hands, blushing. "No, no! Don't be silly! Do you think that if that were true, I'd just... I don't know, drop it on the way in like a pebble?"

"You're blushing," Jane pointed out. "You know something."

Turning even more pink, Rose went to the chair where she often sat, at the foot of their little table. "Well, I mean...

it's not impossible. One of these days. Someday. Who knows?"

Jane's eyes narrowed. "Why don't you know?"

Rose pushed a fist against her lips as though to keep words in. Then she said, too quickly, "Some things I know, some things I don't know. You'll understand, Jane, when you're married." Then she seemed to think again, and added, also too quickly, "Which I'm sure will happen some day."

Jane slid the slate away from her. The sound of it scraping on the table's wood was loud. "Tell me now."

"*What?*"

"Tell me now. Mother isn't here to do it. You're married. You've clearly survived. Tell me what these secrets are that married women all know and I don't."

"But... you're not..."

"I need to know *now*."

"Why?" Anna seemed to wake from the silence of shock, or horror, that still gripped Emery. "Why do you need to know?"

"Haven't you admired Emery's dress yet?" Rose's desperation to change the topic was palpable.

Jane looked at Emery and finally noticed that, instead of her usual much-washed, much-patched gown, she was draped in fine-fitting velvet and brocade. "Oh, *Emery*. You're so beautiful."

"The dress is beautiful," grumped Emery. But she felt her own cheeks pinken.

"No," Anna said, sweeping closer and taking her hands, "*you* are beautiful. My stars. It shouldn't have taken a dress to show us, though you do rather keep your light hidden."

"I don't *hide*. I make bread. I sleep, I get up, I make bread again." This sort of attention wasn't for her. Yet here she was, getting it, with no idea what to do or say about it.

"No, you don't hide." Jane folded her arms across her chest like a man, Emery thought, eyes just as shining as Lady Arnold's, but not the same. Jane leaned back in her chair. "You're just beautiful, Emery, and fine as a gold chain, too. If Aunt Eden could see you now."

"If Aunt Eden had any imagination, she'd have noticed that Emery would be as pretty as anyone when nicely dressed," Anna said with more than a touch of acid, plopping back down in her chair.

Emery considered mentioning that none of them had ever called her pretty before she showed up here in this dress, but let it pass. It was nice to feel like she was no different from them, her pretty sisters. It was nice to feel like for once, she wasn't different.

Though she was planning to go to the opera as Lady Arnold's companion for the evening, and couldn't stop thinking about her lips.

That was likely different, and the two opposing forces were uncomfortable fit inside her at the same time. This was a very confusing evening, and it hadn't even started yet.

"Emery looks beautiful," and some steel came back into Jane's voice. "But I still need to know these married women's secrets."

"Oh no, Jane." Rose's shoulders hunched. "They're for married women and—and strumpets, I suppose. Not for you."

"There's a strumpet in the house right now. I've a right to know as much as anyone."

"*Is* there?" Curious, Rose straightened again. "Where is there a strumpet? Not with Mr. Laurent?"

"Mr. Laurent is a perfectly respectable gentleman." Anna reconsidered a little at the silence that greeted this. "Well, he's very nice. No, it's Lord Zachary upstairs that's got the strumpet. They haven't come back down."

"Can you *hear* anything?" Rose moved to the door and opened it, stuck out her head.

"Hear *what?* Honestly, Rose. Have out with it."

Jane, at least, wasn't letting it go, and though it was clear Rose felt trapped, it was also clear that she wasn't going to leave her sisters entirely hanging. "Well, if you *must* know... This is very personal. Never a word to Mr. Russell."

"I would never." Jane's words were flat and final.

"Well..."

"*I* don't need to hear this." Emery, stomach already twisting around a number of feelings she couldn't name, took the door from Rose. "I must attend Lady Arnold, she'll be waiting."

"No, don't walk alone..." Rose tried to wiggle out the door.

"No escaping!" Jane's voice at the table pulled her back.

Emery watched Rose go back to the table, feet dragging a little. She closed the door... then leaned against it.

She wasn't a married woman. She'd never be a married woman. But she had a feeling that Rose knew what other *women* knew; and she wanted that.

She was a Bickering sister, just like them.

Once Rose had finished, she could practically hear the gape-jawed staring.

"That's astonishing," Jane managed to say.

Rose heard the *snap* of Anna locking her jaw shut. "Honestly, had we known Mr. Russell would be subjecting you to such things, I would have fought your marriage even more strenuously."

Oh dear. Explaining something so *personal* to her sisters had felt like baring her soul, but obviously Rose hadn't explained it well enough. "You don't understand at all. It's delightful."

"That doesn't sound delightful at all."

Jane tapped one finger against the edge of her slate, mind clearly turning over serious thoughts. "Parts of it do. Touching someone. Being so close."

Pleased she hadn't given a false impression, Rose nodded vigorously. "And on the *best* days, it is like... Well, it ends with that... I tried to describe it. It's an *amazing*..." She had trouble saying the word *pleasure* again, but surely she'd already used it enough?

"*Le petit mort.* Little death." Jane's words were choppy.

"What? Who told you that?" Anna sounded suspicious of more knowledge about all this.

"Read it in a book, one of the poems my teacher wouldn't let us have." Jane did not go into detail about how to steal forbidden books. "I thought her excessive. The poem wasn't descriptive at all, and *le petit mort* tells one nothing. Death doesn't sound pleasant."

"Then that's a terrible name," Rose insisted. "It is *beyond* pleasant."

"Puzzling."

Jane seemed wrapped up in contemplation, while Anna was still thinking more broadly. "And that goes on in this house?" Before Rose could point out that she *lived upstairs,* Anna half-shrieked, "With Lord Zachary and his strumpet?"

Moving to the door, Anna opened it to find Emery still standing outside.

"Good night!" Emery finally managed to say, blinking at Anna before gathering up her collection of skirts and darting away down the stairs.

"Sit down, Anna, you can hardly go charging upstairs to check on a grown man," Jane said with evident practicality.

But Anna didn't sit. She didn't feel practical. The things Rose described seemed so... of course, if that was how babies occurred, even her own mother had... it was so very *animal*.

And every morsel of moral outrage anyone had ever expressed at a society ball coalesced into a little cloud of outrage in herself. The very idea that Lord Zachary could be doing something like that right now! In *her house!*

She walked right up past the Russells' rooms without stopping to think how quiet they were, to the staircase at the bottom of Lord Zachary's garret.

"Lord Zachary!" She went up stair by stair but, half-way up, lost her nerve and squeezed her eyes shut. She didn't want to see. She knocked on the stair and then went up another. "You are—"

Belatedly realizing she didn't have an excuse, and ought to have thought of one before she'd come up, she stopped, racking her brain for one.

But Lord Zachary's voice came floating down. "Ah, Miss Bickering. Come see. I do want your opinion."

He wanted her *opinion?*

Trying to decide what opinion she could possibly have of such matters, other than *gah* or perhaps *what?!*, Anna stepped up another stair, then another.

It would be impossible to have any further conversation without opening her eyes, so she did.

Expecting to be assailed with a venal tangle of arms and legs, Anna had to un-confuse herself for a moment, till her mind sorted out that there was Lord Zachary, standing at the easel in a stained smock that went to his knees, and there was the strumpet, sitting on a chair by a candle with her shoulders draped in thick linen.

In fact, "I'm cold," was all the woman said.

"Just a moment. Miss Bickering. It's fortuitous for you to visit. Come and tell me what you think about using blue for these shadows."

Step by step she went the rest of the way up, then across the garret, missing the bowls of pigment on the floor and empty buckets.

"The shadows are brown," was all she could think to say. He wasn't doing... *any* of what Rose talked about. Not even the kissing. He was painting, and she so hadn't expected it she had trouble pulling together words.

"But with a bluish tint they look darker, don't they?" He was utterly fixated on his canvas, eyes bright with concentration, a lock of his hair falling into one eye. He pushed it away and left a smudge of the blue on his face. A dark, smoky blue.

Anna looked closer at the effect of the smoky blue in the work. "It makes her look a little sickly, doesn't it?"

"I'm not," the woman put in lazily, but never moved.

"Dammit. Your pardon, ladies. It does, doesn't it? I wanted a lost, faraway feeling."

Anna looked again. The woman in the chair was far from delicate, but Lord Zachary had rendered her delicately, the shadows of veins in her skin adding blue to the tones he'd used there too.

"Perhaps it's not the right subject?" She wanted to be delicate; the woman was sitting right there. But she wasn't a lost, faraway sort of looking woman.

Fortunately, he seemed to know exactly what she meant. "It's worth something; it's not nothing. But yes, I do see. If I wanted the effect I had in mind."

Anna was so relieved to find him not exploiting a woman in the garret upstairs that she fell easily into inspecting the painting, not really noticing that it wasn't her usual evening activity.

"What time of day is it meant to be, outside that window?"

"Where has Anna gone?"

"Fussing with a neighbor. See here." Jane wasn't interested in Anna. "You do sound as though you enjoy the whole affair. Not just during, but you know, *after*."

Rose shrugged. "Why shouldn't I? He's my husband."

That was a troubling answer. If Jane were to pursue anything like what Rose described, it would be for the *le petit mort* that had sounded so boring in old poetry and now was all Jane could think about. And she had no intention of marrying anyone to get it.

"I suppose one can't do it alone."

Rose pinked again. "I don't think I explained it well at all. It's *not easy,* you know."

"I know." Jane wanted any information she could get.

"Well, one can... with the hands, you remember I said? It's very lovely... together, but one can. Alone, I mean."

"Ah. I see."

This was a whole new world of information. It put Hughes' hand on her ankle in a whole new light. He'd no doubt expected to *proceed,* and now Jane knew why.

And that it wasn't only for his benefit, as she'd suspected, but hadn't been sure.

"Good. So you know why... I *do* hope to have a baby soon."

Ah yes. This was all supposed to end in the production of a baby.

Clearly not every time, but it was an expected result.

That Jane did *not* want. But from what Rose described, counting days in order to avoid that was a bit of a gamble.

Still, it was something.

Yes, this was a great deal of information.

THE OPERA HOUSE WAS A RIOT OF COLOR, THE GILT decorations on the walls and the crystal lamps sending rays of light shooting into every bright gown, every bright head of hair, every jewel, and lighting them up like stars.

Emery was overwhelmed before the players had even taken the stage.

"The story of Orpheus and Eurydice is simple," Lady Arnold said quietly next to her, in a blue brocade gown whose silver tracings also sparkled in the dim light. "It's the terror of a love lost and lost again, really. But I love the music. I hope you do too."

Emery, who had never even attended a musicale, hadn't expected the conversations to go on around her, albeit muted. Hadn't expected to see others gawking around at the fine people the way she did, all their animated faces showing in the light. There were footlights on stage, and the smoke from them made the space in the middle of the theater a little hazy. The players went on performing no matter what, even when a rude lady with a tall feather on her head laughed loudly during a scene when Orpheus was on his way to hell.

But everyone quieted when Orpheus began his journey to the surface again, his lost wife following.

"You see, he mustn't look back or he'll lose her," Lady Arnold whispered, but Emery just patted her hand. She understood.

Then noticed she was touching Lady Arnold's hand.

The man on stage sang longingly, full of hope, as in the orchestra one lone harp accompanied him, his song leading his love back from the land of the dead.

In their box above, Emery took Lady Arnold's hand in hers, not looking, for fear someone would notice, but memorizing every shape of her knuckle, every soft surface, and then melting away all worry inside when the hand turned over, fingers interlacing with hers.

It was all that was really in her thoughts, even as Orpheus made the ultimate mistake and looked back, even as Eurydice, trapped in the underworld by her lover's failure, faded back into the shadows, her song quietly dying away in the now-silent theater.

It was all she really hoped for as she climbed back into Lady Arnold's carriage, riding back with her the short ride to Leicester Square, holding that precious hand all the way, too shy to look into Lady Arnold's eyes while doing it.

So absorbed that she never noticed, as she turned to help Lady Arnold down from the carriage on her own doorstep, that one person passing by at that late quiet hour on Leicester Square, when the night watchman was on his way about and the only walkers were questionable, was a slightly worn, slightly haggard, very observant Jasmine Hayes.

WHEN ROSE FINALLY WENT UPSTAIRS TO HER OWN LITTLE flat, she wondered why Mr. Russell hadn't come down. They often had a little family gathering in the apartment downstairs, and she was always happy to sit on the floor at his feet.

"Rose."

She knew as soon as she closed the door that something was wrong, knew in the next instant what it must be.

His heavy footsteps crossed the room, two, three, and then she was caught up in his arms. His strong, loving arms, just where she most loved to be.

He had the day's stubble on his chin, scratching a little

against her ear as he buried his face in her hair, then down to her neck. He didn't say her name again.

Instead, he said what she knew but didn't want to hear.

"I lost."

Episode 9: Upstairs, Downstairs

The shop was soberly quiet, patrons quietly lined up waiting for service. Sally presided over the cashbox, and Tilly waved her long cutting knife like a saber, pointing with it whenever anyone asked a question.

The mutterings in the shop were dark.

"He didn't win because he's too honest," said one woman to her neighbor, setting off murmurings of grim agreement and disagreement around the room the way a pebble in a pond made ripples.

"'E were too radical," said another. Shocked little gasps exploded around her like pockets of fireworks.

"'E shouted at 'is wife." This primly, from a woman who clearly disapproved and wanted the world to think no one had ever shouted at her.

"He *likes* his wife," another woman answered that swiftly. "That's all. The men don't like a man who's in love."

No one responded to that; whether the silence was because too many women agreed or disagreed wasn't clear.

The air was full, however, of the heavy, angry, despairing

speculations common everywhere in crowds not allowed to vote.

Mr. Wiggs brought a large basket of fresh loaves from the back and the delicious smell curled through the air, soothing some feelings.

"Let's make this quick," said Tilly in the commanding tones she usually reserved for cabbages. "If you're here for bread, this is how we'll do it. For quarterns, line up over here. Cut bread, here. And this line for tuppence loaves. We'll serve you all quick as we can."

But they all knew that there were reasons to be in the bakery—to share in the fellow feeling, or gossip—that went beyond the acquisition of bread.

Upstairs the mood was even more sober.

For once, Mr. Russell was at the center of the family circle, sitting on one of the precious chairs with his wife on his lap.

Jane could tell it was the first time that her sisters had witnessed the deep connection between Rose and her husband. And it felt unbearably intimate to watch, the way it had felt when she had witnessed the aftermath of their public fight. But for once even Anna didn't begrudge Mr. Russell Rose's attention.

"I should have done more." The tears ran silently down Rose's face. She couldn't stop listing reasons this disaster was her fault. "I should have visited more of the ladies and talked to their husbands. Or perhaps I should have talked less. You don't think it was because I talked too much, do you?"

Mr. Russell's sturdy arms tightened. "No," he said with a deep certainty. "It could never be because you talked too much."

"What should we have done?" Emery was typically blunt and clearly felt both her sister's pain and Mr. Russell's. "I suppose we should have done something different."

Anna said nothing, but clearly she too was wondering if they should have turned the bakery into a campaign shop of sorts. Perhaps churning out handbills instead of bread.

Mr. Russell was calm. "Winning an election isn't simple, and losing isn't either. People around here remember the last man, and that's complicated. They wish he hadn't died. And he's not here to give me his blessing. You can never do too much campaigning. But the truth is, ladies, that it was always a long bet. We were trying to get a Friend elected."

The way he said it made the capital letter evident, but the word moved Anna to speak. "And so you are a friend. To everyone, Mr. Russell. I cannot imagine why they did not see fit to give you the seat."

"It was a long bet," Mr. Russell said again, his cheek dropping to lie atop Rose's head. "I did think I had a chance though," he murmured into her hair with his eyes closed.

"Everything is ruined now. Everything." Rose's arms wrapped around Mr. Russell's waist tightened.

"Not everything," he told her softly, "only a few things are spoiled."

It was hard for Jane to stand and witness their sadness. Hard to admit that such sadness had crept up on their little family almost without their notice. They had believed in Mr. Russell; they had believed in their neighbors just as much, and now it felt as if the neighbors had betrayed them. There was no running to the captain for help on this one.

Not that she would, thought Jane, wiping the idea away as fast as she wiped away the tear that escaped to trickle down her cheek.

Down in the bakery proper, Jordan and Wiggs formed loaves, their hands twisting and slapping the bread dough into their soft shapes while Bailey sat on the floor with Mrs. Wallace's youngest baby.

"It's fine if he crawls." Mrs. Wallace, ambitiously attempting to mix three cakes at once in three different bowls, tried not to divide her attention more by glancing towards her odd new baby nurse.

"I can't let him go far," Mr. Bailey countered, "the way he crawls he'll end up in the oven."

Tilly bustled in. "The man from the hotel is here for the cakes."

Mrs. Wallace waved her away. "Send him off. They're still not done."

Tilly put her hands on her hips. "Last time, he came round to the back like he ought, and they weren't done then. What am I supposed to ask him, to call a third time?"

Mrs. Wallace shrugged. "I don't know what to tell you. The cakes aren't done."

The rhythms of the bakery depended on Emery's constant presence and Anna's frequent visits to prompt Mrs. Wallace to do this or that. Without the Bickering sisters, the rhythms of the bakery stuttered like a cart with a broken wheel.

Mrs. Wallace, hair springing up in the heat as she rushed from bowl to bowl, was embarrassed. She ought to have had the cakes ready on time, but without Anna, it had been a struggle to remember the steps. Which was absurd. She was a grown woman and knew how to mix a cake. She did it every day. Why she needed Anna over her shoulder to help, she couldn't fathom.

It also embarrassed her that Jordan, Mr. Bailey, and Mr. Wiggs were turning out bread as if it were a normal day.

Then Jordan made it better. "It feels odd not to have Emery—Miss Emery check the batch."

"Aye," Mr. Wiggs said in his laconic way, "but the bread ain't gonna be different just because she stares at it."

Jordan clearly couldn't shake the feeling that it might well be; there was nothing to be done but keep going.

AT THE BOTTOM OF THE STAIRS, ANNA AND EMERY PAUSED, as if having a mutual thought.

Which they were.

If they turned into the bakery, they could lose themselves in the familiar rhythms of the day. Accomplish something. Make bread, cakes, money.

They could fix whatever was going wrong in there, as there was always something going wrong in there.

Emery had never felt more strongly that she and Anna were sisters than when Anna said, "There must be more to this family than a shop."

They didn't go into the shop. They went out.

Circling the pointed end of the bakery, they walked down Bear Street in silence, then turned onto Castle.

Finally, Anna spoke. "Am I wrong?"

She must feel the pull too. Back to the bakery. Work. Work was everything.

But it wasn't everything.

Nor was marriage; witness poor Rose, who had her Mr. Russell, yet clearly felt her life shattered.

"You're not wrong." It was a struggle, but Emery dug into herself for some words that might say what both of them were feeling. "We've spent so long getting the bakery working. Saving our lives with a little money. This is Rose's life, but money can't help it, and that's all we've thought about. So we're at sea."

Anna nodded, and Emery felt her insides unknot.

"It *is* money, though," Anna said quietly. "Mr. Russell depended on that position. Now, I don't know what he'll do."

"Something. He's young and strong. He won't be a burden."

"I hadn't even thought of that." But then after a moment, Anna said, "Yes, I did. Without words, perhaps, but I did think it. Not truly. But isn't that always a worry?"

"For a woman to be saddled by a husband who won't work? I suppose." It had never been Emery's worry.

"I honestly think that's why Jane won't really entertain being courted. Though I half-think she's more like you, not interested in love at all."

That made Emery shift a bit uncomfortably, legs swinging into steps a bit too long for Anna's shorter legs before she remembered herself. Her hem was too short; she saw that now, after wearing Lady Arnold's velvet gown.

"Anna..."

When Emery didn't go on, Anna prompted her. "What?"

Emery had used up her words. Yet still had to find a few somewhere. "I'm not... *against* love."

"Really?"

Anna's steps didn't stop, but she sounded so astonished Emery wished she'd said nothing.

She braced for questions she couldn't answer; then a man's shout distracted them both.

"Tuppence loaves for a penny! Hot bread! Tuppence loaves for a penny here, get your hot bread!"

The sisters stared at each other. *Gaped.* Then, still wrapped in their mutual astonishment, circled the bread-seller so fast he had no moment to think of escape.

"How are you selling a two-penny loaf for one penny?"

"Why is your bread hot?"

"Do you have a Guild seal?"

"Is the mark on the bread?"

"Why are you selling in the street?"

"Where is your bakery?"

So whirled around by questions that the young man didn't know what was happening, he pulled away from them both. "I'm not telling you!"

Emery sized him up. He was young, nothing notable about him, with a loud voice. Exactly the sort anyone might employ to shout in the street about bread.

And he clearly didn't know that almost everything he'd said was against London law.

Anna examined a loaf. Emery could see it had no seal. As they both must have expected.

"Here." About to put the bread back, Anna changed her mind, giving him a penny.

"All right then," the lad said with some suspicion, pocketing the coin before they could pelt him with any more questions.

"Honestly though, how do you claim to sell two pennies' worth of bread for one penny?"

"Lady, I do as I'm told," the youth said, and, clutching his basket, scurried away before they could ask him any more questions.

And before they could make up their minds to follow him.

"REMY, WHAT THE FUCK ARE YOU DOING?"

Remy-Claude squinted to see Owen in the back of his shadowy public house. "I am thinking about beer but not drinking it."

That was noteworthy enough. Certainly nothing Owen had any right to expect after a year of watching the man drink himself stupid.

But that wasn't what he meant. "You told those girls your name."

"Pffff." The man waved it away. "*A* name."

"A name that's being passed around. That bakery is a hive of bees, man. Someone heard someone tell someone, and now everyone around Leicester Square is calling you Mr. Laurent."

"It's a dignified name." With a burp.

It had been so long since Remy had even thought of *himself* with a name. Any name. It felt like he was being transformed. He'd become a person, with a waistcoat and stockings.

Even Owen didn't know that he'd given a real first name to this person he'd become. *His* real first name.

A sense of impending danger crawled up his spine and made him want a drink.

"I was born here, did you know that?" he asked the innkeeper, wondering why he wanted a drink so badly, and why he didn't have one.

"No." Owen bunched up his bristled face. "But you're French."

"Leicester Square is full of Frenchmen, didn't you... didn't you notice?"

His last purchase had been of a tuppence loaf downstairs in the bakery that warmed his room. It had been light, chewy, and as golden on the tongue as he imagined heaven might be, if he were ever to get there.

Not that he would.

"Owen," he said, "the problem with being alive is filling the hours."

"No it ain't," the innkeeper said with deep conviction, wiping the table in front of him with a rag. "The problem with being alive is staying out of trouble."

No woman was ever turned away from the Ladies' Own Bakery.

So some customers, brushing past the obvious lady of the evening, pulled their skirts aside as they exited; but they said nothing.

Jasmine Hayes righted her hat. It was dustier than she liked, as she had just retrieved it from under a bed. But it was jaunty and blue.

She approached the counter.

"Next bread's not out yet," the plump woman there said instantly.

"Yes, I can see that." The baskets behind the woman were indeed all empty but for the great lump of a loaf from which pieces were cut. Jasmine ignored the heavenly smell and set her shoulders square. "I was wondering... if Miss Bickering were about?"

"No Bickerings here now," the woman cocked her head, "but if there were, you'd need to be a good deal more specific. Unless you don't care which one you get."

"Emery Bickering." In the alleyways, in the mews, Jasmine had felt like she and Emery were equals. Now standing in this warm, delicious bakery, Jasmine felt like a supplicant at the throne. And that wasn't why she'd come.

It put her temper a bit wrong.

"The family," the woman behind the counter said with puffed importance, "is indisposed." Then more conspiratorially, "You hadn't heard about the election?"

Nothing could interest Jasmine less than an election. "Why would I pay attention to any such foolishness?"

The air in the room changed, and Jasmine realized that for some reason, that was the wrong thing to say.

The unwelcome chill and the smell of the bread made her realize that she didn't feel hungry. She ought to; it had been long enough since she'd last eaten, and then some. But she only felt vaguely queasy.

And cold, and angry Emery wasn't here.

The woman behind the counter had narrowed her eyes. "You want a piece of the maslin?" she said with blunt force.

"No," Jasmine replied just as bluntly. "I'll come again another time."

And flounced out, wishing she'd never gone in at all.

WHEN THE DOOR TO THEIR ROOMS OPENED, THE LAST thing Jane expected was for Anna to put in only her head.

Her curly brown head, encased in her bonnet, followed by her gloved hand, beckoning.

Jane slid out, closing the door behind her. "What are you doing?"

"We've seen the most astonishing thing!" Anna's words came in a flood. "We went along Hemmings Row, you know, by the old workhouse? Then down Chandos Street to Bedford."

"No seal," Emery sounded grim and triumphant at once. "No Guild. Half the law's price. Shouting about hot bread. *Hot bread.*"

They sold hot bread every day, but it was technically against the law, and they knew it. So did everyone else.

They didn't, however, shout about it in the street.

"What are you talking about? A bakery?" Heart and head half still in the room with her sister, Jane felt turned around.

"A bread-seller. In the street. Just the seller." There were regulations about that too, as Anna's tone hinted.

"Tuppence loaf for a penny! Just picture us saying that." Now Emery sounded scandalized.

Well, so was Jane.

"You two are out chasing other bakeries? While Rose is in tears? What is *wrong* with you? Have you no feelings at all?"

Anna and Emery exchanged a look.

It made Jane take a breath. Had *she* said that? Was *she* the one objecting to talking about money? Because of someone's *feelings?*

What was *happening* to her?

"All right," Anna said, a little tentative, "but honestly, Jane, what do we *do?*"

"Do?"

"They're breaking all the laws, yet Mr. Keales is in here telling us to close doors." Emery's frown was getting darker and darker. "What do we really *have* to do? Is it just harassment?"

"And that's not even the problem." Anna put her hand on Emery's arm to cut in. "*Someone* is baking that bread, and selling it at half price just a few streets away. What if they come *here?*"

"I don't know." Jane felt exhausted. Watching others be sad was exhausting, the same way watching them revel in their beer at an inn stirred her blood. Other people—and she had always felt this—were a problem. "Is it too late to remind you I *said* opening a bakery was a bad idea?"

"Entirely." Now Anna sounded a bit acid. "Like it or not, it's our livelihood. *All* our livelihood, including, at last count, both Jordan and Sally, and now Mr. Russell. Plus Mr. Wiggs and Mr. Bailey's wages. And Mrs. Wallace."

"You're forgetting Tilly," muttered Jane.

Anna rolled her eyes. "I wish I could. Ladies' Own Bakery is *larger* than us. So now what do we do?"

"You're just glad you can't solve the problem by getting married."

As soon as it was out of her mouth, Jane felt sorry. It was likely true; but it wasn't kind, and today wasn't the day.

Anna folded her lips tight. Then said, "I can solve *any* of this for *myself,* by getting married and walking away. But I would never do that. Would you?"

Yes, a little traitorous voice said inside Jane. *I would.*

But she wouldn't. She had no intention of marrying anyone, and if she did, she wouldn't abandon her sisters.

And now, like it or not, abandoning the bakery would be like abandoning her sisters.

Somehow this family had become equivalent to their affairs of business.

Jane shook her head. That thought didn't feel right; but for the moment, all she knew was it was true.

"So what do we do?"

Episode 10: Manners

"I can't put off Lord Boislegrand's invitation any longer."
Anna turned to Rose. "Would you like more honey on
your muffin?"

Rose was limp in her chair, pale but for the red circles
around her eyes. Mr. Russell, beside her, was also sober.

If Anna couldn't distract them with honey, perhaps she
could with her betrothal.

She poured honey over Rose's breakfast till it ran down
the sides.

"She's going to need a spoon now," Mr. Russell observed.

Anna gave her a spoon.

"My point, muffin, was that I need your advice. I cannot
go alone, can I?"

It was a sign of how deep was Rose's pit of despair that
she didn't catch how absurd it was for Anna to ask her about
etiquette.

The question did pull her a little toward the surface.

"You ought to have a chaperone at least," Rose said
thoughtfully, dipping her spoon in the honey and licking it

without eating the muffin. "I ought to be with you, as the married lady of the family."

"I wondered."

"But I really don't feel up to eating in front of strangers." If Rose used a finger or two to find her food between plate and mouth, strangers might take it amiss.

"Of course you know best."

Jane buttered her own muffin. "It will be another Sunday, I suppose?"

"No; Saturday. His mother will be there, and she chose the day. You'll come with me?" Anna sounded as if it was no question.

"No," Jane said, just as certain.

"I can't let you look unseemly in front of Lord Boislegrand's mother!" The idea roused Rose.

"There you are," said Jane, as if it were all settled who would go. "I will be busy."

Anna wanted to ask how she'd be busy, of course, but Jane never answered those questions. She'd gone from constant excuses about errands to no excuses at all, but still never said where she was going.

Anna turned the other way. "Emery, you ought to go with us."

"Why?" Emery blinked over her porridge.

Anna didn't know why; she'd only wanted to change the subject.

"Yes, it ought to be a show of force," Rose mused. "If his mother will be with him."

"It's not a *war*."

"It's not?" Jane punctuated that with another bite of her breakfast.

"Really. All of you. Lord Boislegrand and I may not be... a conventional pair, but I doubt his mother will be *hostile*."

"I don't doubt it at all," said Jane in her very Jane way.

Before Anna could contradict, Emery, of all people, said, "I'll come with you."

"Why, Emery, thank you!"

"If there's one thing I've learned from being around rich people," Emery said with newfound wisdom, "it's that someone's always stabbing someone in the back."

Anna put down her spoon. "You told us every detail of your night at the theater. I don't recall *that*."

"Oh yes. You remember I told you about people staring, cutting others in public, everyone looking to see the length of my gown. I know some of them recognized the gown as Lady Arnold's. It's cut-throat."

"The women in society do say awful things to each other," Jane agreed.

Emery nodded. "I thought it was just sisters."

"Ugh." That idea put Rose's short-lived burst of energy right back down to the floor. "I can't take any more back-stabbing."

"No one has stabbed us in the back," Mr. Russell murmured quietly beside her.

"No, they stabbed us in the *front*."

Anna found Rose's burst of temper reassuring. It didn't matter to her whether Rose came or not; only that she didn't wallow. "You should do exactly as you please, Rose. I'll certainly have Emery with me."

They all contemplated for a moment Emery in the role of society chaperone. Including Emery.

"I'm off to visit Lady Arnold," Emery muttered.

"Miss Bickering!"

Startled—she was seldom called that—Emery spun on the pavement.

It was Jasmine Hayes. She looked shabbier than Emery remembered her, and Emery couldn't decide if that was because she had now seen Lady Arnold's real finery close up, or because Miss Hayes' appearance had declined somewhat.

There was a dust mark on her hat, and her shoes were scuffed. The shawl in which she was wrapped had no trimming and looked insufficient for the icy weather.

"Miss Hayes."

The woman came right up to her, almost as close as she used to in the mews when she was flirting with Emery. That's what it had been; Emery knew that now.

She didn't know where she'd learned, but she knew.

"Miss Bickering." With a coquettish tilt of the head. "I couldn't help but notice that you have made some valuable new friends. I wondered if you might have a tip for me."

Emery looked down into her face. It looked drawn, as if she weren't eating.

"What sort of tip?"

If she sounded ungracious, Emery couldn't help it. This didn't feel at all like their meetings before. Those had felt special, stirring emotions for Emery that had felt deliciously new. Now Emery felt nothing at all.

And she was, if anything, a bit wary. Miss Hayes looked desperate for something.

And made a noise halfway between a scoff and a laugh.

"Well, the rest of us need to eat too!"

Emery wanted to take a step back, but didn't want anyone else to overhear.

"You sound as if you want work?"

"My kind of work," she said with a slow wink that actually made Emery feel a bit ill. "If you have a plum spot, you might share it, you know? If the lady wants a bit of variety in her company."

It only took a few moments, but in Emery's mind they

were slow, painfully slow. Each realization came together and weighed down like a boulder in the middle of her mind; she could feel it, right behind her eyes.

What Jasmine Hayes was implying about Emery. And what she thought Lady Arnold was doing. *With Emery.*

For money. For the exchange of money.

It all settled into place in horrible *thuds* inside Emery's head, and her response was the only one that she could think.

"Do not," and she stepped closer, looking down at Miss Hayes with an expression that made that woman lean back, "do not speak of Lady Arnold. In any way."

"Oh!" Jasmine leaned away. "I didn't mean anything by it. I mean, if you are merely keeping her company for the fun of it, I wouldn't push you out. Even the food must be—"

"Do not ever say anything about Lady Arnold to anyone. Not anything." Emery's eyes narrowed. "Is that clear?"

"So she's not...?"

Emery had never before wanted to grab someone by the arms and shake them. All that restrained her was her desire not to touch Jasmine at all. "I'm going to say this one more time. Do not. Speak of her. To me, or anyone. I don't want to hear you've ever even mentioned her *name.* Is that clear enough?"

"Why, Emery!" Jasmine shifted, dropping an impatient hip, but she didn't retreat. "I thought you liked me."

Had she been that pretty? She must have been prettier than she was now. Emery hated to think it had all been because of the attention, her obsession with this person.

It likely had, though.

Emery hadn't realized how starved she'd been for attention till Jasmine had given her some. That was something.

But she didn't owe her anything now.

"I did like you," she admitted, for the sake of the person who had finally made her feel seen.

That was all.

Collecting her own shawl around her more tightly, Emery moved along the pavement and left Jasmine standing there. She did not look back.

FORTUNATELY, LADY ARNOLD TOOK THE HIGH COLOR IN her cheeks as from the cold.

"My! Do stand by the fire, Miss Bickering. Let me fetch you a chair."

Emery just waved it away.

This fine room, with its painted wallpaper and porcelain, now felt as familiar to Emery as any. The house did not intimidate her; she called the butler by his name.

But it hadn't been in trade for anything.

"Lady Arnold. You needn't wait on me."

Lady Arnold had never been very formal, even back when she'd visited the bakery to watch Emery cut bread. She seized Emery's hand. "You're like ice! Honestly, stand by the fire. Let me order some tea, and you ought to have some biscuits and jam—if I only had one of your cakes—"

She moved quick, her little figure dashing for the door with fine silk skirts trailing behind her, but Emery followed just as quick.

Emery's hand flattened against the door before Lady Arnold could open it.

Shocked, Lady Arnold turned, and found herself inches from Emery.

Dahlia had the most beautiful heart-shaped face, Emery thought, drinking in all she could see. Delicate features. The way those lashes lay on her cheek when her eyes closed could have been a poem.

"I have not come for you to wait on me," Emery said

slowly and distinctly, wanting every word heard. "I don't come for the dresses, or the food, or the fireplace. You know that, right?"

Lady Arnold's little figure melted back against the door.

"I'd hoped," was all she said. She sounded a little breathless.

"You don't just have to hope. You *know*." Emery felt fierce about this. They ought to be able to talk as clearly as people did walking into the shop demanding to marry her sister. They *ought* to know each other's thoughts. Why didn't *they* have the right? Or the chance?

Feeling behind her, Lady Arnold turned the key in its lock. Fastening the door shut.

It made Emery's insides—she couldn't describe it, but it was like the explosion of the fireworks on bonfire night.

But Emery shook her head. "Someone could try the door and wonder why it's locked."

"Better that than being discovered."

"We're not doing anything."

"Yes, we are," said the little woman, flushed, definitely breathless now, and with a look Emery knew was for her. *Her*.

Slowly the taller woman bent forward, desperate to touch, to taste. To reassure and be reassured. To feel this, here, with her.

Lady Arnold—*Dahlia*—her lips were so soft. Sweet and gentle like all of her. Parting to welcome Emery's kiss.

She abandoned the door and flowed against Emery.

Whatever noise Emery made was shocked, animal, but felt appropriate, just as Dahlia in her arms felt so soft and warm and *right*.

She was the perfect size, the perfect shape, the perfect scent and taste and breath, warm and trusting under Emery's touch, and just to be near so much perfection made Emery's hands shake.

Dahlia looked as surprised as Emery felt when they parted a little, and found themselves still in the same room where they'd begun.

Perhaps she felt as surprised as Emery at how well they fit together.

There was too much to say, and nothing to say.

"How long do you think we can keep the door locked?" whispered Dahlia.

EMERY HAD BEEN THE EXACT WRONG SISTER TO BRING.

Emery had been distracted all week, and now she sat at Lord Boislegrand's supper table completely unconcerned about the finery, the food, or the formidable dowager sitting across the table.

The food was just as fine as it was the first time, but Anna struggled to enjoy it, bearing up under the weight of wondering what conversational gambit was about to come her way.

The Dowager Viscountess was as round in the belly as Lord Boislegrand, but much less soft in her personality. Her eyes, deep in their well of wrinkles, had measured Anna's hems and the thickness of her gown, the number of her petticoats, and the stitches in each inch of her knitted wool shawl.

"I'm glad to see rasped beef on the table," said that lady as she spooned some on to her plate. "That was always a favorite of yours in the nursery."

Lord Boislegrand looked as if he did not wish to discuss his nursery. "Have you tried the beef, Miss Bickering?"

Anna had barely tasted it, while Emery had worked her way through portions of beef, buttered crab, roasted larks, cold sliced ham, and boiled turkey as though she were eating for all her sisters and then some.

"It's very nice." Hoping for something to stir Lady Boisle-grand's interest in their family, she said, "How did you find the beef, Miss Emery?"

"A bit bland."

Anna closed her eyes.

Emery went on. "It's better than potted beef, though; potted beef is so oily. Though any beef is welcome in winter. Have you tried it with curry spices, sir? I imagine it would suit you."

Puffy's eyes widened as if seeing a door to a magic kingdom.

"I *adore* curries. I was just saying last time to your sister—"

"Curries are hardly elegant." Lady Boislegrand plopped this bit of news in the middle of the table, and in the ensuing silence, chewed her turkey carefully. The soft waving of her jowls was impossible to ignore. She swallowed before continuing. "What is the *last time* to which you're referring, sir?"

"I had Miss Bickering to supper, madam. With a different sister."

"I see."

The meal went on that way, every conversational sally parried by Lady Boislegrand as if defending a castle.

Eventually, Anna found herself in the foyer about to depart without ever being directly addressed by her ladyship.

"I've just been in the mood to kick someone lately," Emery muttered, "she seems the perfect candidate."

"This is awful, Emery. I can't marry Lord Boislegrand if she hates me."

"So? Are you going to marry Lord Boislegrand at all?"

"Why do people keep *asking* me that?" Anna felt like stomping her foot.

"Because you're betrothed, Anna. Because he wants to.

Do you like him following you around like a puppy? Or do you simply want him in your pocket as a possible escape?"

And there it was.

Emery had *definitely* been the wrong sister to bring.

"Look around. He's so *lonely*." That was all Anna could think to say.

"And being betrothed is making him less lonely?"

Anna's mouth tightened. Why did Emery have to be so... so *her?*

Meanwhile Emery examined the finery of the Boislegrand walls and floors and porcelain, the way she had examined the windows and linens in the fine supper room. The light of a dozen candles had made the place glitter, but Emery hadn't seemed impressed.

And now she said, "Lady Arnold's home is more comfortable."

"You've changed."

Emery shrugged a little, still looking at the wall's plaster carving. "There's a great deal to see in Leicester Square."

That was certainly the truth.

Was Anna the same person who'd been afire with shame only a few months before after only speaking to Lord Boislegrand in the street?

And now they were betrothed. With the promise of all this glory at Anna's feet.

And all she could think about was the breadseller with his hot tuppence loaves for a penny.

With the threat of immediate starvation lifted, Anna had imagined she would worry about the bakery less. With Lord Boislegrand's proposal, she oughtn't have worried about it at all.

But that hadn't happened. She thought about the bakery *more,* and nothing Puffy could do would help her against the Guild and its accusations. Competition from a rogue baker felt more threatening than Lady Boislegrand's glares.

She didn't know who Emery was becoming, or Jane. But she wasn't them, and she wasn't Rose, with her heart's desire wrapped up in a man. Look how that had ended for Rose.

Not that Rose's life was over; she was still young, she and Mr. Russell, but marriage hadn't saved them from trouble.

Anna still wanted fine things. She wanted to be comfortable. The Bickerings still hadn't earned enough to buy new dresses, and in this weather that was serious business. It was the coldest November Anna could remember.

Surely there was some way to make this betrothal work.

"Wait here," she told Emery.

No servants had followed the Bickerings to wait upon them as they left, so Anna was unaccompanied as she went back through the hallways toward the supper room, hoping to find Puffy, his mother, or some magical gateway to rapprochement with them both.

The room where they'd eaten was full of bustling servants, so she turned aside before she gained it, then wandered on, looking for Puffy.

"Honestly, Augustus."

The sound of Lady Boislegrand's voice, louder and sharper than it had been through the whole supper, made Anna stop.

"If you can't see how common she is, practically a beggar, the lies she tells ought to make it clear. If that woman with her is her sister, I'm Joan of Arc."

"I assure you, madam, it *is* her sister."

"They look nothing alike. Honestly! If this is the sort of company you keep, I ought to move back to the city. You have always been a terrible judge of character, and see what you're doing now. You're a grown man, with grown children! It's as though losing your wife has made you a baby again."

"Madam, I assure you the Bickering sisters are not

beggars. They are of perfectly good family; you've likely met them. Her aunt lives at Walbey Hall, the Baroness Delbinham. Perfectly respectable."

"Augustus, everyone in London claims some similar relation."

"To the Baroness Delbinham? Come, mother, I seriously doubt it."

"To some peer of the realm. It's all lies, and you're a child. You cannot seriously be entertaining the idea of marriage to this harlot."

Feeling herself flush hot, Anna took a step.

"Madam," said Puffy in a tone that made Anna stop. "I have done everything you've ever asked of me. I made a very respectable match; my wife died. I lived a very respectable life; now, I'm lonely. I notice you don't ask if she makes me *happy*. Well, now's the time. Because that's all I care about, at my age. And if you don't understand that, I'm surprised."

Nothing could have startled Anna more than for Puffy to be his own defender.

He went on. "She's a beautiful young lady, and ought to have her pick of London. Her bad fortune is my luck, because she'd otherwise never look at me. You have your dowager house and your friends in the country. Why can't I have something for myself, madam, hmm? I tell you I can, and I will. So stop harping."

"*Harping?* When did you ever learn to speak to your mother like this?" The ancient woman was gasping; Anna thought it from anger. "She'll never be received anywhere. She'll have no society *here*."

"She knows that." Lord Boislegrand had never sounded so certain. "I'll be her company, and she'll be mine."

Anna took a step back. Then another.

Then she turned and ran.

"Where *is* that carriage? Oh, thank you." Anna grabbed

Emery by the elbow and hustled her out at the wave of the driver, never waiting for anyone to notice and announce him.

In the carriage, Emery sat across from her and just stared.

Anna felt she could barely speak above a whisper. All the anger she'd felt, all the shock, pressed down on the few bites of supper she'd had. And all she could imagine was night after night, year after year, of meals like that.

Lord Boislegrand *knew* no one in London would receive her. She had irretrievably stepped down in the world. She was a baker; she was no respectable wife.

The worst part was, he was only asking her to join him in the London prison where he lived. Clearly he had no society of his own, trapped in that fine house alone every night, just as much as she would be, but without anyone's company at all.

This was a problem, not of what society would think, but of what he needed. And what *she* needed.

"Emery," she managed to say, "I really don't know what to do."

THAT NIGHT, ONCE THE RUSSELLS RETIRED AND SO DID Emery, Anna stared at their dining table and wondered where Jane was.

Wherever she was, whatever she was doing, it was unchaperoned and somehow illicit.

And Anna didn't feel like she could scold Jane at all.

They'd fallen out of society. There was no going back. So what did it matter what they did now? Their ankles might freeze till they snapped, but at least the four of them were together. And fed. With a roof over their head.

Wasn't that all Anna had wanted, when she'd accepted Lord Boislegrand's proposal?

She'd feared she'd never be happy. Now she realized, she'd had no idea what would make any of her sisters happy.

She barely had any idea what she wanted herself.

Silently as she could, she crept past their neighbor's closed door, and upwards. She had importuned Mr. Laurent several times, forcing him to shave and bathe and eat; that too had been a welcome distraction, but now she faced the true problem.

She would have to marry Lord Boislegrand, or let him go.

The stairs to the garret creaked worse than the floors, but she trusted Rose and Mr. Russell not to investigate. They must be used to Lord Zachary's comings and goings; he couldn't always use the back stair.

As she'd done last time, her head entered the garret first, and she saw he was there again, candle burning. Blobs of color lay on the canvas in front of him, and he wore a worn woolen waistcoat over his smock as a concession to the cold.

"Aren't you warm enough?" It wasn't what Anna had intended to say, but it came out of her mouth before she could stop it.

He whirled, and she saw him nearly vibrating with tension.

"Don't mock me, not today."

"Sir!" Now concerned, Anna hurried up the last few steps and forward, stepping over scattered pots and rags on the floor. "Are you quite well?"

"Am I well? Yes. Am I a painter? No." Turning back to the inchoate shapes, he ran the hand holding the paintbrush through his hair, streaking a lock of the gold with coral-colored paint. "The canvas should capture a *feeling*. And either I don't have any, or I have no talent."

Anna had the notion she'd walked in on him arguing with himself.

"Of course you have talent. What brought this on?"

"My holiday was a disaster, but at least I tried to sketch some landscapes. They don't interest me, Miss Bickering, and I can't force them to. I don't see what others see in them. There's no *feeling* in a tree. At least, not for me."

"So what is it you've tried here?" Anna's fingertips floated over the canvas edge.

"A woman. Surely a man can have feelings about a woman, right? Surely there's more passion in that than a bowl of fruit. But not me. You saw my work from the model; it was just passable. As if I'd painted a pineapple."

In a sudden burst of motion, he threw the brush at the wall. It left a smear of coral paint and bounced to the floor.

"You always know what's wrong with my art, Miss Bickering. So just tell me. Tell me why I'm a hollow shell. You must know, it must be something you can see, just like you always know about shades of colors. I'm not even as interesting as your neighbor-pet downstairs. Him you drag out and feed, but me—"

"Lord Zachary! What are you on about?"

His left hand loosely gripped the palette, drooping at his side; his right slammed down on his table of paints, making the glass vials jump.

"Lord Zachary," he snarled. "Like a child in the nursery. She was right about that. Do you know I've never used my courtesy title, Miss Bickering? It was from my grandfather, and as a child I found him appalling. Now here I am, still a child, accomplishing nothing. I could have made these drawings in my nursery. I *did*."

Anna had no idea who *she* was, or what might be upsetting him, but... "I've interrupted you at an inconvenient time. I'm so sorry."

"No, don't go." He whirled as she stepped back.

Surprised, she let a foot fall on one of his paint pots, which wobbled dangerously. So did she.

He gripped her elbow fast and steadied her.

Anna looked down at the coral thumbprint on her sleeve. It was the same gown that still bore the mark of a fateful blackberry.

He pulled back his hand as if she burned. "I'm so sorry."

"Never worry about it," Anna said, and she meant it. A stain *wasn't* as important as her problem with Lord Boislegrand. Far less important than keeping her bakery running. And not nearly as important as the real problems of her sisters.

She felt something in her let go. Perhaps the something that had still wanted to be Lady Boislegrand, no matter the cost. Perhaps the part of her that felt responsible for society's demands.

She wished to do something for him, she didn't know what; but right now, she was faced with a more immediate problem.

"Lord Zachary—"

With a frustrated noise, he turned back to his canvas. Slashed across it with the paintbrush in his hand. *Vane.*

"It's my name. It's all I've ever really been. So why do I still chase this absurd feeling I could be something more?"

Anna did not know what was right to say, but had to say something. If it was a mistake, well, she'd put it in her pocket with the rest of her mistakes.

"I suspect, Mr. Vane, that wanting to be better might be what separates would-be artists from genuine ones."

His head whipped back toward her, eyes wide. His lips fell open, but he didn't say anything.

She saw him take a breath, then another.

Then he said, "Miss Bickering. You have better taste in color and composition than anyone I have ever met. I want you to help me. I need help."

Anna knew exactly how hard it was to ask for help; she'd come here to ask it. But help him? Impossible.

And yet... perhaps there was something in the guttering shadows that worked magic on her eyes and his.

Because she could suddenly see what he saw. In all his paintings. In him. He had a beautiful technique, but applied it poorly; and once started, he let his vision go awry.

"We should have to discuss it," she said faintly.

"Yes, of course. It is too late at night to make business contracts," was his swift reply.

"I see the point of it."

"Do you? Of course you do. It must be obvious." His tone implied everything was obvious to her.

"I had come with a different question."

He slapped his forehead. "Of course you did! My deep apologies. Here I am ranting about myself. I promise, Miss Bickering, I do intend to become less vain." He tossed his palette down with another glance at his ironic signature. "Or perhaps more so, in business dealings. Mr. Vane has a solid sound."

He'd turned it back to himself again; but then, men did that, in Anna's experience.

"Let us talk later." And over his protestations and apologies, she curtsied—it was all she could think to do—and carefully started down the dark stairs.

She might no longer have a position in the eyes of society, but she still had a care for herself. At least enough to realize when she shouldn't be in a man's room late at night.

She didn't know why she'd gone there in the first place, but she knew when to rescue herself, and she did.

The problem of Lord Boislegrand and his betrothal would need to find solution elsewhere.

Episode 11: Walks before dawn

It was well before dawn when Rose appeared at her sisters' rooms.

She walked straight in to the sitting room, her appearance pausing all their morning bustle with pots and stockings.

Her back straight, her head held high, she had her hands clasped at her waist like any woman of the Friends on business.

"Mr. Russell is going away," she said clearly.

Then she dissolved into sobs.

BY THE TIME THE HUBBUB SETTLED, ROSE WAS LEANING ON Anna's shoulder, both of them sitting on the floor like they used to do, with Emery's arm around her and Jane sitting near her feet.

"He's so ashamed." The tears had overflowed a kerchief; someone had fetched her a linen bath towel. Rose blew her nose into it. "He still goes out every day to convince more people to support the cause, and subscribe to Mr. Clarkson's talks. I think the abolitionists hoped Mr. Russell would revive the movement. They are discouraged, you know, since Mr. Sharp just died in July."

Jane felt ashamed that she didn't know who Mr. Sharp was, and barely remembered Mr. Clarkson. It felt so odd, when they saw each other every day, to remember that Rose's life differed completely from her own, driven by Rose's own interests.

Which still encompassed entirely freeing slaves, including the ones on sugar plantations; but also revolved around her precious Mr. Russell.

"He's going home, north." Rose blew her nose again. *He* always meant Mr. Russell now. "He wishes to speak to his meeting. Most of the committee here insists that a Friend winning the seat was always unlikely, but that just makes him feel half the time like it was all a waste, and the other half the time he wishes he'd made it happen."

"But why leave?" Anna rocked Rose on her shoulder like she'd done when Rose was very little.

"He says it's to speak to the meeting, but I think he wants to see his family. And I think he has to ask for money. Because without a position, he doesn't have the funds to lease our rooms for the rest of the year. And of course Mrs. Scrope —" Rose spat out the name, "—won't give him any leniency. I'd like to beat her to death with a fire iron."

"Of course you do. Of course you do." Anna kept rocking.

Of all of them, Rose was the least likely to take to violence, Jane thought; but she couldn't deny the appeal of taking a fire iron to Mrs. Scrope.

"I'm so tired, Mr. Laurent, of threats hanging over our head." Anna sounded tired indeed.

They held the meeting after supper: all four sisters at the table, Emery standing, and Mr. Laurent, the neighbor from the closet, sitting in a chair as an honored guest.

Jane found him much changed. Someone had cut his hair, and forced him to wash it, like the rest of him. Anna had patched his clothes. He looked poor, but respectable. Jane had never noticed it before, but when sober, his deep-set eyes pierced like a hawk's.

"I am very sorry, ladies, that I did not discover a weakness of the Guild with which to fight them. But I do know that a lack of weakness may also be a lack of strength."

Emery looked blank. "What?" she said in a way that expected some quick explanation.

"I know nothing about guilds, ladies. But men that don't fight have nothing to protect. *Attend.* A force of men in fear of their lives fight fiercely. A force of men doomed to the gallows? Rarely fight at all. Do you see what I mean? Men who are hopeless, they go limp. And the Bakers' Company, it has no fight."

"No, I don't see." Anna tapped on the table. "I'm terribly sorry, but do explain."

"I could not find one person going in or out of the building to battle the Guild. *D'accord*, the Guild court is one time a year, to prosecute offenders. But that is an old rule, fallen away during the war. They can petition the King to sue, but will the King listen?" One thing he did not have to explain was the difficulty of the crown, with the Prince Regent ruling in his father's stead as that George suffered his bouts of madness. "I think this dog has no teeth."

"Good news," said Jane, feeling it, "but then what do we do? Because Mr. Keales came in again insisting we must close. He's very emotional about it. I thought he was going to cry."

"I'm not sure, but I think Mr. Keales is a zealot. You know the word? He wants to restore the Guild to its former glory." Mr. Laurent's wrinkled nose said exactly what he thought about zealots. "He *is* a master baker tasked with the survey, and he *is* supposed to report violators of Guild rules to the Guild."

"Then why on earth isn't he out catching that cove who shouts tuppence-loaves-for-a-penny?" Jane found this the most exasperating of all. Why harass them? Unless Mr. Keales truly just hated women.

They all turned to Jane.

Realizing what she'd said, Jane quickly revised herself. "Chap. Fellow. You know what I mean."

The tavern's rich vocabulary stuck in her head; now it betrayed her.

But by chance or through mercy, Mr. Laurent came to her rescue. "That is to me the most interesting question. There are so many bakers now, the survey is a farce. Mr. Keales the zealot could be out canvassing the streets for offenders, but no. He focuses on you." At the table, Mr. Laurent held his body tightly contained, but now he leaned forward conspiratorially and waved a hand around the table. "So why you ladies? Is it indeed ill will? Or is there some other reason? I have learned a little of his home, but a person's innermost feelings are hard to discover. A more obvious answer is that someone has pointed him to you."

Emery folded her arms across her chest. "Someone set him on us."

"That is what I think is most likely."

"Fire irons all round," muttered Rose, and silently Jane agreed with her.

Was there no trouble so bad that some cruel person wouldn't pile on more?

"THEN WHAT DO YOU SUGGEST, MR. LAURENT?" ANNA still looked to him for answers, when Rose could have told her that men didn't know what to do any more than they did.

As always when problems dug into their hearts, Mr. Russell attempted to understand all his failures with study and application to the problem. They didn't *fight* about their predicament, not really. Mr. Russell simply went through their options methodically until Rose wanted to scream.

Why had she only seen the good side of moving to the rooms above her sisters? Why hadn't she asked about the pitfalls? Now she realized it was because she hated pitfalls. Well, everyone did.

So she couldn't even scream at Mr. Russell; he had only been trying to please her. True, he shouldn't have, without the finances to back their contracts; but to him, Rose's happiness weighed so heavily on the scale that Rose couldn't fault him. Maybe she should, but she couldn't.

No, it was Mrs. Scrope Rose really wanted to scream at, Mrs. Scrope who would not extend the slightest credit regarding their lease, even knowing Mr. Russell had a steady income that was just, at the moment, too small. Rose would happily have screamed at her; failing that chance, she'd love a chance to scream at the Bakers' Guild or anyone in it.

Surprisingly, Mr. Laurent's thoughts seemed along the same lines. "Take the fight to them."

Fights Rose understood, but not this way. "Explain, please?"

"Mr. Keales threatens you. Call his bluff. Tell him to take you to the Bakers' court. See what he does."

"He might *take us to the court*. That sounds bad." Emery did not like the plan.

"I think he has no teeth. I think the Guild has no teeth."

"But what if you're wrong?" was Jane's question.

Rose understood better now why Jane was always panicked about money. It went deeper than an aversion to poverty. Jane didn't like risk. There was risk in being poor; there was also risk in falling in love.

And risk in marriage that Rose had never imagined.

It would hurt to be separated from Mr. Russell, hurt Rose had thought could never come to her now they were married. He had to go north, and he wanted her to stay with her sisters, safe, warm, and fed. It was logical, but it was going to *hurt*.

Jane was terrified of risk, and Jane might be right.

Mr. Laurent took the question seriously. "When threatened by a tyrant," he said, in a solemn voice, "do you immediately bend the knee?"

That made them all shift and rustle around the table.

But Jane didn't bend. "I suppose the trouble is recognizing a tyrant," she shot back. "Or knowing if your knees are already bent. We've saved twenty-eight pounds—"

"*Twenty-eight pounds!*" Rose pounded a fist on the table. Her hot anger found a new outlet. "Why haven't we got new dresses long since? Aunt Eden's charity gowns won't last forever. Twenty-eight pounds! Jane, you said we had no money!"

"We have no *free* money. If we don't have some cushioning, any blow could crush us. Can you honestly be surprised, after the year we've had? We need enough to pay a month's worth of flour and firewood, at least. And the water bill. Otherwise the bakery could be closed. And I think we need a little more." She seemed to appeal to Anna. "I'm tired of living on the edge of disaster too. *Financial* disaster. If we push the Guild, and they fine us, what then?"

"There are risks in any fight." Mr. Laurent clearly understood that this was no small matter to the Bickering sisters. "But when the fight comes upon you, can you walk away?"

"I want to know who that tuppence baker is," Anna insisted.

"I want to know who snitched about us," said Emery, so darkly Rose wondered where she'd learned *that* word. Its meaning was obvious.

"I want Mrs. Scrope to die a painful death, but who gets what they want?" Rose couldn't help her bitterness.

"Truly? Mrs. Scrope should have an accident?" Mr. Laurent took that quite seriously too.

"No, no." Anna shushed that idea. "You've been very kind, Mr. Laurent. I can absolutely see the value of your advice."

"But this isn't a battle." Jane had not given up. "This is money."

Rose's chin shot up. "Money isn't a battle?"

"Jane, I agree it's an unattractive risk," Anna tried to soothe the feelings in the room. And clearly understood Jane better than Rose had until just now. "But I can't bear Mr. Keales' poisonous little visits. Something has to be done."

"We need it to be less risk," Emery said in her short way. "We need more money, so less risk to the money we have."

"Yes," Jane said with some acid, "let us magically acquire more money to make it less of a risk before we try."

"I'll eat less." Rose had been able to do so little for Mr. Russell. Perhaps she could help her sisters.

"You eat like a bird," Anna brushed that away. "More cakes? But the oven has to be cooler for cakes. Mrs. Wallace and I are already struggling with the timing."

"Open another oven." Emery dropped her answer like a gavel.

And stunned the sisters into silence.

There were two other ovens, smaller than the main one, in the bakery proper. All of them ignored those ovens, the way they ignored the second counter in the shop. They didn't have enough bread to fill the second counter, so it was usually empty; just so, they didn't have any use for the smaller two ovens, so they ignored them, backed as they were onto the great one, sharing the same chimneys.

That was where deliverymen stacked the great sacks of flour, and where Mr. Wiggs and Mr. Bailey now slept.

"Honestly," Anna said slowly, "I never pictured the bakery working at full capacity."

"Nor me." Rose had forgotten those ovens were even there. The empty counter out front she had simply taken as a feature of the store; the empty shelves behind it, she expected would stay empty.

"Forget cakes," insisted Emery. "This bakery was built to do more than we do. Our oven is working round the clock. Open another oven."

Had Emery been contemplating this for a while? She sounded so sure.

"We'd have to buy more firewood, even more flour." Jane sounded less so.

"But as an experiment? For a week or two? Cheaper experiment than calling the Guild's bluff. I'm not asking for dress fabric, Jane. You think we can't afford a fight; so let's get more money."

Anna was clearly considering it. "Cakes make more profit."

"But we have more hands making bread, and it takes less work." Emery's answers were so swift, she must have been thinking of this for a while. "We have journeymen now. We could do it."

They knew how to make money with bread, that was no longer in question.

And it felt so good to latch onto one certainty in life, that Rose became immediately converted to the question. "Yes.

We should open another oven. Feather our nest a little more, if that's needed."

"I need to make some calculations." Jane wasn't entirely converted, but Rose could tell she was interested.

"If I can help," said Mr. Laurent, sensing that the sisters had settled on a path, "you must tell me so."

"Past time for it!"

Rose found Mr. Bailey was all in favor of the idea almost as soon as it was out of her mouth.

She wanted to spend every possible second with Mr. Russell. Even the idea that he would soon sleep away from her made her chest ache.

But he was out talking to Friends about his options one more time, and if Rose had to busy herself at the bakery for the foreseeable future, she would make herself useful at it.

"We could have the maslin in a slower oven," Mr. Bailey added. "Takes longer anyway."

"Ah!" Jordan, stirring a batch of dough, seemed to grasp Mr. Bailey's point immediately. It clearly excited him.

"More ovens is more work." Mr. Wiggs, however, sounded less excited.

Sal, scrubbing half-barrels by the huge trough-shaped sink, snorted.

"What would you need—" But Rose was interrupted by Tilly bustling in.

"Sorry, Mrs. Russell, you have a note."

Tilly bustled back out front as quickly as she'd come, leaving the little folded square in Rose's hand.

"What does she think I'm going to do with this? Eat it?" Rose still felt too prickly to brush off Tilly's thoughtlessness, though she was surely in a hurry, as they all were these days.

"I can read some, miss," Mr. Wiggs offered, but Rose shook her head.

"Never worry, Sal can have her hands dry in a second. Sal, would you mind?"

The girl was by Rose's side in a second, unfolding the heavy paper. "Dear Mrs. Russell."

It still felt so odd to be called that. And so sweet.

Rose forced her attention to the letter at hand.

Sal continued. "We are so sorry to hear of Mr. Russell's loss in the recent election. While it is difficult to put another disa—disappoint, disappointment upon you at this time, we regret to say—"

Sal stopped.

Rose ought to have asked first if it said who the letter was from. "It's all right, Sal, you don't have to finish it."

"We regret to say," read Sal, steadily, "that after all, we do not have a place for Sally Collier in our school. I'm sure you understand—"

"That's enough, Sal. Thank you."

Refolding the letter, Sal silently handed it over.

Then, thrusting herself forward, wrapped her arms tight around Rose's waist.

She was still so young, thought Rose as she hugged Sal back, even as she noticed that Sal's head was nearly to her shoulder now. They were growing fast. They deserved better care too.

Rose found a new way to be angry.

She'd find Sal a good school or someone was going to get a fire iron to the face.

"It's really all right, Sal. It's only one school," she murmured against Sal's hair, giving her a fierce squeeze. "We'll find you a better one. No harm done."

Except a few shattered hopes, she thought, rocking the girl a little the way Anna had done to her just this morning. She knew how shattered hopes hurt.

FOR THE DOZENTH TIME, JANE IMAGINED HER SISTERS'S surprise if they knew exactly how all of those twenty-eight pounds had been earned.

She pocketed her shillings.

She was an old hand now at the Pinfeather Inn. Its proprietor, Mr. Sacks, let her sing whenever she was there, and she even had a few men now who came just to see if she would.

Jane had never seen a sailor in her life until this autumn. Now she felt like they were all old friends. From the oldest, who were toothless and gaunt but still laughed harder than anyone Jane had ever met in London society, to the youngest ones, whether they were wary or loose, they were men who said what they thought.

Jane found them wonderful.

The thought crossed her mind as she went to greet the accordion-player that she liked them just because they were associated, however distantly, with Captain Brice.

But she saw these sailors far more often now than she saw the Captain, and she thought it just as plausible that she liked him because he was like them.

"What'll you have tonight?" The accordion-player had his machine slowly billows-ing back and forth, making a low wheeze.

"I'll pick later." The songs these musicians taught her had a lot of lyrics that would have made her blush a year ago.

Well, would have made Anna blush.

As long as Jane learned a few more each time, and practiced the ones she knew, she could keep the sailors spinning around their tankards. Half the time it didn't matter if she knew the words; the sailors would sing along.

And the women who sat on their knees or kicked up their heels when the dancing started would sing along too.

Jane couldn't have explained why it all felt a lot safer than digging in to argue with Mr. Keales and the Guild. She did know it was simpler, and it was immediate, and it was *fun*. She liked that.

Even when there was Hughes, slouched on a bench against the back wall and sipping his beer, watching her with glittering eyes, waiting for the moment she'd be free from the crowd and go see him.

Perhaps because of him.

Because Jane knew, when it came to Hughes, what she would do.

She knew her gown would smell of beer once she got home; Jane didn't care.

The revelry was dying down, and there was Hughes, one muscled thigh extended. He patted his knee.

She threw herself against him. He could take it. She liked that.

And despite the force with which she dropped into him, his hand, when it came up to cradle the back of her head, was gentle.

The things he could do with his lips were sinful, and Jane liked them best of all.

"Come home with me," he whispered against her mouth.

Jane thought she might stiffen, or push away. Clearly, from the way he lightened his hold on her, he expected it too.

But she didn't.

"I can't get with child." Now that she knew how that

worked, she knew with certainty what to avoid. Even when, as in this moment, it sounded appealing. *Especially* when it sounded appealing. "I mean, it's too risky. I won't do it."

His hand tightened. There was a little desperation, a little pleading in his whispered voice. "I'm clean, and I can please you anyway."

"Clean how?"

"I've got no pox. I promise you, Jane."

If he hadn't said her name, she could have resisted the next kiss. It was masterful, and it made her feel hot, all the way down past her *knees*. He was good at it, and Jane had no doubt he'd be good at whatever he promised to do.

But it was the *Jane* that got her.

"I've never seen where you sleep." She felt shy.

And elated, heady as a drunken tar. She was going to do this. She *wanted* to do it.

He promised to please her, and no one had ever promised her that. Not in her whole life.

She didn't want to be married. She couldn't wait forever for some misty rainbow-like *love;* Anna no longer even believed in it. Somewhere in the middle of that whole messy swirl was just this. Hughes and his hands and his kisses. They *pleasured* her. That was the right word for it.

And if she could get more and stay safe, she wanted more.

"Let's go," she murmured against his lips, smiling.

WHEN SHE WOKE, JANE FELT LIKE SHE WAS SMILING *ALL over*.

The narrow cot was as clean as Hughes had promised, as was he.

Or at least had been, until he'd gone to work on delivering his promise.

He'd only told the simple truth. The things he could do with his *hands*. And that *mouth*.

It had been a long time since Jane had trusted her instincts. She'd been right about that mouth, right from the first time he'd grinned at her under his cap with those sparkling black eyes.

She didn't know what love was supposed to feel like.

But she had decided, somewhere just after she'd reached that second shimmering peak, that this was better.

"Get off," she told him fondly, shoving away the hot arm he had draped around her waist. "I've got to go home."

"Aw, now, Janey," he mumbled against her bare shoulder. It was a startling feeling, and even more startling how much she loved it. "We've got time."

She didn't know what time he meant, but they didn't have it. If she wasn't back before Anna woke, Anna would know she'd been gone the whole night.

That was a river to cross Jane would really rather avoid.

"Get off now. I've got to go."

"Nah, you don't."

The practiced way he rolled her toward him did give her a pang. She wasn't in love, but she didn't like the idea that Hughes had likely had other women in this bed, just like she was.

Was that all love was? *Having?*

"Come on, Janey girl, I kept my promise. You do something for me now." He kissed her nose.

As nice as Jane found the nose-kissing, she didn't feel anything was owed to anyone. She knew damn well he'd had his pleasure; she'd *seen* it. And just thinking about it felt wanton and thrilling.

Didn't mean she needed to see it again right now. "It's not a bill, and there's nothing owed."

"You're teasing me now."

Teasing him? She was naked in his bed. Well, mostly naked; for some reason she still had on a petticoat.

She remembered why now: he'd said he liked the look of it bunched around her waist.

Had he said her name again, she might have been lost.

But her name wasn't *Janey,* and she didn't even like the way he said it.

"Come on now," she shoved off his weight, and bent over the edge to find her shoes. The air was so cold her fingers numbed, but she found the shoes, and her stockings.

He just lay in the cot as she dressed.

Now there was a feeling she didn't like.

She didn't care for the way he watched all her little movements, either.

But she *loved* the fact that she wasn't in love with him at all.

She wasn't Rose, putting all her hopes into a husband who would leave her. This was a lot safer than *that.*

Jane locked away the part inside of her that could have whispered that this was exactly what all those society matrons had seen when they looked at her. That she *was* wanton. Immoral. Faithless.

She might be immoral, but she wasn't faithless. She had faith in herself, in her sisters, and in baking.

And a bit more now in her voice.

"You'll see me at the Pinfeather Thursday night. Tomorrow night now, I suppose." It was still dead dark outside, though Jane felt as if she were glowing, that didn't shed any light.

Just a sliver of moonlight was all she had through the narrow window to find the rest of her clothes.

She found them.

Hughes had laid back in the bed. His chest, sculpted with the hard muscle it took for him to do the work he did day in and day out, bunched into a new shape as he crossed his arms over it. "Maybe I won't be there."

She thought he would. Whatever they had between them, he enjoyed it too; she knew that. He hadn't fought it. And he liked that neither had she.

But she also only said the simple truth when she said, "Up to you."

And left.

THE ENCROACHING COLD POSED BRICE ANOTHER unsolvable problem.

His men hated him for keeping them in dock so long. If the winter kept going this way, there was a real possibility the Thames would freeze.

There was a real possibility of damage to the *Halia* if it did.

He had just enough money left for the licenses to go back to America and perhaps ferry over a load of corn, or iron.

If he wrote to his sisters, he might even arrange some luxury goods. By the time he could return to London, the Continental war might truly be over. The States and Britain were still hostile, but as long as he ignored that trading between them betrayed his family on both sides, he might avoid being shot in the Atlantic and even clear a profit.

If he didn't, he'd sit here going bankrupt. Because Britain would do nothing to patrol the southern ocean for slave ships as long as their attention was on France.

And the States would do nothing about it, because too many of them were built on a foundation of slavery.

"You'd better do something, Brice," he muttered to himself as he sat by his desk, tilting his chair back on two legs, staring out his window into the dark night.

He'd kept himself awake all hours, knowing he was so often in motion that he had to stop to think.

He'd racked his brain hour after hour, with no new solutions coming to him. How could they? He'd been right here in Leicester Square for months, trying to arrange sponsors for his mission; everything in government moved so slowly that he was losing hope something new would present itself after all that time.

From the corner of his eye, he spotted movement.

Someone was walking along the pavement from the northeast corner of the square. At his height, several stories up, he could see them.

He wondered if the night watchman would catch them up.

Must be a streetwalker, he thought to himself, catching sight of a silhouette in the dark that had to be the swish of a skirt.

As the woman drew closer, Brice knew he'd lose sight of her if she crossed the street by Ladies' Own Bakery. The cantilevering of the streets of the square meant Brice could see all the way to the bakery if he put out his head, but the night was too cold to open the glass, and the woman nothing to do with him.

Except—

As she crossed, something about the shape of her profile, or perhaps the way her bonnet sat on her head, made him think he *did* know her. She reminded him of one of the Bickering sisters.

Or rather, specifically, Miss Jane.

No, thought Brice. *Clearly impossible.*

In fact, he'd been hovering around the Bickering sisters all the half year, as if they were chickens needing him to hatch.

He had to cut loose. His ship and himself.

What was he waiting for?

Episode 12: Christmas

"Tilly, you must come tonight for Christmas supper."

Anna hadn't wanted to ask Tilly, so she didn't. Emery did.

Tilly's face lit up, bouncing on her toes. She made the most peculiar flapping gesture with her elbows, then winked an eye. "Will there be punch?"

"Ah, no." Emery looked back toward Anna, who left her to it. It seemed like Emery should apologize. "I'm sorry, we hadn't planned on a punch."

"Sorry then, girls, I'm for the boarding-house. My cousin makes a punch to knock your hair out."

Emery touched the end of her braid. "I don't want, uh, my hair knocked out..."

"That's fine, Tilly," Anna took over. "Just know we'd be happy to have you."

"Sweet of you it is. I suppose that's where you'll eat the gingerbread I've smelled all afternoon?"

For Tilly, it was a very subtle hint. "Sal, run up and ask Rose for a gingerbread for Tilly."

"Thanks! You know, we ought to sell them in the shop."

"Perhaps next year." Anna knew Jane and Emery were watching the results of the second, smaller oven like hawks, calculating new figures every night. So far, the experimental results seemed good, but no one wanted to rush things by trying to sell something new that was as complicated to price as gingerbread.

"That's good. It's a good time to think ahead to the next year. I always try to do that in my own business dealings. If you don't mind, I'll send you all a present to start the year off right."

Anna silently braced herself. "Is it a cabbage?"

Tilly's round cheeks smiled till she could barely see. "I *did* plan on it being a cabbage, Miss Bickering, and you're so clever to think so! One of the fresh ones, you know. None that have been rolled on the ground."

"It's all we could hope for, Tilly," Anna said, meaning it. "You've been wonderful this year, I do hope you know."

"Yes, I know. Kind of you to close early too, Miss! Feast well!"

"We're not... it's not..." But there was no time to clarify that the shop wasn't closing early, because Tilly was gone. Before Anna could offer her a gift of a loaf of bread.

"That's about what I expected," muttered Anna, as she pushed open the door to the bakery itself. "Mr. Wiggs. Has Mr. Bailey gone?"

"Uh. Yes, ma'am. I thought it was allowed?" Mr. Wiggs looked cautious. Which was only reasonable, both as it was his first Christmas with Ladies' Own Bakery and because his colleague had flown.

"It's fine, Mr. Wiggs. We're not keeping you from Christmas supper?"

"I'm to go over to my mother's when you're done with me, ma'am. She's got a pudding waiting." Mr. Wiggs, complacent on the best of days, wore a grin that split his sad-sack features in all new ways. He looked younger.

"Then you must go, and take a tuppence loaf with you. Jordan! There's too much!"

Jordan came out from between the tables, calmly wiping his hands on his apron. He'd grown more than his sister had this autumn, Anna thought to herself. He'd look full grown soon. Not yet, but soon.

"Can't guess what you don't know," he said plainly, reminding Anna of Emery. "We didn't know if we'd sell more than usual, or less, so we just baked a full day's bread."

"Mrs. Wallace. You take a quartern loaf. Are there any more cakes?"

"Only the *galette des Rois* you told me to hold back." Mrs. Wallace's cheeks were rosy with the oven heat. "No, I'm wrong; there's nearly half another."

"Good. Take that for the children. Our compliments, and our thanks. Mr. Wiggs, take a second loaf if you think you and your mother will eat it."

"Thanks, I will!" Mr. Wiggs, who'd felt he had to wait to be told twice, took this as two tellings, and grabbed his cap and coat before diving out the mews door clutching two fresh loaves of bread to his chest.

"I didn't mean right *now*—my stars."

Emery put her head through the door as well. "Don't worry, Anna. It's late, no one will come in. We'll just have more bread for the church collection."

"I know you're right, I just hate it when people assume—"

With that, the bell over the door rang furiously.

Anna peeked past Emery's shoulder. Half a dozen—no, at least eight of the trade women who lived at Tilly's cousin's boarding house had piled into the room, noses blazing with the cold, and laughing for no reason the way careless young people did.

"Bring up a basket of the bread, Mrs. Wallace, quick!"

"I HONESTLY CANNOT WAIT TO LICK THE SPOON." ROSE, that old married lady of the family, stood near the stove while Jane stirred the candy. She'd be lucky not to dunk a curl in it.

"You can wait," said Jane in her practical way, "because you'll melt your tongue if you don't. Sal, you're sure you don't want your father?"

Sal was staying politely at the table, but it was easy to see she'd rather be standing over the candy pot with Rose. "He don't—he doesn't know what day it is, and Emery said we'd fix him a basket."

"That's fine." The candy concerned Jane a little; testing its texture, she dropped another dollop into the dish of cold water she had on the shelf where the candlesticks usually lived.

Those were polished and on the table with fresh tallow candles, waiting for the gathering to come.

The Bickering family had a few Christmas traditions they liked to keep, even though Aunt Eden called them country foolishness. Nothing large; they simply liked to burn a new set of candles as long as they could. The last person to fall asleep got to choose supper on Epiphany.

Jane thought Rose usually fueled the long night awake with sugar.

Though now it was honey, and Jane had never made hard candy with honey before.

"We ought to have tested the prescription," she muttered. The dollop in the dish only formed a soft ball.

"How bad can it be?" Rose had buttered two plates and stood ready to put candy on them, whether it was hard or soft sweet sludge.

"Will Jordan get an extra loaf of bread too?" Sal put in.

"Yes." Jane's answer was distracted. By the time they finished tonight's meal—pumpkin soup, stewed beans, roast buttered turnips, all the bread they could eat, and an actual roast of beef—she doubted Jordan would have room for anything else. But they'd agreed on bread as the gift for the journeymen. And for Jordan. "Because he's an apprentice," muttered Jane.

She was reminding her sisters constantly these days that Jordan was an apprentice, because through Mr. Laurent's skulking around the Guild hall, she'd discovered that if Jordan were a servant, they'd owe a tax on him. The crown didn't care what Sal was, and that was annoying, so Jane wasn't thinking about that tonight.

Politely knocking on the front door, Mr. Russell walked in.

"The smell is enough to make me want to eat a house. I've never smelled anything like it," he said as he stepped up behind his wife to hug her round the waist.

She leaned back against him, making a sweet picture that gave Jane a pang.

She didn't want men hanging around all the time, but Rose had chosen well. Even if he was set to leave after Epiphany for the north, seeking better prospects.

"Haven't you celebrated Christmas before?" Sal asked Mr. Russell, leaning forward over the table on her elbows.

"We keep every day holy, among Friends. Christmas is no great fuss. I don't mind celebrating, though, when we get a supper like this!"

"And tomorrow's Sunday, so no work!" Rose told him, turning in his arms to give him a hug.

The number of times they hugged now, no matter who was watching, would be sheerly shocking to anyone who didn't know how they counted down their days together. Jane ignored it.

"Do you give gifts?" Mr. Russell asked into Rose's hair, unwilling, obviously, to let her go.

"Not really," said Sal with definitive glumness. "I got a book."

Laughing, Jane scraped down the sides of the kettle, knowing the second she stopped staring at the candy, it would burn. "It's Mr. Hill's *Arithmetick*, and if you knew French, you could have had geometry."

"But I don't know French."

"Let Anna teach you some. I know French."

"I don't," said Rose, squeezing Mr. Russell round the waist.

Honey or not, Jane would soon die of over-sweetness if those two did not take a seat. "Go ask Mr. Laurent to come, will you? He said he would come, but hasn't yet."

"What of our upstairs neighbor?" Mr. Russell kept Rose's hand tucked in his arm even as he started for the door.

"Lord Zachary is busy doing... something else." The candy felt sticky, but the texture was approaching the right one. In moments, Jane could have a hard sugary rock for a pot, or cooling candy.

"We ought to have invited Captain Brice," said Rose on her way to the door.

"What for?" mumbled Jane, attention on the candy. "He doesn't live here."

"IT IS REMARKABLE. YOU SERVE THE EPIPHANY CAKE EVERY night of the year, and even on Christmas. Will you serve it on Epiphany as well?" Leaning back from the table, Mr. Laurent seemed more cheerful than anyone had ever seen him. He was sober, his hair was clean, and he even had on his waist-coat. "Or on Epiphany itself, will you only serve turnips?"

"Those turnips were so good." Jordan too had slumped backwards in his seat, patting his full stomach.

Surrounding the table, where the bright tallow candles wavered in the breeze from their laughter, all four sisters had a chair; Mr. Russell and Mr. Laurent sat on the stools the carpenter had sold them, while Sal sat on one of their crates, upended, and Jordan sat on a trunk Mr. Laurent had brought.

It made them tightly packed around the table, all that much more inclined to give each other just a little more food.

"I'm astonished by the sweets. Gingerbread, candy, the almond cream cake, the *flummery.*" Mr. Russell shook his head in disbelief.

Emery laughed at him. "You ate it all. You clearly have a taste for sweets."

"I do," he squeezed Rose's waist again in the chair next to him, and no one reprimanded it, though a few rolled their eyes.

"The flummery was a disaster. I made it in a cake plate and thought it would cool fine outside. It did—it froze solid!" Rose pantomimed chipping the creamy dessert out of the dish.

"It tastes so good." Anna did love flummery. "Even if it wasn't pretty."

"Was it like Christmas dinners you had as a child, Mr. Russell?" asked Rose, reaching next to her to take his hand.

"As I said, the Friends don't make a party of it. Mr. Laurent, though. You must have had many astonishing Christmas dinners."

"Oh yes," said that gentleman, thumbs in his waistcoat pockets, still leaning backward on two legs of the stool. He beamed the beam of a man full of food.

"Tell us about them!" urged Rose.

"Oh no," and he shook his head, still good-natured, but that was all.

Everyone laughed.

"What shall we play?" Anna wanted this moment to last forever. Everyone was in such charity with one another, full of good food, and nothing horrible hanging over their heads.

After a year like this, they were due for some peace.

"Nothing that means moving away from the food." Jordan surely couldn't hold another bite, but staying in his seat meant staying within arm's reach of the rest of the candy.

"Cross questions. I'll ask Mr. Russell if he's come from Bath in a basket, and see what he says." Rose was quick to pick the game she won the most.

"What *do* I say?" Mr. Russell clearly knew nothing of the game.

"You give a silly answer. At the end you have to tell your question and your answer. Wait. I mean, you have to tell the question you were *asked* and the answer you *got*."

It was clear from Mr. Russell's good-natured befuddlement that Friends didn't play many parlor games, either, but he dove in. "So I say, I always travel by bucket. Is that good?"

"Oh, that's very good!" Rose clapped for him. "Then ask Emery a question."

"Did you come from Bath in a basket, Miss Emery?"

"No, a *different* question!"

"I see the game is to be confused. Ah." He had to think. "How many birds are in your pocket, Miss Emery?"

Emery, who had waited till Rose had her husband well instructed, answered with laughter sparkling in her eyes. "I have three wild ones, and two tame."

Rose hitched closer to him. "So then at the end when you're asked, you have to say that you were asked if you came from Bath in a basket, and your answer is three wild ones and two tame."

"It's the question you got and the answer you got, see?" Jane thought he needed a little help.

"I do see, but it seems difficult. And after everyone answers?"

"We'll be up to our elbows in answers, you'll see," said Anna with satisfaction.

MR. LAURENT HAD FADED AWAY AFTER THE FIRST GAME OF cross questions, and then after a game of bluffs, Rose and Mr. Russell walked the children home with their shopping basket packed full of food.

"We'll bring it back tomorrow," Sal promised, between yawns.

Anna, Jane, and Emery sat at the table, surveying the pleasant wreckage. Bread crumbs, glistening evidence of butter on the plates, four small pieces of cake, a plate of honey candy balls, and an end of the best bread in London were all that remained of the feast—those and happy memories, which were the best.

The tapers in the candlesticks had burned hot and quick, making the party bright, and tomorrow it would be a task to clean away their drippings. One fat candle on a saucer, though, kept burning bright, its scent telling that it had beeswax mixed with the tallow; it clearly could burn through the rest of the night and the next day if it wanted.

"I don't think Rose will be back," murmured Anna, uncharacteristically calm as she watched the dancing candle flame.

"No, I doubt it." Jane yawned like Sal had, but covered her mouth. "We should just let her pick Epiphany dinner anyway."

"Mr. Russell will leave right after that?"

"We'll keep her jolly enough. It won't be long."

"She'll still be sad." Emery had offered Rose to come back to their old bedroom, and Rose said she wouldn't, because she was a married lady now. But all three of them doubted Rose would spend all the coming weeks alone in the rooms upstairs.

Or if she did, she'd wind up too intently plotting their landlady's murder.

"Mother was sad sometimes," Anna said, "but not at Christmas."

"No, not at Christmas," Jane agreed.

For a moment all three of them were lost in memories. They were still young, Anna thought. But they had many years behind them, and it was a good night to remember the past years.

For the first time that night, she wondered how Lord Boislegrand was keeping Christmas.

Please, please let him be at someone's house, she thought, with exactly the sort of frantic feeling of dismay she didn't want for her own Christmas.

It had been so easy to include the twins, and Mr. Laurent. Mr. Russell was unavoidable now, and she might have even asked Lord Zachary to eat with them had he been in the house.

That was all. It was only who was nearby. She hadn't purposefully forgot her betrothed.

Perhaps I should dine with him for Epiphany supper, she told herself. But if Rose picked that supper like she always did, there would be roast chicken. Anna loved roast chicken.

Plus if she dined at his house, she'd need a chaperone.

And for the life of her, she couldn't imagine Lord Boislegrand dining here.

Though she knew he would have enjoyed the cross questions.

The dancing candle flame and memories of her mother came together and let thoughts settle in her mind that Anna had been fighting off for a while.

Perhaps it wasn't a question of whether she loved Lord Boislegrand. He was kind and she could learn to care for him. He was, in his own way, as lost as the twins, or Mr. Laurent. Anna was beginning to suspect she had a weakness for lost things.

Perhaps it was a question of who it is she wanted to sit by her, holding her hand and asking her silly questions, on Christmas evening.

In that place, she couldn't imagine any man's face. She knew that. She only had to sort out the mess she'd gotten herself into. Struggling through it all autumn hadn't changed anything; she'd have to change it.

"If Rose wins, we needn't stay up." She suddenly felt quite sleepy. Perhaps that's what *peace* felt like.

"I'm not staying up," said Jane. "It's slovenly, but I say we wait for morning to tend to the dishes."

"I don't mind," said Anna, shrugging her way up out of her chair. "Emery?"

"I'll sit up a while longer," said their tallest sister, still watching the candle burn. "I'm not trying to win. Just... enjoying the quiet."

AS THEY WRAPPED THEMSELVES UP IN BED, JANE FELT perfect peace.

Well... she poked around in her insides, lying with her eyes closed, waiting for the bed to warm from her and Anna being in it. Not perfect. Mother would have thought her terribly immoral now, if she'd known about the tavern and the man. Common.

No, decided Jane, in a hazy glow of food and laughter. Mother would never have thought her common. She'd have been worried and sad, but she would never have called one of her daughters *common.*

And Jane could miss her mother, too, and the life they'd all had, without punishing herself for enjoying this one.

Rose could have her Mr. Russell; Jane had finally learned how to have fun, and the dangers were part of the fun. She admitted that to herself, and regarding herself, who else was owed any answers?

Jane was glad she hadn't kept on like she had, trying to find herself suitable matches, proposing, being humiliated in rejection. Life was bigger than that. She was *better* than that.

She knew she ought to feel bad; that was all the little pricking in her conscience was. That she knew she ought to feel bad, and felt a little bad that she didn't.

EMERY LET THE CANDLE BURN JUST A LITTLE WHILE longer, then pinched out the wick to save the rest.

The moon was new and shed little light as she wrapped herself in their largest shawl and made her way down to the street and turned left as if forces of magnetism pulled her body in that direction.

There was a distant sound of revelry—one of the houses must still hold a party—but few people on the street.

It was a short walk to the southeast corner and Lady Arnold's grand house, and Emery hadn't expected to meet anyone. She was surprised to see a familiar three-cornered hat in the gloom that spread down Green Street, away from the glow of the oil lantern Lady Arnold's house kept lit on the corner.

It was indeed Captain Brice, and he'd seen her too, for he walked right up to her.

"Have a happy Christmas, Captain." Emery never thought about things like menus and guests, but now she wished she had, for she felt they ought to have invited him after all.

"And you, Miss Bickering." His teeth flashed white in a grin against the dark. "You won't be out long? There's a devil of a fog blowing in."

She hadn't noticed it, but once he said it, she saw the haze gathering around the Arnold street lamp. "I'm not far from home."

"I mean a serious fog, Miss Bickering. I'll take you back."

Emery just shook her head, her sedate smile largely hidden by her bonnet. "I'm fine, Captain."

He didn't look inclined to argue, only tipped his hat before moving on. As if an afterthought, he said, "My regards to your sisters. I'm sailing tomorrow, or as soon as this damn fog lifts. Your pardon. I hope to see you in spring."

Startled, Emery reared back. Tall as she was, she had to look up to see all his face. "I'll tell them, sir. Can I wish you safe travels?"

"Why not?" Another flashing grin.

"I don't know if sailors have superstitions about such things."

"Many," said the Captain in good cheer, "but I'll gladly take the wishes. Perhaps I can sail on them all the way home."

For a second Emery hesitated. If the Captain was right—and he ought to know his weather—she could be stuck at Lady Arnold's house in a bad position to get home. Lady Arnold would insist on walking her back to the bakery, and then how would Lady Arnold get home? It would be a terrible game of—wasn't there a riddle about a fox, a hen, and a bag of grain, and how to get across a river?

Then she shook her head. It wasn't like that at all.

The Captain looked out over the square. Wisps of white had settled among the dark greenery there. "I must really see you home."

"I'll be perfectly well." She wasn't coming all this way to leave without seeing Dahlia.

"You Bickering sisters have a taste for late nights. Very well, I won't insist, though I'll wonder all across the ocean if you made it home."

"If you're right, you're not sailing tomorrow."

"True." He had a lightness to him, Emery thought, that must come from excitement. "Loading, perhaps. Fare well, Miss Bickering. You and all yours. And merry Christmas."

"And you."

She knocked on the door, knowing he wouldn't leave till he saw her well inside, and so he didn't. He stayed on the pavement till the footman closed the door after her, and Emery forgot him in a moment.

She hadn't even asked, and there came Dahlia toward the door at a near-run.

Emery seized her hand and tucked it into her elbow. "Your hands are cold. Why are you awake?"

"I went to Lord Clyffe's Christmas masquerade, but it was so dull. I wished I'd ended the evening when I stuffed the children full of sugared plums and put them to bed. But I had a hope for one more Christmas present."

"I think it's the same one I want." Emery closed the parlor door after them, and turned the key in the lock.

"I think it is." Dahlia's arms fit around her waist just as if they were made to, and her lips tasted like spiced wine and gingerbread.

They were growing a little familiar to one another, long kisses punctuated by short ones, nips and little nuzzles on the ends of noses thrown in for good measure.

Emery wasn't going to spoil her Christmas by asking Dahlia if this felt wrong to her. It didn't feel wrong to Emery, and there was her beautiful Dahlia snuggling into her arms just right.

If Rose could have her Mr. Russell, how could it be wrong for Emery to have something like this?

"How are your trees?" Emery rubbed her cheek against the soft hair atop the smaller woman's head.

"I've brought them all in, and kept up the fire."

Emery felt a pang thinking of children who could use that fire instead of trees, but she let it pass. She knew how important her green things were to Dahlia.

"They'll die soon," said Dahlia, with a kind of gentle resignation.

Just the thought of something upsetting Dahlia filled Emery with an urge to act. "What can we do? Is there a better place in the house? Better glass you can buy?"

"It's so cold, Emery, that's all, much colder than usual. And indoors, they can't get much light."

Emery thought of the fog blowing in. "What should we do?"

Dahlia led her over to the settee in the corner, the one behind where the drapes hid the window. There was no view there, but neither could they be viewed.

She settled her head against Emery's shoulder as soon as they sat. "Sometimes there's nothing one can do. Nature does what it will."

"But your shrubs! What if they die?"

"Things do, sometimes."

Emery's arm around her pulled her close. She remembered then that Dahlia had lost a husband. She knew what change was.

Determined to stay only a little while, and even more determined to enjoy every second of it, Emery hugged the precious little woman close.

"I THOUGHT IT WOULD BE WARMER TODAY." ROSE PUT HER hand against the glass in their sitting room.

It was icy cold that morning, and Rose was burningly aware of every coin it cost to burn coal in the little stove, but she couldn't bear to go down to see her sisters. Every minute she had left with Mr. Russell seemed to tick away slowly and rush by all at the same time.

They had a few eggs, and a good loaf of bread, of course, and neither of them would want much more for their breakfast, or their dinner either.

Still in his nightshirt, the hollows of his strong neck open to her touch at its collar, Mr. Russell pulled her back into their bed.

Under the coverlet, Rose's icy feet soon warmed, and she thought to herself that it was particularly cruel that she shouldn't have her husband with her during this cold, cold winter.

"I don't care if it's cold," he whispered against the side of her neck, and made Rose not care either.

"THAT WAS ALL HE SAID? SEE YOU IN SPRING?"

Emery couldn't see what difference it made to Jane. The point was that the Captain had gone. The fog had not been so bad, she'd made it home without incident, but that only made it more likely he'd made good on his plan to sail today.

"What else should he have said?"

"I only wondered."

The three of them rattled about the rooms for most of

the day, the revelry of the night before done, and no plans for the second night of Christmas upon them. There was darning to do, of course, but it was too cold to do much sewing; fingers quickly grew numb trying to hold a needle unless they crouched practically up against the stove.

"It's a new year," said Anna, clearly feeling philosophical. "He ought to start a journey."

"How will this year be that different from the old one?" Jane poked at the dish of candy.

Emery wondered if her sister had had too much of it the night before. She seemed out of sorts. "How do you know till you're in it?"

"Even though tomorrow will be the same as it always is, the bakery warm and all the customers, it will be a new year and it will be different." Anna clearly had set aside a store of optimism for the Christmas season.

"There's five more days in the calendar," Jane snapped.

"Those are just numbers." Emery couldn't say why she felt snappish herself. It had been a perfect Christmas, and she had gotten all she wanted.

Except that she'd woken up alone in her bed, where Rose had her Mr. Russell to herself.

There was no way for Emery to have that, even if Dahlia took their kisses seriously. This was an absurd situation, and she felt absurd for not seeing it coming.

The women of the kitchen salon could have arranged something, for themselves, for her.

But Lady Arnold had a dozen servants watching all the time. That made secrets difficult.

And Emery hated secrets.

"I like this part of the Christmas time," said Anna, calmer than the other two. "Tomorrow will be usual, and the next day, and the next, but counting down to something that will be a surprise no matter what. I think 1814 will be full of good surprises. You'll see. The wheel turns, you know, and we're due some good ones."

THAT MONDAY WAS JUST AS ANNA SAID, AND JANE WANTED to kick her.

She didn't feel philosophical at all about the new year. And had the Captain sailed? She ought to send to the hotel, but didn't want to look interested. She *wasn't* interested. The Captain was only one of many friends they had. *Not even the best*, she mused.

Lord Zachary returned, in an open collar, limp neckcloth, and cocked hat as he wobbled his way inside, clearly much the worse for his Christmas revelry, and Jane wondered what she'd missed at the Pinfeather. She didn't miss Hughes, not much; but she did miss the party.

Tilly brought a cabbage to the shop. "I missed Christmas night, so I thought it could wait," she said reasonably, and Jane had to admit that for a cabbage, it was taut and glossy.

It made a nice supper that night that Jane almost enjoyed. The itch under her skin wouldn't stop, but she could at least feel peaceful that she and her family and the twins and all were safe and fed. Wasn't that the best sort of Christmas celebration?

The idea of the rest of the season unfolding day by day into the new year and being the same as the old, though, didn't give her much peace. Did she need raucous drunkenness now to feel sated? Could she not rest unless caught up in that pace of life?

If that were true, she'd soon have to tell her sisters the truth.

And that she didn't want.

Jane felt happier when she felt free, but it didn't feel free to think of her sisters' faces if they knew what she was doing with her nights. Entertaining. In a tavern. It was the next thing to being a bird of paradise.

And things she'd done with Hughes...

She would never tell that, of course.

ROSE AND MR. RUSSELL JOINED THEM AGAIN THAT EVENING and the vague sense of unease in the room hardly settled, even with a good plate of cabbage.

"Will it be roast chicken for Epiphany, then, Rose?" Anna asked, trying to lighten the mood.

Rose turned to her husband. "What do you like best?"

Knowing it was a gift, Mr. Russell squeezed her hand. "You," he said plainly in front of all her sisters.

All three of whom smiled for their little sister, feeling uneasy in themselves over the display of affection for different reasons.

Late that night, the fog really rolled in.

Episode 13: The Fog

"I know you *want* me to remember her name, but what's it matter if I do?"

Rose tried not to show her exasperation. She'd explained this to Tilly twice. "Because the next time she comes in, she will be more likely to buy bread if you greet her by name. That is the simplest answer."

Tilly swiped the clean counter with her apron. There were no breadcrumbs, because there were no customers.

And there were no customers because the fog outside was like a thick wall.

The discussion of this hypothetical customer took the place of any real ones.

Rose had made the mistake, half an hour before, of saying she wished Tilly would remember to greet the customers by name if she had helped them before.

They'd been around in circles for a while now, but Tilly, it was clear, was growing tired of the game.

"See here, miss." She leaned down on the counter, crossed arms under her chin. "If she comes in, it's 'cause this is the closest bakery, or she likes it here. Either way, me knowing her name makes no never mind to the thing. She's already a customer before she walks in."

Jane was wiping down Lady Arnold's *découpage* vase. "She has a point there."

"Don't support her." Anna sounded tired of the whole thing. In discussions with Tilly, she often sounded tired.

And Rose was learning why.

"It *is* a good point," Rose tapped her lip thoughtfully, "but you could *lose* a customer, too, Tilly, if you're not sufficiently polite."

"Now I object to that. I can keep track of bread and money, but if a customer gets lost, that just can't be my fault."

Jane put the vase down on the second counter and clapped, slowly.

"The perfect rebuttal for today," she said, waving an arm at the windows.

Both the Square side and the Bear Street side of the windows were like dirty chalk, covered with air that was thick, impenetrable, colorless. Not even the green of the Square could be seen across the road, and it was unnerving to hear sounds of the occasional horse, or even carriage, issuing from the faceless bank of fog.

The sounds of the latter meant some footman had disembarked and was leading the horse by hand. Probably, from the sound of things, following the edge of the pavement with his foot.

As the day progressed, the passers-by had grown fewer and fewer in number.

They decided against the last baking of the day, but even so it looked as though the morning's production would not get sold.

Anna tapped a loaf behind Tilly, listening to see if it sounded very dry. "We can't be prosecuted today for selling bread that's too fresh," she muttered, tapping another loaf farther back in the basket.

"It feels as though we're shut in here," Jane said. She sounded quieter than usual, subdued, perhaps, by the blanket of fog.

It made the light in the bakery eerie and dim. That, along with the hour of silence from the doorbell, contributed to the sensation they were alone, adrift at sea.

Then the door did open.

"Whew." Lord Zachary stumbled in, his fine stovepipe hat sparkling with very fine drops of crystal-like moisture from the weather. "I'm spent. It's like a game of blind man's bluff out there, but everyone's blind. I'm sorry, Mrs. Russell, was that rude?"

"Never fear, Lord Zachary, the word *blind* isn't rude and apparently it's apt. I'm so glad you're here. The twins could not come to work today so we must take them a basket." Rose went round the counter, nudging Anna and Tilly aside, to choose a tuppence loaf.

"Take them a *basket?* I've just come in!" He waved toward the window, and the menacing fog. "I don't want to go back out!"

"I know you wouldn't sleep a wink, any more than any of the rest of us, if the twins had no dinner or supper because of the weather."

"Well, I—" His hands dropped in limp defeat. "Now that you've said as much, no."

"We *must* send them something besides bread." Rose tapped her lip again, now she'd picked her loaf.

Anna squeezed her shoulders as she squeezed past. "I'll run and get some honey and butter from the cellar. I wish we had eggs."

"We do!" Jane tipped the jewel-like chalice into its nook.

"We've some boiled eggs; they'd be better than right. I'll get them."

Once Anna had disappeared downstairs and Jane upwards, Lord Zachary just tossed his hat down on the second counter.

Rose asked, "That is your hat, isn't it?"

Startled, he picked it up again. "Yes. Should I not put it down?"

"Not on counters where we may cut bread. I just wished to be sure."

"It has no vermin." Zach studied his hat's brim in the faint light. "Not that I know of."

"I just wanted to make sure it was your hat."

"What other clothing would I slap down on your table, Mrs. Russell?"

"I shudder to think. Would you excuse me for a moment?" Rose moved toward the bakery proper door.

"You think I'm stripping and dropping clothes on your table, but you want permission to leave?"

"Just to speak to Emery for a moment."

His lordship had to drink this in for a minute. "It's an odd combination of carelessness and suspicion, I must say."

"Wonderful," Rose's tone said she wasn't much listening. "I'll just be a minute."

She left him. He put his hat back down on the counter in an empty act of defiance.

"Emery," Rose hissed into the bakery proper. "Has everyone gone?"

"Yes, Wiggs and Bailey took off the second I said baking was done." Without Sal or any other journeyman or apprentice, Emery was at the trough washing the massive bread-rising bowls.

Rose slid right up next to her, as if even in the empty room, she wanted not to be overheard.

"Jane hasn't left today."

Emery went on washing. "No one has gone anywhere they don't have to, today. It's impossible."

"Well, I would have said many of her disappearances were impossible. Still, she hasn't even tried today."

"What does that mean?"

Rose stood wringing her hands in thought over the dish trough for many, many moments, while Emery kept sloshing about in the bowls with a dish-cloth.

Then Rose said, "Doesn't it bother you she goes off so often with no explanation at all?"

EMERY WENT ON SLOSHING WHILE SHE THOUGHT ABOUT this. It felt like a trap. For she herself had *gone off,* as Rose said, many times in the past few months, though most likely they knew it was to visit Lady Arnold.

They didn't know about how she and Lady Arnold spent their time together, but then, why should they know?

It gave her a close feeling of kinship to Jane. Not just that of a sister, but that of a co-conspirator. Even though she had no idea where Jane spent her time.

"Are we our sister's keeper? No, I mean it, Rose. You've likely spent more time thinking about such verses than I have. Are you worried we're not keeping close enough watch to know when to help her, or that we're not keeping close enough watch to make her behave?"

Rose made a groaning noise. "I suppose we ought to know before we start," she admitted grudgingly. "Is losing Mr. Russell making me hold on to everything else tighter?"

"You haven't lost him yet. For one thing, he can't travel in this fog. But he's only going north for a little while to see what he may do for a better living. He's not going to the Antipodes. And he will be back."

Another unhappy noise, and Rose's hands clasped each other. "You don't know what it's like to love someone and be utterly happy, then they're just ripped away."

Emery's arm stilled.

Did she know what it was like to love someone? It was impossible to imagine anyone's face more dear than Dahlia's face, or anyone kinder, or sweeter.

But she'd thought the same thing in the summer, and now the winter was here, she ought to be wiser. Go slower. Think harder.

Give it all time.

What did it matter, anyway? She was not going to marry Lady Arnold and evict Lord Zachary from the garret to set up housekeeping.

"I have a good imagination, though, Rose," she said quietly, resuming her washing.

"I've become dreadful. I'm a dreadful person. Fine, I am." Rose seemed equal parts contrite and tart. "I would like to know where Jane is spending her time. If she's all right."

"She looked fine to me over breakfast."

"Emery, I think we ought to *care* about our sister."

"I do." Emery stopped again. Little knots of dough sluiced down her forearms with the water. "Don't you remember, Jane said she wanted to be happy? Then Mr. Russell sounded like he was going to pontificate and she dropped the question. But is she sad now? Or let me put it this way. Is she as sad as she was when Aunt Eden was sending her to masquerades and assemblies to find a husband, and the men she thought would suit her, dismissed her?"

"No." Rose finally took another bowl and felt for the tiny bits of dough left—for they worked hard to bake every bit, and only a few dollops of their specially-concocted wet, sticky dough escaped. "She seems all right. But that's all the more reason to know what's *making* her all right. Isn't it?"

"I'm not sure. I know this. We've known her all our lives, and she's known us. If she wanted to tell us something, she would. Does it make us good sisters to pry out of her things she'd rather keep to herself?"

"No," Rose answered swiftly. "But does it make us good sisters to just... drift away from each other? Day by day, till year by year, and in the end we have nothing in common at all?"

"We'll always have something in common. We're sisters." The way Rose put it made Emery uncomfortable. She didn't think of herself as keeping secrets, but was her life drifting away from theirs?

"Yes, I know." Rose opened the ball-joint that released the water into the bowl, then shut it again and began sloshing her own dish-rag round the bowl's sides. "I just feel like the world is full of pitfalls we never expected, and we ought to be more, I don't know, careful with each other. We've had awful shocks. I don't just mean losing Mother, I mean about the water bill, and Mrs. Scrope's plots." Here she scowled, proving she had not given up her grudge against Mrs. Scrope. "Things we never expected to turn bad have turned *awfully* bad. I feel we should be far more careful."

"Really? Because I think we weathered it pretty well. We even got the door fixed before the cold weather came."

"That was because of the carpenter's kindness."

"And there've been quite a few kind people along the way."

Rose seemed to consider this as she rinsed away the last sticky drops from her bowl, then set it aside and took another. It had to be hefted with both arms; it was far wider than she was. "I suppose it is only usual for this family if we can't agree whether things are going well or not."

ANNA HAD RUN UPSTAIRS TO TAKE THE EGGS FROM JANE SO she could start their own dinner, then on the way down, knocked at Mr. Laurent's door. She found him surprisingly turned out, which for him meant fully dressed.

He greeted the her plan to venture to the Colliers' with Lord Zachary with genuine concern.

"Madame! You cannot think of it."

"The twins take their supper home every night, and share it with their father," Anna reminded him firmly. "They simply cannot go without food."

"It's quite possible to go a long while without food, but I see your point. I will go with you."

"Will you? I confess I hoped for something like it. Lord Zachary is gallant to go, but he doesn't inspire confidence." Anna did not mention that the gallant Lord Zachary had tried to beg off.

Mr. Laurent made a *phfft* noise that Anna couldn't interpret. Inspecting her basket with a close eye, he grabbed a woolen scarf from a heap on his floor, then closed the door. "For one thing, we must get more. More bread, certainly."

Anna looked at the tuppence loaf. "It will be dry tomorrow."

"And one bad day may turn into more. Is there nothing else we could send?"

Anna sighed. She didn't even want to say it, but she had to. "There's a cabbage."

Tilly had not abandoned her connections to the cabbage trade, and there was usually more than one cabbage about.

"And do they know how to prepare it?"

"I'll talk to them. The twins know so much about cooking. They will understand quickly."

When they reached the bakery shop and Anna set about selecting a larger quartern loaf, Lord Zachary looked quite bemused, and it seemed to be more about Mr. Laurent's presence than choosing new bread. "I don't suppose I—"

"No," said Anna, without turning around.

He tried one more time. "If you feel so strongly that Mr. Laurent is the more resourceful in a crisis, then perhaps I may be permitted to—"

"No," said Anna again, tucking a clean towel around the new mound of food. The fog *looked* dirty. "If something happens and Mr. Laurent must venture away, you can keep me company."

Even as she said this, she slipped out the door, followed by Mr. Laurent.

"Thank you very much," muttered his offended lordship before following them out.

STANDING ON THE PAVEMENT WAS AN EXERCISE IN disorientation.

If they looked away from the bakery wall, it was impossible to know where they were. Even as they stood, a pedestrian trying to pass them walked straight out of the fog and into Mr. Laurent's arms.

"*Pardon,*" said Mr. Laurent, setting the man back on his feet kindly and nodding at his mumbled apology.

"This is insane," said Lord Zachary, settling his own stovepipe hat more firmly on his head.

Now that she was out here, Anna saw his point. Perhaps it would have been wiser to check outside before resolving on the trip, or, and this was the last resort, to take his advice.

But it changed nothing, she realized. She wasn't willing for the twins, or their father either, to go hungry.

"All right, there isn't far to go. Lord Zachary, perhaps you will keep in touch with the wall beside you. I shall stay as close to you as I can, and Mr. Laurent may walk upon the outside and perhaps bar us from any great hits from passers-by."

"An excellent plan, madame. You have the instincts of a general. Lead on." Mr. Laurent's approval bolstered Anna's confidence, and they awkwardly set forth.

She found herself talking, if only to warn others of their presence before they slammed into one another.

"We must meet with Mr. Keales once the weather improves, and I hope you'll accompany us, Mr. Laurent."

"Absolutely not."

This was said with such agreeable assurance that Anna blinked before she realized he'd denied her.

He added, "Dealing with a *bureaucrate* is not my strength. I devote my energies to discovering who directed Mr. Keales to the Ladies' Own Bakery. It is a difficult question as I have not the time or inclination to make friends with him, and I cannot simply lock him in chains until he admits."

Conversationally, this was an awkward bit to handle.

Anna cleared her throat. "Surely you haven't done half the violence you hint you could, Mr. Laurent."

Lord Zachary exploded. "Really, Miss Bickering! You have more sense than you're showing."

"I beg your pardon?"

"A man can't always admit to a lady what he might have done, and if he did, not in the street. In the fog, where literally anyone could be a yard away and we couldn't see. Besides that, Mr. Laurent deserves courtesy! Why must you drag him out of his pen, and clip and dress him, and pester him with questions? He isn't a pet rabbit!"

"Honestly." Anna's tone grew frostier than the fog. "I never have."

"I do not mind being a rabbit," their neighbor said with broad generosity.

Anna gasped. "Mr. Laurent, I don't mean to treat you like a pet!"

"It is being most kind, especially to a rabbit. They are so destructive." Mr. Laurent seemed lost to contemplation of the violence of rabbits.

"Oh dear." To Anna, that didn't sound like rebuttal *or* forgiveness.

"After all, Miss Bickering," Lord Zachary on her other side pressed his advantage, "you may have secrets you don't wish to bare to the world. So why badger others?"

At that, Anna felt how closely both men pressed into her sides. Lord Zachary's arm looped through her right arm, while he traced the stones along the front of Bear Street; Mr. Laurent's was through her left where she also held the basket.

And the basket was growing heavy, but one man was literally keeping in touch with the reality of their situation, lest they wander into the street, and the other shielding her from further hard knocks.

Awash with gratitude for them both, Anna knew Lord Zachary's mention of secrets referred to their plan to continue painting. Together. She didn't know what he thought it would entail, but surely it needn't be secret. She could say as much.

Yet she kept it a secret.

"What terrible weather this is," she said with her voice raised, signaling to them both, and anyone else about to bump into them, that she conceded.

Both Jordan and Sal watched her fry up a bit of the cabbage with such intense interest that it reminded Anna of days when she and Jane stood just that close to the pan and watched their mother.

When had they stopped being a pair? Anna missed Jane in that moment with a pain, sharp and inside.

They'd survived school and Aunt Eden's ghastly attempts at social sponsorship. Horrible marriage prospects and the loss of two parents. Anna always felt safer when Jane was nearby.

Why wasn't Jane there?

Instead of pruning and primping Mr. Laurent, Anna ought to see to Jane's whereabouts. Whatever she was up to...

Anna took a deep breath and let it out slowly.

Whatever she was up to, Anna wanted to know.

Mr. Laurent and Lord Zachary busied themselves shaving Mr. Collier. He looked rougher than when Anna had seen him last. Perhaps the parish ladies had not been in, or perhaps he was growing worse.

The first time she'd seen him, Anna had been overwhelmed by the thought of more responsibilities.

Now, those responsibilities were *Sal* and *Jordan,* and not only did she not mind them, she couldn't imagine life without them.

What a difference it made to have just that little bit more money so they needn't starve. Just to know *something* was in their control.

It was hard for Anna to forgive herself her lack of charity, but harder to remember how little she'd had to give.

"Miss Anna," said Sal, uncharacteristically shy as Jordan went to investigate this new frontier of shaving. "Do you know if Miss Rose—if Mrs. Russell has heard about the school?"

It wasn't just Jane. Anna was losing track of *all* her sisters.

She must do better. She would.

"I don't know, Sal, but we'll ask her. I doubt many letters are traveling in weather like this."

Sal just nodded, fast, and Anna realized she *wanted* to go to school. Frightened, probably, of going without her brother, without anyone from the bakery at all. But she *wanted* to go. Not to learn about the Trojan War, as Sal still considered Odysseus a sneak; but other things.

"Rub the brush into the bristles a bit, like this." Lord Zachary had found what there was of Mr. Collier's equipment, and was showing it to Jordan.

Mr. Laurent broke in. "*Mon Dieu,* warn him to hold the skin taut. He'll slit his throat."

They were an odd pair, Lord Zachary and Mr. Laurent. Likely never friends except for living in the same building. There was a lot of—was it grace? Happiness?—in that.

But they'd never be the same as family, and Anna resolved not to drift any farther away from her sisters.

ONE DAY WAS APPARENTLY ALL JANE COULD BEAR WITHIN doors.

"I must just see what's happening in the square."

"Look outside, Jane." Anna waved her hand at the same wall of gray as the day before. It was so dark in the bakery they ought to light a candle. "If something *were* happening in the square, you wouldn't know it!"

"I'll just dash down to the hotel and see if they want cakes." The day before, the hotel had taken their usual complement of cakes; but it seemed impossible they had had enough guests to eat them.

All of London seemed to have gone quiet, and in the

misty cold, the ringing of church bells in the distance sounded silvery, lonely, stark.

"If you must go, Mr. Laurent would happily go—"

"Heavens above, Anna, it's barely a few yards." Jane had come down to the shop clutching a shawl, and now, winding it around her shoulders under her bonnet, she whipped out the door before anyone could stop her.

The little doorbell's ring echoed the church-bells outside.

"What if she doesn't go straight to the hotel?" Anna moved toward the door.

"Stop." Emery dropped the word like a gate.

Anna stopped.

Rose piped up. "But Emery, what if she gets lost in the fog?"

"And that is what you must decide. What if she does? She's not a child. She won't let you shut her up in a nursery; also, we don't have one."

"It's long past time we found out what was going on with her." Rose stayed firm in her own position.

"And what will you do if you find out? Because you both need to understand this before you make a mess. Jane's life is her own. What if you don't like what she's doing with it? What then, hey? Are you planning to cut her off? Pretend you have no sister named Jane?"

"I would never!" Anna's gasp was so vehement she had to steady herself against the counter; she was in real danger of falling over.

"That couldn't be!" Rose was just as incensed, if less unsteady on her feet.

"Just be sure. Not just saying-so sure. *Sure* sure. Because if she hasn't told us, it's because she thinks we won't like it. But *she* likes it, or she wouldn't be doing it."

These ideas sank into the room slowly.

"What could she be doing that we wouldn't like *that* much? I can't imagine."

Emery wished Anna sounded less worried and more curious.

"I'm just settling this right now." Emery stood firm. "There are more scandalous things happening around Leicester Square than hiding in the mews kissing a politician."

"I *beg* your pardon!" Rose huffed at the top of her voice.

Emery ignored that.

Only said, "Whatever Jane does with her life, if you can't be happy for her, then you should be glad she's not sharing it with you."

Emery waited, feeling her scalp grow hot, feeling a trickle of sweat down her back even though the ovens had cooled so they could sell the bread from yesterday, if they sold any.

She'd like to tell her sisters someday about *her* life. *Her* hopes and dreams. She had those now, dreams she'd never imagined when she was little. Emery was no longer dazzled by the novelty of sheer possibility. She wanted things. She wanted Dahlia. She wanted the freedom to be in love.

She wanted *all* of them to have the freedom to be in love.

Rose had seized her own road and done as she pleased. Whether she was happy with her lot now, Emery wasn't sure. And Emery couldn't ask much without feeling her own silence acutely, even though she *couldn't* speak.

For all she knew, Anna felt the same way. They could tease her and prod her about her betrothal to Lord Boislegrand, but none of them knew how she felt about it, because they hadn't made space for her to say.

Emery felt that there was a risk of being *too* blunt, and wanted to tread carefully, for all of them.

"The bakery is teetering," she said quietly. "I know, if Mr. Keales gets us fined by the Crown, we'll lose it all. Of course

we talk about. But we don't talk about anything else. I think…
I think sisters should."

"It's not really teetering," Rose offered, but Emery shook
her head.

Then said "No," as Rose couldn't see it. "It's teetering. We
have more money than we did in the summer, but this is a
bigger risk. A fine of thirty pounds? That's almost four times
the water bill. We're just ignoring it, because it's too big to
think about."

"No," said Anna. "We're ignoring it, because it was Jane
who explained how big a problem the water bill really was.
And now she's gone."

"We need her to make this bakery work," Emery nodded.
"But I'm saying we also need to stay a family."

"I ought to know what to say." Anna sighed. "I'm the
oldest. It's my job. But honestly, I don't know *what* to say."

"Say anything except a scold. And honestly, let her say
back what she wants to say."

"Letting each other talk is not our strength," put in Rose.

Anna protested, "Not always true," and Rose turned
toward her.

"Really? *I wish to marry Mr. Russell.*" Reminding Anna how
many times she had said that in past months.

Now Anna's noise was recognizably a scoff. "And see what
foolishness that has been."

The air in the room froze. Emery thought it might break.

When Rose marched for the door up to the bakery, both
arms stiff in front of her to find it, then slammed it as she
went upstairs, Emery turned to her last remaining sister.

"Maybe *you* don't say anything at all."

Episode 14: Battlefronts

At the carriage inn, the bustling crowd belied it was a Sunday. All the different accents in the air, and the scents of different food packed for different journeys, mixed at the same place and made travelers of everyone.

"The jam sandwiches are on top," Rose fussed, rifling through the basket one more time. "The ham ones are below. It's the last of the cherry jam we made before bonfire night, so... eat it slowly, I suppose. Enjoy it."

"I will." Mr. Russell took the basket from her with one hand and squeezed her round the waist with the other.

The voices of the crowd seemed to drown Rose out and make her smaller. She couldn't find the right way to say anything else; just threw propriety to the winds and her arms around Mr. Russell.

"Don't go," she whispered in his ear.

"I'll be back before you have time to miss me. Only a month, maybe two. I've had some encouragement from a man in Leeds." His voice dropped, and his lips might have brushed her ear too. "Don't worry, Rose."

"I do. I will. I'll be waiting for you, every minute."

Every dry conversation they had ever had about philosophy and economics faded away in that minute, and the live sweetness of the way they felt about each other pooled around them. It was palpable for anyone who cared to look.

The rest of the Bickering sisters looked.

When Mr. Russell turned away, not bothering to keep a cheery smile on his face since it wouldn't help his wife, he called out, "I'm trusting her to you," before climbing into the huge rocking carriage.

Each sister assumed he meant them.

"No one will blame you if you never speak to Anna again. It will make breakfasts a bit difficult, but they can be that way."

Emery had Rose's hand on her elbow and led her through the crowd toward the Quaker meeting room. It felt awkward and reminiscent of the past. Mr. Russell's absence was conspicuous.

Emery thought perhaps being angry at Anna would keep Rose's mind off the empty space beside her where her husband should be.

Mostly, it worked. "There simply has to be a limit to the things she says when she's lost her mind over something."

Privately, Emery thought Anna was terribly sorry. She'd said so, many times, including through the door, right after she'd said that terrible thing about Rose's marriage. And she'd certainly looked appropriately sad and worried that morning when they'd all gone to the carriage inn to see him off.

But Emery also thought it would do Anna a bit of good to be on the outs with the rest of the sisters for a change.

"She has to be right. She's always been that way."

"Perhaps older sisters start that way, but we're all grown

now. She's got to learn not to push her opinions on the rest of us."

The day one of the Bickering sisters would learn not to push her opinions on the rest of them would be the day all four of them were in the ground. Emery thought that was too obvious to say. She also wanted Rose to go on enjoying her temper.

As long as she was angry, she wasn't crying.

Then Rose surprised her with a change of topic. "She was right that we must decide what to say to Jane."

Emery grunted and steered Rose across the road in front of them, continued on pavement. She held Rose's hand to her elbow tighter. "Don't trip." She considered pointing out that Rose was especially angry because Anna was usually her ally, but decided against it. Rose knew that perfectly well.

As perfectly as they both remembered enjoying stealing Jane's hair-curling papers, and Anna's gloves, because they were the ones always left at home.

"If you really want to press Jane about how she's spending her time, I'll be right beside you. But has any of us ever given up a secret we wanted to keep?"

Rose was silent for so long that Bear Street came into view before she answered.

As they turned down the smaller alley, Rose quietly said, "So let's not talk. Let's just follow her."

How far should Emery indulge a sad sister? Emery thought hard, and hoped it was gentle enough when she said, "Following people to find out where they go? Is that a thing Quakers do?"

"It's not really in the spirit of community, no. But neither is Jane never telling us where she's going."

There ought to be something to add about the moral pitfalls of *tit for tat,* but one of Emery's favorite things about

Quaker meetings was the lack of sermons, and she didn't feel like giving one now.

"YOU'LL COME WITH ME TO CALL ON MR. KEALES." ANNA made it a statement, not a question.

Jane, barely awake, didn't have the strength to fight back.

There had been a brawl at the tavern last night. In her head, Jane called it a brawl, not just *fisticuffs* or *a fight*.

An argument between two of the sailors had spread to include both ships' crews, and at one point Jane had stood on a table to avoid the rolling, fist-throwing brawlers.

It had left her shaken. Jane had never seen any violence before, not personally. She knew many gentlemen attended boxing matches, and even a few ladies, but she herself had never seen the need. Now she doubted she ever would, especially when one could see the fighting skills of any number of men all at the same time for free.

"I'm not feeling up to girding that lion in his den today," she told Anna with a little shake of her head. Then she regretted the shake of her head.

The barmaid had doctored several of the night's wounds with a rag soaked in gin, which had prompted someone in the crowd to produce a bottle, and then more bottles, somehow. Jane had learned to like the taste of beer—after all, it was related to bread—but gin tasted vile. So how had she drunk enough to make her head ache the next day?

It was only that they'd all woken so early to accompany Mr. Russell to the carriage-house. That was it.

"Nonsense." Anna brushed away Jane's refusal as Jane expected. "We should get it over with. From what Mr. Laurent says, it should be the end of it."

"Anna," Jane sighed, "nothing bad is ever *over*. And I don't know why you put such faith in Mr. Laurent. He lives in a room the size of a clothes-trunk and he's often drunk."

Anna sat down in the nearest chair with an audible *thump*. Jane winced.

Anna didn't appear to notice the wince. "Do you know, I'm not sure either why I put such faith in Mr. Laurent." She paused, then added, "Do you think I have developed tender feelings for him?"

Jane blinked. Her eyelids felt heavy. "Are you asking me how *you* feel about the neighbor I just pointed out is often drunk?"

"Lord Zachary says I am toying with him." Anna waved her hands around in front of her in a circle. "Playing with him like a toy, I mean."

"Yes, I know what toy means." Perhaps Jane should take up drinking tea in the mornings. So many of the crowd at the tavern swore by it to prop their eyes open in the mornings. Tea, with plenty of sugar. Honey ought to do just as well. "I'm no one to say, but I suspect you like Mr. Laurent's company because he is very obliging, and you're not betrothed to him."

Anna's hands disappeared under the table.

Jane just let the words sink in between them. Hopefully, no more were needed.

No, Anna had more. Jane tried to push aside her pounding headache and listen. The words seemed to pain Anna, though not as much as they pained Jane's head. "Is it wrong to prefer a gentleman because he's obliging?"

"Only if you like him better than the man to whom you're actually betrothed. Your betrothed is pretty obliging too."

Blessed, blessed silence followed this sally, and Jane hoped she'd be allowed to slip back to bed for a nap while Anna worked out her own thoughts.

But no such luck.

"Jane, I've got to beg off my engagement."

"I know. Everyone knows."

"Oh..." Anna's small scowl faded along with her irritation at Jane's bluntness. "It's harder to do than one would think."

Toast. Jane needed tea and toast. That would set her right. "Would you make me some toast?"

Anna went to the stove to lay some bread on it. "We all should have eaten before seeing Mr. Russell off. That's why Rose left for her meeting in such a foul mood."

"Rose is in a foul mood with you because you know she's married, you know she loves her husband, and you don't seem to care."

That made Anna pause so long she almost burned her skirt against the side of the stove.

"I care that she's *happy*."

Jane rubbed her temples, eyes closed. "She's got what you haven't."

Anna stayed by the stove for so long that Jane wondered if she'd fallen asleep standing up. But no, occasionally she poked at the slices of bread. It would have been faster, and more tasty, if she had used a toasting-fork. But there was so much coal in the stove, burning to fight the icy chill in the air, that the bread toasted on its iron top perfectly well.

"No," Anna finally said. "I didn't say those thoughtless things because I was jealous. I said them because I just want her to be as I wish she were. And that's worse, isn't it?"

Jane wondered if there were something about the after-effects of gin that caused honesty in the morning. If she didn't finish this conversation soon, she'd be describing all the money she'd made with her singing in a tavern.

She was in a bit of a hurry, then, and possibly went about finishing it more bluntly than she would have otherwise.

"Do you remember how Father used to insist everything was fine? Even when we had to move to those little rooms and give up beef except on Sundays? You knew everything wasn't fine. We all knew it. He knew it too. But he felt that saying it made it so. I don't blame you for picking up the habit. But perhaps it's time to let it go."

Anna plopped back in her chair, putting the plate with two pieces of toast in front of Jane, and moving the honeypot closer without looking at it.

"I do that, don't I?" She looked off into the distance, as if into their younger years. "It wasn't his most attractive habit, was it?"

"No, it was not."

The first bite of honey-dripped toast ought to have been delightful, but Jane's stomach lurched. Perhaps she was more delicate than she thought.

"If you want to challenge Mr. Keales to take us to court," she said after she'd swallowed, the bite of toast sitting so heavily she wasn't sure if she could eat more, "let me buy a real ledger and put our accounts in writing first."

THEIR NEIGHBOR WAS USED TO THE BICKERING SISTERS tapping on his door at many hours of the day and night now, so he wasn't surprised to see Miss Emery and Mrs. Russell at his door.

He was, however, surprised at their request.

"Can you teach us to follow someone without their knowing?" asked Rose.

"*Mon Dieu.* No," he gasped, and tried to shut the door.

Emery put a hand on it. "We mean Jane."

"Yes," added Rose, "we'd only follow someone we *knew*."

"That is worse," said the gentleman, using both hands now to try to close the door.

He was reluctant to put his whole strength into it when Miss Emery locked her elbow to stop him.

"We only want to make sure she is well." Rose seemed to think that made it better.

"That does not make it better. See here, there is no good way to spy on someone you love."

"We don't want to spy on her. We just want to see where she's going, what she's doing. Because she won't tell us."

Emery, arm still locked on the door, turned her head a little toward Rose. "You make it sound like spying."

"I'm sure it isn't."

"Ladies," said their neighbor, raising both his rough-nailed hands, "spying goes on between enemies. Not friends."

Now Emery leaned her elbow against the door too, swaying towards it with a boyish lean. "What about sisters?" she asked. "Because sisters are a bit different from both."

BREAKFAST THE NEXT MORNING WAS A STRAINED AFFAIR.

Rose was quite willing it be strained, and indeed every morning. She hated everyone: Anna for being so callous, Jane for being so secretive, and... all their customers for being so demanding.

And Tilly for being bad with the names of the customers.

The only person she didn't hate today was Emery, and the day was young.

"I am going to meet with the ladies' committee for Knight's School," she announced to the silent table. "Mrs. Macy has arranged for them to consider Sal's application."

"Oh dear!" said Anna, "I hoped Mr. Keales would receive me this morning. Never fear, it can wait."

"No need." The frost on Rose's voice was thicker even than the frost outside. "Mrs. Macy will accompany me. She will call for me any minute."

"Fine." Emery finished her porridge and let her spoon *tink* into the bowl. "I want to see that Lady Arnold's greenery is all right after that cold last night. It doesn't look like it will ever end."

They all turned to Jane.

"What?" Jane asked with a little alarm at the sudden onslaught of attention.

Rose heard the faint sound of her teacup meeting the table.

"What are you doing, Jane?"

"Errands," she said unhelpfully.

That settled it. Their neighbor might not think it a good idea for sisters to follow sisters, but there was one thing Rose could settle—aside from Sal's school—and she intended to do it.

LORD BOISLEGRAND, VENTURING INTO THE LADIES' OWN Bakery in search of his betrothed, was surprised to find only the blousy country girl at the counter.

At least for once there was no great crowd of women between him and the counter.

It bore dimly into Puffy's awareness that there were times of the day when the bakery was crowded, and times when it was not. He'd tried mid-morning for once, far earlier than he would usually be up and about, in an effort to arrive when the bakery was not bustling, for a better chance to speak to Anna.

The bakery wasn't bustling, but there was no Anna.

"Where is Miss Bickering, please?" he asked the woman at the counter.

"That's an unspecific question," said the woman. "You look like a man who wants a quartern loaf. I bet you eat your dinner all at once, don't you?"

Puffy, unsure whether there was any other way to eat dinner, looked about. Maybe Anna was hiding behind the other counter.

No, she didn't appear to be.

He'd gone to much effort, affixing a collar around the soft parts of his neck very early in the day. He would not give up. "Perhaps I might have a peek in the bakery?"

The woman found this behavior suspicious. "It's not for peeking in."

"A full look, then." Puffy hadn't meant to seem sneaky.

"No looking. Only baking. And out here, selling." She moved aside and slowly wafted a hand at the tray of tuppence loaves, brown and crusty and smelling delicious. "If you don't have a large family, perhaps you only need a tuppence loaf."

Puffy lost his temper.

He hadn't seen Anna in over a week. The holidays and the fog had left everyone in London testy. His mother still refused to receive his betrothed at any home but his own, his son had written him that his betrothal news sounded like a shockingly bad plan and he'd be down to visit and find out if his father had fallen ill in some way, and *Bridle's Gazette* just that morning had carried an account of a reception at Lady Villeneuve's to which he had not been invited.

Since Lady Villeneuve was well known for ushering about a *coterie* of young girls in search of husbands, Puffy was deeply annoyed at being left out. Not because he wished to meet any young marriageable girls; he just wished to be considered.

Of course, he was betrothed, but Lady Villeneuve didn't know that.

No one knew that, because his betrothed was too busy to see him and he had no one to help introduce her to society.

He'd had enough.

"I am going to sit on that stool till Miss Bickering arrives.

Miss *Anna* Bickering. And I will not budge for God himself until she arrives."

"*Phew.*" This clearly impressed the woman, but she still leaped around the counter with arm outstretched when Puffy made to sit down. "That stool's for the customers, sir, I have to tell you. I'm not to let strangers just come in and sit."

"My good woman." Puffy drew up his chest, unconsciously performing the gesture for which he'd been given his nickname as a six-year-old in school. "I am the right honorable Viscount Boislegrand, and I am betrothed to Miss Anna, as I suspect you very well know. I am *not* a stranger."

"Oh! You know, I did think your face looked familiar. Honestly, I'm not the best at faces. Tough to forget a name like that, though." She screwed up one side of her face. "Though I do think I've forgot it. What was the middle part again?"

With no idea what she would think constituted a middle part, Puffy just gave her the whole thing. "The right honorable Viscount Boislegrand." On second occurrence, it felt odd to announce himself formally.

"So your parents called you Honorable? Or Right?"

"Madame," he said more stiffly than was his wont, "they are courtesies before the title."

"Oh, the title, sure." She blinked. She had long eyelashes, he noted, especially for a woman who blinked so slowly. "So your parents didn't give you any name at all. You just got one, for being born when you were. It makes sense. I have a cousin who calls all her goats by a number; she just counts them as they're born. No point being formal about it; they're goats."

"Madame." Puffy regretted his tiny burst of temper. It never led to good, and now here he was defending his name to a shop girl in a bakery. "My name is Augustus Murgatroyd. I inherited the title of viscount when my father died."

"Oh, now that *is* sad. I suppose you miss 'im."

Puffy didn't. His father had been fifty-three when he was born, a late burst of enthusiasm from his father to ensure the title stayed out of the hands of his cousins, whom he hated. Puffy had few memories of him; none of them stood out as pleasant.

That did not improve his mood.

Flipping back the tails of his coat, he settled himself on a wooden stool near the Bear Street window. It was cold enough that the chill seeped through the glass; he didn't care. He wasn't moving till he saw Anna. "I will wait for Miss Bickering. And if you feel I need to purchase something before I sit," he said quickly to forestall the speech he saw she was gathering, "then give me a tuppence loaf."

"Right away, sir." As soon as he mentioned buying bread, she gave in with all speed.

She brought him one of the smaller loaves, one with a golden color to it and a crisp brown edge. "That'll be tuppence, if you please."

With affronted dignity, Puffy withdrew his purse from his pocket, and the required coins from the purse. Dropped it into her hand and let her hand him the loaf.

He meant to set it on the unused counter, but it was in his hand, and he was hungry, as he'd gotten up early for this.

Breaking off a corner, he tucked it into his mouth.

"It's good," he mumbled ungraciously after he'd swallowed.

It would have been easier to maintain a temper if it had been bad.

Anna wanted to go in and ensure Tilly hadn't sold the bakery, but she could see a profile through the Bear Street window and it looked like the side of Puffy's head. She didn't want to see him.

She still wasn't sure what to tell him.

Hurrying past the bakery window with her bonnet held tight to her cheek, she went in the door to the residences above and scurried up.

It felt pointless to stop and see if anyone had returned to their rooms; the morning had been awkward enough. She kept walking, then on the next floor up, passed the cold and empty rooms her sister had taken. With her husband.

She'd had a failure of imagination, she'd decided on her walk back from Mr. Keales' house, where she'd been disappointed to find the gentleman out.

Rose had a husband now. Anna was having trouble understanding what that really meant.

It ought to be easy to picture Rose in their mother's place, caring for a man who was the head of the house. But it wasn't. Not little Rose, whose childhood nightdresses Anna had helped sew. She just couldn't picture Rose in that role.

Yet she was. So much in that role that here she was, just like their mother, a poverty-stricken woman accommodating her husband's needs.

Anna despised Mr. Russell for putting Rose in their mother's position.

She stood at the foot of the stairs to the garret, hiding her face in her hands.

She did. She *despised* Mr. Russell for this. Anna had loved her mother, and there was no mistaking that her mother's years had not been easy. All because—

All because her father was poor.

How could she let go of her betrothal when it was still her only assurance that she herself wouldn't end up using the same tea leaves three times and sleeping on sheets worn so thin they threatened to tear down the middle?

Slowly she let herself trail up the garret steps. Her gloves felt damp. Perhaps those were tears. If so, at least they weren't on her face.

Lord Zachary was there, two old waistcoats now providing him some cushioning against the cold, worn under his loosely tied smock.

He hunched over a small canvas, making tinier gestures than usual.

"Lord Zachary." It was so odd there was no door, and no one to announce her.

He glanced back. "Oh, it's you."

Well, that was informal too.

"Do you think I have a habit of saying that things are fine when they aren't?" The question just flew out of her.

He shrugged without looking back again, shoulders moving under the fine linen of his shirt. The smock and vests mostly hid their motion. "Not to me. You're devastating when my work is bad, and I hope you still will be."

He pulled back and let her see the painting. It was rather fine, only a foot or so tall, and it captured the droop of the peacock feathers arranged beside a silver bowl of apples quite well.

"That's quite good." She came closer. "You've been practicing."

"Every minute." He cocked his head, looking at it. "Are the peacock feathers stiff?"

"No, you've really made them soft. That's quite something." The colors of the peacock feathers were really beautiful, and true to life. "You've captured those colors."

"Yes, I have the shape of the thing, and the color. But does it make you feel anything?"

Anna considered it quite carefully. Its shapes were balanced, with the long fluid curves of feathers balancing the red-and-yellow fruit. But... "No."

"Damme." He kept hold of his brush. "That's the key. That's what I've got to find out how to do. I don't suppose you frequent the Royal Academy of Art."

"No," said Anna with exaggerated emphasis.

"No, sorry, of course you don't. I saw Turner's *Fishermen at Sea* there as a boy, and that was what made me want to paint. It wasn't the colors or the shapes, though they're incredible. It was the feeling he captured. I felt I'd been to sea when I hadn't."

Anna drew closer to the study of fruit and feathers.

"Perhaps he cared about the sea more than you care about these," she lifted her gloved hand toward the painting and let it drop.

"He did. He did." Lost in thought, he turned back to his canvas.

It was easier to get lost in contemplation of the colors there, and what might give them more life, than her own problems.

Anna let Puffy stew in the bakery while she stood next to Lord Zachary and stared back and forth between his painting and the little table with its bowl full of apples.

She ignored how cold the garret was, how inappropriate it was to be here, or what her sisters were doing somewhere else —several *somewhere elses*, in fact, right now.

"I think you can do it," she said after a long considering stare.

He only nodded at her, one lock of bright hair falling in his eye as he did. He hadn't taken the time to cut it recently.

Then a commotion outside grew loud enough to penetrate even the glass at the top of their corner of Leicester Square.

"What's all that?" he muttered, clearly not expecting her to answer.

Opening his casement window, heedless of the bitter wind, he shouted down. "What's going on?"

Anna moved to look around him. A crowd of men in dark coats buzzed tightly together around the tailor's door across the street, reminding her of bees gathering in a hive.

"Frost fair!" one man shouted back up to him.

Lord Zachary waved, then grunted as he latched the window closed. "It hasn't been that cold, has it?"

"What does *frost fair* mean?"

"Have you not seen one? When the Thames freezes over. Some shops, and performers and such, they get onto the ice. It's a big affair."

"No, I've never seen one. Will it be for Twelfth Night?"

Lord Zachary looked out the window at the milling men. "No, that's almost here, and it will take them a while to plan."

"Plan what?"

"Plan how to hold the fair if the ice hardens. Fairs last for days, Miss Bickering. Perhaps weeks. The merchants will want tents, souvenirs to sell—whatever makes the most of the chance."

"Souvenirs?" All thoughts of her problems fled. Anna rushed to the stairs.

"I'm still painting!" called Zach.

"Think of something to paint that will matter to you! I must see to the bakery. Don't you think, sir, that cold and hungry Londoners will want bread?"

Episode 15: Snow

"Who can live this way?"

Anna stared out into Leicester Square. Into the snow.

Not to the street; not towards the square. Into snow. A white pile of snow as high as her head and more. It lay against the glass; it was all there was to see.

For two days, snow had fallen. Thick, fat flakes, with a susurrus whisper that only grew louder as carriages and horses ceased to come.

"All of London can live this way." Jane had taken her place at the counter, and it would delight Anna to have her there, except it was clearly because it was the only place Jane could be.

Breakfast had been toast. Lunch would likely to be toast as well; Rose, who had descended into the cellar to count the crocks of butter and honey, had not yet emerged, but there was certainly plenty.

Bread, butter, and honey enough for all of Leicester Square for days. And that was about all.

"Are there any eggs left?"

"Likely. Didn't look."

Perhaps it was Anna's imagination, but Jane had talked more and more like this lately. Brusque. Short. Oddly informal.

It didn't sound like Jane; but then in odd ways it did.

Their farmer had last delivered eggs just before the snow began to fall. The delivery was scanty; in general, chickens gave up eggs for the holidays, and the few there were, had to be saved for cakes.

Except Anna doubted the hotel would want cakes.

She called down the stairs. "Is it terribly cold down there, Rose?"

"No," was all her sister said.

Anna waited a moment.

Silence.

"Will you be done soon?" she called again.

"No," Rose called back.

Well.

Wiggs and Bailey were stuck in the bakery along with Emery; they could not disappear today in search of entertainment, because the mews was stacked nearly as high as the street.

They'd taken it upon themselves to keep the drain clear of snow, so that chamber pots could be emptied, and Anna was grateful she hadn't had to ask, and desperate not to know how they were doing it.

In the absence of customers, Jane had covered the second table with the ledger she'd bought and her slate.

"How are you filling in the numbers for past months?"

"Estimates. I've a good memory, and the money is the proof."

"What if the Guild wants more records?"

"They can want whatever they like; doesn't mean they'll get it," said Jane, with a peculiarly careless shrug.

An odd *shh, shh* noise at the shop door distracted them both.

They couldn't see anything, but both of them could hear it. *Shh, shh, shh,* and soft thumps.

"It's a customer," breathed Anna.

"It's an idiot," pointed out Jane.

For who would brave this kind of snow just to buy bread?

Finally, a tap on the door made them think someone wanted it open. It did open, a crack.

Jane put her foot against it to stop it going further. "Don't open it," she shouted, "you'll dump in loads of snow!"

"*Mademoiselle,*" said a French voice frosty enough to go with the snow, "I must."

"Must you, though?"

He shoved, and Jane had to move her foot or have it squashed.

Sure enough, with a *plumph*, a snowdrift fell into the bakery.

Bringing a Frenchman along with it.

He staggered, but kept his feet. "Ladies," he said, straightening his coat as if he had come in to dine. "I must speak with you."

What they hadn't realized was that pent up behind him was a flood of customers who had also struggled through the snow.

They were men, muffled to the ears in all the wool they could lay hands on, looking out of place in the bakery, and covered with blobs of white ice.

"We need some bread," announced one who came in right on Monsieur Boucher's heels. Four friends with him nodded.

"Yes, of course! Ah... quartern loaves?"

All five of the men looked blankly at her as if she'd spoken French to them.

"Look," said the man in front, "My Betty couldn't come out in all this, so she sent me for bread."

"Aye." "Aye, that's it all right." "Couldn't do it, no woman could." "Right mess."

"You all want bread," Anna confirmed.

"*Mademoiselle,*" said M. Boucher, "I also have requirements."

"Just a moment, sir, we will certainly wait on you as soon as we attend to these gentlemen."

Jane had already disappeared back into the bakery. They hadn't put out any loaves, as they hadn't seen a customer since morning the day before; but there was still some bread to sell.

The door opened again.

Realizing she ought to tell Jane to bring as much as she could, Anna dashed after her.

With a sniff, the tall Frenchman looked down his nose at all the neighboring men gathered around him. "*I* opened the door," he pointed out.

None of them looked interested.

Emery came out wiping her hands on her apron.

"We've still got too much of yesterday's bread. Would you have that for less?"

"Not much less," Jane put in from the second counter, a shadow of her old self.

The lead man had settled on a price for the older bread when M. Boucher broke in again. "Ladies, I am *here* for the *hotel.*"

Emery favored him with a long look up and down, and mimicked his tones. "We *know* who you *are.*"

"See here." He bustled Anna into a corner, then gathered

up Emery with his eyes when it was clear that she wouldn't be bustled.

Jane joined them just not to be left out.

Quietly, he said, "The hotel must have food."

"Well, good luck," said Emery frankly.

"We *must*. There is a bit of a shortage at the moment, and it may affect—" he looked over his shoulder at the rough men, none of whom would have ever set foot in Jacquier's Hotel. "—our reputation."

"Sad," Emery pretended to care.

"Emery, stop. M. Boucher, what can we do for you?" Anna was not about to let Emery hurt their relationship with the hotel; in a manner of speaking, they were Anna's customers, not Emery's, with their daily order of cakes.

"We have a number of our men stuck in the hotel because of the snow."

"Stuck." This idea seemed to tickle Jane. "Like a cork in a bottle? Let's go see."

Affronted, the man organized his feelings by tugging on his coat again. "They cannot return to their homes, you see? And we must feed them."

"Feed them duck and calves' liver." Jane was supremely uninterested.

Anna felt inclined to agree with her. "Honestly, monsieur, surely you have food enough to feed them."

"My proprietor has instructed me to give them something filling. We have porridge, but they want bread." He shrugged one shoulder; a wet blob of snow that had clung to his coat dropped off. "They are Frenchmen."

Anna felt a little leap of excitement that the rest of yesterday's bread would not be wasted. "You heard us make a deal with the other gentlemen, sir; we could sell you yesterday's bread for—"

"No."

Jane's hammer-like *no* made Anna look up.

No longer careless, Jane now looked hard as stone. "Full price for that bread, for you. And every man who wants it must come here and apologize to us before we'll give him any."

M. Boucher looked like something smelled bad. "Surely in this crisis—"

"They have had *all year* to repair their manners." Jane's dark eyes snapped. "In fact, it was a condition of the price we gave you for your cakes that you see they were repaired. And nothing has happened."

Immediately Anna's opinion flipped to side with Jane's. "That's true."

Emery just stayed silent.

They could all see that this was the first moment, and likely the last, they could pressure the staff of the hotel in any way. Indeed, it was the first moment M. Boucher himself had come to their bakery since arranging for the delivery of the cakes.

Today, he needed them far more than they needed him.

"We got to be on our way," called one of the last neighbor men, and Jane, after a glare towards her sisters that reminded them she meant what she said, went to wait on him.

M. Boucher looked troubled that they'd even seen him. "I am not here on business for the hotel," he lied, calling out to the men. Anna gasped.

"Don't give a damn," one called back, wrapping his wife's scarf more tightly around his neck before venturing out into the snow again.

Anna saw the advantage and pressed it. "Not only will we need your men to come apologize, M. Boucher, but we must trade. I'm sure you have some food that would be useful for our needs, and we could offset the price of the bread with that."

"What *needs?*" he hissed, pulling his collar around his ears. He really did not wish to be overheard.

"We have many people here, and are unable to shop, and who knows how many days this snow will last? We need some beef," she said quickly before she lost her nerve, "as well as cheese and eggs."

"And ham," added Emery.

"*Impossible!*"

"Is it?" Anna asked sweetly. "Then I'm sure you can feed whatever you have to your staff."

The man hesitated. If he worked the trade right, he'd likely pay less for the bread, and have happier staff. As long as they were willing to come apologize to the lady bakers. For whom they used much more unpleasant terms.

"All right." Clearly unhappy to be defeated, his eyes darted around the shop.

Jane went to the cellar door. "Rose, dear, do you want to come get your apologies from the hotel men down the street?"

It only took Rose a minute to decide whatever was happening upstairs was worth investigating.

"I'll be right up," she called.

WHATEVER M. BOUCHER'S FAULTS, HE SERVED AS A DECENT plow for the snow between Jacquier's Hotel and the Ladies' Own Bakery.

For the most part, it was a pleasant afternoon of embarrassed young men trickling through the snow, cold and wet, to come mumble apologies and put out their hands for a loaf of bread.

"I beg your pardon, I didn't hear that?" Emery said to one hapless young man she remembered. He was a head shorter than her, easily, and had shouted names at her for months that Anna refused to translate.

His mumble sound something like "'m sorry to offend," and Emery took it for what it was worth. A day-old tuppence loaf.

And the knowledge that he would rather eat their bread than whatever old porridge was stirring at the hotel.

In a quiet moment, she sidled over to Rose, and pulled her away from discussing what they must fetch back from the hotel.

Looking over Rose's head to make sure Jane wasn't listening, Emery whispered lightly right into her ear. "We can't follow her if she doesn't go anywhere."

"I know," Rose whispered back, half exasperated, half serious.

"Mr. Laurent said to start by taking note which direction she goes. But that means it'll have to be me, and it'll have to be when I can see out the windows."

"These are the burdens of life," Rose agreed.

"Does she seem happy to you?"

Rose considered. "She seems rested. It makes me realize how tired she's been."

"Makes me think she's doing some kind of work."

"Why?"

"Trust me." Emery didn't think this was the moment to bring up anything sewing related, but they all knew how she'd worked through the night before the journeymen were hired. "It just gives me that feeling."

"That makes sense. Work demands steadier attention than a man."

"Do you honestly think Jane is sneaking out to meet with a man?"

"Why not?" Rose snapped off the end of the sentence, as

if perhaps wishing to end it before Emery realized that was what Rose had spent her summer doing.

Emery didn't. She watched Jane write on her slate. "I don't know. I always thought Jane more likely to take up theft. Or public engineering. Anything but falling in love."

"Women aren't allowed to do either," said Rose with some edge. "And Jane is perfectly capable of falling in love. We all are."

That was the moment. Right now, with no customers and the bakery dead quiet in the snow, and Anna nowhere about, and Jane not listening. It was the right moment to tell Rose that she was right.

That Emery was as capable of falling in love as any of them, and might have done it.

She couldn't quite say it. She wanted to, but then she didn't know what Rose would say back. Poor Rose, prickly over her own husband's absence, might feel abandoned right now if Emery had someone of her own.

She just said, "Me, too?" in a younger voice than usual. Younger than she had sounded for a very long time.

With a little frown, Rose just nodded. "Yes, of course." But she looked confused. Clearly trying to parse together what it all meant. Of course Emery had a heart, of course Emery could love; but she was fairly certain that Emery wasn't sneaking off to the mews to kiss anyone like Mr. Russell.

Emery just left it there. That was as brave as she could be today. She felt disappointed in herself, but also glad. At least she'd said something.

Whatever they found out about Jane, whenever they found it out, she had the oddest feeling that she wanted to ride along in Jane's tracks. Whatever it was would scandalize Anna, and maybe Rose. Emery had the feeling she wouldn't be scandalized; and she was ready to take advantage of the resulting chaos as long as she, Emery, was able to get away with a scandal or two of her own.

Mainly the big one.

"How's it look, Mr. Wiggs?"

The young man had impressive enough shoulders, which was why Emery thought he'd be a good companion to check on the neighbors.

But she couldn't see round them.

"I could get to the hotel," he said, clearly dubious, "but not much else."

Finally Emery wedged in beside him.

There was a groove in the snow that led down what was usually the pavement, all the way to Jacquier's Hotel. Clearly more people had taken advantage of it since M. Boucher had ventured forth.

But it also didn't go far. Dr. Shelton's door was between them and the hotel, and a few others; but going beyond that looked impossible.

Turning, Emery saw that the way to the tailor shop, across Bear Street, was also impassable.

How could one flail their way through so much snow? It was wet enough to pack, but not packed enough to walk on. If she did shove her way through it, she'd wind up soaked.

"All right," she sighed, "make sure all's well down to the hotel, and I'll check on Mr. Morley. It's the best we can do."

That wasn't what Emery wanted. She wanted to go all the way down the east side of the square and see if Dahlia was all right.

She certainly was; she was a rich woman, with a full house of servants, and the sense to stay in out of the snow. Of course she was all right.

It was only that Emery wanted to hold her and be sure.

Cranky with the weather, Emery turned toward the tailor's. She'd brought a broom outside, but it was clearly to no purpose. She left it by the door.

Shoving her way forward, she found that the muscles it took to press through a chest-high snowbank were quite different from the ones it took to make bread.

Had she been a different person, and subjected, perhaps, to different sermons on Sunday, she might have taken all this snow for retribution for her sins. She had lived her whole life in London and had never seen anything like it.

"And what do you do?" she muttered at the statue of whatever George stood immortalized in bronze in the Square. It was only a rounder heap of snow among all the other heaps of snow, but it was something to berate. "Nothing. You do nothing about all this."

Exactly what kings should do about snow, she wasn't sure, but if anyone should be able, it was them.

It seemed to take hours to flail her way across the street and pound on the tailor's door.

And a long time for someone to answer. So long that Emery began worrying something had really gone wrong. What if he'd suffered a fit of apoplexy from swearing at all this snow? What if his fire had gone out? What if his wife had taken the chance to tip him out the window?

She had no evidence of the woman wanting to do such a thing, but if she were married to Mr. Morley, she would.

Finally he answered.

In a finely quilted dressing-gown that went down to the floor.

"*What?*" was his ungracious greeting.

She couldn't take in all of what she was seeing. Mr. Morley, as befitted a tailor, was always completely turned out, in finely made trousers, shirt, waistcoat, and coat.

The dressing-gown just didn't suit.

"Everything all right then?"

He just waved his arms as if to encompass the snow-covered world. "Clearly not."

"I mean, with you and the missus?"

Emery had never said anything like *and the missus* in her life. Mr. Bailey said it often, though, and it was the phrase that came naturally to mind.

As soon as she heard herself say it, she cringed inwardly. What if she said something like that in front of Dahlia? It would only prove that she was too common for such a lady's company.

She cleared her throat. But Mr. Morley didn't seem to notice. Of course, he thought her and her sisters common already.

"No customers. Nothing is all right when there's no customers. Surely you know this."

"Actually, we've sold most of our bread to the hotel. We wanted to make sure you and Mrs. Morley didn't need any before we disposed of the rest." *Or made more*, she thought to herself; there was the new challenge of keeping journeymen occupied when there was little work. She'd never faced it before. Mr. Bailey had taken to carving shapes out of pieces of firewood.

"Aye, I'd take a loaf," the tailor said a little sullenly, as if not wanting to admit that food would be welcome.

"Good." Emery turned back toward the bakery.

"How long will you be?"

"What?"

"How long till you bring back the bread?" Mr. Morley asked slowly and loudly, as if that would help this conversation.

"I'm not bringing it back. You're all right. Come on and get it. I have to see to the rest of the street."

Because seeing him there just made it more urgent that she see Dahlia. Mr. Morley, who didn't deserve to be, was right as anything all wrapped against the cold. Dahlia ought to be the same.

"I'm not wading through all that snow."

"Guess you're not that hungry, then." Emery shrugged and turned her back. There was a *v* in the snow back across its thick expanse to the door of the bakery, and it should be easier going back than getting here; but it would take effort, and time she didn't want to spend.

"It's the least you could do for your employer, bring us some bread!"

His words snapped something in Emery it would have served him not to snap.

She turned, and loomed over him.

"Mr. Morley, you're not my employer. You gave me work some time ago, grudgingly and rudely, and I gave you good value for your money. Since I stopped coming for work, you haven't spoken to me twice. I don't owe you anything."

"You stopped coming without a word! Just like a woman to be so unreliable. Never should have helped you in the first place." The way his anger twisted his wide jaw was unattractive.

"I'm sorry." Emery hadn't thought about it that way. "Perhaps you should expect your workers to abandon you without explanation when you're so abrupt."

"No," he shook off any blame, "a proper man doesn't do it. I knew you women were wrong from the start, and I just let kindness get the better of my judgment. Should never have let you in the door."

The profound unfairness of this attitude pricked Emery just the wrong way. She hadn't intended this to be the day to set fire to what remained of her relationship with Mr. Morley; but apparently thick snow had that effect.

"Mr. Morley." She leaned in until he folded his neck down to get away. "Blame me for a poor leaving all you like. But my sisters are proper women. So am I. And here's a thought for your reflection. *You* are not the person who gets to decide if you are kind. *All of us*—" Here her arm waved over the snow-covered silence of the square, "*we* get to decide if you are kind. And sir? You're not."

His eyes bulged a little as she leaned closer and closer, looking far more threatened than even an angry Emery should inspire.

He put up both hands. "I didn't do anything!"

Of sisters, Emery had only Rose younger than her, but that had been an education in the habits of children. Sal and Jordan would never had said such a thing, but five-year-old Rose would have, and Emery knew what it meant when someone who hadn't been accused of anything suddenly defended themselves.

"What did you do?"

Without further discussion, he slammed the door shut.

Well, thought Emery. *Whatever he did he feels guilty about, I hope he starves in there with it.*

She didn't want to stop at the bakery to discuss it. Once she'd flailed her way back to the door, she went beyond. She'd catch up to Wiggs; she could just see his hatted head, bobbing in the white ahead of her. A few other men pushed through the slightly shallower snow in the street. That's what she should do; if she wanted to get all the way to Dahlia's house, she could go in the street. They were in no danger of being run over today.

She could have spent the whole way down the side of the square steaming about Mr. Morley. About all the times he'd been short with her when she'd been nothing but nice to him. But he had at least given her work, and Emery didn't like holding grudges. There was too much to do for that, and also he wasn't what was important.

What was important kept her going long past the time her legs felt like melting candles, her muscles burning, skin clammy and cold. It seemed like a year till she finally struggled up the steps to the front of Lady Arnold's house, but a short year, because thinking of that sweet face kept her occupied the whole way.

The butler looked surprised when he opened the door to her and Mr. Wiggs.

Just seeing him made some part of Emery feel silly. Dahlia was fine. She had this whole big house.

But she didn't feel right in her heart until Lady Arnold herself darted in, hair in a braid down her neck, crisp linen cap and shawl wrapping her warmly even inside the house.

"Miss Bickering!"

She came to Emery fast as an avenging angel, and took both Emery's hands in hers.

"Your hands are like ice! Is everything well? Nothing has happened to the bakery, I hope? Your sisters? You are surely in good health? But you must come in and get dry! You'll catch some terrible fever."

"Not at all." Just seeing her made Emery feel lighter, and warmer. Perhaps there was a silly smile on her face; if so, she couldn't help it.

"No, this won't do! And Mr. Wiggs. Go right to the kitchen and ask the cook for some port. Miss Bickering, you must take your sisters some port. These wars are terrible; we ought to have brandy."

Mr. Wiggs didn't need to be told twice to go in search of port; the butler led him away.

"I'm fine," Emery said more softly as they were left standing in the entryway, Emery's skirts dripping on the carpet.

"It's really not fine. If one of the children came in like this, I'd—"

Emery stopped her worry with a kiss.

She liked the way it made Dahlia blink, and her words trail away.

She *loved* it.

"I'm quite fine," she said quietly, "now that I see you are too."

Dahlia seemed to fight down the gentle smile that didn't match what she wanted to convey. But the smile insisted on emerging.

"Honestly, if one of the children came in like this, I would be very cross. What are you doing?"

"Just seeing if any of the neighbors need help. Do you need any bread, Lady Arnold?" Emery kissed the tip of Dahlia's nose.

Had the nose been cold, she would have bundled Dahlia straight off next to a fire, ignoring how she had just refused to do the same thing.

But it was warm, and that melted the last worry in her heart.

"And the children are fine?" Emery wanted to carry her off to a quieter room now for much more kissing, but dropped her hands when she nodded. This was her entryway, after all. "And your plants?"

Now that she could see something besides Dahlia, she saw that the door to Lady Arnold's seldom-used ballroom was open, and if she wasn't mistaken, she saw some green in there.

"It has become an obsession, trying to keep some of them alive." Dahlia's self-deprecating little laugh was also rueful. "Poor Miss Williams is kept busy trying to be diverting to the children, who are tired of being inside, while I write to my father's friends just to see how their collections are faring. But then the letters cannot travel! No mail for days, and who knows when there will be? There may not be another dahlia in England when all this is done, and what will have become of all my father's work?"

"There will be the most important Dahlia left in England when all this is done, as long as you stay warm and stay fed." Emery couldn't resist one more kiss. Dahlia's nose was so soft. "Your father would feel the same."

It was only what she felt, but Dahlia sighed and murmured, "Thank you," as if Emery had given her a great gift.

It was so easy to make her happy.

"Send someone down to the bakery when you can. I'll make sure you get today's bread."

"I'd rather have you," Dahlia murmured, moving to hug Emery without raising her eyes.

Emery wanted that hug, but she'd soak Dahlia through. "Hold a moment," she said, hands on those little shoulders. "Better to stay dry than be hugged."

"Obviously not," the lady said with a twinkle in her eye, finally meeting Emery's gaze. But her burst of girlish feeling seemed to have passed, and she was the fine lady again, well able to manage her house and her botany collection.

It still felt good to Emery that she had helped, perhaps, a bit.

"At least no one will think it odd for me to make all this effort to see you in such an emergency." It took some of the shine off the moment that Emery had to think of such a thing, but she did.

And so did Dahlia. She knew that by the other woman's quick nod. "I thought something similar," she admitted. "I wish we had emergencies every day."

ABSOLUTELY NO ONE EXPECTED LORD BOISLEGRAND TO arrive in a sled.

They couldn't see it, of course; the snow had stuck to the glass higher than anyone's head but Emery's, and she'd been lost in her own thoughts since returning to the bakery and changing her dress. She wasn't looking.

Jane was in a mood to shoo him away, but left it to Anna.

It was oddly peaceful, being snowed in here; but she was losing money every night the inns were closed. The fog had cut down her earnings, and now this snow was doing the same. If the whole winter went this way, she wouldn't be able to sleep for counting the shillings she didn't earn.

It might have been pleasant spending the day with just her sisters, except Rose was still not speaking to Anna, which Jane found sympathetic, and slightly amusing.

She wondered why it was so much easier now to see their lives as their own and separate from hers. Was that truly the effect of simply leaving their company from time to time? Was that how men managed to be so uninterested?

If so, Jane liked the effect.

When his lordship shoved through the door, a wet slide of snow adding to the puddle gathered on the floor, Jane just opened the bakery door to call out, "Lord Boislegrand is here," and gave him a nod.

It felt a little odd not curtseying to a viscount; but she could manage it.

"Oh! Lord Boislegrand! How astonishing! I'm so glad you're here!" Anna came out of the bakery with hair flying and eyes blazing.

He looked struck by lightning. "Delighted!" was all he could say. "Delighted!"

"I have been *so* worried about the Colliers. We have a basket nearly packed. Would you be so good as to take it to them? We have bread things, of course, but also a little meat and another cabbage. And some parsnips." Bargaining with the hotel had been productive all around.

Lord Boislegrand just stood there, mouth gaping open, arms dangling at his sides like two caught fish.

"*No!*" he finally said. It wasn't a shout, but it was the top of his voice. "No, I won't!"

"Sir!" Anna stepped back. "I have never thought you mean before!"

"I have come to see my *betrothed!* I won't be sent off to run errands! Won't sit here all afternoon looking like a dunce in the window, either!"

This was very new.

Jane sidled toward the bakery door to tap on it, but Emery and Rose had already peeked through.

They both slipped in as Anna pressed a hand to her chest. "Your lordship! I can't recall we have ever had reason to raise our voices to one another."

"I'm not raising my voice!" Now he was fairly shouting. "I am insisting on my *rights!* Just as I deserve to get *married!*"

Now Anna folded her arms and narrowed her eyes. "What, right now?"

There truly was a tantrum-type effect to his speech.

As if noticing it in himself, he subsided a bit. "No, of course not. I only wish to have reassurances."

Anna burst out, "My stars, sir, this is no time for wavering! There are two children going hungry while you fuss about whether you're sufficiently reassured."

"That's because I'm not reassured! Just tell me when you wish to be married!"

"I *don't* wish to be married! I think that's perfectly clear!"

"Oh my," Jane muttered under her breath, nudging Emery's shoulder with hers.

Emery in turn nudged Rose, who nudged back.

It had all been obvious for some time, but no one had expected Anna to just say it.

Least of all Lord Boislegrand.

"Oh." He deflated like whipped cream left out overnight. Slowly, with one step back, then another. "If that is your feeling, Miss Bickering, of course I wouldn't dream of holding you to your promise."

The word *promise* hung in the air like a knife. "Oh, sir." Anna moved forward as if to lay a hand on his arm, but he stepped back again.

And into the puddle of melted snow, where he slipped slightly.

For a moment Jane truly thought he was going to fall, making the moment more pathetic than it could bear.

But he didn't.

"Yes. I see, that's how you feel. Of course I do see." He looked about as if noticing the rest of the Bickering sisters for the first time. "Yes."

Jane glimpsed, just for a second, what it would be like to have Puffy for a brother-in-law.

He would have been fine, in his own way. Not really a match for Anna, but not a bad sort.

She thought he'd bear up eventually.

In fact, it took him only a few seconds. "No, I think I will have to hold you to your promise after all."

"*What?*" Anna went from commiseration to incandescence in an instant.

"No, I don't accept it. No. I don't think I shall."

Anna just backed against the counter, hands pressed to her mouth, shaking her head in disbelief.

Jane could well understand the disbelief, but would rather this didn't get worse.

"Rose," she said loudly enough to be sure everyone could

hear, "if Lord Boislegrand is elsewhere engaged, could you run up to the garret and see if Lord Zachary is here?"

And in fact, just at that moment, Lord Zachary came in the door from the stairwell, shrugging on his greatcoat.

He had his painting smock under it, along with a vest or two for warmth, and Jane suspected that, from his snow-free garret windows, he had seen Lord Boislegrand's sled.

He took in the scene in front of him and said nothing about Anna backed into the counter, hands covering her mouth, and Lord Boislegrand standing in a puddle of water.

"I thought I'd come see if you needed any errands," he announced to the silent room.

"Yes," Jane caught up the thread of conversation quickly. "We've packed a basket for the Colliers and had just asked Lord Boislegrand if he might take it."

"I'll go," said Lord Zachary carelessly.

When Anna turned to look at him, hands still muffling any sounds she might make, her eyes just asked *why?*

And he answered. "You need someone to do it, right?"

Jane, assuming this was as many lords as the job required and maybe one extra, reached behind the counter for the basket. "Thank you," she said, shoving it into Lord Zachary's hands.

And then Lord Boislegrand reached far down into his reserves of gallantry, or manhood, or desire to impress Anna, and said, "I'll drive you there, sir."

It made Jane feel more sympathy for him than she ever had.

And indeed, she wasn't alone.

For after Lord Zachary had left, shoving his way out through the chest-deep snow, followed by Lord Boislegrand, all four sisters went to the open door instead of closing it.

The air had that cold taste that was peculiar to snow, and they stared as the driver reached out an arm to haul Lord

Zachary up into the two-seater sled, and then after him his lordship.

The horse had a struggle ahead of him, as the snow drifted higher than his belly; but another cart or two had been by, and at least some of the way was broken.

"It's so much worse since he offered to take Lord Zachary there," Rose said as the sled *shhh'd* away.

"So much worse," agreed Anna faintly.

"Especially after he said all that about not wanting to leave you," Jane added. It was a new low, even for his lordship.

"Especially after he refused her refusal. He can't do that, can he?" Emery was clearly more astonished than anything else.

"No," said Anna, still faintly. "He can't make me marry him."

"Sounds like he wants to, though," said Rose in a thoughtful way.

Then Rose shut the door, blocking all their views.

"Can't imagine why," she added before going back down to the cellar.

Episode 16: An icy new light

"Jupiter jackstraws," said Tilly as she surveyed the cellar shelves. "It's all frozen."

"What?" Anna called down the stairs to her. "Do come help, there are some men waiting."

The new influx of men had not stopped. Snow still lay everywhere, and even walking was dangerous. Anything that could stop in London had stopped, from the mail to the Thames.

The men who came to the shop had an air of urgency about them, but no instructions. Or, Tilly thought to herself, likely they just didn't remember what they were told.

"It's all frozen!" she called back.

If she got a spoon, she could dig some hard honey out of the top of one pot; it gave a little to her fingernail, but it wouldn't pour. And the butter? Hard as a rock in the butter tubs.

They'd had weeks of high snow and every morning, beautiful patterns of frost melted slowly from the bakery windows as the ovens slowly pumped heat into the shop and a weak sun rose in the sky.

Tucking a pot of honey into the crook of her arm, she carried it upstairs.

"You want the maslin?" she snapped to the first man she ran across. And the second, and the third.

The bakery was stocked for the things it usually made. White bread and maslin. So they tried to bake as usual, though less. That meant there were loaves of maslin, including the half-peck giant.

But the men were unused to telling even the difference between a tuppence loaf and a quartern. The option of maslin absolutely floored them, and it wasn't selling.

Tilly took that as a personal affront.

Thumping the honey pot onto the counter, she gave Miss Anna a hip-push aside. "I'll get it for 'em."

"I don't know that they all want maslin, Tilly, I—What on earth has happened to the honey?" Anna picked up the pot and tipped it, and nothing happened.

"Frozen. All of it frozen. Half pound for you, sir?"

"Astonishing. I suppose it will thaw?"

"Everything'll thaw someday. Why don't you take this genn'leman's coin, and I'll serve the next."

Anna touched the surface of the honey. "Still a little sticky. It looks the same, but it won't pour!" She turned the pot upside down over her eye, leaning back. "Perhaps it will pour very slowly?"

"Miss Anna. Put it by the bakery door and it'll thaw all right. Perhaps you'd like to sell some bread."

Miss Anna shook herself. "I'm sorry, Tilly, I'm not sure what has me so absorbed by a pot of frozen honey! I hope it will be all right. The hotel does want cakes." Her subdued tone made clear the difficulty of baking cakes when there were few eggs. It meant little cake money. "I suppose the butter's frozen too?"

"Like ice," said Tilly, sawing off another hunk of the heavy brown bread.

"OH MY."

It had taken ages to struggle down through the narrow streets, and it was harder for Rose than for her taller sisters as the streets were still piled with snow and topped with dangerous crusts of frost all the way to the banks of the Thames.

Rose had not much wanted to come. They'd seldom had reason to walk by the river, of course, because it wasn't a place for fine ladies. Usually it was a place for mud and dead things and refuse in smelly water. And sailors. None of it palatable.

Today... She heard Emery's indrawn breath.

"What is it?"

EMERY STRUGGLED TO FIND WORDS. SHE STOOD ON THE heaped snow, knowing that far underfoot there were still ancient stone walls with steps that led down to the river. A river that nearly always rose and ebbed, carrying ships and barges and boats into London and out again.

But not today.

"I can't... The whole world's turned to ice."

"What does it look like?"

They'd come about half a mile, through buildings and streets. The same distance stretched out before them, but...

"Open air, of course, because the river's still here. But it's not a river. It's like a frozen wasteland. It's solid. Covered in jagged blocks of ice. Just... everywhere. There's a couple of boats stuck in it. Nothing is moving. Forever ice. As far as I can see."

"You don't mean it's solid!"

"I can't see any plain water. But there are skaters everywhere."

"I thought you said it was jagged!"

"Someone has smoothed it, here and there. And people have all brought their skates down to the water. Hundreds of people, Rose. Maybe thousands!"

"This sounds terribly dangerous." The pink cold of Rose's nose was forgotten in the surprise of it all.

WHERE ROSE HAD EXPECTED TO HEAR A BUSTLE OF WAGONS and sailors calling, or at least the flapping of sails, there was… nothing. Just the shouts of people in the distance, and cold, cold quiet.

At least, until someone shoved something hard into her hip.

"Mind yer business, lady!"

"You mind yours!" snapped Rose. None of this snow had improved her mood. Nor had Anna's broken betrothal. It ought to have, perhaps, but it hadn't.

She was still irritated with Anna.

Hard to blame someone for never having been in love, but there it was.

Emery filled in the scenery. "He's taking a ladder down the stairs. Well, sliding it down. The stone steps to the water are so covered with snow and ice that the quickest way of getting the ladder down is to lay it on the stairs and slide it."

"Sir! Why a ladder?" Rose called.

The man might have stayed snappish, but the way his voice softened a little told Rose he'd noticed she was blind.

"Building a booth!"

"For the fair?"

Because the merchants who'd been gathering at Mr. Morley's talked of nothing but.

That was why Rose had insisted she and Emery make their way down to the water. None of the men were coming into the shop to tell them anything, nor would they give any details if the Bickering sisters simply stood behind them and eavesdropped. But from what little they could gather, if there was to be a Frost Fair, it would be down on the Thames, and as soon as the ice was solid.

"Just so!" shouted the man back cheerily, and Rose heard him sliding away, catching himself a little and grunting as he drew himself, and presumably his ladder, over the chunks of ice.

"He's foolish," murmured Emery. "If it's to freeze solid, I heard it will be down past Blackfriars bridge. I wouldn't carry that ladder all the way down there on the ice."

"But there's so much snow and ice on the streets! Maybe it makes no difference to him."

Both of them stood there for a moment, waiting for the man to fall through the ice; but he didn't.

"Emery, do you think we could make it down to the Blackfriars bridge?"

"Absolutely." There was a pause while Emery considered. "But I do think we should do it on the roads. A hundred people with skates all look fine till they fall through the ice together."

JANE STRUGGLED IN THROUGH THE DOOR, SHOVING IT SHUT with one shoulder. The broom they kept there let her sweep the snow away from her feet, but there was nothing to do with it but let it melt. The cool damp in the shop crept further and further in, threatening to defeat the rush of heat from the bakery proper.

"Anna—Oh. Tilly."

"Miss Anna's gone upstairs," Tilly told her, barely looking up from her game.

Slowly Jane stepped closer.

"I can't believe you're playing solitaire on the bread counter."

For before Tilly sat a wooden box, holes carved in its top, and a set of pegs resting in a variety of holes waiting for Tilly to make them hop to their appropriate spaces.

Tilly shrugged. "I can't believe I've had two dozen customers today. It's like hell froze over but no one cares. Just going about their business buying bread." She moved a peg. "I suppose that *is* what happened, without the hell part."

Jane didn't ask her to expound. Life was better when one just let Tilly be Tilly. "Where did you get that game?"

"A girl in my boarding house, her brother works in a wood-shop and they're turning these night and day."

Moving closer, Jane saw it had writing on its side. She picked up the box, trying not to disturb any of Tilly's pegs.

Played upon the Ice

it said, with a blank space underneath on the smooth wood.

"They're going to ink the date on the day they sell the game," Till informed her.

"What? Who would buy such a thing?"

"Who would buy such a thing? Who *wouldn't?* Why, the girls at the boarding house are all working late and early getting ready to set up shop on the ice. Tents everywhere. I mean on the ice, not at the boarding house. Beer, skittles, so many books you can't imagine. The printers are going to set up right there on the ice and print tickets. *Printed on the*

Thames, they'll say. And gambling, a'course. And other things I know nothing about," Tilly hurried to add.

"Music?" The idea lit a fire of excitement Jane hadn't felt in weeks.

"All sorts of music, and dances. There's a play going to use one of the frozen-in boats as a stage. They're paying the boat owner eight shillings to do it."

But Jane didn't care about plays. Dancing! And music! It had been so long since she had any fun.

She hadn't seen Hughes anywhere around the square, not in ages; but everything was so topsy-turvy, she didn't really expect to. In any event, time had settled a few things in her head. It wasn't him she craved; in the end, he had been dull company. She craved people letting go the stuffy London rules that tried to crush the life out of them all.

It didn't sound like there would be too many rules down on the ice.

"Do you know where Anna went? There's two letters; I had to pay for them to the post-boy, there's no way of knowing how long they've waited."

"Haven't seen her for an hour. She disappeared just after I showed her the stiff butter."

"It did what now?" Jane slipped the letters into the money box and settled down to spend the time it would take to work out what Tilly was talking about.

"I CAN'T DO THIS."

Anna felt that peculiar embarrassment that came with not keeping a promise. In fact, she'd felt little else since breaking her betrothal promise to Lord Boislegrand. He still arrived every few days at the shop, sliding in his carved sled, and made half-hearted attempts to get her to agree to marry him again. He looked broken as a kicked toy. She felt constantly soaked in guilt, and covered it a little, she hoped, with the bonnet she had taken to wearing inside to keep warm.

She couldn't bear more guilt; but she also couldn't do this.

"Of course you can." Lord Zachary gestured to the loose platform of crates where he'd placed a rickety chair, covered with sheepskins, and atop it all, a woman whose curves threatened to spill out of the velvet robe wrapped round her.

The model wore a gown, of course, but his lordship had tucked a lace fichu all around the neck to make a gauzy cloud. Rather, the woman had tucked it; if Zachary himself had actually tucked all that lace around all that skin, Anna would have fled.

The model herself didn't seem to care about anything but the cold. "You said it'd be warm."

"It's warmer than most of London right now. I apologize, Miss Porter. If you would only let me put down a sketch."

"I'll do what I can," she said a bit ungraciously, pulling the velvet robe up over her shoulder, only for Lord Zachary to wave that she should push it down again, a bit farther.

"I honestly cannot." Anna had an overwhelming sense of the inappropriateness of the woman, and far worse, being alone with her and Lord Zachary in his garret.

As for him, like the model, he was businesslike. He stared at the model, but the more Anna looked—for she couldn't bear to look at the model—the more she saw that there was nothing, well, warm in his gaze. His stare was intent, to be sure; but it was the kind of intent that translated into sweeps of line with the silver pencil on his drawing board. That was all.

Anna tried to breathe.

She *was* the sort of person who mixed with people like these. In her bakery. She was the sort of person who broke engagements, right in front of everyone. And broke a heart.

How she could make it up to Lord Boislegrand, she didn't know. Why she'd felt she had to, she wasn't even sure.

Atop it all, Rose's low opinion of her felt justified.

Well, if she were a heartless scold, she might as well do her best at it.

"Why a portrait, again?" she asked faintly, trying to gather her mind from the places to which it fled.

"Turner fills whole skies with emotion. I've been trying to do it with flowers, and it doesn't work. The sketches I made at Gravesend just prove to me that I'm not Turner. I don't have those landscape views here, but when I was there, I didn't care for them. It just doesn't move me. So why not try people? There's good money in portraits, if I can do them better. And Miss Porter is an excellent model."

It was easy to see of what.

The woman had no concern for being stared at, and gradually Anna began to breathe.

"All right," she said from her position near the stairs. She didn't want to come closer, but from her place she could also see both the model, barely lit by the icy window, and the drawing paper Lord Zachary had pinned to his board. "All right. The background must be dark, because it is, and perhaps you can do something interesting with the shadows of it."

"To suggest a tunnel, perhaps." He took a step back from his drawing to consider it more widely.

"Nothing so literal. You want some of Turner's emotion; where will you put it? It could be shades of black suggesting that the world beyond her goes on, or closes in."

Zachary shook his head. "No. I'm not interested in the *space;* I'm interested in *her.* I saw something in the colors of her skin that suggested that kind of tumult to me, when she blushed. One of Turner's skies. Can you blush, Miss Porter?"

"Not like this," Miss Porter said easily.

"What were you doing when you blushed?" Anna asked from practical curiosity.

The model turned her head an inch and dropped Anna a slow wink. Then put her head back where it had been.

The woman clearly understood the work of being a model far more than Anna understood that wink.

Lord Zachary obviously did, as he demonstrated *he* could blush quite easily, despite the chill in the air.

Anna closed her eyes. She didn't want to know. She didn't want to know where Lord Zachary encountered such a woman. She'd only recently begun to think better of him. And his carrying food to Sal and Jordan—who were still staying safely at home with their father, and by report, very bored—did not necessarily mean that his character was all it should be.

Anna was afraid if she kept creeping into grayer and grayer areas of morality, she would not realize when she was wholly in the black.

"Lord Zachary. If I may speak to you a moment."

"Of course."

She led the way down the garret stairs and around the corner to where Rose's apartment with Mr. Russell stood empty. She didn't wish to insult Miss Porter, after all.

Very quietly she said to him, "Is she your mistress?"

"No!" After his first explosive sound, he moderated himself. "I assure you, Miss Bickering, I have no such thing." He shifted a little. "I can't afford one," he admitted to her a little sheepishly.

Anna wanted to shout at him *not to tell her that,* but she didn't. This was awkward enough. "Is she a lady of ill repute?"

"Well..." Lord Zachary looked behind him, perhaps to check that Miss Porter had not followed. "What sort of ill? And how much repute?"

She couldn't do this. "Lord Zachary!"

"All right, I'm sorry. The sort of women one meets at a gentleman's club are not ladies. The sort of women who let you dress them and draw them are not ladies. Miss Porter…" Here he looked up at the ceiling, and his blush came back. "Is definitely not a lady. But I'm asking her to do nothing untoward. And she has that look I want to paint. That wild red hair, and her skin is flawless."

Anna had to admit the woman's skin *was* flawless.

"All right. I simply… cannot believe I am doing this without a chaperone." *Or at all,* Anna admitted to herself.

"Well, so is Miss Porter," said Lord Zachary with a distinct lack of awareness for the differences between the two women.

There are differences, Anna told herself firmly, even as it became harder and harder to see what they were. Miss Porter, after all, was here to work for her money, as Anna did every day. And Anna must like the idea of working for her money better than the idea of marrying Lord Boislegrand, as she'd thrown him off.

There was something wrong with her.

"Well," Anna said slowly, "she's not going to blush. And you won't try to make her," she said quickly to forestall any such attempt. He just put up warding hands as if to say he would never. She went on, "And if you try to paint a blush, you'd have to be so delicate to avoid too much contrast between the colors of her skin. You'd have to have them the way nature provides. It could look blotchy. Don't you think? So why not use the color of her hair against the robe? Two entirely different warm colors, the brown and the red, but not where the viewer expects. As brown hair is so much commoner than the red kind."

Lord Zachary snapped his fingers.

"You have something there. You organize your thoughts

so clearly before I've even put paint on the canvas. That's what I need, someone to organize some thoughts for me."

"I'm sure any thoughts would help," Anna said faintly in an echo of the barbs she used to toss at him.

But her heart wasn't in it. She had always known, looking at the serviceable engravings and portrait of a lady under a tree that her father had inherited—an ancestor, but long ago sold—that someone had decided to organize the lines and colors just that way. Art did not spring from the ground; someone had to make it, just as she made bread. And though she had little ability, despite efforts to develop it into a talent that would make her a more interesting candidate for marriage, practice had helped her develop her instinct for what kind of work it was.

Every fine house she'd visited during that season of parties had its share of pretty paintings, and Anna had seen far more in that one year than in all the years of her life up till then. And all those paintings, bought by people with money and taste, had certain things in common. There was a composition to them, an intention, as well as a great deal of expensive pigment.

And someone had to think them through and decide how to make them look.

Today, that was Lord Zachary.

"Usually portraits are of fine ladies." She just wanted to point that out.

"In the rooms *you* frequent."

He was implying that there were many rooms ladies did not frequent that held paintings of very different women.

Had he not gone on, she might not have found it in her to go back upstairs.

"Miss Bickering. I'm not trying to become an artist who churns out salacious coloring for pleasure clubs. Though there would be money in it," he added wryly. "If I can paint a better portrait, I'll have something to sell to the fine ladies you just mentioned. I must have *something,* and I have spent weeks trying to find a topic sufficiently interesting to me that I could try to capture it the way Turner does an ocean sky. I haven't found it in nature, I must admit. Dogs and horses don't interest me, nor do dead pheasants. I apologize that I am not a better man, but I think I could paint a portrait of Miss Porter that would have something fine in it. Not because of Miss Porter's morals. Just because of her looks. I'm very clear about that. There's nothing particularly appropriate about it. But I must try."

He was so earnest. So honest. There was nothing gray about that.

"Yes, of course," Anna said, still faint, but more sure. "I think this is the best plan. Remember how harsh the separations were in the colors of the flower petals last time you tried those? That's exactly what I mean by blotchy. Focus on the shape of the robe and the hair and you'll have something."

"Thank you." He looked ready to shake her hand, he was so elated. "Do you... will you come back up, or should I try without you?"

It ought to have been more flattering that he wanted her guidance, but in the moment, it didn't feel so.

"I'll come up," said Anna, committing herself to the black.

IT WAS DARK, AND NEARLY TIME TO CLOSE, WHEN EMERY and Rose finally stomped back into the shop.

"I'd started to worry!" Anna swept as much of the snow back out as she could and shut the door. Jane came to help unwrap the shawls and shake them out as her younger sisters peeled them away.

"You cannot imagine how many people are down on the ice." Rose shook out her bonnet.

Emery wanted to do the same, but only brushed the bonnet clean while leaving it on her head. The difference between the warmth of the shop and the cold outside was stifling. But in half an hour she'd feel chilly again, unless she went back to the bakery proper. "Did Wiggs bed down the coals?"

"Yes. And the butter has thawed."

"Had it frozen?" Rose sounded surprised, as if all the time she'd spent in the cellar recently ought to have kept it from getting too cold.

"*And* the honey! I'll make cakes tomorrow. There's still no sign of Mrs. Wallace," said Anna as she shook the shawl, sending white ice crystals flying.

Mrs. Baby, as they still thought of her, had not been seen since the beginning of the fog, which now felt like years ago.

"Never mind the cakes," said Rose, "unless you can take them to the river. Anna, there are *hundreds* of people on the ice. Maybe thousands. It's a roaring crowd, but all on the river! Solid ice where the water used to be."

"Never say so!"

Emery folded the knit woolen shawl in her hands. "There's men building booths everywhere on the ice. Hammering them together right there. And tents, more tents than I could count. Some men are carving verses on the stone piers of the bridge."

"Why?" This surprised Jane. "When will anyone be able to read them again?"

"It's the spirit of the moment, I think. When *will* they? It's been years since the Thames froze over. None of us were even alive last time. Well, I think you were," Emery looked at Anna dubiously.

"Thank you for that." Anna patted a curl into place as if staunching a wound. "Has it frozen smooth?"

"No, there's great jagged chunks everywhere. Except a few places someone flooded, I think, to make better skating. Come to think of it, that bit of thaw we had on the week-end must have flooded things the way it flooded the street. Iced over again immediately, just like the road. Perhaps that made the skating park. But the rest of the water you can walk on, or climb, more like."

"Carefully," Rose put in, rubbing her hip as though she'd failed once or twice. "The point is, everyone in London seems to be setting up shop."

"Tilly brought a game one of her boarding house girls showed her. Played on the ice, it said." Jane looked around, but it was gone.

"Yes! There's whole print shops being set up on the ice. Handbills, tickets of all kinds, anything foolish. So long as it says *printed on the ice,* they think people will buy."

"Who has the money to spend on such things?" Anna's face echoed the surprise in her voice.

"Apparently," said Rose, "a lot of people. And my chick-adees, we must be there too."

"Never say so!" Anna exclaimed, but Jane looked thoughtful.

"We must." Rose had that firm look to her, the same one she'd had about being married. "The river isn't flowing, but the money is, and we might make back some of what we have lost in the last few weeks of business."

It was a sign of how sensible they had all become to the flow of money that no one argued how welcome it would be to have more. They all knew the dip in earnings they'd suffered the last few weeks endangered their footing, but what could they do about it? Now, here, was an answer.

So there was no arguing over the desirability of making money. It went straight to the conducting of the affair.

"How many cakes could we safely carry without crushing them?"

"The bread baskets could be heaped with two layers. Maybe three."

"We could charge more for the tuppence and quartern loaves, and never bother with the half-pecks."

"Buns!" Rose flapped her hand to quiet them all. "We could charge far more per bushel of wheat if we make them into buns, and people can carry them."

"Can we mark them *Baked on the ice?*" Jane looked utterly serious, and they all took it so.

"I suppose now we wish we had one of the Guild's seals," Anna said wryly.

"Well, if we did, it wouldn't say that." Emery had no interest in trying to stamp all her loaves.

"And we won't bake them on the ice. Anyway, what would be the point? People will eat them, and they'll be gone. Not like the tickets. They'll keep those."

"One of the printers is planning to do a whole *book*," Rose told them with disbelief.

"Buns," said Jane with decision, "if we can use the regular dough to make them. Can we, Emery?"

"I'm sure we can. They'll bake too fast, but... we'll have to watch them." She cracked the door to the bakery. "Mr. Wiggs!"

"Yes, ma'am!"

"Add some wood to the fire, we'll do some baking."

"Oh thank Christ," they heard Mr. Bailey muttering in the background. Clearly the men had been bored doing little but flip knives and trying to gamble, which the sisters had made them stop.

"Fire up the second oven," Anna called around Emery's shoulder. "For cakes."

"Yes, ma'am!" Wiggs called back.

She nodded to Emery. "If you can bake all night, I can."

"You must sleep too," warned Rose. "If we're to make this happen quickly, it will take all of us."

"We should send Lord Zachary to fetch Jordan and Sal in the morning."

"They won't want to miss it!"

"We didn't see any bakers today." Emery already felt cheerier at the prospect of putting on her apron. She'd have something to *do*. Suddenly she understood the bustle of merchants on the ice. They were all eager to have business again, money flowing, and work. "I'm surprised now that we didn't. If we do, we must try to keep watch for Guild marks. I'd like to know who will compete with us."

"Oh!" Jane slid behind the counter. "I think one of the letters we got is from Mr. Keales."

"Letters?"

Jane handed one over to Anna, who broke the seal and unfolded the little packet as Jane did the other one.

Anna read hers first, and the words threw a cold blanket heavier than snow over the energy the sisters had felt just a moment before.

"Dear Miss Bickering, I have the sad privilege of informing you that the questioning regarding your bakery, selling without the full force and privilege of the Guild of Worshipful Bakers, will begin on February the first. Why, that's tomorrow."

"I'm surprised the letter got here at all," said Jane, trying to read over Anna's shoulder in the evening gloom.

"You can't bake all night, Anna, if you must answer to the Guild tomorrow." Rose's firmness was wavering.

"Yes I can." Anna's, however, solidified. "Our business has nothing to do with the Guild. All they've done is tell us to close, and we won't. You're quite right, this opportunity won't come again. Think of how much we could ask *for each slice of cake!*"

"I'll have to come with you."

Anna looked at Jane as if she'd suddenly reappeared out of the floorboards. It rather felt like she had, mused Emery.

But Anna wasn't about to turn down support of any kind. "Thank you. *You* should sleep."

"I'll sleep a little. So will you. But even if I've never had your talent with the cakes, I'll mix whatever you tell me. Rose, you and Emery shape up some buns. Can we make something in the shape of river ice?"

With a few words, Jane brought the determination back.

"I don't think so. But buns we can make. Rose, I think if we lay them in a circle we can nearly fill the oven with them. They'll bake in minutes. We'll have to watch every second. Come to think of it, we may have to add flour to the dough after all."

"Yes, let's—"

"This letter is from Knight's School." Jane's voice stopped them before they went through the door.

They did all stop, and words too. The silence was grim.

Jane read. "*Our pupils often begin with us after the new year, but the weather has made us all quite confined within the school, and as it is a delicate age for girls, the headmistress thought that perhaps Miss Collier would find it more comfortable to wait.* What does that mean?"

"They don't want her?" Emery was so grateful never to have attempted school. Such a convoluted sentence surely wasn't useful.

"They think she won't suit," said Anna. "That she won't have friends, perhaps."

"Sal doesn't need to be comfortable." Rose wore a little scowl. "Sal is braver than all of us."

"With Jordan," Jane said softly, and there was no arguing that.

"I am not giving up."

"Nor should we." Anna was different these days, thought Emery. Perhaps jilting Lord Boislegrand had been good for her. She had always been bossy, but now she recovered quicker from blows. "We must work quickly, my chickadees, that's all. Jane and I will see the Guild tomorrow, Rose may argue with the school, and Emery must bake faster than she's ever baked before."

"I do need someone to accompany me," Rose pointed out.

"Are you willing to have Lord Zachary?"

"No, we've imposed enough on his lordship."

"He'll do it," said Anna, a little darkly, which made no sense to Emery. "Even if he'd planned to work."

"No, I'll ask Mr. Laurent. He's had little air since all this began, and while I'm glad he's also had little gin, he must be terribly bored."

It was a sign of the bustle that had taken over all the sisters that no one stopped to question the questionable idea of having their rough neighbor accompany Rose to a girls' school. After all, Mr. Laurent had had his hair cut, and his waistcoat patched. He looked quite respectable, if shabby, in good light.

And the omnipresent ice seemed to excuse everything.

Episode 17: Of fairs and knights

Until the moment the headmistress of Knight's School came into the room, Rose forgot that she did not call on people in society without Mr. Russell.

She remembered it when the lady's voice, so cultured, settled over her like a quilt. "I'm sorry to keep you waiting, Mrs. Russell. Did I forget an appointment? The weather has so rattled London I'm afraid it has rattled me as well."

Rose did not have an appointment and had intended to argue Sal's way into the school, so the gentility, and the reminder that she was there uninvited, took some steam out of Rose's temper.

Mr. Laurent, who had accompanied her, stood when the lady entered the room, and Rose was so spun round for a moment that she stood too.

He put a hand on her shoulder and squeezed. Just a little, to remind her he was there. Slowly Rose sat again.

"And this must be Mr. Russell," said the headmistress.

Before Rose could say anything, Mr. Laurent answered.

Smooth, instant, and with a flawless English public school accent. "Indeed."

Rose's head spun. Of course, a married woman would not visit a school headmistress without her husband. Would it have been better to come alone? No, she should have brought one of her sisters. But Emery and Jane were at the Frost Fair, and Anna dealing with the baker's guild. There was no one.

Snow and ice could fall on London all year and they would still have work to do.

Not that she could expect anyone at the school to understand women with business pursuits. The headmistress went on. "I am Mrs. Crantock. Delighted to meet you both. Are your feet dry? The fire is just warming the floor. Or maybe it isn't. I trust you have been well during this horrifying weather. And Sally."

"Yes," said Rose, adding no detail. Sal was bored to tears, as far as Lord Zachary reported, and Jordan the same. Trapped in their room with their father, they had even resorted to reading a book of plays between them, Sal acting most of the parts and Jordan chiming in when they felt a man was needed. Jordan's voice was sometimes now deep enough to portray generals and kings.

Mrs. Macy from the women's committee had given them the fifth volume of a set before the weather had gone bad, and it only contained two plays. Both children now knew them very well.

The schoolmistress was accustomed to doing much of the talking. "And to what do I owe the pleasure of this visit? Did you receive my letter about postponing Sally's arrival? You must know how girls, well, they tend to cluster in tight groups, and when their delicate social organization is upset they can be so horrid to one another. I doubt young boys are ever so horrid."

"I'm sure you're right," said Mr. Laurent solemnly, still in his English accent.

"You see, I'm sure she can accomplish the schoolwork; I'm more concerned with the social element. You understand. If you'd like, I would be happy to furnish you with the list of books she will need once she comes."

Maybe Mrs. Crantock's gentle nudging worked on women who had never had to deal with a water bill, but Rose was not there to be nudged.

"I would be happy to take the book list. But Sal is quite capable of handling any social gatherings, and she is well past our ability to educate her at home."

"Oh," with a sad little half-sigh, "you don't know how difficult groups of girls can be."

There, there came a spark of Rose's temper back, and she grabbed it tight. "I have three sisters, Mrs. Crantock."

"Oh. Yes, I see." That flummoxed her for a moment. "Let me order you something bracing. This weather is *so* bad."

She rustled out of the room and Mr. Laurent leaned close.

"She's giving herself time to think," he murmured in his more usual voice.

"Oh. Thank you. That didn't occur to me," Rose murmured back.

"Your sisters don't do that sort of thing, which is why I mentioned it," he said before sitting up as Mrs. Crantock came back in the room.

That gave Rose no time to take offense.

Very well, she would take the hint. If Mrs. Crantock wanted a slightly slower fight, Rose would give her one.

"WHERE'S YOUR HUSBAND?"

The abruptness of the question felt out of place in the rich dark wood of the hall, with its sweet burning candles.

The room had felt to Anna almost like church until the man's harsh question reminded her this was not a place of solace.

"I am not married, Mr. Wainwright," she told the warden of the Worshipful Guild of Bakers as frostily as she could.

"There is no baker in residence at the Leicester Square bakery, sir." Mr. Keales had always struck Anna as an officious, slightly forlorn fellow, but here in the Bakers' hall he was quite at ease. As he argued, there was a glint of eagerness in his eye Anna didn't like.

"Yet you say here the business sells quite a bit of bread." Mr. Wainwright, plump and gray-haired, had a wattle under his chin that shivered in an officious way whenever he looked up from the sheet of paper.

"Indeed, sir."

"Not just cakes?" He bent his head to search the paper in his hand.

"No, sir." Anna had not come all this way in the ice to pretend her bakery wasn't exactly what it was. She couldn't stop Lord Boislegrand from dropping in and looking at her sadly; only the ice had done that, and once it melted, he'd be back. She couldn't stop Jane and Emery and Rose from venturing out all over the square or, at least in one case, getting married; she'd already failed there too. She couldn't stop herself being drawn in by the painting Lord Zachary was creating in the garret, choosing colors that melted together to give a live, hot impression of flushed skin; it was for some reason an experience that was melting into *her* own skin and down to her core till she couldn't stop thinking about it.

If she could stop this guild from harassing her and her sisters, it would be the biggest work of which she was currently capable.

She was the oldest; this was her job.

Mr. Wainwright was clearly confused. "So who does the baking?"

"We do, sir."

"We? You said you weren't married."

"Indeed. My sisters and I are the bakers."

"They've got two journeymen working for them too, sir," Mr. Keales put in with that flash of eagerness.

Mr. Wainwright looked up through bushy eyebrows at Anna. "You can't have journeymen without a master baker."

Anna shrugged one shoulder with a disdain she'd learned in ballrooms. "And yet, we do."

"No no, that's no good. Those men need *work,* Mrs. Bickering. When you marry up and leave them, how will they earn their livelihood?"

"One of my sisters is married. She still bakes and waits on patrons. If the rest of us marry, I suspect it will be the same." She did not lean forward, but she clasped her hands tightly, standing before his wide oak table, feeling like a schoolgirl. The position was intended to make her feel so, and she knew it. "Unless or until I marry, my name is *Miss* Bickering."

He frowned. "Trying to be respectful, madam. As you've reached an age."

Perhaps he meant it. But Anna didn't wish to be called *missus* by virtue of her age any more than she did by virtue of her marital state.

Mr. Wainwright was happy to be less polite if she preferred it. "You can't do this to these men." He tapped the paper, still holding it half off the table with the other hand. "They won't be able to find a proper place after your bakery closes."

"We don't expect to close."

He sighed. "Why do young people think the world will be so different for them? Have sense, young lady. I entered this hall as a lad and here I still am, forty years later, serving the Guild. I did what my betters did, and worked to be like them. I didn't expect it to be different just for me." He looked a little sad as he said it.

"My parents died, Mr. Wainwright. Would you rather we starved?" These men. These old men. Anna knew her cheeks were flushing hot, but couldn't help it.

"You shouldn't starve, you should *marry*. I don't have to explain that to you, you're old enough!"

The man's obsession with her age began to grate.

Anna was not going to explain the whole evolution of her family to a fat man at a table. "At the time we opened the bakery, none of us had husbands."

"Then get them. This isn't difficult. I don't understand what's difficult about this. Do you, Keales?"

"No sir," said that man instantly.

"We decided," Anna enunciated the word clearly, "not to. We *decided* to open a bakery. As you see, we have."

"Can't do that."

"Yet," and here Anna spread both hands wide as if to encompass the entire empty hall, "we did."

"Do you understand it is not permitted to bake for the public without the guild seal? We ensure you don't mix chalk in your flour. We ensure you don't cheat on weight. We ensure the food you make is healthful for the citizens of the city." Mr. Wainwright's wattle shivered again with the sheer majesty of his responsibility.

"We don't mix chalk in our flour. You are welcome to check our weights at any time. Our bread is entirely healthful, which Mr. Keales could have determined by himself on his first visit. He did not even try our bread. He only demanded that we not exist. Well, sir, we do exist. We are going to keep on existing, because there is no alternative."

With that speech, Anna leaned back on her heels, chin in the air.

Jane would be proud of her. She'd said it all by herself, without Jane having to come to her rescue.

"OY, LOOK OUT!"

Jane ducked just in time to keep from being knocked aside by the rickety cart of toys the young man shoved across the uneven ice.

Ducked, and kept tight hold of her basket of rolls.

"Tuppence a roll!" she called, knowing it was an outrageous price and not caring. This whole Frost Fair was outrageous.

It was marvelous to stand *on* the river, *under* London Bridge. It felt like a dream, something impossible, till she realized that of course others had seen these stones from this angle; but they had been moving on water, and she was standing on her own two feet.

Children of all sorts clambered over the toothy wooden edge around the stone pier that supported the bridge in the water. One tall boy carved something into the stone.

"We must bring Sal and Jordan tomorrow."

Emery's cheeks were pink from cold, making her hair look brighter. "If we dragged Sal and Jordan out of their safe, warm room, it should be to bake bread." She'd been up with Wiggs and Bailey much of the night, and was now out here selling while the journeymen baked more and napped as they could by the fire. She was cranky.

"Rose can help bake tonight, and Anna. And you can sleep. But they shouldn't miss this!"

Jane swept her arm over the whole scene.

Skaters slid and screamed with excitement on patches of the river smooth enough for their skates.

Three printing presses, complicated spiders of metal, had set up within sight of each other, one turning out tickets that said *Printed on the Thames,* another doing handbills exclaiming *Printed during the Frost Fair, 1814,* and another turning out whole booklets of some popular scene from a play. The play printer looked bitter at the wool-coated men surrounding the smaller items; Jane hoped he had not decided on too ambitious an offering.

The rolls had been a perfect choice, as the cold made everyone hungry.

A puppet show had a gathered crowd and set them laughing, and children leaped and slid over big and small chunks of ice, ice that had trapped the usually mighty Thames in one moment.

In more shadowed spots, hunched men threw games of dice, while others spun wheels of fortune or flipped cards.

Down the center of the river a stream of people strolled as best they could over the ice, laughing, pointing, eyes wide at the unusual sights and marking a moment that might not come again for decades, if ever. They promenaded towards Blackfriars Bridge and back.

"The children can't miss all this!"

Selling the bread for egregious prices might have been the draw, but the excitement in the air was palpable.

Emery just shrugged.

"Take a bit of grog, you're tired and cold." Jane jerked her head toward the tent where revelers shouted and danced.

In truth, Jane wanted to be in that tent. A violin was playing an irresistible reel, and Jane wanted to sing. To dance, even, maybe.

She'd spent so many days trapped in the bakery; she knew how Jordan and Sal felt.

"If I have grog, I'll fall asleep and freeze to death." Emery didn't seem to care for the crowds or the excitement.

Jane could tell, though she didn't really understand. "I won't let you freeze."

"You could hare off after some new thing at any time." Emery met Jane's eyes.

She knew.

She knew something. She knew Jane was up to things, late at night in the dark.

Jane didn't know how she knew, but she could see it in Emery's tired, unguarded face.

"I wouldn't leave you to freeze." How could Emery think that? "I'm still your sister. Just as you are mine."

She tried to tell Emery back with her own eyes. *I know. I know you have a secret life too.*

Something must have passed between them because Emery looked down at her basket of bread.

"I didn't know when we started all this it would make life so different."

Jane knew exactly what she meant. "Me either."

"It's good, it's just... there's so much I never expected."

So much to do, to be, to learn. Jane wanted to talk about it. She and Emery used to be able to talk.

Though mostly it had been about Anna and Rose and how they indulged each other into doing things Jane and Emery didn't want.

Emery became angry when Jane and Anna began school. She never stopped being angry. Had Aunt Eden deemed Emery marriageable, she might have had school too.

Looking back, Jane could understand how Aunt Eden's judgment made Emery angry. Everything to do with it was unfair. Why shouldn't Emery have had school, just because she'd intended to spend the rest of her life with their mother? Why shouldn't she have school just because she *wanted* it?

Had she had school, her life might have turned out differently.

"Do you wish you'd gone to school like Anna and me?" Jane had to ask. It felt like there was a gulf between them right now wider than the Thames.

"Of course," Emery said instantly, not looking at Jane again.

"Do you think your life would be different?"

They plodded on, carefully picking their way round chunks of ice, trying not to get caught in the flow of people walking the other way. Several stopped to take a roll and drop a coin in one of their mittens. Jane suspected she could have charged a shilling for those rolls and some walkers would still buy.

"Different," said Emery finally, "of course, but not better. I'm glad we came to the square. I'm glad for the bakery. It makes me feel like I can do something useful, that there's a place to be useful. I used to think I'd just sit in a corner for the rest of my life."

"I'm sorry." Jane felt now like it was her fault.

"Never you fear, I put blame where blame is due; on Aunt Eden." Emery flashed Jane a toothy grin. "And on Mother, to be honest. She didn't fight me, but she didn't fight for me, either."

It was a relief to have someone say something about Mother that wasn't worshipful. Rose barely allowed it. Jane sorely missed her mother as a confidant and at the same time was glad for the chance to breathe deep in whole new worlds that would never have fit in her old life.

"We should write Aunt Eden a letter."

That made Emery laugh. "She'd be shocked to get a letter from us with no trouble to report."

The real trick would be if Aunt Eden wrote back. "We can

do that. At least, once Anna sorts out these bakery men, and once the mail is traveling again!"

A new swirl of voices shouted and squealed up ahead, distracting them from the proposed letter.

There, a hundred yards down the ice, someone had persuaded an elephant to climb down the banks and stand on the frozen river.

Jane and Emery both stood still, jaws dropping.

"That's an elephant," said Emery.

"It must be." Jane had seen gray shapes in picture books, but this animal was real.

"There's an elephant on the ice."

"It is."

As they watched, the man leading it and several of his friends behind convinced the elephant to walk across the frozen river. It didn't like the hard bits of ice on its feet any more than Jane did, and picked its way gingerly, pausing once to let out an astonishingly musical roar before continuing.

Jane and Emery stared at each other. Back at the elephant. And at each other again.

"We really must bring Sal and Jordan tomorrow," said Jane.

Anna stood outside the door of the meeting room and, abandoning her decorum more completely than she had since the fateful day she ran out to meet Lord Boislegrand's carriage in the street, listened at the door.

Faintly came the voices of the men, but Anna could hear.

"What do you expect, Keales? The King doesn't want to hear our business. What does it matter if it's because he's busy or wobble-headed? The effect's the same."

"Sir, the Guild exists to enforce the rules." Keales sounded absolutely scandalized.

"Well, if the Crown don't care, there's not much we can do."

Anna leaned her face against the door. She'd felt sure that Mr. Laurent was right, that the Guild was barking more than it could bite, but she hadn't been *certain*.

She wondered when she'd become the gambling type, and listened.

The Warden went on. "He won't take our business, and that's that."

"But... but..." This hit Mr. Keales hard. "If that's not our business... what do we *do?*"

"If you ask me, pretty soon, not too much." Mr. Wainwright sounded bitter. Then he rallied. "Now don't take it like that, Keales, you look like I kicked your sister. We do important work. You know yourself that you haven't seen all the bakeries we tasked you to inspect, and that's aside from kicking up nests of these sorts of feathers."

"It's beyond the pale."

"So it is, but what about that baker you found ignoring the assize laws altogether? Bread and flour still have weight, and so do we. We ought to press down on *that* fellow."

"I don't understand, sir. This Ladies' Own Bakery by rights shouldn't exist."

"By rights, Keales, it doesn't."

Anna flattened her ear to the door to hear Mr. Wainwright's lowered voice.

He said, "These sorts of things are unnatural, and like all unnatural things they soon die. Your attention breathes life into its staggering form, keeping it upright. Let it sort itself out. The girls will marry and the bakery will close and it'll all end. Too bad for the journeymen, but you say you warned them."

"But what if the bakery doesn't end, sir? I've kept watch a while now, and they haven't budged an inch."

"So what if it doesn't? By rights, they don't exist. As years pass some women here and there might try to open a shop and sell bread. But if they don't have a seal, they aren't in the Guild records, and without being in the records, memory fades. That's what makes them disappear. Soon enough they're gone and no one else will even suspect they were there. Honestly, Keales, you do more to encourage rebellion by writing their names in an official report than you would have done simply passing them by. Someone might read this."

"But sir." Keales seemed absolutely lost. "They're selling *bread*."

"To a few houses. A street barely bigger than Cheapside. Come and bother me when they take over east London. Better, come talk to me when they put peas in the flour. Now that riles the public."

"Sir, they *were* noticed breaking the rules. That's exactly how I found them. I received a complaint."

Who had complained about the Ladies' Own Bakery? Anna had not really suspected that a patron of their shop—or a neighbor—would have done such a thing. But there Keales confirmed it.

In that moment Anna felt alone.

She had been proud and tall, but the thought that one of their neighbors had drawn the Guild's attention to them, tried to close their doors, made her feel small.

Determination not to feel small in front of those men, paradoxically, made her brave again.

"Excuse me," she said, tapping on the door and opening it before they answered. "I must attend to my business, I've been away the whole morning. You know where to find me, Mr. Keales, if you have any more questions? I do apologize, Mr. Wainwright, but you of all people understand."

"It doesn't matter, Miss Bickering," said the Warden, waving a pudgy hand. Keales' thin face looked stricken.

Even in dismissing her, he couldn't bear to admit she existed.

Well, at least Anna had what she came for. The Guild was toothless, and she knew it.

"So you see, Mrs. Crantock, Sal has a talent for maths that shouldn't wait another second." Rose had warmed to her subject all through a long explanation of Sal's talents, and had to force herself not to start explaining them all over again once she reached the end.

"I do see, Mrs. Russell, but you must admit that a young lady's social connections are just as important as her intellectual ability." Mrs. Crantock stirred her tea, happy to continue discussing it all afternoon as long as she had something warm to drink.

Rose stood.

"No, Mrs. Crantock, I don't. Yes, it is important for Sal to make friends, and of course she should be happy. But she has gifts, gifts it hurts her not to use as best she can. I'm not asking you to make her ready to marry a duke. I'm asking you to give her teachers. She deserves that."

Mr. Laurent stood next to Rose, apparently in solidarity.

Rose still found it hard to stop. "Sal is brave and bright and no stranger to hardship. She *wants* to learn, *wants* to work. You only have to make it possible. She'll make friends as well, because she can't help it. She's a winning soul." Which was true, Rose thought, underneath Sal's sometimes thorny exterior.

Being exposed to the Bickering sisters day and night was not making her sweeter, and school could only help.

"Mrs. Russell." Mrs. Crantock didn't get up. "You of all people should know it is only a road to disappointment for a girl to try to do something she simply isn't able to do."

The silence crackled till Rose could feel it, and she wasn't sure why till she played the words over again in her head.

Was Mrs. Crantock saying Rose ought to know that some things were impossible, because she was blind?

Mr. Laurent certainly seemed to take it that way, because from standing beside her, he put his hands flat on the table in front of the schoolmistress and leaned. Rose heard him, heard the boards creak.

"Mrs. Crantock," he said, still in an English voice but silky and dangerous. "It's not hard to imagine *you* being overcome by an obstacle. But do not presume to know what others can or cannot do by measuring them against your short, short yardstick."

"Oh, I—" The headmistress' flow of words had finally stopped.

Rose couldn't leave it like this, couldn't simply flounce away. These were the hard things she had to do, staying the course till Sal found a place. "You do understand that we know Sal best, don't you, Mrs. Crantock? You understand we would never ask you to disrupt your school *or* put Sal where she couldn't be happy. We must just try it, surely. You do see that, don't you?"

"Well, I—" The woman stopped again.

Had Mrs. Crantock been different, the lady could have dug in her heels, insisting she knew what was best for her school and, more foolishly, for Sal, when her acquaintance with the girl was only by report.

Instead, to her credit, she bent.

"Of course you know her best, Mrs. Russell. And the ladies' committee has recommended her highly, else we would not have this discussion. The school was founded to give chances for young ladies who wouldn't have them elsewhere. I have to turn away so many each year I've become timid, perhaps, when there is one I can afford to accept. Of course, let us start Sal next week."

"Thank you." All Rose could think to do was curtsey.

"Thank you, madam." Mr. Laurent straightened.

She let Mr. Laurent put her hand in the crook of his arm. The gesture was so like Mr. Russell and yet so different that, on top of Mrs. Cranstock's thoughtless remark, Rose felt her eyes fill with tears.

Mr. Laurent led her out through the front door of the school. A school she herself would have liked to study in. But if they found it difficult to make allowance for a girl starting in the middle of the year, had they been tasked with educating a blind student, they would have claimed it impossible.

"If I cry, will she see?" she asked in a tight voice.

"Don't do it yet," said he, with a falsely careless air.

He whisked her into the street and down a tiny alleyway, the kind that usually hosted vagabonds and cats.

There Rose sat right down in a heap of snow and cried.

"Now, miss. Oh, *horreur*." Mr. Laurent, back to his usual voice, was distressed.

But Rose couldn't help it. Not even to ask why he'd suddenly sounded so English. She didn't care right then if he *was* English, or Portuguese, or somehow Russian.

No one else had made her feel so small, not in a long time. She thought once she'd learned to stand up to Aunt Eden, to walk proudly at Mr. Russell's side, she was past such things.

Would she ever be past them?

"I don't think Sal should go there," said Mr. Laurent, in a way that said he was plotting revenge even as they spoke.

"They have an excellent teacher of maths who is a woman

herself. It will be the best place for Sal, truly." Rose hiccupped.

"She's cruel."

"She's foolish. And as you said, Mr. Laurent." Sighing, Rose stood, and tried to brush snow off her skirt. "She measures the world by too short a yardstick. I think you did her good."

"I don't like the idea of Sal under her thumb."

"I don't think Sal would stay under anyone's thumb. And in my experience, the worst thing one can do is to trust that someone else cares for your child as you do. We will visit often, and not take Mrs. Cranstock's word for how things go, but Sal's."

"Sal will know that she *is* our child. Just as you say, Mrs. Russell. She belongs to everyone in our building."

"Everyone at the bakery."

"All of us," he said, brooking no disagreement, and Rose felt better.

JANE FELT DRAWN IN BY THE REEL AS SURELY AS IF IT TIED itself around her waist.

The fiddler had a jaunty way with a tune and an Irish drummer keeping him racing, too.

Dancers scattered under the tent that served ale and spread out on the surrounding ice. They watched for lumps in the ice, and sometimes missed them till it was too late, tripping and sliding on their rumps, and not caring much. Partly from beer, partly from high spirits. Everyone was glad to be free of the fog and snow.

When the music paused, and the dancers cheered, Jane felt bold enough to approach the fiddler. "I don't suppose you'd like a song while the dancers caught their breath?"

"I could use a rest for my fingers and that's the truth. What'll you give them, though?"

"*Lord Jamie Douglas?*" Jane sounded a little doubtful. She'd only have a few minutes, really, before Emery came back. But the music was irresistible, the crowd in high spirits, and she wanted a little fun too. She was as glad as anyone for a drop of freedom.

"La!" His sound was like a scoff, but his face split with a wide wrinkled grin. "That's a man's song, girl! What would you know about ships deep in the water, or being so in love you don't care if you sink or swim?"

His words stabbed deep into a pocket of feeling Jane hadn't known she hid inside.

Too much, she thought to herself. *Not enough, and far too much.*

She'd only wanted to sing. To sway while others danced. She didn't want too much for herself, not really.

Not for the frozen Thames to split wide and let the *Halia* sail straight up the river to her feet.

Not for Captain Brice to climb down the rigging, whole and safe.

She didn't wait for Emery to catch her there, or for the man to say one more thing. She ran.

Episode 18: The Shattering of the World

"It's funny. Only a few days and it seems like the ice has always been here." Jane shifted the big basket around to one hip, gripping it with her mittened hand.

"Is it funny? It seems more—Aggh!" Rose jumped, nearly dropping her own basket. "Someone pinched me!"

"What?" Jane looked around. Skaters were walking everywhere, trying to find bare patches of ice where they could slide, plus there were jugglers, the whoops of their audience drowning out the ringing clacks of the printing presses making handbills behind them.

Yes, there went a group of working men ambling toward the tent that had turned out beer and music nearly non-stop. One of them winked back at Jane.

"I never! The villain. I'd like something to throw at him."

Rose recovered herself. "Don't throw the rolls, we want to sell them." She paused. "I've never been pinched before."

"Well, not like that."

Jane was sensible to the fact that stepping down from their aspirational poverty to the bakery was one thing, and mixing out here on the ice with everyone London offered was quite another.

Surely there were lords and ladies among the stream of onlookers gawking at the extraordinary sights on the frozen Thames. But they had retinues, maids and footmen, very like the visit the Duke and Duchess had made to the Ladies' Own Bakery last year.

She and Rose were simply stirred in with the rest of London's everyone—from beggars to titles, everyone was visiting the ice.

"I'm so hungry. That puppet-player told me about the sheep they roasted on the ice and now I wish they'd do another."

Rose wrinkled her nose. "Didn't they scorch off the wool? The smell must have been horrid. Isn't it horrid enough when we scorch a skirt? Eat one of the rolls."

"I want to sell them all."

As ever, Rose was practical. "The journeymen and Emery have been baking every hour of the day and night for three days. We have piled up every basket we own and made bags of clean petticoats to bring them here, and they've all sold. We can afford to eat a roll."

Jordan came running, nimbly hopping over every chunk of ice in his way. Jane noticed his legs were long enough now to simply step over most of them. "Can I have another penny? There's such a fun game!"

He'd come from the direction of the gamblers. "What game?" Jane asked suspiciously.

"He said it was rooje et nwar. Funny name."

"That's *rouge et noir* and it's gambling, and remind me to teach you some French."

Jordan's face fell and Rose said, "What's the use if you won't teach the naughty words? You never translated half the things the men at the hotel used to yell."

"Well, they don't anymore." There had been little travel between the hotel and the bakery since the great snows, but what little there was had been blissfully free of insults. A few of the men even looked down with some appropriate shame when Jane passed them at their work, emptying dustpans in the street or holding the carriage horse of some visitor.

"Can't I gamble if I win?" Jordan wanted to know.

"That's why it's called gambling; you don't, not always. Where's Sal?"

Jordan pointed. Sal was standing ten yards away, feet in woolen stockings widely planted on the ice, and staring up at a man on stilts. Who was, Jane had to admit, impressive.

The children had come to work, but after so many days cooped up in their room with their father, always pleasant but so heart-breakingly vague, they wanted to move. And they moved everywhere.

If only she had the money to simply give them to play, Jane thought. All the children on the ice were twice as excited as the rest of the people, and half of them had left work of their own to be here. Apprentices of all sorts, from small chamber-maids younger than Sal to little boys covered with soot from sweeping chimneys and big ones carrying the stains of London's sewers.

"Sal?" called Jane.

Sal twisted, feet still in place, to point up at the man balancing on his stilts on the ice. Her mouth was a huge open O of astonishment.

Jane laughed. "Tell me when you're free," she teased, happy to let the girl go on gawking.

Agreeably, Sal bounced toward her over the bumps in the ice, holding out her hands for a basket. "I'll sell! I'll sell around his legs. Just give me the bread."

Laughing again, Jane handed it over.

"Around his legs?" asked Rose.

"It's a man on poles!" shouted Sal, louder than usual in her excitement.

"Stilts," said Jane.

"How tall?" Rose wanted to know.

"The poles are as tall as Emery, almost!" and Sal dashed away, wide flat bread basket in her arms.

"Heavens." Rose seemed impressed.

"THE LITTLE OVEN'S TOO HOT."

Emery was tired. Tired through to the bone. She'd been tired before in the months since they'd opened the bakery, but this was the height of it. Lifting every footstep was too much effort, yet somehow she did.

Wiggs lay flat on a pile of flour sacks snoring, chin pointed to the ceiling. Bailey had his hands on his hips, the flour-smattered apron nearly stiff. They had been baking, baking, baking, baking, and there was no time to launder it. At least the flour was clean.

"It is and that's the truth," Mr. Bailey admitted, frowning at the dark brown tops of the rolls. With their bread prescription, the crust should be brown, but not that brown.

"I thought we knew how to set this fire." Emery peered into the little oven with dissatisfaction, as if it contained someone unhelpful who fanned the coals too hot.

"We're still getting the measure of it. And we hadn't used it for bread, mostly cakes."

"Oh, uh, there's a ladyship here," said Tilly, sounding more awkward than Tilly ever felt, and Emery turned to see Lady Arnold—Dahlia—standing there in her bakery among its tables and tubs.

It was indeed as though a flower had bloomed in the middle of chaos. Dahlia's braid peeked out beneath her blue cape, its hood edged with embroidered leaves. She looked girlish and beautiful.

She came toward Emery immediately. "I had to see how you fared. Mr. Bailey. Oh I'm sorry, I didn't see Mr. Wiggs." She studied the way Wiggs' chin pointed to the ceiling and listened to the deep sounds coming out of him. "I suppose he would not have waked even if I blew a trumpet."

Mr. Bailey, who spit in alleyways and cheerfully swore like a pirate with the flour delivery man, became as shy as a young girl at her first late party.

He tried to sweep off his cap in respect, then realized in the heat of the bakery he wasn't wearing one. The realization made him blush. It was an odd effect on such a burly man. "Beggin' your pardon, your ladyship."

Dahlia merely gave him an indulgent smile, her attention turning straight back to Emery. "Miss Bickering, you look ill. You simply must rest."

Emery felt about as tongue-tied as Mr. Bailey. This was her element, and she was at home in it; but she didn't want Dahlia to see her looking like this. She must have terrible circles under her eyes. The look on Dahlia's face said that and much more.

She looked down at her own hair and saw how much flour dusted the braid.

"Lady Arnold, we are baking all we can." She said it quietly, calmly, so Dahlia would think she wasn't about to fall asleep on her feet. "Mrs. Wallace has not returned yet, and we can bake very few cakes in winter. We must take advantage of selling at the Frost Fair while we can."

"You'll be ill." Dahlia did not look persuaded. She looked more like she had just discovered one of the children digging in the garden.

"Mr. Bailey," Emery turned to him where he stood blush-ing, "put some water in the oven and let's have some tea.

With honey. Lady Arnold, you must let me show you to some-where more comfortable."

Emery hadn't forgot the over-browned bread. It was just that spending a few minutes alone with Dahlia was more important.

Mr. Bailey didn't question it. If there was one thing he grasped from this apparition of delicate beauty in their kitchen, it was that she was more important than life itself.

"I'll get Wiggs awake here in a minute and we'll make up those next pans," he assured Emery, who pasted a little guilt over her excitement as she led Dahlia out of the bakery proper.

"Anna, help Mr. Bailey shape that next batch of rolls, would you?" Emery asked as they passed through the shop.

Anna jumped, as if suddenly remembering where she was.

Then she said, "Yes, of course," without questioning further, and left Tilly the counter.

Emery followed Dahlia up the stairs hoping that would keep her from noticing how much of a struggle each step was.

More than a chance to rest, Emery was glad she could offer Dahlia a chair in their own little parlor. "I should have baked some biscuits. I didn't expect you."

Dahlia ignored the chair she pulled out. "I'm dying to kiss you."

Emery was awake *now*. "I'm covered with flour," she said, suddenly nervous of her feet.

"You *must* rest." Instead of taking the chair, Dahlia looked around the neat little apartment. "Where do you sleep?"

She took off her blue cloak, showing the fine woolen walking dress beneath. It had tassels all around, halfway down the skirt. The bakery would have destroyed it in five minutes.

Or set it afire, Emery thought as Dahlia deftly discovered which room was hers.

Rose was back in their room now that Mr. Russell had

gone, but Rose was out on the ice selling rolls, with Jane. And the children.

No one was here.

"You'll ruin your gown," she murmured as Dahlia untied the tapes that held up the bib to her dress.

"Nonsense."

"I feel like I'm being scolded like one of your children."

"Do you?" With a bold little look, Dahlia slid the overdress down Emery's hips for her and motioned her to step out. "You are not."

And as soon as Emery was free of her flour-stiffened outer things, Dahlia flowed up against her, right into her arms.

She should have felt cold, standing in the bedroom far from the banked stove; but she did not.

Indeed, she felt suffused with warmth as Dahlia's arms went round her waist.

She leaned her cheek against that soft temple and closed her eyes. "Surely you shouldn't have come."

"Why?" Tucked into the circle of Emery's arms, Dahlia sounded both irritated and relieved. "You think someone would suspect how I've been worrying about you day and night, wishing I could be here to make sure you ate and slept? You think they would know how it felt to see you down there like a walking statue, all gray and dusty?"

"I should bathe."

"I don't mean that." Dahlia's arms tightened. Emery could feel the warmth of her hand through the linen. It spread across the small of her back. "They wouldn't know. They'd never guess. Women are pure and delicate, haven't you heard? I could stand in Leicester Square and shout that I love you desperately, with all my heart, and they would only think us good friends. And me dramatic."

The expanding feeling in Emery's chest was not just new, it was miraculous. She slid her fingers down Dahlia's cheek, down to cup the point of her delicate chin, her thumb caressing the soft skin there. Pulled her up to meet her eyes. "I love you too."

There was a little nervous look around the edges of Dahlia's eyes that fled, and she threw her arms around Emery's neck, pulling her down into a kiss that was neither pure nor delicate.

She was the miracle, thought Emery as she cradled Dahlia there, feeling how warm she was, how soft, how steady even though she was so small.

Too magical for what Emery must say.

"Don't ever do that, shouting in the square," she murmured, caressing her cheek against Dahlia's. "Do not take risks for me."

"I *want* to. I've never taken a risk for anything. I married as I was told, had children as I was told, lived the life I was told to live—*you* are the first excitement I have ever had."

Emery loved hearing that. She had never been anyone's excitement.

Still she said, "I'm not exciting. I'm a baker." She pulled away a little, thinking she'd be more persuasive if she weren't wrapped entirely around Dahlia's person. She saw that she'd blotched flour onto the smaller woman's cheek.

She hadn't realized she was smiling till it faded.

Brushing at the dusty white spot, she said somberly, "I am a baker, and you a fine lady. And that is all aside from the way the world does not want us to be in love."

"They don't care!" A wild wave at the window unlike Dahlia's usual calm. "They only see what they expect to see."

"But when they see something they don't expect, they may get angry."

She couldn't wait another moment. She had to kiss away the angry, anxious look on Dahlia's face. So she did.

Yes, there was the taste of flour on her lips, but that was

her own fault. Dahlia was sweet, her lips softly warm, the taste of them better than tea, better than wine, waking up every inch of Emery's skin and warming her with no need for a fire.

When Emery pulled away again, she adored the sleepy look of distraction as Dahlia's eyes fluttered open.

"Look," she said softly, "I've already stained you with flour."

"I don't care," said Dahlia, pouting like a child but pulling Emery back into another kiss like a commanding lady.

The winter, the ice, everything fell away as the two of them got lost in the adventure of their kisses.

When they parted again, Dahlia's lips pink, the air between them sweet and warm with her breath, Emery said without thinking, "I wish bread didn't matter so much."

"It doesn't!" The wildness came back to Dahlia's eyes, this time a fire of excitement. "You should come live with me. I would happily have your sisters. Even Mr. and Mrs. Russell, if they like."

Dahlia must hear how absurd the idea was, Emery thought the second the words were out.

She rubbed the tip of her nose against that precious nose before her.

"You will not take in a family of bakers," she said, softly but firmly. "And I will not give up our bakery to spend a life in your velvets, accompanying you to the theater. It's a pleasant dream in its way, but that won't happen."

"That is just what would happen if I were a man!" Dahlia's eyes flashed with something else now; Emery thought it might be anger.

She would happily spend the rest of her life getting to know this woman's moods and better learning to read the feelings in her eyes.

But that wasn't going to happen. For too many reasons.

"No," said Emery, "it wouldn't. That is just what Lord Boislegrand offered my sister, and she didn't go."

"Anna doesn't *love* Lord Boislegrand!"

"True. But no one would have questioned why she might marry him. If I lived under your roof, it would only be charity; we can't marry. It's too many secrets, Dahlia, and it would be forever. Your servants already must wonder, and what would you tell your children when they get older?"

"I'd tell them I'm in love for the first time in my life, and it *matters!*"

Her brave, honest beloved.

"And your house," Emery said, just as softly still, "does it even belong to you? Where would you go, if your son put you out?" She tried to make a joke of it, tried to turn Dahlia in her arms to look around her cold, bare room. "Where would we put your velvets?"

Dahlia wouldn't budge.

"I won't let you give up on this, on *me*, before you've even truly tried." She gave Emery one more kiss, rather fiercer than the others, then moved to the bed. "This isn't over. But you need to sleep."

"I can't sleep." She could, though. Dahlia's kisses were like wine, warming through her middle and making her arms weak.

"You will. You're going to get in this bed and lie under the quilts perhaps for multiple hours, and rest. Because you can't be ill. I won't let you."

Perhaps Emery liked that stubborn streak in her ladyship because it was familiar. Like family.

The little crackle between them as Dahlia pushed her to sit down on the bed, though, was only theirs.

She looked up, for once shorter than Dahlia.

Who blushed a little. "Yes," she said, trying to keep her eyes on Emery's and failing, glancing toward the window and the door. "I would happily lie down there with you and never rise again."

Well, thought Emery. She was too astonished to think anything else. No one had ever said anything like that to her before.

Plus, the words flooded her with images of what that would be like, how soft and warm Dahlia would be *everywhere,* and she couldn't really speak.

But Dahlia just went on, "But not today. You look truly ill and if you don't sleep, you will only get worse. Even bakers must sleep."

"My lady, they don't." Surely she'd seen Bailey and Wiggs downstairs. Bakers often did work all hours and every hour.

"But you must. I know you are a baker, Emery. You were when I met you. But you are also only mortal, and you must sleep."

The linen sheets were freezing cold, but Emery knew they'd soon warm from her body, the way she'd been warmed in turn by Dahlia's kisses.

The little hand was gentle against her face, brushing back her hair, heedless of the flour.

"Sleep," she said, and despite Emery's conviction that sleep was impossible, she had slipped into its dark comfort before Dahlia even moved away.

Anna felt guilty leaving the counter to Tilly.

But she had shaped two more batches of rolls, they were rising in the pans, Mr. Bailey had both ovens full and in just a few minutes he'll pull those out to cool with Mr. Wiggs' bleary help.

Then Mr. Bailey ought to nap as well, but Anna felt a bit desperate to keep her appointment.

"I'll be back directly," she told Tilly, taking off her apron and laying it across the second counter.

"No worries," said Tilly cheerily. "If you don't come back soon, I'll help Mr. Bailey myself."

"*No!*" The idea of Tilly touching the ovens was more than alarming.

Tilly looked offended. "Only if he needs a bit of help."

This was foolish, sneaking away like this.

But everyone else had done it. Even Emery had Lady Arnold for company, and all Anna wanted was half an hour to herself.

Well, not to herself.

By the time she crept all the way up to the garret her skin was cold.

"You cannot expect to keep Miss Porter in this chilly air."

For once Miss Porter, who never seemed to mind being half-draped, agreed. "She's got it right, I can't stay."

"Just let me get this shoulder." Lord Zachary himself had a pink nose from the cold, yet his eyes fixed on Miss Porter's shoulder as though it were the last diamond in London and he had to have it in his pocket.

"It's too cold for—the dress Miss Porter is modeling."

It was too cold for how much skin Miss Porter was modeling, and that was so apparent surely Anna didn't need to say it.

"That shade of pink." Zachary pointed with the handle of his paintbrush as if seized by a fever.

"It's *frostbite.* Miss Porter, I do apologize. Lord Zachary is beside himself. You must wrap up and get warm."

"No! I just need—look, if Miss Porter must go, you sit there."

Anna felt that she'd turned to a block of ice.

Had this been inevitable?

Had she *wanted* this?

"Miss Porter, do wrap up. Are your feet quite warm? Lord Zachary." She turned away from the model as the woman hurriedly dropped the fichu she had tucked around her shoulders, and wrapped herself in a woolen dressing robe before throwing her cape over it all. "I'll return in a moment."

She walked Miss Porter down the stairs. A week ago she would have blushed to send the woman into the bakery. Now any embarrassment she felt escorting Miss Porter was secondary to the embarrassment she felt over Lord Zachary's indecent suggestion.

She returned to the garret alone.

He was still painting. He must have grasped a view of what he wanted to capture, as he did indeed seem desperate to get it down in oil before the short winter daylight faded.

"Sir."

"Oh good, you're back. Just sit—"

"*Sir.*"

He looked over his shoulder with genuine impatience. "Can you just save your lecture about my stupidity until this is done? I have been desperate to paint, it's been days, and I just have the idea of how to color this. Give me a moment."

"Then you must do it from memory. You have made an indecent suggestion, sir. I reluctantly agreed to help your painting. I never agreed to disrobe."

"Is it disrobing?" He still sounded distracted, daubing bits of color on the canvas.

Anna had to admit the daubs were coming together rather well.

"To uncover my shoulder? Yes."

Half of her didn't want to interrupt him. She wanted to see how the finished painting would look too. There was a magic to it, the colors coming together to make an image of warm woman's flesh that nothing else had quite achieved, not while she had seen Lord Zachary's paintings.

But she felt like she had to make herself quite clear, if only to herself.

"I am a baker. I am *not* a lady of the night."

"Well, no one said you were." He still didn't look.

He was there, but he wasn't with her. He was lost in a world where all the thoughts and feelings mixed in his head and came out his fingers.

She had to do this alone, she supposed.

"I am *not* a lady of the night," she muttered this time to herself. "I may have fallen, but I am not worthless. I have a profession, and a bakery, and my sisters. I will not marry Lord Boislegrand, no matter how he hangs about the bakery like a sad puppy and no matter how guilty I feel for leading him on. I will not take off my clothes for you to ogle, and I will not become less respectable than I already am. I won't do it."

He looked up, looking largely surprised she wasn't already in the chair.

Then he looked back, and it seemed her words threaded through the fog of his consciousness and he understood them.

He frowned, a lock of blond hair falling into one eye.

"I do not wish to compromise you, Miss Bickering."

"We are alone in your room!"

He looked about as if noticing that for the first time too. "Purely in a business capacity."

While it was fair for even unmarried women to visit men alone to conduct business, surely he knew that was rare, and people did not mean this kind of business.

"Miss Bickering. Can I assure you I only have honorable intentions?"

"No," she said plainly. "Even though—"

Even though he'd made no untoward moves.

He had done nothing lascivious toward Miss Porter, not even with his look. And surely he meant the same now.

She wasn't really going to disrobe.

But she might sit in the chair.

"Would it help for me to sit in the chair?"

"It wouldn't hurt," he said, blowing the hair out of his eye.

Reluctantly, she picked her way through his mess of tables toward the spot where the last light was fading.

"Here," he said impatiently, and took her hand to help her up.

His fingers were warm. *Alive.* There was a spark in them, something she could feel. Was it because he could paint?

He also seemed to stop at the sensation.

It was for only a moment, and if their eyes had met, it would have crossed the line into an inappropriateness Anna could not bear.

But he didn't meet her eyes.

He turned back to his canvas.

She didn't see what help she could be when he wouldn't even look at her now, only said, "Perhaps you could take off your shawl?"

Well, if it helped, she would. Even though as she unwound the wool, an icy breath of air seemed to freeze the front of her dress.

This far, no farther. She repeated it in her head over and over, while Lord Zachary used the curve of her shoulder to help him paint Miss Porter's skin from memory.

"Mr. Laurent. Did you want a tuppence loaf?"

He'd only stopped in the bakery shop to make sure things were going well. The harsh December had worsened all through January, and February showed no signs of stopping. While the energetic young ladies of the bakery never seemed to flag, he knew extended campaigns tired a person, and wanted to make sure one of the young ladies had not overextended themselves.

It was beginning to bear down on him that he was a drunk living over a bakery off the stale loaves his neighbors gave him.

Today, however, he only shook his head at Tilly's question. "Not just now, thank you."

She, a *bonbon* of skirts and yellow curls, was jerking her eyes constantly to the right trying to drag his attention to something.

There was only the sad viscount whose broken *fiançailles* with the eldest Miss Bickering had rendered him despondent.

"Is all well?" he asked under his breath, in case *mademoiselle* felt harassed.

"Mr. Lord Boislegrand is waiting to see Miss Bickering." Tilly's eyes kept shifting back and forth as if she could lift his lordship with them and deposit him outside in the cold.

"Ah."

It had borne in upon him, early in the ladies' tenure in this building, that the four sisters living next to his closet had no champions. He had been able to do little, but in his own small way he had tried to help, and the young ladies seemed to appreciate it.

It had bolstered his feelings, truth be told; not toward them, but toward himself. He had walked a long road back from dark places, and the young ladies reminded him that there were still good and bright things in the world. And that perhaps he might walk among them, even if he were not so good himself.

He'd noticed his lordship's presence several times, and perhaps today he could be of good service.

Mindful that Miss Bickering would not want his lordship frightened away—though that would be the simplest solution

—he approached the sad man slumped on a stool before the Bear Street window.

"Sir, did Miss Bickering expect your call?"

"No, no." The man waved him off.

This was a challenge.

He could simply lift the man and move him. Or perhaps he couldn't. Drink and sloth had taken much from him.

Of course there were other ways to move the man, but he kept at the top of his mind that Miss Bickering might not want the caller, say, rolled out the door.

He took a sneakier approach.

"How can I help you, sir? It pains me to see a fellow man so despairing, and in a bakery of all things."

Lord Boislegrand looked up as if just noticing that he was, in fact, in a bakery.

As the bakery had been turning out rolls day and night, there were few loaves for sale; still, the baskets behind Tilly held a few tuppence loaves, quarterns, and instead of a half-peck, more quarterns of the maslin that could be cut to a patron's requirements.

The gentleman on the stool looked as if he might be interested in the bread for a moment, then he slumped back. "Nothing, thank you."

"I did not mean just bread. Truly, sir, you cannot simply sit here day after day souring the milk with that look."

That made Lord Boislegrand sit up. "I'm not offending you, surely." He seemed to puff out his chest a bit with his denial.

"The young lady at the counter is not benefiting from your company, I will tell you that."

As if noticing Tilly's existence for the first time, Lord Boislegrand's eyes shot to her. She gave a little curtsey, clearly unsure what to do about lords looking her way.

The neighbor suspected that *mademoiselle* Tilly was not

that young; but neither was she old, and she was the kind of bouncy confection that a man liked to look at. Especially a man with a *tendresse* for the eldest Miss Bickering, who was also of generous figure and curling hair.

"Surely you wish to keep up manly appearances," he said, leaning closer to Lord Boislegrand to make the words more private.

"Yes, I do see your point." The fellow stood and brushed off his coat-tails. With the fury of baking, and several of the ladies out selling rolls nearly all day and all night, the shop was full of flour.

"Come, let us find a drink somewhere more *amicale* and you may tell me tales of your woe."

"No offense," said Lord Boislegrand, straightening his watch-chain, "but I had hopes of feminine company."

"And while I fully support your dreams, here we are. *Allons-y*."

And with that, the gentleman left the bakery on his own two feet, with a good-bye curtsey from Tilly.

All in all, a triumph.

HE RECONSIDERED HIS TRIUMPH ONCE THEY SAT AT A rough plank table over at The Bitter Rose.

"Now then, Remy," said his friend Owen, bringing them two tankards of beer while the barmaid across the room served the rest of the people streaming in now the sun was going down.

"I say." Lord Boislegrand peered around in the gathering gloom as if he'd never visited an inn before. Perhaps he hadn't.

His drinking partner sighed and settled himself in for a

long night of being punished for his good deed. That was what happened when one tried to be heroic in winter.

"So tell me your troubles," he said, never showing his reservations.

And not noticing the man in an oilcloth coat on the bench behind him, who jerked upright when he heard the proprietor say *Remy*.

TILLY DIDN'T KNOW IF SHE SHOULD LOCK THE DOOR ONCE the sun went down. Street custom had practically stopped weeks ago. Since the snows, many husbands continued to come, but less often. Women came, but not in rushes when the bread was fresh; now it had more to do with when they could pick their way through the snow and ice.

"Letter for you," said a boy even as he jingled the door bell.

Tilly gave him two farthings and studied the thick paper as the last of the sun went down. Letters were interesting; she wished there were an invisible way to open this one.

But it was folded tight, with a wax seal on the back, and no hint of its direction.

In the absence of all the ladies of the bakery, she wouldn't take the liberty.

"UGH!" GRUNTED ROSE AS RUSHING BOYS JOSTLED HER AGAIN.

"See the donkeys! Aren't they cunning?" Sal laughed, no doubt pointing at the animals on the ice.

"You see donkeys every day like that on the square," groused Jane.

Rose felt no panic, but she was tired of being shoved. No one gave her any quarter, and the crowds pushed close. Apparently donkeys on ice were high entertainment.

"Not these days," Sal pointed out with perfect logic, making Jane contemplate how long a month lasted to a child.

"There will be donkeys again. Rose, are you all right?"

"I think so."

In truth, Rose was fighting down tears, and not sure why. After all the tribulations of the last six weeks—Mr. Russell leaving, the fog, the snow, the ice, all the work that had gone into making the most of the Frost Fair—there was no reason to cry over a bump, or even donkeys on ice. Yet she wanted to cry.

They ought to go home and come back. They'd sold their bread, and there would be more waiting at the bakery. Every penny they made on this venture put back in their coffers what they'd lost over the last weeks on cakes and loaves.

Not that they had *coffers*. They had a money box, and Jane counted it. And it needed more coins.

But the thought of walking all the way back to Leicester Square, climbing the icy bank on its slippery stone steps, picking through the street with the children helping her so she didn't put a foot wrong on a frozen lump underfoot, all was exhausting to contemplate.

Some heavyset fellow, full of beery cheer or donkey excitement or both, stumbled into Rose, sending her flying forward.

She caught herself on her mittened hands, feeling one hand cut on the ice.

"How dare you!" she shouted with all the force in her small body.

Jane was there. The sound of Jane swinging the big square basket straight at the offending clod was very satisfying; by the sound of it she had used both hands. His *oof,* too, was satisfying.

Jane helped her up. "Clumsy oaf! Are you all right? We should go."

"We should come back with more bread but... Jane, I don't think I can."

"Never mind it. I can come back if need be. Come up now."

Standing quickly, Rose felt something she never did. She felt *queasy.*

Her mother had not been a fountain of information upon matters of marriage. Rose had felt many times in the past months grateful that Mr. Russell was such a kind, indulgent husband. Of course, that was exactly the kind of husband she wanted, so it was self-congratulation of a sort, but still, Rose felt it keenly.

She wished he were here with all her heart.

But he was not, and she had a suspicion too big to keep to herself any longer.

"Jane," she whispered, "I think I might be with child."

"What?!"

Rose hadn't meant it so, but Jane took this as a signal to clear their path off the ice faster than a whirlwind.

She held Rose's arm tight. "Jordan, watch where she puts her left foot. Sal, watch the right. No, *donkey later.* You! Move out of the way!"

"I'm fine, Jane, really," Rose tried to protest as they hauled her bodily across the width of the Thames.

A little snow had fallen that morning; it muffled the sounds of donkey hooves, making the Thames more quiet. The further they got from the revelers, toward the bank, the more Rose could hear something faint and far away.

Well, not that far away; it sounded like water.

"Listen."

They all stopped. Maybe Rose had imagined it?

But no, Jane heard it too.

She must have, because she took a deep breath and said, "Look around, children. It's been my whole life and more since there was a Frost Fair like this, and who knows when there will be another one?"

The children paused, and they must have taken in the sight. Rose could hear the tents with drunken singing and dancing and laughing, and all the babbling voices of people walking, gawking, buying trinkets, amazing themselves.

"How long will it last?" asked Sal, apparently impressed, which was quite a feat for a girl who felt that the Trojan Horse was only a rude idea.

"I think not much longer," said Jane. "And that's all right. One moment like this can change your life."

She grasped Rose's mittened hand in her own and squeezed. Rose knew what she meant.

"You mean selling the bread?" Jordan was nothing if not a man of bread.

"That, and... just think." Jane would not share Rose's news, but the children should remember this too. "You've climbed up on stone piers that are otherwise always surrounded by rushing water. You've seen London the way most don't. Your ordinary world stopped, and you had time to do something different. That's worth something. Change, and excitement, and fun matter." Jane sighed, and Rose wondered why.

"It wasn't all fun," muttered Sal with the grimness of someone who had spent too many days barricaded inside by the weather.

"No, it wasn't. But some of it was, and that's worth remembering," Jane told her.

Rose took a deep breath. This *was* a special place, and a special moment in time. It wasn't the way she'd have it; she wanted to have Mr. Russell right beside her. She'd rather that than even a seat in Parliament, for him.

But she was lucky, because Mr. Russell was still all right, and he would come home, and she had her sisters.

And, perhaps, a very exciting present for him when he returned.

ANNA TRIED NOT TO LOOK GUILTY WHEN SHE DISMISSED Tilly, but Tilly didn't care. It was only fair, as she'd have slow work picking her way across the ice to get home.

When she ushered Tilly out, she stood by the door, looking out over the square. The thawing and freezing ice, mixing with snow and frosted by fog, made the pavement a cold, craggy mess; the road itself even more so. In the square itself, the greenery looked defeated, its shoulders all sagging beneath wintry weight. The bright, bright moonlight made everything look white, streaked with the black of the park fence iron bars and the statue looming above it all.

Even in the cold, she wanted to cover her face with her hands. She had never felt less like a lady than sitting in that chair. Yet the painting that was emerging on Lord Zachary's canvas was one of his best. He could see it too, and he'd been so pleased.

Theirs was a peculiar cooperation. Anna had had drawing lessons; she had no great talent for putting images on paper. She didn't need to use any of Lord Zachary's expensive oils to know that the medium would make no difference.

He had that talent; yet he couldn't imagine the whole composition from its start without her prompting. With it, he was doing something really fine.

She watched the few people in the square. A guest descended from a fine carriage before Jacquier's Hotel; Anna thought for a second of Captain Brice, and hoped he was well. Lady Arnold's house at the far corner looked lit and cheery; while on the other side—

Was that the tailor Mr. Morley? Out walking?

With Mr. Keales?

Anna couldn't be sure, not even in the bright moonlight; they were far away, her breath fogged in front of her, and her mind was full of other things. She didn't care what Mr. Keales did anymore, after all.

Why must she live her whole life constantly worried about others watching? Was it born in her, or could she not shake the training?

And if she no longer cared about Mr. Keales and the opinion of the Bakers' Guild, why was it so disconcerting to put herself in front of Lord Zachary's gaze, subject for his paintbrush?

Anna went back inside. The bakery bled heat out the door as she closed it behind her. The shop had been cool before she'd gone outside; now, coming back in, it felt hot.

Only seconds later, it opened again; she hadn't seen her sisters coming.

"Stop baking." Jane yelled it before she even had the door open.

Anna accepted it was urgent. She was in no mood to argue, for once. "Mr. Bailey! Stop the baking," she called through the door to the bakery proper as her sisters struggled in the door.

"Where's Emery?" asked Jane, flushed and gripping Rose's hand as if she might blow away.

"Sleeping upstairs. Why ever—"

"Sal, go wake her. Tell her to hurry."

Sal bounded out and up the stairs as Anna took the bread baskets away from Jane. There were three, awkwardly bound together with twine; Rose had another, and Jordan two more.

He took his with him into the bakery to see what stopping baking might entail. Any dough in progress, of course, would have to bake.

"Did anything happen?" Anna went to help Rose off with her shawl. "And here I was worried about the letter."

"What letter?" asked Rose. "Oh, is it from Mr. Russell?"

Sal bounded back. "She's right behind me!"

She was. In shift and petticoats.

"*Really,* Emery!" Anna was aghast. Here she had felt shame all afternoon for sitting in a chair and letting Lord Zachary stare at her clothed shoulder, and Emery did *this.*

"Sal said an emergency. Is there? What's happened? Is anyone hurt?"

"Not like that! Go help Jordan, dear," said Anna, and Sal tripped off to find her brother.

"Is the letter from Mr. Russell?" demanded Rose.

"What letter?" Emery rubbed her eyes. "This is what comes of sleeping."

"We'll open the letter, but first the news." Jane—*Jane*—was bouncing up and down on her toes.

"What news? Why did we stop baking?" Anna was more confused by Jane's excitement.

"We stopped baking? What happened?" Emery peered around the room, blinking hard.

"The ice is melting." Jane brushed that aside as if the once-in-a-lifetime frozen Thames was a paltry afterthought. "We heard it. Rose, tell them the *news.*"

"I'm not even sure of it!"

"Well, you might as well tell us." Anna thought this all called for some oldest-sister-ing, but wasn't sure how to do that when she felt like hiding her face.

"But is the letter from Mr. Russell?" Rose was nearly crying, and that Anna didn't expect. No one expected.

Quickly, Anna broke the seal. "No, it's from Aunt Eden."

"Oh." Then Rose *did* cry.

"Oh no, darling, it's all right!" Anna crowded in to hug her, along with Emery and Jane both.

She murmured reassurances and smoothed the curls that had escaped Rose's braid.

"I know, it's all right, and I'm so lu—*lucky!*" Rose burst into full-blown sobs.

After a few more moments of soothing and shushing, and Rose wiping her face on Anna's apron, it was clear Jane was literally jamming her own teeth shut to keep from saying more.

Anna thought maybe the oldest-sister behavior called for here was just a calm question. "Are you all right, Rose?"

"I think so. A bit ill in my stomach, and... I think, all in all, I might be having a baby."

She nearly whispered it, and the silence was indeed a moment they'd all remember, longer than they remembered the Thames in ice.

Then Emery picked up Rose bodily and whirled her in a circle, and Anna *whooped*.

Jane burst out laughing. "See? See?"

"Oh! Emery, put her down, don't do that!" It seized Anna that Rose mustn't be crushed.

"I'm sure even increasing ladies get hugs, Anna," said Emery, who put her sister down but could not stop her huge grin.

"Mr. Bailey says the bakery is—uh, what?" Sal, head through the half-open door, gaped at all four sisters, Emery in her underthings.

For once, Anna didn't care at all about the bakery.

"We'll be in after a minute. Let's upstairs, my chickadees, and have a minute to ourselves, shall we? And a dress for Emery."

Emery ran up the stairs first, screaming for joy, with Jane

after, clearly unable to stop laughing. Rose followed them, sobbing and laughing at the same time herself.

The joy felt like it went all the way down to Anna's toes. Down to her fingertips. All the way to the ends of her *hair*.

She followed more slowly, but she was no less delighted than her sisters, and no less grateful.

THAT NIGHT ONCE THE FIRES WERE BANKED, MR. WIGGS and Mr. Bailey sent to get much-earned sleep, the children home, and the dinner served, Jane remembered the letter. "So what does Aunt Eden say?"

"Did you write to her?" Emery could not stop patting Rose on the shoulder, as if for a job well done.

"I never did."

Anna fetched the open letter from her apron pocket. "Ah, quite a bit congratulating us for not writing, as she won't give us a bit of help, et cetera et cetera... Oh, my."

"What?" Rose was curious, as her last encounter with Aunt Eden had been very educational.

"She wants Jordan."

"What on earth?" For once Jane had nothing else to say.

"She wants to give him a place at Walbey Hall, see if she can find a profession for him."

"He *has* a profession. Baker." Emery shoved food into her mouth with the speed of someone who'd baked for three days straight.

Anna tapped the corner of the paper against her lip. "But if he found something new to do? Sal is going to school, after all."

"Sal *wants* to go to school, and she has gifts. Jordan's gifts are bread," said Emery with her usual simplicity.

"Oh, we can talk about Aunt Emery tomorrow. What a

sour biddy she is, after all. And tonight's no night for that."
Jane had stars in her eyes; they sparkled just like the ones
outside had done before all this long, cold winter had
descended upon them.

Jane's eyes reminded Anna that one day, the stars in the
sky would sparkle again too.

"Jane, I love you."

That made Emery's fork pause mid-air.

"I know, dear." Jane reached over and patted Anna's arm,
too. Everyone was in a patting mood.

"I mean I love you no matter what you do at night that
you won't tell us about."

The good feeling in the room settled a bit, became
heavier.

"I know, dear," Jane said more slowly. "Thank you."

"I hope you—" Anna couldn't confess what she herself
was doing. This wasn't a time for confessions; maybe only
broad forgiveness. "I hope we all remember that we love each
other, that we are *family*, wherever we go, whatever we do."

"I hope so too," said Emery, staring down into her plate of
bread and cabbage.

Anna jumped up out of her chair and ran around the table
to hug Rose. Just around the shoulders, afraid to touch her
anywhere else. "We should *celebrate*, Mrs. Russell!"

"Well, we've been too busy to bake any cakes!"

They all laughed louder than Rose's remark perhaps
deserved. The laughter freed all kinds of tensions that had
jabbed them for a long, long time.

THAT NIGHT THE THAMES STARTED TO THAW.

The center of the river softened first, and several of the
printing presses broke through the ice. Those who saw them

carried away in the rush of black water ran to the dancing tents, and there was a general rush toward the banks.

The thaw moved slowly enough for people to escape, but too quickly for the tents. The one closest to the printing presses collapsed slowly as one of its pegs was carried off, and when the water grabbed the edge of its tarpaulin, it dragged down with furious force and the tent was sucked into the water's flow.

A groan traveled through the rest of the people even as they scrambled for the harder ice closer to the bank.

The fun was over. The Frost Fair was done.

Episode 19: Breathe

"Where's the piss pot?" Bailey groaned and turned over on his pallet.

Wiggs muttered something about *cellar.* Sometimes in winter they kept it upstairs, as it froze in the cellar; but the past few days had been so busy it was still down there.

"Nah," grumbled Bailey as he staggered to his feet. The neverending days had stiffened his muscles, and he rolled his shoulders before stumbling towards the mews door.

"Wait."

Bailey paused as Wiggs pushed with his arms and jack-knifed his own body to standing, then lurched to the side like a much older man.

"Whuffor?" mumbled Bailey. He was blurry and needed to piss.

"No reason to open the door twice." Wiggs, showing his reverence for the warmth pooled around the banked ovens, waved a hand to show he'd follow along.

The bite of the outside air was indeed brutal, and both

men pulled their woolen collars tight as they shuffled over the remaining, persistent ice toward the sewer drain.

Both shrugged into position with the delicacy of grown men on such occasions. Careful to point, but not look. The winter sky, so furious these last few weeks, was fogged and quiet.

Then the door to Ladies' Own Bakery slammed shut with a crack in the night like a thunderclap.

THE OPEN DOOR HAD LET COLD AIR ROLL HEAVILY ACROSS the floor, raising the warmer air above it.

Inside the littler oven's chimney, that warm air nudged a clump of ash that had been quietly smoldering for the previous two days. The warm breath of air blew the small spark into a flame.

The same air contained motes of flour, which floated everywhere in the bakery. On the floorboards, on the tables, and most importantly, in mid-air.

Just enough flour to ignite.

A column of flame and hot air rushed up the chimney, sucking the door shut.

And spilled down out of the chimney as well.

Quicker than thought, every speck of flour floating in the bakery ignited its neighbor.

All their strength, meant to feed the lives of hundreds of Londoners, burst into flame in a moment.

The explosion burst out both doors, the seams of the chimney, the flames a mighty roar.

THE SOUND WOKE ALL FOUR SISTERS AT ONCE.

The sound, and the *thud* underneath them, a noise so fast and hard on the floors, the very walls—they knew at once something had happened that should not have happened.

Jane, who kept her shawl by the door, flew down first. Each step of her bare feet slapped against the wooden stairs.

The door between the stairway and the bakery stood ajar.

She ran through the silent shop. Blackly scorched, the door to the bakery proper lay on the floor, and a similar mark stained the ceiling above.

Anna arrived just behind her.

"What happened to the door?"

"It's broken."

"It's burned."

"Why is it on the floor?"

Their voices broke over each other, interrupted each other with their confusion. The door shouldn't be on the floor. The black scorch mark made no sense.

The acrid smell added to the confusion. It wasn't just that their bakery never smelled this way. It was that they had never smelled anything like it.

Emery arrived with her dress strung around her neck like a scarf, obviously still stung from rushing downstairs without a dress earlier in the day. Rose was behind her, moving slowly stair by stair. "What's happened?"

Anna reached the bakery itself first.

Black scorch marks were everywhere, clustered above the second oven, the top of which hung sickeningly askew. There was a hole in its chimney. That made no sense either. There should not be a hole.

Jane crowded in next, and Emery.

"Fire! Fire above!"

Afterwards no one could remember which sister shouted it. They all heard it and felt it at the same time, even Rose as she bumped into the door-jamb rushing to follow her sisters.

She tripped over a half barrel, the sort they used to mix the dough. It shouldn't be in the middle of the floor, but it was. The tables were knocked over, all the bowls, askew everywhere, many cracked or broken.

The crackling sound of fire was ominous, and now that the sisters could see it, they saw it everywhere. Everywhere little licks of flame clung to the old wooden beams, eating, growing, and getting faster.

And everywhere the awful acrid stench of something burning.

Mr. Bailey and Mr. Wiggs were there, beating at the flames with woolen jackets. Behind them the door to the mews hung askew on one hinge, the bottom one.

"She's on fire!" Mr. Bailey shouted, perhaps unnecessarily, but in the confusion his words made sense. They were all that made sense. The flames, the scorch marks, the smell, and increasingly the heat, none of that made sense; but the more times someone said *fire*, the more real it became.

"Don't let it reach the flour," shouted Wiggs.

Rose gained her feet again and shuffled back the way she had come.

Emery ran to the trough, opening the ball joint and letting water flood in. Snatching off the dress around her neck, she dumped it in the water, then took the sodden mass to the far wall to beat at the flames as well.

Jane turned and ran.

Of all the things Anna could see, that was the one that made her feel the most frightened. "Jane!"

"I won't let our money burn," Jane shouted.

Everything went so slowly that Jane expected to pass Rose on the stairs.

But no, she found Rose already at the top, pounding on the door of their neighbor.

"Mr. Laurent! Mr. Laurent, you must get up."

Jane rushed into their rooms, to her bedroom, the one she shared with Anna. It seemed fine and whole, but still she scrambled under the bed for the money box that she stored there each night after she counted its contents.

"Mr. Laurent! Mr. Laurent!" Rose still shouted in the hall.

Jane heard Zachary come pounding down from above.

"Miss Rose—"

Jane heard no more words. With a rending crash, the door to the little closet next-door was rent from its hinges; Jane heard it hit the floor. Rose had not done that.

"He's not here," she heard Zachary say. "Your foot is cut. Can you find yourself some shoes?"

Jane just kept telling herself how she mustn't lose the money. If the box fell open while she ran, the money would go everywhere. It was all they had. Terror pounding in her head, Jane ripped the sheet from their bed and wrapped the box, shouting all the while, "I'll find them for her!"

His steps down the last flight of stairs sounded heavy. Jane did not realize till many days later it was the sound of him carrying Rose down.

Cradling the money box bundle under one arm, Jane ran toward Rose and Emery's room before remembering she and Anna should have shoes too. The need to run in two directions at once froze her in the parlor, a little bubble of terror inside her whispering that this was how she would die. Burning alive because she couldn't decide which pair of shoes to fetch first.

She *could not die yet.*

Dashing to Rose and Emery's room she threw shoes, stockings, whatever was in reach atop the bed's quilt. She ran with the quilt to the parlor, and put in her sheet-wrapped box and her mother's silver candlesticks.

Shoes. In an instant she grabbed her own shoes and Anna's, for some reason skipping stockings or any of the linens that she took in the younger sisters' room. Her mind was no longer a single spool of thought, and nothing went in a straight line.

When she arrived back in the bakery shop, unable to remember anything about coming downstairs, Rose was there gripping the bread counter.

"Should I run outside?"

"I don't know. Not yet. Let me see what's happening in the bakery."

"It's on fire, I know it's on fire."

Through the empty door, Jane found Rose was right.

SMOKE BLOCKED ANNA'S VISION PATCHILY, HERE AND there. All the air was gray haze, and above her smoke billowed from the freely burning ceiling planks. It even seemed to gather about her feet.

Anything could have come out of the haze, but what did was Lord Zachary.

He took a flour sack from the pallet where the journeymen slept, and ran to the sink, plunged it into the water. Even as he did, he shouted "Get out!"

He couldn't make her. This was her bakery. Protecting it was her job. She was the oldest.

Wiggs and Bailey had seen Emery's example. They stuffed their jackets in the water, trying to make the wool soak instead of float, then used them to slap around themselves everywhere.

Anna was doing it too, with her flour sack.

Even as Lord Zachary copied them, slapping upward with heavy dripping cloth, he shouted at her.

"Go! Anna, you must get out!"

That made no sense. This was her bakery.

Emery and the journeymen chased licks of fire crawling across the floorboards. They fed on the flour dust that lay everywhere.

Still-full flour sacks lay nearby on the floor.

Anna saw another flame flicker behind the oven, crackling on the wall.

The wall the bakery shared with the houses next-door.

Perhaps she should have had imagined the entire square bursting into flames, but all Anna could think was that this was her bakery. Her bakery. She darted everywhere she could reach to slap her wet sack on the flames.

It seemed to go on for hours, though it could've only been minutes.

There was so much fire and her sack was so small. Every inch of the room seemed to welcome the fire with open arms, and it hid in the cracks and around corners.

When Zachary turned to assure she was gone, she was still very much there, behind the oven, swinging her arm as hard as she could to slap wet cloth all the way to the ceiling.

Swearing, he crossed the room in a few strides, kicking broken half barrels out of his way and shoving aside the toppled tables.

Dropping his sack, he seized her round the waist with one arm, and then swung the other under her knees.

"At least go into the shop." His voice was fast, urgent, completely unlike it had ever been before.

"I have to help." Anna kicked a little, but didn't want to hurt him. "I have to help, you can't stop me!"

"My art is all I have, which means you are half of something irreplaceable." He said nothing else, only dumped her on the floor next to Rose and strode back into the bakery proper.

"Anna, is it bad?"

Anna turned to her sister and realized Rose must be in

her own agony, not being able to see what was happening. "There's fire everywhere. On the ceiling. The second oven has come apart. I don't know what happened."

"What *could* have happened?"

Anna had no idea. But if she could not go back in the bakery, she must—

There was no other option. Lord Zachary had his interests to protect, but she had hers. She *would* go back in.

"Rose, you are always brave. You know where you are. If I yell to run, you run out the front door."

"I'll go now!"

"It's so cold. You'll get ill. Only go out if you must, and if you do, I'll find you."

"I'll take the bundle."

That was the first time Anna noticed the bundled quilt on the counter. And where was Jane?

Was this really a time for Jane to disappear?

"If you can; if not, leave it. I'll be right back."

She hoped as she ran back into the bakery that she was telling the truth.

Never in her life had Jane expected help from men.

Now she ran for it.

She burst through the foyer of Jacquier's hotel, senseless to her bare feet on its rich carpets, already shouting. "Fire at the bakery! Fire!"

An officious young man came forward between the receiving room's heavy gilt chairs. "Miss, this is a respectable—"

Jane grabbed the lapel of his coat and jerked him closer.

"If we burn, you burn with us," she said, with every ounce of vicious conviction she could muster.

He only looked at her for a moment.

"Fire! Fire at the bakery!" he took up the shout, and Jane saw maids and footmen come running in various stages of dress.

Trusting for once that a man would do what she needed, Jane ran on.

The doctor's house was only a few doors away. She wanted him.

The butler at Dr. Shelton's house answered the door in disarray. His eyes nearly bulged from his head. He too was extraordinarily concerned with propriety at this horrific moment. "Miss, this is—"

Jane shoved past him and shouted as loudly as she could, "Dr. Shelton! Dr. Shelton, we need your help."

Perhaps the gentleman had already been woken by the commotion. He ran into the foyer himself, untucked shirt billowing around him and without boots. "What is it? Gunfire?"

"A fire. A fire in the bakery. They're putting it out. I fear burns."

"I'm not a surgeon, madam, I am a physician—"

"Don't you think I know the difference? You've studied medicine and you must know something. Today you can help someone more than just holding their hand." Jane grabbed him by the sleeve and dragged him towards the door. His choices were to come with her or lose a sleeve, possibly an arm.

"Mr. Bushill, fetch my old boots."

EMERY LET HER SICK ANGER TOWARDS THE FIRE TRYING TO destroy her bakery drown out the despair of betrayal.

She couldn't have loved this room more had she built

every board of it with her own two hands. What had happened? How had it turned on her?

For a second she imagined with wild terror that the children had been here. But no, they'd gone home to sleep. It felt like months ago. It had been hours.

She lost count of how many times she ran to the sink to soak her dress then back to the bags of flour still stacked on the floor. It was a fortnight's worth of flour, and water would ruin it. But better that than have it burn.

Wiggs was coughing, so hard that it forced Emery to notice her own coughing. Bailey seemed made of iron, but ventured so close to flames that Emery feared he too would be scorched.

She had never felt so helpless. She ought to send them away; wouldn't a master baker do that? But she needed their help. She couldn't do this alone.

She had no idea where her sisters were, only a sharp drawing in her mind of every flame in the room, and a dogged determination to chase them all down and stomp them out.

ROSE NOTICED THAT THE SHOP WAS FULL OF SMOKE. How long had it been there? She coughed, her throat feeling dry and raw.

Gathering the edges of the quilt bundle, she dropped lower.

It was a little easier to breathe. If she must, she'd crawl to the door.

Around her strange men appeared. They didn't speak to her, only shouted among themselves. There was running to the bakery proper; she couldn't tell how many of them went through.

She clutched the quilt close and wondered every second

how she'd know to abandon her spot and go out. *Was this the right moment? Was this?*

DIMLY ANNA NOTICED LORD ZACHARY SHAKING HER shoulder and shouting in her ear.

"Is there more?"

She came out of her fog of repetition. It was hard to see, hard to breathe.

There were so many more men. She hadn't seen them come, but they were everywhere, shouting, some of them dunking bowls in the sink trough and throwing water on the walls. She couldn't see any more flames.

That bright orange color had become all there was in the world, and she peered hard. "I don't see more?"

"Wiggs!" Lord Zachary had Anna's wrist in his hand now, but turned to where Mr. Wiggs knelt on the floor, coughing so hard Anna feared it would injure him, batting weakly at the scorched wood with his jacket.

He finally looked up at Lord Zachary after he shouted the third time.

"Wiggs, we must get out of here. We need air."

"Don't open the door," Wiggs mumbled; Anna could just hear it.

But she didn't know why he said that. The smoke was thick. They must clear it out.

"Where's Bailey?" His lordship was urgent.

She recognized other men now, young men from the hotel down the street, men who had come to get bread and apologize during the storm.

They were there in coats and no coats, some in boots, most with no hats, and they poked under every table, looking for flame. They coughed too.

Anna shoved at Zachary's arm to set her free, then ran behind the small oven.

Emery and Mr. Bailey were there, shoulder to shoulder, and they too were still whacking wet wool against the walls, but there were no more flames.

"We must go out!" Anna shouted, yanking on Emery's arm.

Later they would decide the deep gouges on Emery's skin were Anna's fingernails.

Looking around, Emery grasped Mr. Bailey by the collar.

"Out!" she yelled, as if the noise of the blast and the smoke had made them all deaf.

He nodded. Seeing Emery turn seemed to wake him and he turned too.

It wasn't till they were coughing together in the mews, the smoke drifting away into the black sky, that Anna shouted "*Rose!*" and started back in.

"Anna, *stop!*"

This time Lord Zachary shoved Anna into her sister's arms. Maybe Emery could keep her in place.

"Stay here and breathe. I'll get Rose."

Crouched on the floor by the counter, arms wrapped around the bundle Jane had left her with, Rose wondered if everyone forgot her.

Or if all her sisters had died.

She shivered, she didn't know why; the shivers shook her from top to bottom and she just clutched the bundle tighter.

She wanted her husband, wanted his arms around her desperately.

She wanted her mother.

She didn't recognize any of the footsteps or voices. She had not been so confused since she'd fallen blind. Who they were, she didn't know; only gripped the bundle tighter.

Then she heard Lord Zachary's voice. "Miss Rose!"

"*Sir!*" She had not meant to scream.

She felt his arms go around her and he lifted her; with her viselike grip on the bundle, he lifted that too.

Then paused.

"I don't want to carry you through the bakery. It's full of smoke. I must look above and make sure the fire has not traveled. Will you be well outside for a moment? Your sisters are in the mews. They're not hurt."

"Yes, I'll be fine." As long as her sisters were fine.

It was cold on the pavement; the ice burned like fire. Shivering, Rose wanted to sit if only to take the weight off her feet.

Neighbors had come, drawn by the noise, the explosion and the shouting. She didn't recognize any of them either, but now she was cold, too.

Anna had been right. Anna had been right about everything. It was icy here, and Rose felt like she was dying from the feet up.

Then she heard Jane's scream. "*Rose!*"

Not noticing how similar it was to the noise she'd just made, Rose didn't dare let go of her burden but she wanted to. She wanted to reach for her sister. "I'm here, Jane!"

Then Rose heard some sort of scuffle. "There. Dr. Shelton. *Do* something."

"I am not a surgeon," Rose heard him mutter, but someone's hand touched her cold foot.

"We must get her inside. She's bleeding."

"She is? We must get her shoes on!"

"A bandage first," said the man Rose recognized now as Dr. Shelton, their sometime customer, "and for you."

"Me?"

"Look at your feet. You ran on the ice with bare feet."

JANE WASN'T WORRIED ABOUT HER FEET. ROSE MUST GET warm.

Rose wouldn't be out here if the inside were still hospitable. Jane looked about wildly.

Her eyes landed on Mr. Morley's tailor shop across the street.

"You." She grabbed a man in a coat who stood gaping on the pavement. "Find my sisters, will you? We'll go to the tailor shop."

"They're in the mews!" yelled Rose, only slightly muffled by being gathered against Dr. Shelton.

The man shouted agreement and ran down Bear Street, tripping and falling almost as soon as he started.

Jane moved to help him, but he clambered up, waved. "I will!" he called over, keeping Jane where she was, and kept going, rather more slowly.

Dr. Shelton looked—Jane couldn't describe it; something between panic and shock. "I can't carry her across the street."

"Yes you can." Jane felt able to do it herself; she would, if Dr. Shelton tried to leave Rose on this ice.

Rose, shivering so hard her teeth rattled, said, "I'll walk."

"I'll do it."

Jane faintly recognized the man who spoke from the pavement, one who'd come in often since his wife couldn't brave the snow. He wore a rough gray scarf and heavy brown coat.

She'd remember his face the rest of her life.

Without another word he caught Rose up crooked in his arms, staggered forward across the spikey ice to the door of Mr. Morley's tailor shop.

Jane pounded on the door the way she had the rest. "Mr. Morley! Let us in. We must come in, just for a few minutes. Have mercy."

It wasn't Mr. Morley who opened the door; it was a woman. Jane didn't care. Only rushed past her, gesturing to the man carrying Rose to follow.

Mr. Morley, nightcap flying, appeared before Rose was settled. "You can't come in here! My shop will stink of smoke!"

Here was one obstacle to which Dr. Shelton felt equal. "Call upon your humanity, man. I'll buy your damn wool scraps, just give me a few. I must make a bandage."

"Blood!" screeched Mr. Morley. "On my floor!"

The woman—surely the unfortunate Mrs. Morley—had more heart, or more presence of mind. She disappeared behind a narrow door and reappeared with a handful of wool pieces, most of them no bigger than a few fingers' worth.

Dr. Shelton didn't mind.

"Here, let me put that down—" He tried to take the bundle from Rose's arms.

"*No! I have to watch it!*" screamed Rose.

HAVING BUNDLED LORD BOISLEGRAND INTO HIS WAITING carriage, still as sorry for himself as earlier, but drunker, the neighbor from the closet strolled up the icy street.

It was an odd circumstance that made drinking partners of him and a viscount, in a disreputable tavern no less.

Odd, or perhaps peculiar; but he did not think the young ladies who had taken over the bakery peculiar.

No, he thought them miraculous.

As he drew toward the square, he noticed there were unusual numbers of people out and about. Always alert to danger, next he smelled smoke in the air, then saw people pointing.

Shouts in the distance.

"Fire! Fire at the bakery!"

He broke into a run.

All along the north side of the square he could see smoke, black and gray, drifting away from the bakery doors, and people gathered, standing, staring and pointing, some running.

As he drew closer, he heard a scream—not from the bakery, but from the tailor's shop just steps ahead.

"*No! I have to watch it!*"

Little Mrs. Russell. Little Rose.

He burst through the tailor's door still running.

A cluster of people stood around Rose on the floor.

"What happened? Are you hurt?"

"Oh, Mr. Laurent!" And for some reason, faced with someone recognizable and kind, Rose's tears began to flow.

Unhesitating, he knelt beside her, putting his arms around both the bundle and Rose. "There there, *ma petite*," he shushed her, rocking her slightly while Dr. Shelton tucked clean wool around her feet.

"I wish I had a stocking," muttered the physician.

"Yes!" Jane loosened a corner of the bundle in Rose's arms and untucked a wad of stockings.

"Perfect," murmured the man of lancets. "And you next, Miss Jane."

"I must go and fetch my sisters—"

"*Anna!*" Rose cried as if she were little again. She would not entertain the idea of her sister leaving, that was clear.

"I will get them. Where are they, Miss Jane?" Mr. Laurent cast a wary eye toward the door. "Not inside the bakery?"

"In the mews. He said they were fine. We sent a man. I don't know how long ago."

"I'll find them," he said without hesitation, taking only seconds to put Rose back on the floor with a *shh, shh* in her ear before racing back out.

"She's bleeding on my floor!"

Rose, braced a little by Mr. Laurent's appearance, shouted up at the tailor. "Be *quiet!*"

Emery coughed so much her belly hurt. Her throat and chest—everything hurt, including her hands. She might have burned them, or rubbed them raw swinging the wet sacking; she couldn't tell.

There were voices shouting in the bakery, but no flames. Emery couldn't see any.

She wanted her sisters. To be quiet in their rooms again. To watch them sleep.

She only had Anna, sitting on the cobblestones next to her; she gripped her sister hard, and Anna gripped back.

The hazy gloom in the mews showed the smoke's course, how it drifted and smudged over the moonlight.

Pounding shoe leather came toward her. When she looked over her shoulder, it was their neighbor. "Miss Emery!"

"Anna, it's Mr. Laurent. He's fine," said Emery, she didn't know why. Maybe because Anna hadn't bothered to look.

"Can you walk?" asked Mr. Laurent, puffing as he drew near. "Are you hurt?"

"No!" insisted Anna, then bent double with a fit of coughing that shook her down to the ground. "No," Anna wheezed, "we're not hurt. Have you seen Jane?"

"She's in the tailor's with Rose. She's asking for you."

"The tailor's!"

Anna struggled to her feet, just as Mr. Wiggs shook again in another fit of coughing.

"Do you know anything of physic?" Anna put her hand on Mr. Wiggs' shoulder where he lay on the stones. "They need help."

"Dr. Shelton is at the tailor's too." Clearly calculating how many people there were in both places, Mr. Laurent's eyes reckoned the physician should come here; but in the end he did what Rose asked. "Let me take you there."

And helped Emery to her feet.

She hadn't realized she wasn't standing. Her legs felt like water; she couldn't breathe.

She wanted to go back inside.

But she wanted her sisters more.

"Come," she said, and stumbled.

Mr. Laurent saved her from falling with a hand to her shoulder, roughly.

"*D'accord.* Stand a minute. Just a minute."

And running to the mews door, he shouted in French. Several young men appeared, clambering over the broken portal.

Two of them on either side hauled Mr. Wiggs and Mr. Bailey to their feet. Mr. Wiggs looked gray; Mr. Bailey was silent, head hanging down. Emery was terrified he was dead.

Coming back to her, Mr. Laurent looped her arm around his neck, used his other arm to brace Anna by the waist.

"It's not far," he said soothingly, like he would to children, and Emery had the unshakeable sense he'd done this before.

"WHAT IS THE NOISE, MR. SPARKS?"

Lady Arnold felt utterly safe in her large house, but it bore upon her that Mr. Sparks, as he teetered toward the front door in dressing-gown and nightshirt, was no one's great idea of protection.

He stood in the open door, unwilling to brave the cold, and peered out.

"Commotion up the street," he said, his choppy words emphasizing how he'd been asleep only minutes before. Lady Arnold descended another stair, then two; she wanted to see, but it *was* cold, and the bitter air crept in.

"Where? Is it in the park?" It wasn't impossible some ruffians had broken into the park, perhaps set off fireworks. Maybe that explained the odd sound she'd heard that had woken her light sleep.

"Just up our side of the square, madam. Perhaps the bakery."

"The *bakery!*" Lady Arnold raced down the stairs and stood in the doorway.

Yes, there was a crowd of people at the bakery, and she could just hear their noise.

"*Josephine!* I must dress! *Josephine!*"

ZACHARY SEARCHED EVERY SPACE HE COULD.

The sisters' rooms, over the shop and the bakery proper, showed no flames. They smelled of smoke. Everything smelled of smoke.

Beside them, the tiny plain room with its wool pallet on the floor still held a locked trunk, though its door sagged open under the lock he'd broken.

He didn't know where that burst of strength had gone. He felt weighted down as he climbed to the Russells' apartments, but no one was there. Had there been more sign of fire, even the slightest tinge of orange, he'd have investigated; but they were surely empty.

As it was, he left it.

The side of his garret held the bakery chimneys, reaching up through the roof. There were four there. He put his hand on one, not sure which led to the destroyed oven.

It was warm; they were all warm. He had no way of knowing if one held a fire lower down, or above him. No way to know if the sparks had reached the roof.

The smoke smell was fainter here.

He looked around. Most of his paintings were covered. Only the recent one was still open, abandoned where he had last put his brush to it. He'd thought of it as his flame painting, capturing Miss Porter's fiery hair and warm skin. Now he winced at the idea.

Even as he felt he might have conjured disaster with it, he realized again he had never done anything so good.

He wanted Anna standing here beside him to look at it. And at the same time, to go back to her. To convince her it was only because of the painting.

To convince himself.

For years he'd imagined his talent would burst free and he would stand in the Royal Academy of Art, his father and mother with him, beaming with pride. He would have no more time to drink with the men his age; he'd travel, painting work that made men catch their breath.

He would no longer need to prostrate himself before his father, or his brother, for money. His living need no longer be modest, for he would make a fortune along with his fame.

He'd never felt a blow to his pride like the one he'd felt when he'd realized Anna Bickering had something he lacked.

A sense of color, a sense of taste. He'd never felt lower than the moment he'd asked her to help him.

And he'd never felt higher than he did now, seeing what he could do with her help.

This painting meant more to him than anything he'd ever had.

Now he knew it meant nothing next to Anna herself.

He would have happily given it, this house, this square to the flames to ensure Anna survived.

He hadn't known that before.

Her precious bakery had not burned down. He left his garret as it was to go make sure she was all right.

HORRIFIED AT HIMSELF, ZACHARY REALIZED HE'D forgotten Rose on the pavement while he searched the house.

Realized it as soon as he returned, because she was gone.

There was shouting. He followed the sound. It seemed likely to lead to some or all of the Bickering sisters.

Oddly, the shouting wasn't from the sisters.

"You warty toad! We will get them off your precious floor if you help us!" Mr. Laurent was so red in the face Zachary hoped he had no weapon.

Surprisingly, Mr. Morley faced off with the man, clearly emboldened within his own shop.

"Who will pay me for all this wool? It stinks like fire in here!"

Zachary felt an urge to throttle the tailor himself. "We'll fix that. Give us a moment."

There was Anna on the floor, cradling Rose, arms tight around her sister's shoulders. Rose held on to a bundled quilt on her lap.

Rose's feet were oddly wrapped in bulging stockings, but Anna's were bare.

Dr. Shelton's attention was on the journeymen, who lay flat on the floor. He beckoned to Mr. Laurent. "We should tilt them," he murmured. "They'll breathe easier."

Jane sat next to the journeymen, her feet wrapped oddly too, and beside her Emery slumped forward over her own criss-crossed knees, petticoats draped to the floor.

In fact, all the sisters were in chemises and petticoats. Zach hadn't even noticed.

"Miss Bickering," he said softly, trying to catch Anna's attention. "Do you have shoes?"

"Yes." It was Jane who answered. Unwrapping a corner of the bundle on Rose's lap, she drew out eight shoes, spent a moment unraveling them. She put four of them next to Emery—no doubt for both her and Jane, who were of a size—two little ones by Rose, and two by Anna.

"Why don't you put them on?" he said just as quietly, still to Anna, patting her hands to help them loosen their grip on her sister.

Anna just shook her head *no*.

Nor did she move as Zachary traced her leg down to her feet, tucked underneath her.

The delicate bones looked undamaged; the skin on the soles was black with ash. Reddened spots here and there could have been from burns, or the ice; there were some scratches, but nothing deep.

Gently, Zachary moved her hips to one side with both hands. It seemed horribly intimate, which made no sense after he had hauled her around like a sack of flour half the night. Unfolding one of her legs, he slipped her small foot, careful not to scrape any of its cuts, into the loosened leather of her shoe.

When she didn't stop him, some conversation drifting

past him from each sister to the other, trying to make sense of the night, trying to understand, he shifted her the other way and did the other one.

The tiny structures of her toes were such a poor reflection of everything she had inside her. Inside Anna was a tower of fire; that painting should be of her.

In Zachary's hands, her feet were so fragile and small.

The door to the shop opened; in marched a lad in a livery coat. "The Lady—"

"Yes, François, that's fine." Pushing past her footman, Lady Arnold swept in, her cloak brushing the floor.

Unerringly her eyes flew to Emery, slumped over herself, blonde hair lank and wet and soot-stained.

"*Emery!*"

She flew to the baker's side, knelt down and put her arms around her.

Heedless of the soot and water, Emery turned into her shoulder. Zachary saw the tracks of tears in the dirt on her face.

Lady Arnold made soothing noises, rocking Emery a little, up on her knees to hold the taller woman.

Silence descended. Even Mr. Morley had nothing to say as a cocoon of peace, of relief, formed around the two women in the middle of the floor, Emery's soundless tears giving some kind of release to all of them.

When Lady Arnold finally moved again, it was to brush back Emery's hair. She spoke as if she meant all of them, but her eyes stayed on Emery's face. "We must go to my house. I'll have some baths prepared. You need warm beds. Soup. Does that sound all right?"

Dr. Shelton put in from behind her, "These men need to rest. With their heads above their feet."

"And you do too, don't you?" She said it to Emery, still smoothing back Emery's hair.

Emery spoke, and her voice was shockingly hoarse. "I'm well."

That was such a bald lie Lady Arnold didn't address it.

"François. Gather some men from outside. I'll pay them for their trouble. We must move all the Bickering sisters to my house, and their journeymen." She looked around as if noticing the others for the first time. "Lord Zachary? Mr. Laurent? Are you hurt?"

Zachary just shook his head no. He hurt, but couldn't have told the physician where, and wouldn't have said why.

Lady Arnold wasn't terribly interested. She did not wait. "We'll get everyone to my house and treat their ills. Dr. Shelton, you will come." It was an order.

"I want to know who will pay for my wool!"

The tailor's outburst finally made Emery look up. That or she drew some strength from Lady Arnold's presence. "You heartless pig. Did you do this?"

That seemed to wake Anna from her ritual soothing of her littlest sister.

Anna's head whipped around. She stood, steadying Rose. She faced Mr. Morley. "Did you do this?"

"I didn't do anything!"

The man was so palpably frightened, so palpably lying, that even Zachary wondered how he had the sheer gall to lie to the sisters' faces.

They were all, perhaps, shocked into silence for a moment.

Then with icy resolve came Anna's voice, low, menacing. "I'll kill you."

Indeed she lunged for him, and Zachary had to make a twisting leap over and past the other sisters to seize her around the waist before her hands reached the tailor's throat.

She wasn't screaming or shouting. Only icily hard, like stone. "I'll kill you," she said again, and Zachary believed her.

Clearly Mr. Morley did too. "Not the fire! That's nothing to do with me! I didn't do it!"

Zachary had lived over the sisters' bakery for months. He would have expected Jane go after the man, perhaps even Emery. Rose would have talked him into his own shame.

Anna had burned down to pure emotion and she truly wanted his throat.

"All right, all right now," he murmured as he struggled to keep Anna in his arms, feeling stupid even saying it; but it would be disaster to let her go.

"I'll—" She stopped before she said it a third time.

Zach only hoped that meant she was coming back to herself. He noticed how well fitted to the inside of his arms she'd become in very little time.

He carried her back over Rose's legs towards the door. "We'll find out what happened."

"Did he burn my bakery?" She looked at Zachary, and he didn't recognize her eyes.

"I did no such thing!" shouted the little tailor behind them.

"He's a coward, not a killer," Zach told her under his breath. He wasn't even sure he believed it; just wanted to snap her back to herself before this went any further.

"We cannot stop here." Lady Arnold very obviously didn't care about anything but getting Emery off the floor. "Good. François," she called, and her footman reappeared in the door. "Dr. Shelton, will you direct him how to move everyone?"

"Carry the ladies and—"

"No." Anna marched over to Rose's side. "I'll walk out of here."

Across the room Emery shakily donned some shoes, but when Jane tried to follow suit Dr. Shelton took her hands and wouldn't let her. Zach saw how her feet were covered in blood.

Lady Arnold saw too. "The men must carry Miss Jane and Miss Rose. François, I'll have the ladies in the blue room next to mine. Don't go above that floor, I don't want the children disturbed. Give these men the Chinese drawing room near the kitchen. Tell cook I want broth, both hot and chilled, for everyone."

She spoke as if ordering tea. Her footman leaped into action; Zach heard him shouting on the pavement. His chosen men trickled in.

Mr. Morley looked as if he wanted to complain about the soot and ice they tracked in, but he stopped himself.

Lady Arnold went to the door to call once more. "And François, everyone must bathe. All the tubs you can find, and hot water."

"Of course, madam."

Lady Arnold surprised him by looking over her shoulder back at him. "Lord Zachary, of course you will come?"

He wanted to. A wave of exhaustion threatened to knock him down.

But he didn't want to leave the bakery—the house—wide open. Half the square was out there, and too many doors broken.

"I'll have to watch the building, madam."

Standing, Dr. Shelton took both his hands, turned them over. "You're burned."

Zachary looked down, fearing for a moment he'd lost his hands and hadn't noticed.

"Not badly." Now that the physician drew his attention, he felt the burns, and the sore skin, and sore muscle down to the bone.

"I'll send some salve. Lady Arnold, let us waste no more time."

Having given all the necessary orders, that lady led the street men out, small but bracing under Emery's shoulder as she insisted on walking.

Mr. Laurent might have turned his attention to their wormlike reluctant host, but he too stood and came toward Zachary. "I understand," he said, making Zachary wonder wildly *what* he understood. "I will make the doors secure. You must rest."

Zach wanted a bath too, and brandy. He could have followed Lady Arnold down the side of Leicester Square to her house; she would have given him both. He could have found a hackney cab to take him to his family house, where his mother would have lavished him with nursing care. Even his sister might have stirred to do something about his condition.

Instead, he dragged his boots back over the tailor's threshold toward the Ladies' Own Bakery, and home.

ROSE SPOKE AS SOON AS THEY CROSSED LADY ARNOLD'S threshold. "This must stay safe."

She'd carried the bundle all the way from the tailor's shop, and Emery didn't even know what was in it.

Neither did Dahlia, but she took it and went upstairs ahead of the carrying men, saying, "I will lock it in my cupboard myself."

"You did fine, Rose," Jane said tiredly as she was carried up the stairs after the lady of the house.

The house had many vessels and soon every fire hosted cauldrons, cook pots, even milk pails warming as much water as the footmen could pump and carry.

Her ladyship swept open the doors to the room beside hers, previously his lordship's private chambers. Soon it became a hospital suite featuring both her own copper tub and two tin-lined wood tubs from the servant's quarters.

"I don't need to bathe," said Emery, arms wrapping around her waist.

"Nonsense," said Dahlia, trying to settle Emery on the bathing linen draped over an embroidered footstool.

Emery didn't want to settle. She didn't want to get anything else dirty. Everything in the world was broken and awful and the worst would be if she dragged all that horror into Dahlia's house too.

Time must have passed before the cook brought up a pot and a pitcher, both full of beef broth, and bread and butter sandwiches.

"I'll bring up what's more substantial as soon as I can," said the good woman with a curtsey to Dahlia.

Emery wasn't hungry, so Dahlia took a wet napkin and wiped the soot off her hands, making low murmuring sounds over the burns she saw there, cleaning them delicately. Then gave her a square of bread and butter.

"Please," she said under her breath, so Emery took it, but she didn't want it.

Tirelessly, gracefully, Dahlia ministered to all her sisters, washing their hair herself as the sun peeked up and shed watery light on the still-cold world outside.

She wrapped them all in wool cloaks from someone's closets and put them by the fire, urging them to shake out their hair and let it dry.

The bath was to smell better, but Emery didn't think she ever would. "I smell like smoke," Emery objected as Dahlia's footmen emptied a tub.

"Only a little," Dahlia lied.

Then her ladyship showed her first sign of indecision. "This bed is very large. Can you bear it if I keep your sisters here, and you sleep in my bed?" It was clear she'd rather not have Emery out of her sight.

Emery looked to her sisters.

"It's fine," said Anna, and Emery knew she meant it as a gift. The rest of them clung to each other, and perhaps Emery might too in other circumstances; but right now she felt raw, and wanted nothing but quiet.

"I should stay with you," she heard herself say. She wanted that too. She wanted to be with them.

"It's fine, Emery," said Jane, holding out her hand. It was clean, but Emery took it anyway. The smudges from her hands would wipe off.

With the skill of someone who had coaxed before, Dahlia persuaded them all to eat a little, and drink broth. Emery's throat was like fire; the cool broth washed down what tasted like soot, and her throat eased a little.

She was still too cold.

The re-filled tub was barely hot, hurried as all the water preparations had been, but it hurt as it washed over the raw places on her skin. Dahlia hissed in sympathy, helping her ease down.

One by one Emery saw her sisters' eyes closing by the fire, their hair warming and weighing down their heads and making them sleepy.

At Dahlia's quiet call, a footman placed wool-wrapped Jane in the bed, and Anna limped over to crawl beside her; in seconds they were both asleep.

Rose's thick mane of hair took the longest to dry, and she fell asleep lying on Dahlia's settee, her hair hung by the fire like a curtain.

Finally Dahlia could devote herself to Emery's bath. Her fingers in Emery's hair were slow and soothing; the fatted soap gave off a scent of laurel that soothed Emery's nerves.

Dahlia must have made note of every cut and burn; she

avoided them all as her soft linen washcloth rinsed away as much of the soot as it could.

She'd put one of her own chemises over Rose's head, and it fell past Rose's feet, wrapped in new bandages according to Dr. Shelton's whispered instructions as he stayed with the men. With another beckoning of the footman, Rose, clean and warm, was placed in the bed beside her sisters.

They stayed asleep as Dahlia helped Emery stand and wrapped her in drying cloths. Steadied her tall, teetering body as she climbed out of the tub; walked her to the next room. She left the door open.

There, in the quiet of Dahlia's luxurious room, her ladyship shifted the logs in the fire grate herself to make it warmer.

Emery wondered if she ought to be frightened of the little fire in the grate; but bore no relationship to the stuff that had spilled out all over her bakery.

Without a word, Dahlia led Emery to her own dressing table bench, sat her there, and combed the length of Emery's hair till it was dry, smooth and shining.

A warming pan had already been placed between the clean sheets. From too hot and too cold, Emery finally landed in a world that was gentle and welcoming, the warmth creeping up her legs as she settled herself among feather pillows. Dahlia made sure she reclined there, her head higher than her legs.

"It will be fine," Dahlia whispered, and Emery let the soothing lie carry her off to sleep.

Episode 20: Aftermath

"Why are you lecturing me about how dad eats his mush?" Jordan preferred to walk a step or two ahead of his sisters, looking for traps in the icy snow; but she stayed close enough they could still grab each other's hand like they would have last year, even though they were so much bigger now.

"Because you eat with him every morning, but I'm not sure if you notice. I think you can be kind of... Airy." Sal swung her arms on both sides of her body as if trying to waft away any sense of accusation.

"Airy? I'm not airy." Jordan looked down at his increasingly solid chest. "No one could be airy who eats like we do now!"

"I don't want to have to worry about you or Dad while I'm trying to concentrate on lessons—" Sal stepped into the mews and stopped.

The cobblestones lay pocked with slush and snow. But across the way, the door to the bakery, Ladies' Own Bakery, hung askew on its hinges.

Silently, they reached for each other's hands.

"I don't want to touch it." At the threshold, Jordan stood and looked at the scary thing. He couldn't see inside and didn't want to.

"We have to look, don't we?" Sal sounded uncertain, and Sal being uncertain unsettled them both.

Finally, Jordan pushed it aside.

The inside of the bakery looked like the end of the world had come and gone. Floor, walls and ceiling were all blackened, water pooled on the floor, the chimney to the second oven hung at a crooked angle, and there were mushy wet flour footprints everywhere.

"Do you think everyone's dead?" Sal's voice shook.

Jordan knew a lot of things no one credited to him. He knew a lot about bread, and he knew more than he wanted to about cakes, which weren't as interesting. He knew a lot about babies from watching Mrs. Wallace try to mother and cook at the same time, and he knew a lot about what happened in taverns from the things Mr. Bailey said when no one else was around.

But he also knew one thing no one else did, and that was that his bristly sister was easily shaken.

And hated to show it.

So Jordan took her hand again and made sure her shoulder squashed his. "No one's dead," he said, as if he knew things. "Something's happened, that's all."

It was eerie to walk across the silent black floor, scattered with pieces of bowls and half barrels. Eerie to stare into the half-full sink, soot floating on top of the water and settled to the bottom. "Should we drain it?" Sal wondered.

"Not without someone saying so."

It was understood between them that the person whose permission they needed would be someone full grown, hopefully Miss Emery, but any of the ladies would do. Even Mr. Bailey or Mr. Wiggs.

Honestly, they wanted anyone who could tell them what to do next and what had happened.

People didn't always explain things to Jordan and Sal. Sometimes it was because they couldn't; but only sometimes. They had no idea why their father was so vague and unable to understand the simple things that happened day after day. They had no idea where their mother had gone, or what they were supposed to do without one. They'd started work at the bakery because Miss Emery had taken their hands in the park and promised them bread.

But losing her, *all* of them, without explanation was too much uncertainty to weather. They'd rather have the ladies than bread.

By unspoken agreement, they didn't touch any broken or burned things. They picked their way across to the door that ought to lead into the shop. That also was a gaping hole.

Jordan thrust his head through first.

Two men lay rolled up in quilts, sleeping back to back on the floor.

Tiptoeing towards them, Jordan squeezed Sal's hand, trying to silently ask her if they should wake these men.

But one of them, the one they knew as Mr. Laurent, opened his eyes as they stepped close.

"It's all right," he said, as soon as he blinked and saw the children there, staring at him.

"The ladies aren't dead?" Sal asked in a small voice.

The seriousness of the gentleman's reply was reassuring. "No, no one's dead."

"Not even his lordship?" Jordan prompted, because the lordship in question, lying next to Mr. Laurent on the floor, hadn't moved.

"No." Though on this Mr. Laurent sounded less certain.

Groaning, Lord Zachary turned over, one soot-stained

hand wiping over his eyes. Jordan hoped it helped him see better, because it certainly didn't help him get cleaner.

"I'm sorry," rasped Lord Zachary. The children had seen him several times, ferrying them food during the storms. They knew who he was. "I should have come early to stop you coming. My apologies."

"Never say so—" Jordan was prepared to deny the need for apologies the way he had heard the bakery ladies do many times.

The front door swung open, hitting the bell that dangled above it, which appeared to be the one untouched item in the place. Although the shop itself was less devastated than the bakery proper, the smell of smoke hung in the air.

"Good morning?" The lady hesitated, then pushed the door wide, surveying the disaster inside as she did.

For a wild moment, Jordan was afraid that she wanted bread.

With a fearful groan that came from deep inside him, Lord Zachary pushed to his feet. Mr. Laurent followed suit, standing beside their puddle of quilts.

"We heard about the fire," said the slight woman at the door. "The ladies' committee wishes to help."

"What ladies' committee?"

"The Friends' ladies' committee, of course."

Jordan began to wonder if Lord Zachary had hit his head amid whatever horrible thing had happened last night. When the gentleman said nothing, Jordan helpfully offered, "The Quakers, you know."

"Yes. I do grasp it." Lord Zachary's clothes were striped with soot, and if Jordan wasn't mistaken, he wore a flour sack over his wool waistcoat and linen shirt. One shirtsleeve was torn and hung open over his hand. "I simply don't know what you ladies may do in the shop before the Misses Bickering have returned."

"Well," said the lady before them as a handful of women in somber dresses with buckets crowded in the door after her, "I doubt they'll argue the place needs a good cleaning."

JANE TIP-TOED BACK INTO THE GRAND ROOM WHERE HER sisters lay sleeping, carrying a tray.

She'd minced as far as the kitchen on her hurt feet, wondering what she could do for anyone and so hungry her stomach made utterly unladylike noises.

The maid had wanted to bring up the tray but Jane decided she'd do it herself in case her sisters were still asleep.

The vast golden silk canopy overhead was the most luxurious thing she'd ever seen, but not half as precious as Rose's and Anna's heads on those pillows.

Jane had spent a lifetime worrying over what could happen. Now she saw she'd always worried about the wrong things. She'd always fretted about money when there were more important things to lose.

Rose sat up, her feet slipping toward the floor.

Jane rushed to put her tray on the table beside the bed. "Don't," she whispered, putting a hand on Rose's knee.

Rose put out her own hand to take Jane's. "You shouldn't be walking either."

"It doesn't hurt much." It did, but it was bearable, at least once she passed the pangs of the first few steps. Jane wasn't ready to put on boots and march across the Thames, but she could stand.

"I'm glad to hear it, as we can't spend the rest of our lives in this bed." Slowly, Rose tipped over to lay on her side again in the vast featherbeds, quilted coverlets heaped around her making her look very small. "Then again, perhaps we can."

Jane looked over her. Anna was still sleeping.

Wordlessly, she helped Rose sit back up and handed her a bowl of porridge with honey.

"What are we going to do?" Rose whispered over her spoon.

"Something." That was all Jane knew. "Right?"

Rose kept her head bowed over the bowl.

THE SUN WAS TOO COLD AND DISTANT TO LIGHT UP THE bedroom.

Dahlia's smile did that.

She turned over when Emery touched her shoulder, shyly.

"We should go—" Emery didn't know why she'd said that. All she wanted was to be here, like this.

"Where?" Dahlia met Emery's first thought by snuggling closer. She'd finally shed the hastily donned winter gown somewhere in the night, and in her chemise she was soft and warm.

It was too far to hear voices in the next room; Emery would have to go look to see if her sisters were awake.

Which she would. In a moment. Emery closed her arms around the snuggling form of the dearest woman in London and closed her eyes.

She wondered if everyone felt more foolish the older they got, or if it was just her. Just a few months before, she'd been convinced that Jasmine Hayes hung the moon.

Jasmine had made her feel ten feet tall and, for the first time in her life, beautiful.

Dahlia was like a magic queen in a magic castle, yet she made Emery feel wanted. Comfortable.

Home.

But she couldn't assume the welcome would be everlasting. "We won't impose," she murmured softly into the glossy locks of hair that streamed behind Dahlia's ear. It felt natural to nuzzle there.

"You must." Dahlia said it with such vehemence Emery had to pull back to see her face.

Her ladyship was tired, with blue circles beneath her eyes. There were tangles in her hair Emery longed to brush out. She'd worried a red spot into her lip.

And she looked very, very determined.

"I spent every moment of my life doing exactly as expected." The words rushed out of Dahlia, urgent and fierce. "I've lived on tepid feelings, like eating bland food without salt. Every *day*. I won't any more. I know how fast the years go by, how quickly everything can change. I won't go back to having nothing. I want you."

Petals Emery hadn't even known were there unfurled around her heart. "You are the kindest, most generous, most beautiful woman in the world. Dahlia, surely you know you have me. All of me." Emery felt a hot flush across her cheeks but kept talking. "I never imagined I'd have the chance to love someone like you. I'm honored. I'm in *awe*."

Dahlia snuggled closer. It was shockingly intimate and sweeter than honey all at the same time.

It couldn't be an accident, how well she fit just inside Emery's arms. How well the curves of her fit against Emery's curves, how well her lips fit against Emery's lips, how well their breath mingled together in the depths of the fluffy featherbed.

Surely, thought Emery. *Surely this was meant to be.*

And Dahlia must have thought something similar, because she said, "I never in my life imagined what I was missing till I saw you. I think I always felt a little hollow, but I told myself that was what happened when you married a title. You gave up living. I didn't realize how empty my life was till I saw you—covered in flour!" She rocked her forehead against Emery's shoulder, chuckling a little. "Golden hair and green eyes and radiating *strength* I'd never seen before, that I wanted all to myself, greedily, as soon as I saw you. I waited all my life for you. I won't give you up no matter what anyone says. You have to know that."

The words felt heavy. Like promises. Like vows.

"I'll give you everything I can. Everything I have. I don't know what else to do." Emery pulled her in tight, held her close. "I wish I could marry you, but even if we could... You're so fine. You belong here. And I can't leave the bakery. My sisters. My work."

"It's part of you. Something else fascinating that I love." Then Dahlia wiggled up a little higher so Emery could see her incandescent smile. "I love you too, you know."

Emery hadn't exactly said that she did, but it was a relief that Dahlia knew. A gift for her to say that. Always making her dreams come true.

Always making things easier on Emery.

"I love you," she whispered against Dahlia's skin, and they both sank into a kiss among the silks and featherbeds that wrapped the two of them up together for a long, long time.

When they parted, it was just slightly, and Emery found herself leaning against the pillows with Dahlia fitting into the space beside her.

"So what do we do?"

Dahlia was supremely unconcerned. "You are the cleverest woman in London, and I am in love with you. No one can tell us what to do. We'll do whatever we like."

She seemed to think sweeping thoughts when Emery only meant *after last night*.

"What do *I* do?" Perhaps Dahlia had an answer.

She did. "You're going next door and talking to your sisters. And whatever you decide, you will let me help."

ANNA SURFACED SLOWLY, UNWILLINGLY, FROM A SEA OF BAD dreams. Cold and hot mixed till she was lost in a scorched black land of ice, looking for everyone, alone; but she'd still rather stay there than wake.

The sounds of Jane and Rose whispering beside the bed finally pulled her up from sleep.

Warm softness wrapped around her, her clean hair a curtain under her cheek. When she opened her eyes, she saw the little fire in the coal grate.

And all the crushing weight came down on her.

"How long should we let her sleep?"

"Will the physician return to look at her feet?"

"*Her* feet? *Yours!*"

"Yours too. How did we ever get to be such a mess?"

There was a fire, thought Anna, wondering how to make words. Her words wouldn't come; in fact, she didn't want them.

Words would only make it all real.

When she closed her eyes, she saw the scorch marks again, the men coughing, the flames licking up, crawling all over their bakery like insects, like demons.

"Zachary!"

The image of him pulled her upright.

Rose simply took it for a bad awakening. "He stayed in the building. He's watching the bakery."

It *was* a bad awakening. She thought she understood art, but it had driven the man mad. How dare he behave as though it gave him a claim on her? He'd tried to give her orders.

The madness must have been momentary, because he'd never been overbearing; that was the last thing he was.

Which was good, because she wished him well, wished

good things for his art; but she had no more room in her for people telling her what to do.

Aunt Eden had tried, Lord Boislegrand had tried, and the truth was Anna couldn't stomach it any longer.

Wouldn't stomach it.

She rolled over in the unbelievable softness of the bed.

There were Jane and Rose on the bed, looking at her. Jane's dark hair streamed around her shoulders; Rose's draped in walnut-colored waves all the way down to the snowy sheets.

"You're both so beautiful." It was true.

Had she ever seen how lovely her sisters were before? Had it changed something in her to practice her eye on all that art? Or was it just the preciousness of seeing them alive, whole, after the horrors of the night before?

Carefully they both moved closer, leaning into the softness, a sea of velvety warmth making everything that had happened the night before unreal.

But it had been real.

Rose said what Anna thought. "Is it reasonable, do you think, to feel as if we dreamed it all?"

"It must be," Anna told her, "because I do."

"I can't remember half of it, and the other half I don't want to remember." Jane's little groan as she hiked her knee up on the bed, letting her still-bandaged foot hang over the edge, said volumes.

Rose reached out and took Anna's hand in hers. Both of their hands were sturdy against the linen. Baker's hands. "Anna," she said, "what do we do?"

There were a thousand thoughts crowding into Anna's head and drifting right back out again. She couldn't keep hold of any. She hoped her mind wouldn't be like this the rest of her life; she wouldn't be good for much.

She had little feeling left either. As if the night had wrung her out like a wet rag and left her to dry in front of Lady Arnold's fire.

"I don't know," she admitted aloud. "We must talk to Emery."

SUMMONED LIKE A GENIE, EMERY EMERGED FROM THE NEXT room, the tall oak panel that reached far above her head barely creaking as it opened and then swung back shut.

"Are you awake?" she whispered.

"Everyone's awake," Jane answered back, still soft, but easily heard.

Emery crawled up the foot of the bed to the middle where the sisters all sat together, reclining in their bed of soft confusion and silent exultation that they were all here. They were here, and alive.

"We don't know what to say," said Anna, almost lightly, like she meant it as a little joke. It was very unlike her, but felt good in that moment; Emery had almost been afraid that the world would crack depending on what Anna said first.

"We don't know what to *do,*" added Rose.

Emery reached out and threaded her fingers through the hand of Anna's that Rose wasn't holding. "I don't know what to say *or* do, but we must go to the bakery, mustn't we? Once we check on Mr. Bailey and Mr. Wiggs. The physician was with them. Then we must go to the bakery."

Anna's soft brown eyes, so unlike hers, held Emery as if in a tight grip. Their feelings had a whole conversation in that moment, and later when she could describe it to herself, Emery felt as if they had just met each other. She saw more determination in Anna's eyes at that moment than she'd ever seen before, and it wasn't just because she was the oldest and it was something she felt she must do.

"Yes," said Anna finally, "we must go to the bakery, and see what must be done."

"For what?" Jane's voice quavered a little. She was not despairing, as she had been over the water bill. She was steady now. Just asking. After all that fire, all the smoke, all the water, what *was* there to do?

Rose said what they all needed to hear. "You *are* asking how we'll put it all right again, aren't you? Not whether we'll bake again."

Jane took a long, shuddering breath.

"Yes," she said, more firmly now. "That's what I'm asking."

Then Anna looked at all of them.

She still had that look, in her eyes, in her face. "Are we... Are we too far apart to start again?"

"I don't know what you mean," said Rose, the only one who didn't.

Emery looked at Jane, who looked back.

"I'm not ordering anyone to give up their secrets." Anna found a way to be both delicate and direct. "I don't want that. I just want to know if perhaps we've all drifted too far in new directions. Maybe we don't *want* this now, not like we did before."

"Nonsense." The very idea made Rose frown. "Here we all are."

"*You* got *married*." Anna let her tone be pointed.

"Yet here I still am." Rose's answer had a bitter flavor.

"I just mean... We opened the bakery so we could live together. So we didn't have to live lives we didn't want. But perhaps some of us want something else now."

"None of us want to give up." Rose said this with a certainty none of them felt until she said so. Her words made everything they felt real, assumed, and therefore created, their common purpose.

Made none of them alone.

It was the moment to speak. Emery felt it. She should say something.

But Anna was asking about the bakery, not Emery's life, and Emery still felt that her heart, her love, didn't matter to the rest of them.

Or at least wasn't welcome.

"Good," said Anna. "There will be ever so much work to do."

They might have smiled, or laughed; but they didn't have it in them. Not yet.

But they would again one day.

The ball of tension in Emery's gut didn't go away. Not about Dahlia. Not about being in love. But at least she and her sisters were together, and that felt better.

It did.

She'd keep thinking that till it was true.

"I can't imagine what we will do about money," Anna sighed, sounding more tired than anything else. "What must it cost to repair things? Even clean them?"

"What *happened?*" asked Rose. "You said the second oven came off its pedestal."

"I don't know what happened." Emery frowned. "But we must know, to make sure it doesn't happen again."

"Anna, do you honestly think Mr. Morley had something to do with it?"

Emery didn't let Anna answer. "He did something, and I will find out what."

"I have no idea, but I hate him," said Anna, more limply than anything else she'd said yet.

"Yes, you conveyed that last night." There was almost a smile in Jane's voice; almost. "I've never seen you like that."

Anna just slumped against the cushions. "I've never had my bakery burn down before."

"It didn't burn down." Emery was already making lists in

her mind of everything that would have to be done. Like a receipt for restoring the bakery. "It's damaged, but—"

"Ooooooh." Jane slouched onto a pillow as well. "Mrs. Scropes!"

"Oh my stars. We must get there before she does." From a picture of exhaustion Anna shot upright in the bed, then leaned over, searching the floor, perhaps for her shoes.

There were a million things to do, and a million thoughts battling together in Emery's head.

Everything was more urgent than being in love.

But the secret of it weighed in her gut. Just minutes ago, Emery had been so happy she felt like flying. Now the secret made her happiness heavy. She couldn't carry it forever.

She couldn't carry it even one more day.

She didn't deserve to. It was so heavy it hurt.

She tugged Anna's chemise to get her to sit upright and listen as Emery approached the thought carefully, more carefully than she'd ever done anything in her life. "First things first. We'll need money."

J ANE WATCHED EMERY'S BROWS KNIT TOGETHER.

"Lady Arnold wishes to help us," her sister said, each word coming slowly, as if Emery thought hard about each one before she said it.

"That's very kind of her," said Rose, just as Anna added, "We can't take charity from Lady Arnold."

"What if we arranged to borrow from her?" Emery was picking each word so carefully it made Jane's elbows hurt.

"We cannot afford debt, can we, Jane?" Anna looked toward her.

"If we wished to have a loan," added Rose, "the ladies' committee can do such things. There are funds available for the Friends in dire straits." She ran her hand over the linen in front of her as if very conscious of the contrast between their circumstances and their immediate surroundings. "We are in a *sort* of dire straits."

"Lady Arnold wishes to help. She has always been keen to help our business, you know that. And it is her wish."

"Oh, now." Anna shook her head. "I don't know if our association with Lady Arnold is close enough to make such a thing seemly."

Jane could see Emery's flush, see her searching. Words didn't always come easily to Emery, and she was struggling so hard right now for the right ones.

Jane did not want her to have to struggle.

Jane's mouth opened and the words came out without conscious decision. "I have six pounds of my own."

"*What?*" That made Anna try to spin a little in place, her legs tangling in the chemise and sheets.

"I sing in taverns."

The silence following this announcement was absolute. As if it had emptied the room of air.

"I beg your pardon?" Anna finally asked.

"I sing in taverns." Now that she'd said it, Jane felt like it was a small, absurd thing. Compared to the fire, it was hardly the biggest thing in her life, even though at the time it had felt like a path to happiness, perhaps to freedom.

Freedom from what? Her sisters? She didn't want to be free of them.

"That's where you've been going?" Rose's punch on her shoulder reminded her of when they were all much littler. "Why didn't you tell us?"

"They're *taverns*, Rose."

Anna's eyebrows climbed as high as they went. She put a hand to her cheek as if to hold back any blushes. "As in, more than one tavern?"

"A few, yes." Why must she make it sound like Jane had been... well, whoring? No matter. There was no point now to holding anything back. "I made a guinea in the dancing tent on the Thames. I went back late that night."

"Oh my stars," Anna's voice was weak.

"You can't complain about having *extra money*." Emery's tone straightened Anna's back a little.

"No, not at all, just... let me settle the idea, will you?" Anna couldn't even look at Jane.

Jane didn't mind. She'd done what she did on purpose, not by accident, and that made it feel... right. Anna would get a grip on herself, and she'd just said she wanted them to be together.

Jane couldn't offer any more togetherness than to offer her money.

"This is... startling news," Anna said, and then to Jane's shock, she put out her hand and covered Jane's on the linen. "Did anyone else know? I hate to think of Jane in such a place alone."

Just the idea that Anna's first concern was for her safety made tears well up in Jane's eyes.

They were stupid, there was no reason for them, but still they dropped, one after the other onto the linen sheet below them all, and she moved her hand out from under Anna's and hobbled forward on her knees to wrap Anna in a hug.

"Thank you," whispered Anna as if Jane's money carried the same weight as giving her little sister her approval.

"I have a little money," said Emery while her sisters still held each other in the center of the bed. "But Lady Arnold can loan us much more."

Arms still around Anna's shoulders, Jane gave her sister a little shake of her head, knowing Anna wouldn't notice and Rose wouldn't see. Emery didn't have to bare her secrets.

Emery met her gaze calmly. "If you can, I can."

"Can what?" Anna pulled out of Jane's arms. "Don't tell me you make money in taverns too. Is it dancing?" For some reason she was crying too, wiping the tears away with delicate movements of her fingers.

There was a bite to that comment, but Jane still felt more good than bad. Anna had expected to hear a terrible secret; she'd forgive her; Emery should just leave it.

She shook her head warningly at Emery again.

Emery reached across the space between them to grab Rose's hand in hers, making Rose jump a little.

"I wish I had half your gift for talking," she told their littlest sister, and Rose, open-mouthed, just squeezed her hand in return.

Then Emery said slowly, "Anna. Is there anyone from whom you'd take a loan to fix the bakery?"

Very confused by the portentous way Emery said it, Anna tried to stuff her hands under her apron, then remembered she wasn't wearing one. "Aunt Eden, of course. Mr. Russell, had he any funds. Perhaps, when we were betrothed, Lord Boislegrand, but that was a very different situation."

Still holding Rose's hand as if for strength, Emery stayed calmly, evenly looking at Anna and said, "No. It isn't."

"*What??*" squealed Rose, as Anna's face ran through a complicated battery of expressions.

Jane just let Emery speak. If she were so determined to do it, she should do it.

Rose had no shortage of words. "I'm confused and amazed both. Do you mean that you and Lady Arnold are betrothed? But you can't be! But you don't sound like you're teasing at all!"

"I'm not teasing." Finally Emery did smile, the first real smile after the fire, and Rose stretched out her arms, opening and closing her hands in a beg for a hug.

Laughing a low quiet laugh, instead of wiggling in undignified fashion across the sheets, Emery stood and walked around the bed to hug Rose. "Don't let me bump your feet," she murmured.

"Bother my feet. I'm so confused, but *Emery!*"

"She loves me." Emery knelt beside the bed, hugging Rose's legs, careful not to bump her toes. Her words were quiet but clear, and full of emotion, more emotion than Jane could remember seeing Emery show. "Can you believe it?"

"Of course I can believe it," Rose half-scolded in return. "You know you are quite amazing enough for anyone to love."

"What does it mean?" Anna's voice cut through the little swirl of congratulatory celebration.

"What does what mean?" Emery's voice was still steady, but she reached up again for Rose's hand, and Jane gave hers too. "Love?"

"No, I understand—well, likely I don't, but that's not what I mean. Or maybe it is. Heavens." She wasn't looking at her sister, but down at the bed. "I don't understand how it's similar at all. You cannot be married. It can only be love."

"Yes," Emery said, with a rich exultance in her voice. "That's it exactly. It can only be love."

The very sound of her made Anna look up.

See Emery aglow with emotion, trembling in front of her. Expecting her judgment.

Anna's expression still said she was confused, and being asked to understand a lot. But her hand reached out to touch Emery's cheek.

In a near-whisper, Emery said, "I know we have our differences, and we will never be much alike. I was so jealous when they sent you out into the world to get married, our whole family, and you insisted you'd rather fall in love. You just assumed you'd find something I never thought I could have. Well, it's happened, and no one is more amazed than me. We have far more in common than just our last name. We are sisters. Can you not be happy for me?"

That was when Anna's face came out of its thinking contortions and only smiled.

"I'm much happier for Lady Arnold," Anna whispered back, patting her cheek. "For look how sensible she is, to love you."

Leaping up, Emery fell among them, hugged Anna so hard they all heard the breath *whoof* out of her. There might have been a few more words, but they made little sense; it was just that general sounds of agreement, approval, affection, all had to come out of them somehow.

It was quite some time before the sisters all recovered enough to speak again, and when they did, it was Emery first.

"The first step is that Lady Arnold's carriage will take us to the bakery," she announced like the carriage was her own.

Or maybe she had just picked up that tone of command from Lady Arnold.

"Nonsense," said Rose immediately, always ready to argue with a tone of command. "It's barely a few hundred yards down the street."

Anna had not given up directing. "And you have bandaged feet, little one. And a little one of your own to take care of!"

"There's no baby in my feet," muttered Rose, but conceded the point for the moment, which was how they all knew her feet still hurt.

EMERY RANG FOR A MAID WHO BROUGHT THEIR DRESSES.

Laundered and pressed, the dresses were clean, and Rose felt the wonder of a life in a house full of servants.

Would Emery get to live this way forever? She wondered as

her sisters helped her hobble down the hall, down the stairs. The idea was awe-inspiring.

She hoped Anna would be easier on Emery for finding love first than she'd been on Rose.

In a room full of silent carpets, Dr. Shelton's voice was distinctive, low and professionally reassuring. Even so, he sounded concerned.

"Good morning, ladies. I came early to check on your journeymen here."

"'M fine." *Rasp* didn't do Mr. Bailey's voice justice. He sounded like his throat had been sanded.

More worrying, Mr. Wiggs said nothing at all.

Anna forced her cheer. "We are so grateful for all you've done, both of you. We won't forget, ever. Dr. Shelton will do anything you need."

Among their talking, Rose found herself patting Mr. Wiggs' hand.

It felt too cold.

They trooped into the next room where Dr. Shelton said, "Do sit down, Mrs. Russell. Miss Jane. I must see to your dressings."

"Is Mr. Wiggs well enough?" Rose kept her voice down; it seemed clear they did not want the men to hear.

"Mr. Bailey will take time to heal. Mr. Wiggs is struggling."

"What can you do for him?" Anna asked quickly for them all.

"His lungs seem wounded. He can't breathe in enough air." Her sisters must have looked as impatient as Rose felt, because he did rush to add, "I do think I can treat him. I'm no surgeon—"

"Yes, we know," Jane half-snapped.

With forbearance, the physician went on. "—but I followed the work of the Pneumatic Institute in Bristol. I know an apothecary where I may get vital air, and the Bristol gentlemen published some very encouraging reports. I believe it may be what Mr. Wiggs needs."

"Then go get some!" Having survived, the night before, what felt like an eternity of waiting, Rose was through with it.

"Mrs. Russell, I am happy to help in dire circumstances. I would like to do what I can for a neighbor. But I cannot provide—"

"We'll pay for it." That was a full snap, from Jane. Why she was so impatient with the man, Rose couldn't tell; hadn't she fetched him? "Should we also hire you a cab?"

"Unnecessary." He sounded, not just forbearing, but indulgent of Jane's short temper. It was nice of him; at least Rose felt so. She wanted all her sisters to be treated very gently right now.

"With your permission, I will also consult a surgeon I know whose experience with the medicine of wounds far exceeds mine. I tend to apoplexies and gout, if you must know, and ladies' complaints. He served in war."

"We'll pay for him too." Rose felt wildly reckless. But there was no question Mr. Wiggs must have everything he needed, even if it meant closing the bakery.

It felt odd, when only moments before she and her sisters had just agreed to keep the bakery open; but she didn't need to consult them to know they felt the same.

Anna supported her. "We are not accustomed to consult physicians, Dr. Shelton. You must advise us how to proceed. We are trusting you not to take advantage of our precarious position, as a neighbor and a gentleman."

Answering Anna, his voice was even more gentle. "I am honored, Miss Bickering. Let me venture to Lord Rawleigh's house immediately, and the apothecary; I won't hesitate, I promise you."

"We will rely on you," and from Anna it sounded more like a warning than thanks.

EMERY HAD TO TAKE A DEEP BREATH BEFORE FOLLOWING her sisters out of the carriage.

The drive had only taken moments, but Emery didn't want to see.

When her feet hit the pavement, she found that perhaps her sisters felt the same way, for they stood waiting for her, even though Rose and Jane should not be on their feet.

The front door was still there, closed. From the outside, nothing looked terribly wrong. Only the inner glass of the windows was fogged dark.

As she watched, a rag wiped at the glass.

She seized Anna's hand and pushed open the door.

It was a hive of activity. There were women everywhere. She recognized many of the women from the ladies' committee of Friends, and there were more.

Women who had been in the bakery nearly every day for months. Women who gossiped and laughed in there. Women who knew them.

There were some of the trade girls from Tilly's boarding house, and Tilly herself, skirts hitched high to keep from dipping into the water on the floor. Wives and maids and housekeepers, chandlers and vintners and seamstresses. The latter looked a bit brightly colored for the work, then Emery saw at least one of the night ladies who came in sometimes, with an orange skirt pulled as high as Tilly's for the same reason.

Stupidly, she stood there, unable to take it in.

"Ah, Miss Emery." Mrs. Swofford picked her way through

the milling women to greet her. "We thought the place could use a woman's touch."

The phrase struck Emery to the heart and bloomed there next to her Dahlia. This was a day of emotional bursts. Emery would hate it if she cried in front of these people.

"That is just what it needs," she managed to say without tears.

"Come through. We've nearly done the cleaning out here, but the bakery itself needs so much more."

"Where is Lord Zachary?" Anna asked from behind her.

"I haven't seen him lately." The narrow little woman looked about as if she'd just misplaced Lord Zachary somewhere. She must have seen him.

"I'll check upstairs."

"Wait." Emery still had Anna's hand, and didn't want to let it go.

She didn't want to see the rest without Anna.

And it wasn't because Anna was the oldest. It was because she wanted Anna's strength.

Squeezing back, Anna let go. Only long enough to take up the two stools in the corner where the windows on Leicester Square and the windows on Bear Street converged.

"Come on," she told their sisters, and Jane and Rose hobbled along behind. Their unbuckled shoes made room for their bandages, and they shouldn't be walking at all, the physician had said.

Silently they walked over their door, which still lay on the floor, its handle making it teeter.

The bakery looked burned. Black marks streaked the ceiling, the floor; the broken chimney of the second oven was blackened where it had burst. Soot lay on everything. Everything looked shattered.

Water dripped everywhere too, and the smell was indescribable. Emery would remember it the rest of her life.

Anna put down the stools, and her sisters sat. They just looked at the mess, the bustle in the room quieting as the pool of stillness spread out from them, the effort it took to absorb everything they saw.

If even one of them had said that it was *too much,* that rebuilding it was *too big,* Emery might have wavered.

They didn't. They only sat and looked.

Had they said it, Emery would have believed, because she felt it now. It was too much. Too big to imagine it back as it was. All the work it would take.

And no idea how to pay for it all, as even with Jane's money and hers, even with Lady Arnold's, how would they make it pay when they had barely been managing as it was?

Someone knocked on the empty door-frame to the shop. Emery turned to look.

"I've been told you need a carpenter." A man wedged his way in, his muscled bulk flattening the teetering door into silence.

"*Mr. Harding.*" Anna looked for a moment as though she were going to launch herself into the man's arms.

So it was. The carpenter who had planed the counters and fixed the doors.

He stood in the middle of the damage and peered around. "Not too bad," he said.

That sounded crazed, but Emery was grateful for it. He knew things. Wood was his business. If he said it wasn't that bad, he must know whereof he spoke.

He laid a hand on the crooked stovepipe. "Huh," he said.

Then Anna did go to him.

"Can you fix it?"

"Oh sure. You never saw that collapsed floor by the Queen's Mews, did you? That was a mess."

If he didn't think this place a mess, Emery didn't want to know what sort of work he usually faced.

Of course, this was the same man who'd taken months to plane their door so it didn't stick. Once she thought about it, Emery would have doubts.

But she didn't have room in her for doubts right now.

Jane didn't have doubts, she had practical concerns. "You will estimate for us how much you expect to bill before you begin, I assume," she called from her seat.

"Oh, sure," he said again with simplicity Emery chose to find reassuring.

The women had flushed water over and over through the wash trough; Mr. Harding stuck his head in to see it. "Pipes still working," he said in his brusque way.

It was soothing. *Pipes still working.* They had those. Emery could rest assured they had those.

Then a thought hit her, and she ran out into the shop.

There it was, Lady Arnold's vase, still sitting in its nook above empty shelves.

It had come forward to the edge, as if the blast that had burst the door from its hinges had pressed it forward too. But it was still there, unsinged, unharmed.

Gently, Emery took it down.

Back in the bakery she handed it to Jane. She hoped Jane took it the way she meant it; she was out of words. She'd used them all up for the day. But surely they weren't needed; the vase said everything. It was beautiful, and theirs, and they had friends, and they had a great deal more than nothing.

Jane cradled it and nodded.

To Mr. Harding she called, "Have you ever seen anything like it?"

"Oh, sure."

That was all he had to say?

Before any of her sisters could prompt him, another voice came from the broken door. "I'm afraid it's all too common."

It was Mr. Keales.

"What do you mean?" Rose's calm kept Emery in check when her first inclination was to toss the man out so hard he slid all the way to the Thames.

"Fires like this, in mills and in bakeries. The flour fills the air, you know, and it's flammable."

"Flammable?"

"It ignites. All at once. It's like a bomb, it explodes."

Emery felt ten feet tall again, this time from fury.

She strode to him purposefully; it felt very slow, the process of gathering up his collar and neckcloth in her fist.

Her baker's muscles nearly lifted him off the floor.

"And you never saw fit to tell us this?"

His expression stayed sad and condescending even as his face reddened

He still managed to speak. "A real master baker would have known."

Horrified, she dropped him.

The man staggered back, straightening his clothing, but Emery stood still as ice, shackled by the truth of what he'd said.

A real master baker would have known.

Her sisters, however, did not stay silent.

"Why didn't you tell us?"

"You made *bakery seals* sound so much more important!"

"All those weeks complaining we should close and no *help?* No *advice?* No wonder the Guild is dying!"

"It was more important to you to squash our bakery than ensure we made good bread!"

"You think that should be a *secret?*"

"We will take *you* to court! For endangering the entire square!" Anna was red-faced and shaking her finger an inch from the man's nose. "After all your threats! Your pressure, your—"

She stopped.

Emery looked where she was looking, past Mr. Keales' shoulder.

Through the door opening, they saw Mr. Morley, the tailor, peeking around the jamb of the door.

He reared back as Anna glared at him.

"I'll kill him," said Anna, not as stone-hard as she'd been the night before, but clearly meaning it.

Emery reached her before she could move.

"He's a mean old—"

"He put Mr. Keales on our doorstep. Didn't he, sir?" She turned back to Mr. Keales, and this time he stepped back from what was in her eyes. "He complained to you of us, didn't he? Brought you to report us to the Guild?"

Emery didn't want to believe, didn't want to be that foolish of where she'd put her work and her trust.

But looking at Mr. Morley cringing out past their door, she knew it was true.

Mr. Keales didn't deny it. His narrow, mottled face shook as he settled his collar. "We rely on reports from the public in our annual census of—"

"Get out." There were two words Emery had left.

Anna had more. "You could have come to offer us assistance as part of your worshipful company. You would for a brother, wouldn't you? For a man? We'd have bought your seal if you let us, and we could have helped each other. But you chose this. You wanted us gone. We will *never* go. And as for Mr. Morley—"

"Get out." Emery said it again because she couldn't bear to look at the man another moment.

Turning in as dignified a manner as he could, Mr. Keales departed over the broken door.

"Well. For once I thought you might be here because it was *quieter,* and I see I was right." Lord Zachary filled the portal where Mr. Keales had just departed.

He looked awful, filthy and tired, and his hands had red marks on them Emery knew were burns.

Anna couldn't believe that he still hadn't bathed. "Sir! You *must* go home, or if not, Lady Arnold would gladly let you visit."

"I'll go." His aristocratic profile was smeared with soot. It made his smile, and his eyes, look lopsided. It was an eerie yet humanizing effect.

The black in his golden hair, however, made him look scorched.

He looked down at his hands. "Perhaps Lady Arnold will have me first. If I went home looking like this, it might make my mother faint."

"And rightly so!" *Shooing* him with her hands, she urged him through the shop to the stairs.

He looked hollow-eyed, too.

"Have you slept?"

"Some."

Behind her, someone tugged on Anna's gown. She turned.

There was their neighbor, Mr. Laurent. He didn't look nearly as bad, only slightly worse than normal, she had to admit.

"Mrs. Scropes will come. She may have already heard. When she comes... Please remember that I have lived in the garret at Lord Zachary's request for a long time."

Anna wanted to explain that this was no time for surprises. She wanted to explain *many* things. She had not done venting her spleen at that odious Mr. Keales, and as for Mr. Morley...

She had three younger sisters, and that had taught her the value of not assuming others meant the worst. They squabbled enough without thinking poorly of each other, and their mother had trained Anna especially to indulge the younger ones, give them the benefit of the doubt.

She'd clearly taken that lesson too far, and she wouldn't be taking it any farther.

She disliked bitterness, and they were all generally too busy to hate.

But Mr. Morley was an enemy, pure and simple, and she'd find a way to pay back what he'd put in motion if it was the last thing she did.

These were all unfamiliar feelings, and she didn't have time for their ragged neighbor to pose riddles. Still, she felt she wouldn't sleep that night unless she knew what he was talking about.

"Why?" she asked with infinite weariness.

"I, ah... You may have been under the impression that I rented my room."

Anna just stood there, trying to let the words slot themselves into some order that made sense. It had been a day of too many revelations already and she had to do a great deal of work.

"Mr. Laurent," she finally said, "are you telling me you never paid rent?"

"Ah, you know, an open door... it was a long time ago," the gentleman said with a sheepish shrug.

"Whatever you say." She hadn't interest to spare. She was still tired, it had been a taxing hour, and Lord Zachary clearly needed someone to mind him and see him home. It wouldn't be Anna. "Would you be so kind as to accompany his lordship to Lady Arnold's?"

"You needn't big-sister me, Anna." When Anna turned to look at him with confusion, Lord Zachary immediately corrected himself. "Miss Bickering. I'll see to myself. Mr. Laurent may wish to stay here."

With that settled, Anna nodded. "I must confer with Mr. Harding. There is a great deal to do."

She couldn't interpret the odd look he gave her, but he nodded, and Anna went back to her sisters, confident that he, at least, had been dealt with.

EMERY FELT HEAVY. JANE STOOD NEAR ENOUGH TO CATCH her if she wilted, as well as she could with Lady Arnold's vase in her arms; she didn't want to put it down on the wet, sooty floor.

"Don't listen to him, Emery. He's just being vicious."

"He's got to be right." Emery looked pale again, stricken. "A real master baker would have known. I thought just because I could bake bread—"

"*Stop* it. You can't just bake bread, you're brilliant at it. We could not have come this far without you. Don't doubt yourself."

"We should have known."

"How? By magic? Anna was right. If that guild truly meant to serve London they'd have told us what we should know. Keales had every chance; instead he harangued us."

"But now Mr. Wiggs and Mr. Bailey..." Emery couldn't go on.

Two small sets of arms came around her waist. "Are they dead?" asked Sal in a very small-for-her voice.

"No! They're at Lady Arnold's." Jane reached out to gather Sal against her; from the looks of it, Jordan squeezed Emery as hard as he could, which was quite hard indeed.

"If they are, you can tell us." Sal still barely spoke above a whisper, and Jordan nodded. "We'd rather know."

"Have I ever lied to you?" Jane murmured to the girl shaking against her side.

"They're ill." Emery still sounded gutted. "Fire's very dangerous. If we open again..." She stared around her as if the devastation looked different now. "We must know more. Be more careful."

Jane worried a little that out of her sight, Anna might really do someone some damage. When she looked about, Anna was still gone, and Rose had disappeared.

Mrs. Swofford approached their little group. "You want the bowls scrubbed too, don't you, Miss Bickering? If we can save them?"

She'd get Emery back on an even keel again, as the sailors said. She'd learned a lot from those sailors about coming out of a fight, treating your wounds, and soldiering on.

"Yes," Jane told her with conviction. "Yes, Mrs. Swofford, we do. We can't thank you enough."

NO ONE HAD MENTIONED ANY FIRE ON THE STAIRS OR UP IN their apartments, but the smell hung in the air and Rose felt like it had invaded her home just the same.

She had to examine it for herself. She moved slowly from room to room, feeling the bedsteads they'd brought from their childhood home, the clothes pegs, their precious table and chairs.

The porcelain plates gifted by the Duke and Duchess of Talbourne were all secure in their stacks against the kitchen wall, where Mr. Russell had put shelves for them. She lifted one; it felt cool on her cheek. It was still wintry outside, but she felt warm.

Please come home, she sent the dream winging his way, wondering how many miles there were between them, and when he'd be back.

The door creaked, and she dropped the plate.

"*Aiee!* Mrs. Russell. I did not mean to startle you." It was Mr. Laurent.

Crouching low, Rose started to gather the pieces. "My clumsiness, Mr. Laurent. Never you mind."

"It was not your clumsiness but mine. Here, let me." The gentle *clink* of the broken porcelain seemed the last drop in a bucket Rose couldn't hold full any more.

She felt her eyes fill with tears, felt them drop.

"Oh no! Mrs. Russell!" Leaping up as if tears were a far greater catastrophe than a broken plate, or even a fire, their neighbor took the liberty of plucking her up out of the shards and moving her closer to the door.

Rose was tired of being moved around, and she was tired of shock after shock.

She should be enjoying married life. Her husband should be here. They should be enjoying the prospect of their own little boy or girl.

She was tired of mourning.

"Mr. Laurent." She wiped the tears away with both hands, but they just kept coming. "Does life ever get easier?"

He seemed to sense she didn't want to be hauled about any more.

Moving one of the chairs to her side, he touched her hand to it. "You should sit."

Her feet throbbed; she sat.

But she was a grown woman now, with a husband and a baby on the way, and all she wanted was to curl up in her mother's lap and cry. She really needed to know. "Does it, though?"

"For you, *ma chérie?* Definitely."

It was a relief to get off her feet, but it still felt cold, lonely.

Rose slid off its seat to land next to Mr. Laurent where he crouched down.

"I know it's awfully inappropriate of me," she said as properly as she could, "but if I could just cry here for a little while."

As if worried she too would shatter like the porcelain, he gingerly patted her back as she leaned into him and let go of the rest of her tears.

"WELL, MISS EMERY, WE'VE FINALLY COME."

Emery thought it was a feverish dream. The vision of Dahlia, hair bundled up in a length of rough linen and wearing an apron over a worn blue dress, drew her out of the inner scoldings in which she was drowning.

But it was real. There was Dahlia, clapping her small hands together as if relishing the prospect of getting them dirty.

"You can't be here," Emery said stupidly, and Dahlia only laughed.

She snatched her vase out of Jane's arms and darted out to the shop to put it away, then came back.

The twinkle in her eyes was very real as she looked up at Emery. "For better or worse, Emery. For better or worse."

Then she spread her arms wide in greeting to Mrs. Swofford, releasing Emery from her gaze but not her spell.

Please don't ever release me from this spell, Emery hoped fervently to herself.

"My maids have come too! All but Miss Williams; she did not want to dirty her fingernails. Just as well, I left her with the children." Lady Arnold treated this as a vast joke. "But you've left us nearly nothing to do!"

One thing the Friends had in common: titles didn't startle them.

"This way, Lady Arnold," said Mrs. Swofford in complete calm.

"I think Mrs. Russell would rather be with her sisters." Mr. Laurent poked his head in diffidently, and both the children ran to help Rose hobble in over the scorched floor.

She had something like a wooden plank under her arm.

"I have improvised her a little crutch," Mr. Laurent said with the same self-effacing shyness.

"And lifted my spirits," said Rose, just as Anna returned as well.

"Lady Arnold came to help clean." It felt stupid saying it, but she was *here*. She could have stayed in her fine house, but she'd come. For Emery.

"Someone should go find some paper. Let's write down everyone's name so we can thank them when all this is through. Everyone who helped last night, too." Rose sounded a little older than she had an hour before, and calmer. Very much Mr. Russell's campaigning wife.

That helped.

Jane noticed it too. "Mr. Russell will want to know how the Friends have rallied round us while he was gone. Surely he'll soon be home."

"And Captain Brice too," said Rose with a satisfied nod, as though counting down the hours till the people she wanted back in the square were here.

"That would be nice," Jane said, a little more softly.

"*Good God!*"

That was Lord Boislegrand, arriving in the door of the shop as if struck by lightning.

Anna rolled her eyes. She clearly had no time for *that*.

"Tilly, would you please escort Lord Boislegrand to his carriage and let him know what happened?"

"Well, I can only give the gist of it, as I wasn't here," said Tilly reasonably, wiping her hands on her apron, "and the gist is pretty clear from looking around. But I'll do what I can." She curtsied to his lordship. "Fire, obviously, but may I walk out with you?"

"She's lost her awe of him," muttered Anna as Tilly dragged a struggling Lord Boislegrand out by the arm.

"It was never going to last," observed Jane.

Rose, near-strangled by hugs from the children on both sides, had nothing to add.

Emery could only stand there, more humbled than she'd ever been in her life, grateful every one of her sisters was there too despite all the damage and destruction, despite not knowing how any of it would be fixed, despite not knowing what the future held.

Stared at her Dahlia blooming among the wreckage.

"We'll be all right." Emery didn't need to prove it. She felt it, and that was enough.

WANT MORE LADIES' OWN BAKERY? GET YOUR EXCLUSIVE bonus chapter for Season 2 and you'll get the news of LOB first!

Historical Notes

I keep a page of historical notes for Ladies' Own Bakery on my website, where I can update it as the series goes along. **It's for readers and has spoilers, like this section** - be careful!

Season 2 of *Ladies' Own Bakery* would not have been possible without Sylvia Lettice Thrupp's 1933 excellent book, *A Short History of the Worshipful Company of Bakers,* tracing the development of the Guild down through the ages since its founding in 1155. This rare book was provided by my local— and wonderful—library system. **Please support your public libraries!**

An organization changes a great deal in almost nine hundred years, and nothing in *Ladies' Own Bakery* is intended as a factual description of any real person or policy or action of the guild.

You may apply to join the Guild today, and these days they do indeed focus on education and charitable works.

They did indeed admit widows of master bakers in the past, but not women who were not widows, although many baked a great deal of bread to keep London fed down through the centuries.

Explosive fires are still a problem in bakeries and flour mills, and such facilities use extensive air filtering to keep such incidents to a minimum. Take heart; our sisters will recover. (As readers of *The Lord Trap* may have guessed.)

If you still have questions, take heart, for we are only halfway through the planned four seasons of this series. By downloading the bonus chapter you'll be among the first to hear when Season 3 debuts!

Thank you for taking this journey with me, and I so look forward to seeing you again.

Enjoyed the Ladies' Own Bakery?
Invite your friends!

The story doesn't end here—I hope we'll see each other again!

Season Three will be coming!

Sign up here to be among the first to know when more LOB drops, and (*psst*) you can even elect to get new episodes right in your inbox. **Four seasons are planned!**

Right now, you can get Seasons One and Two at your favorite bookstore. And if you download the bonus chapter, you'll be signed up to receive future episodes *free* as they come out!

(If you want to chat about Ladies' Own Bakery there's a Facebook group just for that, or feel free to send me a message via my website. I love to hear from readers even more than I love baking.)

Questions? They're probably answered on the Ladies' Own Bakery page of my website.

Looking forward to the future of the Ladies' Own Bakery!

About the Author

Judith Lynne writes rule-breaking romances with love around every corner. Her characters tend to have deep convictions, electric pleasures, and, sometimes, weaponry.

She loves to write stories where characters are shaken by life, shaken down to their core, put out their hand...and love is there.

A history nerd with too many degrees, Judith Lynne lives in that other paradise, Ohio, with a truly adorable spouse, a small domestic jungle, and a misgendered turtle. Her screen-writing and science fiction efforts ranged from aspiring to award-winning and back again. Now she writes passionate Regency romances with a rich sense of place and time.

If you enjoyed Ladies' Own Bakery, *keep these books coming - share a review at your favorite bookstore, Bookbub, or Goodreads!*

Sign up for the author's newsletter, including exclusive book news and sneak peeks,
at judithlynne.com.

Also by Judith Lynne

Lords and Undefeated Ladies

Not Like a Lady

The Countess Invention

What a Duchess Does

Crown of Hearts

He Stole the Lady

No Titled Lady *Series prequel*

Maids Done Waiting

The Lord Trap

The Lady Escape *Forthcoming*

Cloaks and Countesses

The Caped Countess

The Clandestine Countess

The Castaway Countess *Forthcoming*

Ladies' Own Bakery

Ladies' Own Bakery Season One: The Collected Episodes

Ladies' Own Bakery Season Two: The Collected Episodes